WINDS

WINDS

A Novel

Paul Dale Anderson

Publications

Rockford, Illinois USA

2AM Publications
3211 Broadway
Rockford, Illinois 61108-5941
www.2AMPublications.com

Publisher's Note: This is a work of fiction. Names, characters, places, and incidents are a product of the author's imagination. Locales and public names are sometimes used for atmospheric purposes. Any resemblance to actual people, living or dead, or to businesses, companies, events, institutions, or locales is completely coincidental.

Book Layout © 2014 BookDesignTemplates.com
Author photo on back cover by Timothy Hatch

Winds/Paul Dale Anderson -- 1st ed., October 2015
2nd ed., January 2018
ISBN-10: 0-937491-16-0
ISBN-13: 978-0-937491-16-4 (pbk.)

For Tammy and Teddie and Susan and Gretta.

For Dianne Walters-Butler.

For Barbara Puechner.

And for Lizza, who urged me to kill again

"There are more things in heaven and earth, Horatio,

Than are dreamt of in your philosophy."

Hamlet I,V, 166

Prologue

Shortly after midnight, on the sixth night following the eleventh full moon of the year, a massive Canadian cold front clashed violently with warmer air rising high above the waters of Lake Superior.

The much cooler polar air, turbulently deflected southeastward along lines of least resistance, resulted in a savage wind tunnel generating intermittent gusts in excess of 90 miles an hour.

Not unlike crazed banshees, fierce arctic winds howled across the northern half of Wisconsin, downing trees and power lines and ripping rooftops off houses and barns directly in its path.

Despite the raging wind, Ellen Groves ran three miles through thick woods to her nearest neighbor's house and begged Sara Nelson, a pre-adolescent girl secretly tutored over the past eight years, to skip a day of public school and accompany her on a mission.

"Hurry!"

Disaster was written on the wind. Ellen, a sixty-four year-old social recluse, knew how to read the wind like a book.

Suddenly, the winds changed again.

Not their direction. They still blew straight from the north and the northwest. Not the temperature, either. The deadly wind-chill still induced dangerous frostbite in a matter of minutes.

What changed was infinitely more subtle. The banshee no longer sounded crazed. It sounded scared.

"Run, child! Run and hide. Quickly. Do as I say, and do it now!"

Sara ran. At first, Ellen was afraid the youngster would waste precious time by demanding a logical explanation. But she obviously gleaned the urgency in Ellen's voice and realized this was not a time to ask questions.

Nor did the eleven-year-old ask where to run. She intuitively knew safety resided within a circle of ancient pines where she'd be protected from more than just the wind.

Fleet and graceful as a fawn, she darted across both lanes of the two-lane asphalt highway that separated the Nelson farm from the eastern edge of Ellen's undeveloped property.

Sara disappeared into dense underbrush at the periphery of the forest while Ellen, encumbered by an attack of arthritis aggravated by the arctic winds, had yet to clear the steep embankment on the far side of the road.

The fifty-plus-year difference in their ages became painfully apparent.

Rising above the wind, rumbles of half-a-dozen fast-moving vehicles racing down County Trunk O at break-neck speeds told only seconds remained to make it across the highway or die trying.

Evil surprised her when she was most vulnerable. Unless she reached the protection of the trees, there was nothing she could do to save herself.

She urged slow-moving feet to move faster. She felt, as well as heard, the frantic vibrations of twenty-four steel-belted radials asynchronously pounding paved asphalt less than half a mile distant. All six vehicles barreled close enough to see with the naked eye if she turned her head half an inch to the right. But she harbored no desire to look violent death—especially her own—full in the face.

Run! Run! Run!

Run as if your very life depends on it!

Although Violet, her older sister, repeatedly warned powerful men would stop at nothing to get what they wanted, Ellen refused to listen. "Oh, pshaw," she insisted each time Violet brought up the subject. "They won't hurt me. They only want my land. And they can't have it."

Unfortunately, manipulating the law of the land, through political pay-offs and high-priced corporate lawyers to get whatever they wanted wasn't enough. They viewed her as an obstacle standing in their way.

An obstacle to be eliminated.

The roar of approaching high-powered engines became deafening. Ellen crossed the double yellow lines that divided the two-lane highway and signaled a no-passing zone. Though she sensed she'd never make it to the other side in time, she urged her feet faster as the oncoming vehicles bore down on her five foot-two frame with a fatal vengeance.

Two abreast—one in each lane like testosteronized teenagers dragracing in a George Lucas film—a black Dodge pick-up and a silver Ford Explorer closed the gap at 90 miles an hour. Now she could actually feel the heat of their engines on her face and arms, smell the stink of gasoline fumes and boiling motor oil polluting the air, hear pistons knocking, valves opening and closing, spark plugs firing and misfiring.

Sudden impact shattered every bone in her body, ruptured blood vessels, severed various arteries, and separated limbs from torso, head from neck, body from soul. Ellen Groves was pleasantly surprised to feel no pain. Her mind continued to function without sensory input. Then normal consciousness ceased.

Momentum carried the lead vehicles a quarter mile down the road before the Explorer and Dodge Ram finally screeched to a halt. Two of the trailing vehicles slowed, backed up, and deliberately ground what was left of Ellen's scattered remains into the asphalt. Then they drove over her again. And again. And again.

The first vehicles made wide U-turns and came back. Two men— one unusually tall and lanky with immaculately coiffured hair unruffled by the wind, and the other short but powerfully-built who wore a broad-brimmed hat to mask male-pattern baldness—threw open the doors of the silver Explorer and waved cohorts out of the other vehicles.

Ten men with woodland-camouflage-patterned fatigues, holstered sidearms buckled to hips, and semiautomatic rifles in their gloved hands paced up and down the pavement searching for scattered body parts.

"Over here," called the short man. "I think I found what's left of her head."

"Can you confirm?" asked the tall man. "Is it Ellen Groves?"

"Hard to tell." He picked up a severed head in gloved hands and looked closely at the smashed face. "Yeah! It's the Groves bitch," he shouted.

"Left hand over here," announced a young man with a freshly-shaved scalp who foraged in brush near the shoulder of the road. "I got part of her left hand. One of the fingers is missing."

"Bring the head and hand to me," ordered the tall man. "The rest of you begin normal clean up. When you're certain the area's sanitized, return to base."

After locking Ellen's severed head and bloody hand in a specially-designed refrigerated metal box bolted to the floor in the rear of the Explorer, the tall man and his powerfully-built partner entered the front of the vehicle and sped away.

The others, utilizing heavy-duty push brooms and snow shovels, scraped as much of Ellen's remains as they could from the asphalt into a small pile at the side of the road.

"Stand back," warned the young man with shaved head as he unscrewed the cap of a five-gallon gasoline can and splashed volatile diesel over desiccated flesh.

Then he struck a match and turned night into day.

Book I

"What fools these mortals be!"
--*William Shakespeare, A Midsummer's Night Dream, Act III, Scene II*

"The wind goeth toward the south, and turneth about unto the north; it whirleth about continually, and the wind returneth again according to its circuits."

--*Holy Bible, King James version. Ecclesiastes, 1:6.*

CHAPTER ONE

Diane Groves knew.

Even before she spoke with her younger sister Nancy in the student union and Nancy whispered, "Ma's dead, Di," she knew.

Her mother had been cut to pieces and the pieces burned. She felt the emptiness. The emptiness was unlike anything felt before.

"She's not just dead, Di," added Nancy. "She's gone. She's completely gone. I can't reach her at all."

Nancy's voice broke as she burst into a torrent of tears. Diane Groves didn't cry. Unlike her sister, she never displayed emotion. She kept hurt bottled inside until it exploded in anger.

"I know," was all she said. Her voice sounded cold and devoid of personal affect, the same voice she used to inform a student she knew had plagiarized a paper.

Deep down inside herself, Diane tapped a secret cache of strength Ma insisted she tuck away for a rainy day. Literally and figuratively, today was a rainy day.

Since early this morning, gods of irony deluged Madison, the capital of Wisconsin and home to the state university where Diane taught graduate courses in ancient history and Nancy taught undergraduate linguistics classes, with four inches of inconsolate tears. It was as if heaven cried over the loss of a beloved daughter.

She placed one arm around Nan's shoulders and drew her closer so no one else in the crowded student union heard what she said next.

"Have you seen her, Nan?" Her whisper sounded so thick of tongue it was more grunts than meaningful strings of words. "She came to you in dreams?"

Nancy answered in the same weird tongue. She sniffled, dabbed at eyes with a Kleenex, momentarily managing to dam the miniature Niagara Falls flooding her freckled face. "I only caught whispers on the wind. But when I tried to reach her, I couldn't find her. It was as if she'd never existed at all. She should've devised a way to meet if she made it through the veil. But I can't find her. That means something or someone is keeping part of her here in this world, deliberately preventing her spirit from reaching the other side. Di, I think Ma's been dismembered."

"And parts of her body taken as trophies? Or eaten?" It was more a statement than a question.

Nancy's face lost all its natural color. "Who would do such a terrible thing? Who would even know what to do?"

"Can you find out, Nan?"

"Maybe. If I could cross all the way over to the other side. But something's blocking me, Di, a rift between worlds I can't cross. I don't think anyone can cross. The only way to communicate now is through dreams, and dreams are always ambiguous."

"If the door between worlds were open, Ma would have seen what was about to happen before it happened, and it wouldn't happen at all. She would have taken steps to prevent it. But it did happen. She's gone."

"We're in danger, too, aren't we?"

"Yes," Diane agreed. "With Ma gone, we're *all* in danger."

How strange it was to feel vulnerable! Even here—in this metropolitan area of a quarter million people and where some small percentage of that population were murderers, rapists, religious or political fanatics, lunatics, or worse—Diane had always felt safe, secure, protected. But with Ma gone, the world had suddenly become a scary place.

By sheer force of will, she fought feelings of panic that threatened to consume her. Her breathing slowed. Her eyes lost their focus.

Part of her went deep inside herself and called upon primal senses to warn of impending danger.

Her heightened sense of smell tasted the air, moving quickly beyond the innocuous odors of greasy fried hamburgers, French-fried potatoes, grilled onions, steaming coffee, the sickeningly-sweet smell of colas and flavored lattes, the perfumed, cologned, and feminine-hygienized bodies of students that regularly permeated the student center. Wafting in from outside, the fresher smells of pine trees, raw earth, decomposing leaves, and pools of lake water drew her spirit. She let herself go there.

Her spirit sped past the domed capital building, and the noxious fumes of unleaded gasoline and diesel assaulted her nostrils. She sought refuge in raindrops pelting Monona and Mendota, Madison's twin lakes. The myriad conversations in the Union, lectures in surrounding lecture halls, and the familiar street noises of downtown Madison faded away as she tuned into sounds the wind made.

She shivered with the cold as her spirit soared high above the lake like some swift-winged, sharp-taloned bird of prey. She split her senses and fanned out in all four directions at once, seeking help from the guardians of the watchtowers of the four winds.

Her spirit called out in a language they could understand. When no answer came, she returned to her own body.

"Something is very wrong," Diane said in the ancient tongue as her eyes swam back into focus. "We should be wary of everyone and everything. How soon can you be ready to leave for home?"

"Give me an hour," Nancy replied in that same ancient tongue.

"Take two. We must arrange for someone to teach our classes during our absence. And we need to reach Tom. Do you know where he is?"

"Ma gave me two phone numbers to use in an emergency. Some general's office in Washington, and the American Red Cross. I'll call both. Maybe they can get a message to him."

"Tell him we need him to remember Ma. I'll contact the rest of the family. We don't have much time. You know what this means, don't you?"

Nancy shook her head. "With Ma gone, it could mean anything."

"It means," said Diane Groves in English, "that, despite all our precautions, someone knows about us. And if they know who we are, what we are, where we are, and how to destroy us, nothing sacred is safe."

CHAPTER TWO

L ieutenant Colonel Robert Sean McMichaels refused to admit he fought a losing battle trying to keep both eyes open at three o'clock in the morning.

Bob considered himself a special breed of super-soldier, one of the best of the best in this man's modern volunteer army. He'd never acknowledge he couldn't win any battle.

At 3:30, he half-seriously considered propping his eyelids open with toothpicks. At 3:45 he mentally kicked himself in the butt for allowing ordinary human weakness to slow him down.

It had been more than twenty-four hours—closer to thirty and still counting—since he'd accepted his special assignment. The adrenalin rush that propelled him into immediate action had long since dissipated.

The only thing keeping him awake now was caffeine.

If Major Groves didn't show soon, Bob would surely be asleep on his feet when he eventually did. Where the hell was he anyway? General White dispatched a team into the field hours ago to locate him and bring him back. How the hell could one man be so difficult to find?

Bob refilled his empty cup with black coffee. The cup overflowed and he let out a string of epithets that would have made a drill sergeant proud. Blame it on jangled nerves, frayed from too little sleep and too much caffeine. He set the mug down, wiped wet fingers on wrinkled uniform trousers, and regained control of his nerves by sheer willpower.

Needing to keep active, he paced back and forth in front of his computer, trying to fit pieces of the puzzle together in his mind. The big picture eluded him.

So far all he had were scattered bits and pieces that didn't make a whole lot of sense. Why would a pack of professional hit men take out a sixty-four year old woman in northern Wisconsin? Was Mrs. Groves' violent death an act of terrorism against the United States or a personal vendetta against an individual? Was this a solitary act or the first of a long string of planned hits that impacted national security? He needed additional intel before he could begin to guess. But he wouldn't have more information until Groves got back from field training.

He returned to the well-worn, GSA standard-issue desk in one corner of his temporary duty senior officers quarters, picked up his reading glasses from atop a sheaf of papers, propped the frames between the bumps of his thrice broken nose, and carefully keyed— careful now, every keystroke counts, because they'll lock you out if you make a mistake—a critical sequence of top secret codes into his personal laptop computer. Distant mainframes acknowledged his right to ftp information and automatically dug up requested files from various network-linked systems. As if by magic, billions of bits of highly classified information scrolled across the laptop's screen in the blink of an eye.

Lieutenant Colonel Robert McMichaels loved piecing together puzzles, especially puzzles no one else had the expertise to solve. Every day of the week for the past 2 years, Monday thru Friday, from 7 AM to 4 PM, he'd diligently pieced together parts of the big picture for the Defense Intelligence Agency. Sitting behind a desk in Arlington, Virginia, and analyzing sensitive computer data was all he'd done for the past two years. Hell of a thing for a dedicated combat soldier to be doing.

But with the cold war over, there wasn't much demand for senior combat soldiers in the real world. He'd already completed five tours in Afghanistan and wasn't slated to go back. Other than annual requalification on the range, he hadn't touched a conventional weapon in more than a year.

Officially assigned to an obscure position in the Table of Distributions and Allowances of the Deputy Chief of Staff for Plans, Operations and Training, he'd been secretly detailed to anti-terrorist intelligence gathering operations in the office of the Chairman of the Joint Chiefs of Staff. That meant he had a low-profile desk job that seemed to most of his co-workers, and sometimes even to him, as useless as tits on a boar.

At 42, McMichaels had regimented life into a comfortable routine more and more difficult to break by the minute. He usually went to bed before nine, got up before five. He shit, showered, shaved, ran four laps around the parade ground, did two complete sets of calisthenics, ate a high fiber breakfast, caught the six-thirty shuttle from Fort Meyer to a crowded office in a Pentagon annex in downtown Arlington, and started work at precisely seven sharp. Now his forty-plus year old body refused to function with less than a full night's sleep.

Did that mean he was too old to do field work anymore? Hell, if staying awake seemed so goddamn hard, what the fuck would he do if there were a war on and he had to go into combat? He hated to think about getting old. Old meant making a whole lot of personal and career decisions he wasn't ready to make.

If he got his promotion to bird colonel—he'd been informed his records had been submitted to the DA selection board and his name had been placed on the coveted short list—then he could put off making any personal choices for another five, maybe ten years. If and when he did make full bull, he'd be grandfathered in for a full thirty before facing mandatory retirement at age 55. And, if he was lucky enough and good enough to make brigadier before finishing his thirty, he could stay in the Army to age 62.

But if, for some unfathomable reason like an unexpected Reduction in Force that cut the rolls for colonel in half or he fucked up royally and received a horrendous Officer Efficiency Report, then he'd be forced out at twenty plus, sent back into the civilian sector long before he was ready to turn into a couch potato like so many of his friends once they retired from the army.

The U. S. Army had been his life longer than he cared to remember. When he thought about it, he was surprised to discover he'd spent more time in uniform than out. Even before he entered the real army as a shavetail at age 22, he'd worn dress uniforms during four years of Reserve Officer Training Corps drills at the university and battledress during annual summer camps. What would he do when it came time to hang up his uniform for good? He didn't like to think about it.

When he'd entered the regular army at age twenty-two, he volunteered to give his life for his country, fully expecting to end up in a plastic body bag with a bronze star, a purple heart, a good conduct medal, and a belly full of shrapnel. He'd been surprised to pass his fortieth birthday and find it hadn't happened. He'd missed Korea and Vietnam entirely. He'd missed the first Gulf War, too. He'd been a second lieutenant, first lieutenant, and a captain in Iraq, a major and then a light colonel in Afghanistan. Now he was forty-two and still alive.

While waiting for data to download and Major Groves to return from the field, he had plenty of time to think about things he'd rather not think about. He shoved those thoughts aside and refocused on the problem at hand.

Ellen Groves was the mother of Major Thomas Groves. Her violent death had national security implications that required immediate attention. Tom was no ordinary soldier. He'd been selected by the Joint Chiefs to train and lead rapid deployment special ops teams that had successfully accomplished top-secret missions in Iraq, Iran, Afghanistan, and Syria. No one else had been able to do what Groves had. The Joint Chiefs considered him a vital asset, and anything that threatened Tom or his family was a threat to national security.

They'd met four times over the years: once in Iraq in the Green Zone; once in Germany during a NATO training exercise; once stateside during a three-week planning session with Pentagon brass; and once in Afghanistan while searching the hills for Taliban insurgents. He remembered how impressed he'd been with the kid's no-bullshit professionalism.

Although the brass admired and respected and utilized Groves' unique abilities, they didn't like him as a person. He wouldn't play the usual Pentagon power games, and that made Washington insiders uncomfortable. Tom was a rarity in the modern military: a professional soldier, a man of action, a warrior born. Give him a combat assignment and he'd meet or exceed all expectations. Invite him to a cocktail party at the officers club and he'd stand off in a corner. Casual conversation was as foreign to him as combat was to most mess officers. Such no-nonsense soldiers were considered indispensable in wartime. They were usually the first to get RIFed in peacetime.

Rumor had it that Groves, as a young 2nd lieutenant, had saved the life of the son of a politically connected three-star general. General Lemminger had been commander of US Army Forces Command at the time and had subsequently flagged Groves for special handling by the officer assignment desk at what was then the Military Personnel Center (MILPERCEN) and was now called the U. S. Army Human Resources Command. So when the Rapid Deployment Force created new special ops infiltration teams, Groves was selected to lead and train several of those teams. It was a rare case of the right man given the right job, something that happened in the military with the frequency of a blue moon.

Now it appeared the man's family had been targeted by terrorists, and Bob was assigned to discover why.

He tapped the escape key twice to blank the computer screen when he heard a knock on the door. For an instant after opening it, he had the eerie feeling he stared at his own reflection in a full-length mirror.

Major Thomas Groves stood 6 feet 2 inches tall and had the same large body frame and muscular build as McMichaels. Both men kept the sides of their heads virtually shaved, and both wore identically-patterned battledress uniforms. Although the colonel's own close-cropped sandy-brown hair now sported flecks of intruding gray, his football-player's physique remained firm, thanks to a spartan diet and daily workouts.

McMichaels escorted Groves into the room and invited the major to pour dregs from the nearly empty Mr. Coffee.

"How much have you been told?" he asked as Groves filled a cup.

"General White informed me my mother was killed in an accident while I was field training. He said to see you, and you'd supply details. When and how did my mother die, Colonel?"

"Around sunrise day before yesterday." McMichaels offered Groves a chair, then sat at the desk to log his laptop off the network. "The sheriff's department is still investigating. But according to the sole eyewitness, an eleven-year-old neighbor named Sara Nelson, your mother was deliberately run down by multiple SUVs and pick-ups while crossing a two-lane highway near her home. Unfortunately, the Nelson girl wasn't close enough to get a good description of the perpetrators and she couldn't indentify makes of vehicles."

"What do you mean my mother was deliberately run down? And why the hell is a senior intelligence officer investigating the death of a civilian?"

"Someone murdered her. They ran her down in the middle of the road, deliberately drove over her body, backed up their vehicles, and drove over her again."

"Why? Why would anyone do something like that to a harmless old woman?"

"That's exactly what the Pentagon ordered me to find out. Do you know if your mother had any enemies?"

"None. At least none I can think of. A few townspeople may have thought her a little weird." He seemed to debate with himself whether to say more. "Okay, to be perfectly honest, they thought her downright eccentric. But no one hated her. Certainly no one hated her enough to kill her."

"Someone did," McMichaels said. "Someone wanted her dead."

Groves fumbled in a cargo pocket for a cigarette. "Is it okay to smoke in here?"

"No, but go ahead. Use the wastebasket as an ash tray. The Nelson girl counted six vehicles, two men to each. Your mother's murder was apparently well organized, premeditated, and carried out with military-style precision. After the twelve ran your mother down on the highway, they poured diesel fuel over her body and torched the remains. There wasn't enough left to positively identify. If Sara hadn't witnessed the act, your mother's murder might be classified as a missing person's case."

Groves clenched his teeth and bit through the filtered tip of his cigarette. He spat pieces of filter into the air, crumbled what was left in one massive fist, and angrily flung paper and loose tobacco into a wastebasket next to the desk. "Why the fuck would anyone go to all that trouble to kill my mother, Colonel?" He slammed his fist into a wall and left a dent in the drywall.

"That's what Army Intelligence needs to know. Think for a moment. Is it possible Al Qaeda or a foreign government—Iran comes immediately to mind—might be launching a series of terrorist attacks against families of military officers? How about the Islamic State in the Levant, ISL or ISIS? Terrorist attacks have become common in Europe and the Middle East, but relatively rare in the U.S. Is it possible your mother was killed in retaliation for your participation in the Iraqi war? Or Afghanistan? Or Syria? Was she targeted because you're an integral part of our Rapid Deployment Force? Do terrorists think they'll demoralize the RDF by targeting families of RDF officers?"

"Possible." Groves reached into a cargo pocket for another cigarette. "But highly unlikely. I'm only a minor player in this game, Colonel. To demoralize the RDF, they'd need to go after someone far more important than an O-4 team chief."

"Suppose you're just one—the first—of many? Suppose they've targeted the families of other officers, too, but your mother happened to present a convenient target of opportunity?"

"How can we know, Colonel? How can we know for certain terrorism was even involved?"

"We can't. Not unless they strike again and establish a recognizable pattern. Meanwhile, I need to check out all possibilities. What about your father, Tom? Does your father have any enemies you know about? Business rivals? Is it likely someone may be trying to get at your father through your mother?"

"I don't have a father."

"C'mon now. Everyone has a father. You mean your parents are divorced? Your father deceased?"

"No. My mother never married."

"Oh, I see."

"No, I don't think you do, Colonel. My mother is—was—a very independent woman, much too independent to be a housewife. But she did want children. So she had three kids on her own, each fathered by a different man. She never told us who our fathers were. She said she never told any of the men they were fathers, either. She didn't think they needed to know."

"Anyone blame her for that?"

"Sure. People in town thought it scandalous, even downright immoral, to bear three children without benefit of wedlock. Our neighbors—most of them upstanding Christians—avoided us like the plague. Actually, I think a few husbands were afraid their wives might get ideas if they associated with a free-thinking woman, or maybe wives feared their husbands would get ideas around Ma. Kids in grade school called me a bastard once or twice, and I got into a few fights over it. Neither my sisters nor I were accepted. But it didn't bother us. We didn't let it. We grew up, earned college scholarships, made something of our lives. That's more than the rest of the town did."

"And you haven't been home since you went away to college?"

"No. I haven't."

"But you're heading home for your mother's funeral?"

"No funeral. A private, family-only memorial service. General White authorized two weeks emergency leave. I'll be on my way soon as I take a shower."

"Flying or driving?"

"Driving."

"How far is it to your home?"

"Nine hundred miles. Give or take a mile or two."

"Are you in any shape to drive 900 miles tonight? I know I'm not. Wait till morning, and I'll help you drive."

"Thanks, but no thanks. I'm an experienced driver, Colonel. I know my personal limitations. I'll stop when I'm tired."

"I'm going with you. Orders from the Puzzle Palace. We can ride together or take separate cars, it's up to you. But I'm ordered to stick to you like stink on shit until we know why your mother was targeted. Understand me, Major?"

"You look in worse shape than me, Colonel. Oh, hell. After three days in the field without much sleep, I haven't the energy to argue. If you want to tag along, fine. Pack your duffel bags. I'm going to hit the shower. I'll meet you in the BOQ parking lot in twenty minutes."

A half hour later when Groves—dressed in faded jeans, sneakers, University of Wisconsin sweatshirt, and black army overcoat with insignia of grade removed—carried a packed suitcase and a battered AWOL bag down to the parking lot behind the BOQ, McMichaels— also wearing jeans and an identical trenchcoat—was impatiently waiting in the early morning rain.

Groves unlocked the trunk of a metallic-blue Ford Focus and threw his own suitcase, the Colonel's suitcase, and the AWOL bag atop a space-saver spare tire.

"You drive, Colonel," Groves said, tossing the keys. "But wake me before we reach Indianapolis. We'll stop for breakfast at a greasy spoon outside the old south gate of what used to be Fort Benjamin

Harrison. After eggs, bacon, and half a dozen cups of coffee, I'll spell you at the wheel."

Because soldiers learn to sleep anywhere and anytime they can, especially after three days and nights playing war games in the field, a warm, dry car was as good as a bed. Groves settled into the passenger seat, buckled his seat belt, and ten minutes later was fast asleep.

McMichaels drove. From time to time, he had to slap his face really hard to stay awake.

* * *

Wildly disjointed dreams, part nightmare and part reminiscence, oddly mixed with boyhood memories of his mother. He saw himself at four or five, uncut blonde hair as long as a girl's, his scrawny half-naked body scratched and bleeding from an unending, mad, headlong dash through untamed woods near his mother's house. It was a stiflingly hot midsummer's eve, well past midnight to judge from moon and stars high overhead, and young Tom, awakened by unfamiliar sounds, searched everywhere for his mother and couldn't find her. She wasn't in her bedroom next to his own on the second floor of the big old wooden farmhouse. She wasn't in the living room nor in the well-kept kitchen that dominated the first floor. Nor was she in the pantry that looked out onto the back porch. He even checked the outhouse and went down into the dark, dank root cellar where his mother stored canned vegetables and dried herbs from summers past. Where was she? Why couldn't he find her?

Nor could he find either of his sisters: Nancy, the two-month-old snotty-nosed crybaby whose empty crib remained beside mother's abandoned bed, or Diane, the three-year-old whose empty room was adjacent to his on the second floor. He had the horrible feeling something bad had happened to his mother while he slept. Had something bad happened to Nancy and Diane, too?

Feeling afraid, feeling abandoned and all alone, he ran into the night and wailed his mother's name to the wind.

"Maaa!" he half shouted, half cried. "Maaaaaaaaaaaaa!"

But the wind didn't answer.

Then the dream changed. He was much older now. Seven or eight. Again, he wakened in the middle of the night. Again, he was all alone.

Why? Why did his mother abandon him like this? Why did she take Nancy and Diane with her and leave him behind? Didn't his mother love him anymore? What had he done to make her stop loving him?

Suddenly, he metamorphosed into a strapping teenager. Now nothing frightened him, certainly not the night nor the tall trees. Ancient oak, elm, and 80-foot pine, once so foreboding to a small boy, became his closest friends. The animals of the forest were his constant companions. He ran with the deer, hunted with the fox, hid alongside the rabbit, climbed trees with the squirrel. Night was his favorite time of day.

He no longer depended on his mother for food nor shelter. He felt free as a bird. Though he still had a room of his own on the second floor of the big old wood-frame farmhouse where he stashed his school clothes and several hundred well-read paperback books, purchased with his allowance at the IGA store in town, Tom now lived in the woods. Each day when the yellow school bus dropped his sisters and him off at the corner of county trunks O and Double N, he dashed home, shucked his regular school clothes, slipped into comfortable jeans and sneakers, and quickly disappeared into the forest.

There, a quarter mile from his mother's house in a secret place he thought of as his personal space, he explored his own body and—while meditating on the beauty of the feminine form as exemplified by mental images of his female classmates and an ideal woman with red hair he pictured clearly in his mind—experienced his first orgasm. From the spring he turned thirteen until the summer following his sixteenth birthday, Tom Groves devoted an inordinate amount of time to private meditation in the forest.

During his sixteenth summer, while spending all night under the stars in his secret hiding place, he was awakened from a dreamless slumber by the sound of laughter floating on the wind. Rubbing the remaining sleep from his eyes, he sat up on his bed of dried pine needles and strained both ears to focus on the voices. One—soft, soothing, and in tune with the whispers of the wind—was instantly recognized as his mother's. Another—lower pitched, more earthy, strained from smoking three to four packs of cigarettes a day over a period of twenty years—belonged to his mother's older sister, Aunt Violet.

There were probably close to a dozen others in the woods, judging from the sounds they made, and they were all coming his way.

Why were so many people—all women, judging from their voices—wandering these woods at night? They weren't lost, were they? What a ridiculous notion! His mother knew these woods like the palm of her hand. Even without a moon, and tonight's moon floated silvery-full in a cloudless sky, Ellen Groves could navigate woodland trails better than most forest animals.

Were they searching for him? Why? Did his mother doubt he was old enough to take care of himself? Should he run to her and tell her he was all right?

Now the voices veered northward, towards the very heart of the forest. His curiosity tweaked, Tom followed.

Within minutes he was close enough to see a parade of diaphanous silk gowns—robes so sheer he was sure he saw brief flashes of naked flesh through that flimsy fabric flitting through the woods. Did the women wear nothing beneath identical see-through garments? Or was it only the magic of moonlight, filtered through thick branches and dense leaves, playing tricks on a sleepy teenager's imagination?

There were indeed twelve women, not counting his mother, varying in age from eleven to forty-five. Besides Aunt Violet and his two sisters, Tom immediately recognized several of his closest neighbors and their adolescent daughters, including Roseanne Martindale, a girl he'd had a schoolboy crush on since the second grade.

It was Roseanne Martindale's teen-aged face and body that Tom fantasized about nearly as often as he imagined the red-haired woman when he went to his secret hiding place. Just the thought of Roseanne's divine visage—her hair, her face, the swell of her breasts, the shape of rounded thighs sheathed in blue denim—could cause an instant reaction.

Every time he got close enough to talk with her, however, his tongue literally tied up in knots and he fled like a frightened jackrabbit. Whenever she happened to look up from her desk during the school day to smile at him as if she knew exactly what he'd been staring at and exactly what he'd been thinking, he blushed from head to toe.

So what was Roseanne Martindale doing out here now in the middle of the night dancing half-naked through the moonlit forest with a dozen other women that included his own mother and his two sisters?

That was precisely what all these women were doing. They danced on the wind.

Even the awkwardly tomboyish Nancy, almost turned twelve and just beginning to flower as a woman, glided effortlessly over fallen logs as if floating on thin air. Diane, two years younger than Tom, pirouetted over the earth with the unbounded energy of a yearling fawn. Ellen, his transformed and revitalized mother, laughed and giggled like an adolescent schoolgirl. And Aunt Violet—thirty-three years Tom's senior and an associate professor at a prestigious private ivy-league college somewhere in New England who hardly ever visited the Midwest—hopped and skipped like a madwoman while crooning a tune Tom didn't immediately recognize.

In a foreign language that seemed hauntingly familiar.

As the other women—his mother, sisters, and Roseanne Martindale included—joined in, he tried to translate their words.

Right on the verge of knowing, a warm hand nudged his shoulder and he snapped instantly awake.

"Indianapolis," Bob McMichaels announced. "We're approaching the junction of I-65 and I-465. Which way to breakfast?"

CHAPTER THREE

S heila loved the view through tinted floor-to-ceiling windows on the 76th floor of the XIIMI building.

Even on cloudy nights like tonight, she could peer out those windows and see endless swells of white-capped waves spiking and cresting to the east. Long red trails of departing taillights snaked northward toward suburban Evanston and Highland Park, continuous swarms of headlights approached the Loop along the Outer Drive, thousands of soot-stained brick and ceramic chimneys dotted the flat rooftops of nearly identical rows of apartment buildings and storefronts, and—far below, on the bustling sidewalks of Chicago's North Michigan Avenue, oblivious to eyes observing their every movement from high above their heads—crawled human beings no larger than ants.

Peering out the floor-to-ceiling windows that lined the entire north wall of the elegant mahogany-paneled boardroom, Sheila Ryan felt like a Greek goddess viewing the world from atop magical Mount Olympus. It was, she'd long ago discovered, a feeling that seemed irresistibly appealing to a woman like her.

Lake Michigan, buffeted by unusually unruly winds even for mid-November, threatened to spill past concrete breakwaters to swamp the easternmost edges of the Outer Drive. Purely on a whim, Sheila raised the palms of both hands toward the onrushing tide and tried to will the water back—push it away—from the city. Despite her half-hearted attempt to divert the fierce onslaught of mother nature, the chaotic waves of Lake Michigan continued to crash against the fragile shoreline like millions of liquid sledgehammers.

So much for trying to play goddess.

The door behind her whispered open, and she felt her pulse rate double as the ghost-like reflection of a tall, tastefully-tailored man in his late forties—Philip Ashur, the man who owned this building and thought he could own her—appeared beside her reflection in the floor-to-ceiling window.

"Sorry to keep you waiting, Sheila," apologized his Oxford-accented voice from behind her as she watched his incredibly handsome face in the window lip the same words. "May I offer you a drink? Brandy, perhaps? Sherry? Something stronger?"

"Coffee, please," Sheila replied, fighting off the need for something to calm her nerves. "Black."

A moment later he reappeared with two china mugs filled with steaming-hot, freshly-brewed Brazilian coffee. He placed them side by side on a polished mahogany conference table in the center of the room. Then, silent as a ghost, he pivoted on his toes with the elegance and grace of a professional dancer and stared appreciatively at Sheila's backside.

She felt naked. Ashur's eyes didn't look *at* her but completely *through* her—through her expensive clothes and lacy underclothes, through flesh and bone—peering directly into her heart, ferreting out her innermost secrets, touching her in mysterious ways that made her feel more than merely uncomfortable. Philip Ashur made her feel violated.

He had that effect on women. And on most men as well.

Reluctantly, Sheila turned away from the window and, self-consciously, walked to the conference table in the center of the room. Forcing her hand to remain steady, she reached for one of the cups.

"Okay, what's the deal, Phil?" she asked, wanting to get this over with so she could rush home, down a stiff drink, and scrub herself clean beneath a hot shower. She slid an oversized captain's chair away from the head of the conference table, modestly tucked her navy-blue skirt under both thighs, crossed shapely, nylon-encased legs above the knees, and dropped her derriere into plush leather. Pulling a pack of Benson and Hedges 100s and an engraved gold-plated Dunhill butane lighter, a gift from Phil for services rendered in the past, from her Gucci purse, she casually lit a cigarette and inhaled. "Better be something really big to drag me out of bed in the middle of the night, Phil," she said, smoke leaking from her lips. "I'm billing XIIMI overtime for this, you know. And my time isn't cheap."

Ashur smiled. "I take it, then," he said, pausing to sip his coffee, "you'd rather bill us an hourly rate than pocket a percentage?"

"A percentage of what?"

"Fifty million, give or take a million or two. It could be more, I suppose. Are you a gambler, Sheila? Are you willing to take a chance?"

She uncrossed her legs, sat up straight in her chair. "Keep talking, Phil. You have my complete and undivided attention."

"The corporation needs an exceptionally sharp attorney for an extra-special job. An unscrupulous attorney who is experienced at playing both ends against the middle. Someone with no known ties to XIIMI. Someone who's an excellent actress and can deny, unequivocally, that she represents XIIMI interests. Someone who knows the score and has a healthy respect for what money—big money—can buy. Naturally, Sheila, your name came instantly to mind."

"Naturally. Cut to the chase, Phil. Who do I have to screw for a piece of fifty mil?"

"The heirs of a recently deceased tree farmer in upstate Wisconsin."

"You gotta be kidding! Since when are trees worth fifty mil? Must be a hell of a lot of trees."

"The trees aren't worth diddlysquat. It's the location. The land they're on is part of a very important package XIIMI is developing for a group of private investors. Our profit on the deal should exceed fifty million dollars."

"And you're willing to offer me a third? Just to close?"

"A third? Don't be silly. Six percent."

"No way. Twenty-five percent."

"Eight percent."

"Twenty."

"Nine percent."

She shook her head. Her long flame-red hair shimmered and danced like a runaway forest fire. Sheila's emerald eyes challenged the two black holes beneath Ashur's bushy brows. She and he had played this game before.

"Fifteen," she countered.

"Ten percent. And that's as high as the board will authorize me to go."

"Twelve."

"Ten. We're talking ten percent of fifty mil here, Sheila. That's five mil for you, hon, less expenses. Naturally, we expect you to front all your own expenses, including whatever you pay out to the grieving heirs to gain clear title to that property. You deliver that land to me, Sheila, and I hand you a certified check for five million bucks. It's really that simple. Do we have a deal?"

"If it were that simple, Phil, you wouldn't need little old me, now would you?"

Ashur's smile widened. Sheila smiled back and pretended to sip at her coffee while silently calculating the pluses and minuses of Phil's offer. She didn't trust him as far as she could throw him and with good reason. But Ashur was one of the richest and most powerful men in the world, and Sheila's father—the late Burt Ryan, God damn his good-for-nothing soused-and-mortgaged-to-the-hilt soul, may he roast in hell forever—had been one of the weakest and poorest. To the little girl who'd grown up on the south side of Chicago in such abject poverty that she wore hand-me-down underwear until she was fourteen and had to lie about her age to land an after-school waitressing job that barely paid a third of minimum wage but earned enough in tips to allow her to dress like other kids, the temptation to be a player in such high stakes poker games was overwhelming.

Sheila Ryan had slaved long and hard to overcome the shitty hand that fate, and her less than worthless father, initially dealt her. And now, when years of hard work and long-range planning were beginning to pay off big time, could she afford to hedge her bets?

Hired straight out of DePaul's law school by a large LaSalle Street law firm that turned out to be one of XIIMI's secret subsidiaries, Sheila had earned corporate favor and come to Ashur's personal attention by aggressively tackling difficult cases no other attorney in the firm, certainly none of the blue-blooded Harvard or Yale educated males who dasn't think of sullying their lily-white reputations by bending the law, dared litigate. When she finally amassed sufficient money and experience to venture into private practice, XIIMI continued to throw a substantial amount of business her way.

XIIMI cases paid the office rent and kept her in top-of-the-line undergarments from Macy's. Would her practice survive if XIIMI withdrew their support? She wasn't certain she had the guts to find out. The little girl still inside Sheila Ryan urged her to leap at Ashur's offer, while the grown-up lawyer part of her brain warned her to beware. If neither he nor XIIMI expected her to play by the rules, she shouldn't expect them to play by the rules either.

Intuition cautioned that he was withholding vitally important information about this project, and, normally, she would have listened to what her intuition was trying to tell her. But tonight the thought of a quick five million dollars kept intruding, pushing her intuition aside. Sheila wasn't about to blow a five million dollar deal because of vague feelings that Ashur wasn't telling the truth, the whole truth, and nothing but the truth. Obviously, he needed her talents badly enough to promise a cool five million. What else might he be willing to promise?

And what, exactly, did he expect her to do for so much money?

"I'll demand a bonus if the total exceeds fifty mil," she told him, squashing her cigarette in a crystal ashtray he'd taken out of a credenza and placed on the mahogany table in front of her. "And I want your personal guarantee that I'll pocket ten percent of the entire gross. You clear fifty-five, Phil, I take five point five. Fair enough?"

"Fair enough," he said. "Do we have a deal?"

"We have a deal," she said, offering her hand.

As Ashur's long, slender, perfectly manicured fingers touched the sweaty flesh of her palm, a spark of static electricity snapped across the tabletop like a fiery bullwhip. It made the hairs on the back of her neck stand on end and the nerves in her fingers scream. She jumped back.

"What the hell?"

"Damn weather," groused Ashur. "We haven't seen sun for a week, and the air is filled with enough static electricity to fry John Wayne Gacy twice over."

"Winter is sneaking up on us," sighed Sheila, licking her tingling fingers with the tip of her tongue. "Sunshine's a rare commodity around Chicagoland in the wintertime, Phil. If you want sun, book a vacation to Florida."

"Maybe I will. Want to come along? After you close the deal, of course. Call it an added bonus."

Sheila vigorously shook her head. A week of fun in the sun with Philip Ashur might be tempting, but it was much too dangerous to seriously consider. He was the kind of man who used people up and, when they no longer served his purpose, discarded them like sacks of refuse into rat-infested dumpsters in a dark alley.

She promised herself she wouldn't let Burt Ryan's little girl be treated like a pile of garbage. Not by Ashur. Not by anybody.

No, if she and Philip Ashur were going to play house, it would be on her terms, not his.

"Now," she said, forcing a smile, "I'll take that brandy you offered earlier, Phil. And you can tell me everything I need to know about these Wisconsin tree farmers of yours to legally steal their land out from under them."

CHAPTER FOUR

After a brief stop for food and fuel at a tollway oasis north of Chicago's O'Hare International Airport, McMichaels and Groves switched seats. Bob took the wheel again while Groves slouched sullenly in the passenger seat and chain-smoked cigarettes.

Mile after mile of denuded cornfields flowed hypnotically past the windshield like slow-motion frames in a silent film. Groves stubbed out his cigarette in the butt-filled ashtray below the dash, laid his head against the passenger-side window, and soon appeared sound asleep. McMichaels had a four-hour nap between Indianapolis and Chicago and no longer worried about dozing off at the wheel. Nevertheless, as the metallic blue Ford sped northwest on Interstate 90 at 70 miles an hour, past green and white exit signs for towns labeled Elgin, Marengo, Belvidere, Rockford, Machesney Park, and Roscoe, he found it increasingly difficult to keep his mind on the road.

Slowing only to pay a final toll, they crossed the state line and entered Wisconsin at two-twelve in the afternoon.

Forty-eight hours ago, Wisconsin had been the last thing on his military mind. What he'd been looking forward to then was seeing his two children.

How long had it been since he'd had quality time with his kids? Two years? Three? It seemed impossible that Susan was now a freshman in high school, and little Sean—not yet as tall as his father, but showing signs he soon would be—was already a teenager.

But why should that be so surprising? His divorce from Donna had been final six years. My God, how time flew when one was having fun!

Earlier this year he'd heard she'd divorced her third husband, that fast-talking salesman. What the hell was his name? Sam? Yeah, Sam. And last week she'd phoned to tell him he could have the kids all to himself the entire week before Thanksgiving while she and her latest boyfriend flew to Aspen for the opening of the ski season.

Bob had accrued four weeks of excess leave—use it or lose it before the end of the year, said Army regulations—so he'd put in his leave papers. He'd planned to fly down to Dallas/Fort Worth on Tuesday, rent a car at the airport, pick up Sean and Susan in the affluent Texas suburb where they now lived, and the three of them—Sean,

Susie, and Bob—would spend some quality time getting to know each other all over again.

Maybe it wasn't too late to be a real father to his kids.

Then the dream had been shattered and his plans changed radically. His previously-approved leave had been canceled, and he received new orders to investigate a possible terrorist attack on the family of a service member.

After successful terrorist bombings ripped apart the homes, private vehicles, and off-duty hang-outs of military personnel and their families overseas, similar incidents occurred in California, Colorado, Texas, Virginia, and North Carolina. A car bomb exploded in San Diego, killing the wife and two children of a Navy Captain. An Air Force pilot and his family were killed in Colorado when the brakes and power steering on their family car failed and the vehicle dropped off a forty-foot cliff because the brakes and steering had been tampered with.

Terrorists also gunned down the family of a Marine Corps Lieutenant Colonel in North Carolina in the parking lot of a shopping center, made to look like they'd accidentally wandered into the middle of a drug war crossfire.

Consequently, the Defense Intelligence Agency asked the FBI to report any stateside activity that smelled vaguely like terrorism. Within hours after Ellen Groves had been murdered, computers matched her name and address with the name and point of entry into military service of a flagged army officer. And Lieutenant Colonel Robert S. McMichaels became the senior intelligence officer assigned to investigate.

This was considered a top-priority assignment by the Pentagon. If families of military officers were being targeted by terrorists, the President of the United States was prepared to direct a timely retaliatory response. A full report was required within ten days.

Official orders, expeditiously faxed from the Adjutant General's office, authorized LTC McMichaels to carry concealed weapons aboard commercial aircraft. As an interim measure, he was authorized to use whatever force he considered necessary to protect the families of military officers in the continental U.S. Civilian law enforcement agencies were requested to cooperate in every way possible, but the nature and extent of his investigation was highly classified and he was advised to exercise discretion during contact with civilian authorities.

He had ten days to find out what was happening and report to the Director of the Defense Intelligence Agency. The head of DIA would personally hand the report to the President.

Yesterday afternoon he'd telephoned Donna from his quarters to tell her that a military emergency he couldn't discuss with her for reasons of national security had unexpectedly come up, and he was really sorry, but he wouldn't be able to take the kids next week. Could he have them for the week between Christmas and New Year's instead?

She had ranted and raved and yelled and screamed for better than fifteen minutes.

"You lousy son of a bitch! How dare you do this to the kids and me again? Where the hell am I going to find someone who can watch two teenagers at this late date? And what am I going to tell them, huh? Their father isn't coming to see them because he loves his job more than he loves his kids? They've really been looking forward to seeing their real father for the first time in years, and then you go and disappoint them. No wonder they hate you. Don't you even want to see your kids? They are yours, you know. Don't you care about them at all? And what am I going to do with *your* kids while I'm gone? I sure as hell can't take them with me to Aspen. Maybe I should just leave them here. Leave them all alone. Would you like that? You just don't care about them, do you? Well, think of your kids all alone while you're off playing soldier, you son of a bitch! Think what might happen to them because you're not here with them! You care more about the stinking Army than your family, don't you? You always have. If something bad happens to your kids, it'll be your fault, not mine."

Donna was right. He did care more about the Army than her.

But he did love his kids.

He'd requested and received a download of Groves' permanent 201 file, including the results of psychological, emotional, and aptitude tests routinely administered to Ranger candidates and members of the RDF. According to efficiency reports and detailed background checks from the major's national agency investigations, Groves appeared to be a dedicated career officer with highly developed combat skills.

His social skills, however, left a lot to be desired. Still a bachelor at 33, he had no steady girlfriend. According to investigators, he seemed to have no social life at all, no close friends, and hadn't seen his family in years. According to his psychological profile, he expressed no interest in marriage or long-term relationships of any kind.

Groves displayed classic tendencies of a sociopathic loner who didn't want or didn't know how to comfortably interact with other people socially. But he made one hell of a fine soldier. He'd commanded the respect of his men in every combat assignment he'd been given.

McMichaels wondered if Tom's father might have been responsible for the tragic death of his mother. Would a man who'd been denied parental rights—denied even the acknowledgement that he'd fathered one of her three children—go to such an extreme?

If Donna refused to let Bob see his kids, would he get angry enough to want to kill her? Domestic violence in this day and age was certainly not unheard of. But would anyone become angry enough to pay a professional hit squad to take out the mother of his children, especially grown children? Would anyone really spend the money necessary to field twelve professionals just to avenge a perceived slight to his manhood?

And why wait thirty years to do it?

If an organized attack on the mother of a military officer were a terrorist action by America's political enemies, then why did the killers attempt to cover up what happened? And if this were indeed a terrorist political action, why hadn't some group claimed credit for the kill?

Terrorism only generated fear if potential targets knew they were vulnerable to attack. Terrorism's primary purpose was to cause enemies to alter normal behavior patterns in response to perceived threats.

Wasn't that exactly what happened with 9-11?

McMichaels glanced in the rearview mirror, then looked at the speedometer. His speed had inched up to 90. He checked the rearview mirror again, moved into the right lane, eased off the gas, and slowed to 65, allowing cars to pass in the left lane.

Despite the rain and wind, traffic seemed to be moving at a brisk pace. Only one vehicle, remaining three or four car lengths behind the Focus, noticeably varied its speed.

As he sped up or slowed down, so did his shadow.

Groves sat up and rubbed sleep from his eyes.

"Take a look in the rearview mirror. There's a dark green Nissan Altima three or four cars back. See if you can make the plates."

"I can't read the numbers." Groves adjusted the mirror on the passenger door for a better look. "Front plate's spattered with mud, I can't even make the state. What's so special about that Nissan?"

"It's been following us since we left Chicago."

"You sure?"

"Positive. Two other cars tailed us earlier, a silver Mazda from Fort Campbell all the way to Indy, and a beige Honda after we left the restaurant. That Nissan took over when we left Illinois. We're being leap-frogged by professionals. Watch what happens when I increase speed."

Groves continued to watch the Nissan in the rear view mirror. When McMichaels accelerated to 85, so did the Nissan. When the Ford slowed to fifty. the Nissan slowed.

"Obvious bastard. Can you shake him?"

"I can try. Hold onto your seat."

McMichaels slammed the accelerator to the floor. Weaving in and out of traffic at better than a hundred miles an hour, he searched vainly for an exit from the expressway. A sign said the next exit was thirteen miles ahead. He pushed the speedometer to 120 and flew forward.

The Nissan swerved into the left lane.

Suddenly, from a row of scrub pines in the median between north-south lanes of the freeway, a Wisconsin State Patrol cruiser raced onto the expressway, red lights flashing and siren wailing. The Nissan immediately slowed, slipped inconspicuously back into the stream of traffic, and disappeared from the rearview mirror.

McMichaels swore. He slapped the steering wheel with the palm of his hand, eased his foot off the accelerator, pulled onto the shoulder, and braked.

The cruiser joined the Focus on the shoulder of the road at the very moment the green Nissan sailed past at a legal 70 miles an hour.

Two men hunched down in the front seat. Both wore hats. He wasn't able to see enough of a profile to recognize either if he saw them again.

"Please step out of your car," commanded a loudspeaker mounted near the center of the cruiser's lightbar. "Keep your hands where I can see them at all times."

As they stepped out of the Focus, freezing rain pelted their bare faces. A frigid gust of arctic wind made Bob's teeth chatter.

"Please place both hands on the trunk and leave them there," directed the trooper's voice. "Don't move until I tell you to."

From the corner of one eye, Bob watched the middle-aged, overweight trooper radio in the out-of-state plates. Within minutes, he obtained registration data and reports of outstanding warrants and/or moving violations.

"You boys are sure a long ways from home," the portly trooper drawled as he approached the car. His right hand hovered an inch from an unsnapped leather holster housing a 9 millimeter automatic. The name tag pinned to the flap of his left pocket read "Seifert." "Welcome to the dairy state where we take the speed limit seriously. Which one of you is Groves?"

"I am," Tom said.

"You in the Army?"

"Yes, sir. We both are."

"I thought the Army gave safe driving lectures before they let you leave base. When I was in, they made us sit through a boring hour-long safety lecture. I clocked you at..." he glanced down at a paper-filled clipboard he held in his left hand "...well, sir, let's just say you were traveling at an unsafe speed at least 40 miles per hour over the legal limit, and that's a felony here in Wisconsin. Very slowly now, please remove your driver's license and military ID from your wallet. Keep your other hand on the trunk. When you're finished, your friend can show me his license and ID."

After the trooper recorded names, addresses, dates of birth, heights, weights, and colors of eyes on a form on his clipboard, he patted both men down for weapons.

"Okay. Slowly, now," he said, apparently satisfied they weren't armed. "You can turn around. As soon as my backup gets here, we'll all drive down to the district station and arrange for a bond hearing. I'm arresting the driver on charges of reckless endangerment, exceeding posted speed limits, and driving way too fast for current conditions. I'm holding the passenger as a witness. Your car will be impounded until released by the court. Any questions?"

"Officer Seifert," McMichaels said, "you have no authority to hold either of us. Major Groves and I are on official business in a matter of national security, and I have written orders in my pocket that exempts us, as federal officers, from state and local statutes. Under the Homeland Security Act, federal authority takes precedence over local ordinances. May I show you my orders?"

"The hell you say. Show me. Carefully remove your orders and slowly—very slowly—hand them over."

Using two fingers, McMichaels pulled a stapled set of written orders from his coat pocket.

"Please read the special instructions. Then ask NCIC to patch you through to the Attorney General's office. The AG will verify Groves and I are exempt from local and state jurisdiction while on official business."

The trooper studied the orders. "These look legit. But I gotta check. You boys'll have to wait here in the rain while I run a check with Madison. This could take a while."

Fifteen minutes later he returned, his chubby face red with embarrassment.

"Sorry I stopped you," he said, handing the orders back to McMichaels. "You're free to go."

"Thank you, officer. I appreciate your cooperation. No hard feelings?"

"Just doing my job," Seifert grunted. "Drive safely. We wouldn't want you getting in an accident now, would we?"

"He thought you were trying to bullshit your way out of a ticket," Groves laughed. "But you weren't bullshitting, were you? How do a pair of grunts rate this kind of VIP treatment?"

"I'm on a priority mission. Until we find out who murdered your mother and why, I answer to nobody but the Pentagon. You, on the other hand, are on emergency leave. I could've let Seifert throw you in jail, if I'd felt like it."

"But you didn't feel like it?"

"Tomorrow I might feel differently. Meanwhile, I need you to keep your eyes peeled for our tail. He's probably waiting on an entrance ramp up ahead."

It was already dark by five o'clock, and tiny snowflakes swirled in clusters in front of the Ford's headlights. Groves recommended they turn off Interstate 90 at the Wisconsin Dells exit.

No lights followed them.

Just to be sure, Bob drove around the block twice in downtown Dells. Then he doubled back and parked in front of a boarded-up souvenir shop. When neither the Nissan nor any other car with out of state license plates appeared, he shoved the Focus into gear and continued north on State Highway 13.

Snow came down thick and heavy. McMichaels' neck felt stiff and his backside hurt by the time they stopped for dinner at a family-style restaurant in the heart of Wisconsin Rapids.

"Rapids used to be a papermill town," Groves remarked between bites of meat and potatoes. "Loggers herded timber downriver on the Wisconsin, and later by truck and train on roads and tracks that paralleled the river, to sawmills and pulp paper factories at Rapids, Port Edwards, Nekoosa, and Necedah. Hundreds of mills sprang up and prospered during the second half of the 19th century. Most of the state was pretty much logged out by the end of the Second World War, and these days, despite token reforestation efforts by the state of Wisconsin and the U. S. Department of the Interior, local mills import timber from Canada. Foreign competition from rain forests in Malaysia and South America threatens to kill the domestic paper trade altogether."

"You said your family owns a tree farm. Did they supply timber to the mills?"

"Never have, never will. Ma earned a living selling seedlings to nurseries. She also planted acres of fir and scotch pine to accommodate the annual Christmas tree market. She sold mostly to locals who'd drive out to the farm for the perfect tree for their living room. Ma hated loggers, and wouldn't have anything to do with people from the mills. Over the years she turned down hundreds of offers to sell. 'The land doesn't belong to me,' she told them. 'I'm just a caretaker. How can I sell what doesn't belong to me?'"

"Only a caretaker? Your family rented the tree farm and didn't actually own it?"

"Figure of speech. Legally, Ma owned the farm and everything on it. She inherited clear title to 1800 acres of mostly virgin timberland from a great aunt, under very strict conditions none of the old growth trees in the heart of the forest ever be felled. My mother thought of herself as sort of a caretaker of the land, and she considered it a sacred trust to pass that land on to her daughters."

"To her daughters? Not to her son?"

"No," Groves said. "Not to her son."

"Why not?"

"Nurturing trees is a woman's job, not a man's." Groves shoveled another forkful of potatoes into his mouth. "Ma felt it was a woman's obligation to take care of trees, much like the obligation to take care of children. You see, she was more than just a caretaker. She was a caregiver. She loved to protect and nourish trees almost as much as she loved to protect and nourish her children. It's the kind of thing women, not men, do."

"And what kind of things do men do?"

"They hunt," Groves said. He laid his knife and fork across his empty plate. "At least, that's the way it is in my family. But, then, my family is a bit unusual."

"Unusual? How so?"

"Wait until you meet my sisters. You'll see just how unusual we are. You ready to go? It's my turn to drive."

Sixteen miles north of Park Falls, the Focus bogged down in a four-foot high snowdrift that stretched across both lanes of State Route 13. It reminded Bob of sand dunes he'd seen in Saudi Arabia. Fortunately, Groves kept an army-issue entrenching tool next to the spare tire in the trunk. It took only twenty minutes to dig through the drift; but, by the time they finished digging, blowing snow had cut visibility to less than ten feet.

"If anyone's still trailing us, they won't be able to see us any easier in this storm than we can see them."

"They know where we're headed. They stuck to our tail long enough to be certain you were going straight home. When we get to your family's farm, they'll have a vehicle waiting to pick us up again."

"You make this sound like a game of tag. Or maybe a high-tech game of cops and robbers."

"They followed us across state lines, so I don't think they're cops. But they use the same tactics. A few years back, I was assigned to an MI detachment for training in covert surveillance. Newcomers went TDY to Quantico for six weeks and learned tactics from experts at the FBI Academy. Whoever's trailing us learned the same techniques. They're well-trained, well-disciplined, and well-equipped. If they're not cops or former cops, they're military intelligence. Unless someone's running a double blind, I don't think they're American intelligence."

"You think they're the same men who killed my mother?"

"I intend to find out. Sooner or later they'll tip their hand. And when they do, I'll be waiting."

"We'll be waiting," amended Groves. "If they killed my mother, I want a piece of their hides."

Tom pulled off SR 13 and headed down a side road flanked on both sides by solid stands of 35-foot tall white pine. Snow clung to the upper limbs, making weighted-down pine boughs look like low-lying clouds.

"Almost there," said Groves, turning onto another road. "The Nelson farm's just around the next bend."

"None of this looks real," Bob whispered, feeling awed by the never-ending panorama. "It's too picture perfect, like a scene in a plastic snow globe. I've never seen so much white in my entire life. The whole world's white."

A mile beyond the Nelson farm Groves slowed, turned off the highway, and cautiously edged the Focus onto what appeared little more than two wheel-width ruts between parallel rows of trees.

"Fire trail," he explained. "State law requires us to cut and maintain trails through the forest at predetermined intervals so fire-fighting equipment can be brought in. This one leads up to the house. It's the closest thing to a driveway we have."

The Ford's headlights penetrated the snow enough to unveil the natural beauty of the old-growth forest. On both sides gigantic 35 to 40-foot-tall white pines, some stretching as high as 70 or 80 feet into the air with trunks nearly as wide as a car, rose skyward in a pyramidal succession of branches that formed protective arches. It was as if they drove through a natural green and white tunnel that stretched as far as the eye could see.

"How old are these trees?" Bob asked. "They look positively ancient."

"No one knows. According to Marquette's diaries, they were here when white men first explored this part of the world in the late 16th or early 17th centuries. Conifers, unlike humans, don't die of old age. Did you know that, Colonel? Unless felled by a lumberman's ax, infested by fungi, eaten by insects, uprooted by strong winds, or starved by drought or a lack of minerals in the soil, trees can live forever."

"Wasn't the entire state leveled by glaciers during the last ice age? Seems to me I read that ice destroyed native vegetation about fifteen or twenty thousand years ago when glaciers pushed through."

"Parts of Wisconsin escaped, believe it or not. Some of these trees survived all three Wisconsin glaciations. Of course, there's no way of knowing a tree's true age without chopping it down and counting growth rings."

"And your family won't allow that, will they?"

"No. The only way any of these old-growth giants will be felled is over the dead bodies of the entire Groves family—mine included. And I'm not as easy to kill as my mother."

CHAPTER FIVE

T he woods opened up like the parting of the Red Sea, and there, straight ahead, in the exact center of a thousand-foot clearing surrounded by ancient pines, stood a white two-storied wood frame square box with a snow-covered cedar-shingle roof.

It looked exactly the way he imagined Santa Claus' house at the North Pole might. That is, if Bob McMichaels still believed in Santa Claus.

He was surprised to see two cars, a late model Silver Mercedes Benz and a blue Toyota Prius, half-buried in an immense snowdrift near the front porch. Three other cars, only partially covered as if they'd arrived within the past hour, were parked off to the side nearer the trees.

"Once," Groves explained, "a sizeable stand of oak and hard maple occupied this very spot. The house itself is constructed exclusively of timbers hewn from those hardwood trees, felled nearly two centuries ago by my ancestors."

"I thought you said your family didn't allow any trees on this land to be cut."

"None of the trees incorporated in the building of the house was more than four hundred years old when ancestors of mine cut them down."

"And that made it okay to cut them down? Their age?"

"No. The reason it was okay to cut them was the trees themselves gave my ancestors permission. At least, that's what my mother said the people who built the house believed."

"That's crazy."

"I warned you my family was weird." Groves parked the Focus next to the Mercedes. "When you meet my sisters and the rest of the family, you'll see what I mean."

A massive granite-and-mortar vine-encrusted chimney climbed the east wall of the house, and McMichaels caught a whif of fragrant wood smoke wafting from the two-stack chimneytop as he pushed open the car door and swung his cramped legs into ankle-deep snow. Groves exited the driver's side, tromped through snow to the rear of the car, popped the Ford's snow-covered trunk, extracted both suitcases and the AWOL bag, and tossed McMichaels his own suitcase.

"Careful!" shouted McMichaels, grabbing for the suitcase with both hands. "My computer's in there!"

As the two men hurried up half a dozen steps to seek the shelter of the verandaed front porch, a massive oaken door opened inward. The most beautiful woman he'd ever seen—tall, slender, raven-haired, and dressed in a flowing white gown that seemed so thin it looked virtually transparent—materialized in the open doorway. She held a flickering candle in her ringless left hand, and her eyes sparkled like cut diamonds in the flickering candlelight.

She looked exactly like he thought an angel would look, if he still believed in angels.

Despite the raging wind, the candle's flame did not go out. In fact, as he stared in fascination, the pulsating flame only seemed to flare stronger and brighter in the oxygen-rich wind.

"Hurry," said the Most Beautiful Woman in the World, stepping back to allow Tom through the door. It's already eleven. Ma's remembering starts at midnight."

"I came as quickly as I could." Tom slipped his free arm around the angel's waist and gently brushed her cheek with his lips. "The others all here? Vi? Cynthia?"

"Aunt Vi flew in yesterday. Aunt Cynthia arrived about an hour ago. Great Aunt Hazel isn't well rnough to travel. But Great Aunt Anna is here in her place."

"Do we have enough people?"

"Now that you're here, we do."

Bob followed Tom and the woman inside, catching only scattered bits and pieces of their conversation. The raging north wind whistled and howled at his back, drowning out most of the words.

Careful not to track snow onto the spotlessly-clean varnished hardwood floor—a floor that looked starkly naked except for three oval-shaped hand-braided rag rugs near the entrance—he set his suitcase down, closed the door behind him, and wiped the soles of his snow-drenched shoes on one of the rugs.

Tom and the Most Beautiful Girl in the World continued reminiscing about family as they walked through the house. Bob followed them into the living room, huge by today's standards, though not completely out of character for a house constructed well before the turn of the last century. All four walls and the high ceiling were paneled with varnished pine planks identical in appearance and texture to the hardwood floors. Two good-sized shuttered windows broke up the monotony of the north wall, and several dozen potted plants, strategically-placed on the floor in front of each window, added touches of color to the room.

What made the oversized room seem even larger, was the complete absence of normal curios and bric-a-brac found in the typical family room of the modern home. There was no large-screen television set, not even a radio, to take up space. Where, he wondered, was the usual bookcase stuffed with Readers Digest Condensed Books, old National Geographics, unread self-help books, and the family Bible? And where were the normal pictures, family portraits and dozens of snapshots of kids in various stages of growth, that decorated the walls and tables of nearly every home he'd ever been in?

Warmth in the room radiated not from heat vents but from a roaring fire in a monstrous stone fireplace that filled most of the east wall. Two tapered candles flickered in silver candlestick holders on a bare-wood mantle over the fireplace, and a glowing kerosene lamp on a four-foot-long maple coffee table in front of a well-worn, comfortable-looking sofa, plus the single lit candle that the Most Beautiful Woman in the World still clutched in her left hand, contributed illumination. But not enough. Despite the woman's breathtaking beauty, Bob thought the room seemed cold, inhospitable, sinister, and filled with brooding shadows.

"Bob," said Tom, gently turning the woman around to face McMichaels. "Allow me to introduce my sister Diane. Di, meet Colonel Robert McMichaels. Bob has been assigned to investigate Ma's murder."

Diane Groves' robin's-egg blue gaze sized Bob up, and then promptly dismissed him.

"As you can see," she said, her voice colder than the outside air, "we have neither central heating nor electricity in this drafty old house. You won't like it here at all. You *were* planning to start back immediately, weren't you?"

"Diane, please," Tom pleaded. "Have you forgotten your manners? The roads must be totally impassible by now. Let him stay the night, and he can head back in the morning."

"You know that's impossible." The chill in her voice was even colder than before. "We have friends and family staying tonight and tomorrow. Every bed in the house is taken. Trust me. It'll be better for all concerned if your friend looks for a motel out on SR 13."

"I really don't want to intrude," said Bob, knowing how a third wheel felt on a bicycle. "If you'll lend me your car, Tom, I'll find a motel."

"You'll never get through those drifts, Colonel. Winds have piled snow six-feet deep in places, and county road crews don't plow until the snow stops. Who knows when this storm will end? If you leave here tonight, you'll only get stranded in a snowdrift between here and Highway 13. Do you really want to spend the night sleeping in a cold car?"

"I'll take my chances. I've slept in worse places than a car."

"Ma's snowmobile is in the shed out back," Diane offered. "It's not as warm as an automobile, but the Ski-Doo will get him through drifts. Tomorrow, if the snow stops, you can drive your friend from the motel to the bus station. Okay?"

"Are you sure this is necessary?" asked Tom.

"Absolutely. It's already eleven-thirty. Ma's memorial begins at midnight. He must leave now."

"You'll need a heavier jacket, overshoes, gloves, and a ski mask," said Tom, sounding reconciled to the idea. "I have some old clothes tucked away upstairs. Wait here. I'll be back in a minute."

Left alone with the Most Beautiful Woman in the World, Bob felt like a schoolboy on his first date. God! She was beautiful! Beautiful and...cold. Was she this cold to every man she met?

Or, he wondered, is it only me? Something I said, maybe? The way I look?

Diane turned her back on him, cutting off any chance of engaging her in friendly conversation. As she casually sauntered over to the fireplace, he felt mesmerized. Though she had to be aware he was openly staring as she bent down and selected a split log from a three-foot-high pile of cut wood, he couldn't keep his eyes off her.

She added the log to the fire. Her body was silhouetted by firelight. The nearly sheer gown shimmered like a gauzy halo around her perfectly-shaped body.

Was she naked beneath that flimsy fabric? He'd bet a month's pay she was!

Tom returned with a fur-lined parka, knit ski mask, and woolen mittens.

Bob quickly turned his eyes away from Diane's backside. He felt like a small child caught with his hand in the cookie jar.

"These fit me when I was a high school student," Tom said, handing the garments to Bob. "I haven't grown a hell of a lot since then. I figure you're about the same size as me, give or take an inch. Try them on and see if they fit."

Bob removed his trenchcoat and slipped the parka over his sweatshirt.

"A bit tight in the shoulders," he said, "but it'll have to do. I'm sure the mask and gloves will fit just fine."

"Then come out back and I'll show you how to run the snowmobile. Leave your suitcase here. You can get it in the morning."

Groves grabbed the kerosene lantern from the coffee table and led McMichaels through a spacious kitchen, then through a well-stocked pantry, out the rear door, and into a garage-sized wooden shed which housed a wide variety of garden implements, assorted hand tools, and a 50-year-old black and yellow Bombardier Ski-Doo. The snowmobile sported a pair of aluminum skis mounted in front, twin tractor-like rear treads, and a set of chrome handlebars that mimicked the handlebars on a Harley Davidson.

"You ever drive one of these before?"

Bob shook his head.

"It's like riding a motorcycle. If you've been on a big bike, you'll have the feel in no time. Turn the handlebars, and the skis turn the same way. Squeeze the right grip to give her gas. Squeeze the left grip to brake. Take it real easy on the gas, though, until you get the feel of the machine. She'll do forty or fifty on a straightaway, but forty on hills or curves will flip you over and you'll likely break your neck. Here," Tom handed Bob a padded plastic helmet and plastic goggles. "Better put these on over your ski mask."

"Where do I find the nearest motel?" Bob donned the helmet while Tom topped off the tank with an oil and gas mixture from a five-gallon can.

"Follow the fire trail back to County Trunk O. Turn right on O, then turn right again when you get to double N. You'll hit Highway 13 about twenty miles or so up the road. Turn right on 13 and you'll see a mom and pop motel a good half-mile on the left. They should have plenty of vacancies this time of the year. If, by chance, they're full tonight or closed for the season, try the cabin courts about five miles farther on."

"Tom, I don't mean to intrude on your family during their time of grief, but I have a job to do. I can't leave the area until I dig up answers about your mother's murder to satisfy the big-ass brass. I know you understand. I do hope your sister understands."

"Come morning, Diane'll be a different woman. Wait and see. As soon as the snow stops, county plows will clear the main roads. When they're open again, I'll meet you at the motel. Then we can drive back here or go talk to the sheriff, whichever you like."

Tom showed him how to adjust the choke and pull the rip cord. On the third try, the Ski-Doo growled to life like a mother bear waking cubs from hibernation. Bob circled the house twice to test the controls and get used to straddling the saddle-like seat. When he felt comfortable balancing the front end on turns, he threw Tom a quick salute and zoomed up the fire trail at thirty miles an hour.

Close to the ground, with nothing overhead to block the spectacular view of the majestic pines, Bob was suddenly overcome by a sense of awe. He hadn't experienced anything like this since he'd been a small boy attending Catholic mass on Sunday morning. It was as if he'd suddenly become a child again. He stared up at the trees.

He felt like he'd entered a magnificent cathedral and he half-expected to see the Savior hung on a larger-than-life-sized cross above the sacrosanct. Totally awestruck, he slowed the snowmobile to a snail's crawl. Half-way between the house and the highway he killed the motor.

The sudden silence was overwhelming. No birds sang. He heard only the whistle of the wind passing through snow-laden pine boughs.

Bob felt in the presence of the Holy. Not even the deserts of Saudi Arabia compared with this. It made a man feel totally insignificant in a world he hadn't made and couldn't control. Man's fate, like the fate of the world, rested in the hands of a higher power.

McMichaels wasn't a particularly religious man. Raised Roman Catholic, his faith had been diluted over the years, replaced with hard-hearted practicality. When his fervent prayers went unanswered after his father deserted them and his mother fought her losing battle with cancer, he doubted God cared or even existed. His doubts were confirmed by the atrocities of war in Iraq and Afghanistan. How could a loving and caring God allow such things? How could any father, heavenly or not, watch his children kill each other and do nothing to stop it?

He didn't think much about God at all anymore. And if God really did exist, he didn't think He gave Bob McMichaels much thought, either.

But here in the heart of the woods, he felt an unmistakable religiosity that had very little to do with faith. Rather, he became conscious that man was only a tiny, insignificant part of a much greater whole, as if an individual human were no more than a single cog in a vast chain of being that stretched on forever.

Were these trees really as old as they looked? Did some of them actually pre-date the glaciers? How old were they? These pines were certainly tall enough to have seen Ellen Groves run down on the highway less than a mile away. What else might they have witnessed in the millennia they'd lived in this place? What stories might they tell if only they could speak?

C'mon, Bob. You're starting to sound crazier than the entire Groves family put together. Better get your butt back on the damn snowmobile and find a motel before you freeze to death!

He adjusted the choke and cranked the motor. Once again the hibernating bear growled to life.

Five minutes later he reached the county road, turned right, and headed east toward State Route 13.

Lost in thought, he didn't notice a four-wheel-drive Ford Explorer—one of two vehicles waiting along the side of the road without headlights—pull onto the road and follow him at a discrete distance.

CHAPTER SIX

S heila Ryan never expected to be stuck in snow.

Following highlighted roadmaps and detailed instructions Ashur's secretary had supplied along with extensive dossiers on the entire Groves family, Sheila departed Chicago shortly before noon. Despite an incessant drizzle that turned blacktopped pavement treacherous at speeds above sixty miles an hour, she achieved excellent time on the Interstate as far north as Eau Claire.

She did notice a blustery wind blowing snowflakes this way and that in front of her leased Lincoln MKZ's windshield when she turned off I-94 onto US 53 north, but Sheila paid little attention to the gradual accumulation of white stuff until overworked wipers became clogged with clumps of hard-packed snow. She had to turn the defroster on high just to see the road.

By the time she reached Barron, where she picked up U.S. 8 east and dutifully followed the winding federal highway through Ladysmith to link up with the narrower two-lane Wisconsin 13 outside Prentice, blowing snow was already two feet deep and coming down in blinding sheets driven by a powerful northwest wind. If she'd been smart, she would have stopped for the night in Philips, the last decent-sized town on the map before Park Falls. But she wasn't weather-smart, and Sheila Ryan—as her opponents in court knew only too well—never knew when to stop.

Now she was floundering in a snowdrift someplace miles north of Park Falls on State Route 13, and it looked like she'd be spending the night stranded in her car out here in the middle of nowhere. She hadn't seen a town, or even a crossroads gas station, for more than an hour, and crawling along at barely five miles an hour she entertained doubts she'd find any type of shelter in this storm before morning's light. There was nothing but trees and snow, and more trees and more snow, on both sides of the road as far as the eye could see. And even with high beams her vision barely extended two feet beyond the hood of the leased Lincoln MKZ.

WBBM, Chicago's Newsradio 78 and her last connection with the real world, faded in and out somewhere north of Portage, and 780 on the AM dial now broadcast more static than news. Scanning the dial, all she managed was a Minneapolis station playing classic country like "Achey Breaky Heart" and "Nobody's Fool." She cursed herself for not bringing along a few classical cds to feed the car's empty cd player. Country-western music had always been her father's favorite, and Sheila Ryan hated country-western music with the same passion she afforded her late father.

She was stuck in a snowdrift that even the sturdily-built Lincoln found impossible to navigate. She tried to rock the car back and forth but got nowhere. She wasn't even sure anymore which lane the car was in. She had tried to use her cell phone, but no signal roamed this far from civilization. There was nothing to do now but wait out the storm and pray the gas in the tank held out until morning.

She was glad she refilled the tank at Ladysmith, glad the fuel gage still hovered near the three-quarters mark. As long as she kept motor and heater running, at least she wouldn't freeze to death. And, if she were truly lucky, maybe a snowplow would come along to plow her out before morning.

Never wanting to waste a moment of valuable time—time was money, her father had repeated so often that she'd grown up believing it—Sheila turned on the overhead light, opened her briefcase, and brought out four thick files on members of the Groves family that Ashur's secretary had handed her in Chicago.

Ellen Groves, 64, matriarch of the family: five feet 2, 103 pounds; recently deceased. Ellen mothered three children: Thomas, Diane, and Nancy. She never married. Groves was her maiden name. She inherited 1800 acres of timberland from a great-aunt, Emma Wells. A grainy thirty-year-old black and white photograph showed a blonde-haired woman in her mid-thirties. Other photos, older but clearer, showed a smiling college-age girl with delicate facial features and bright blue eyes. A recent photo, shot with a digital telephoto lens from a great distance, showed a diminutive grey-haired grandmother-type wearing a blue chambray work shirt, Osh Kosh bib overalls, and brown Timberline work boots. The boots were splattered with mud. The grey hair was tied back in a bun. Not bad looking. Too bad she didn't know how to dress or use makeup. She could have been a stunner when she was younger. Probably was. Probably turned men's heads.

Thomas Groves, 33: 6 feet 2, 210 pounds; Major, Infantry, U. S. Army. Currently assigned to the Joint Chiefs of Staff Unified Command Rapid Deployment Force. Detailed for temporary duty to train stateside units on counterinsurgency tactics. Not bad looking either, if he let that straw-colored hair grow out to a reasonable length. A real hunk, actually. Nice tush. Looks like he'd be fun in bed. Maybe tomorrow or the next day she'd find out if he was as good as he looked.

Diane Groves, 31: 5 feet 8 inches, 127 pounds; BA, MA, PhD, Doctor of Divinity; Associate Professor of History at the University of Wisconsin, Madison. This woman didn't need to use any makeup at all. Her shoulder-length, raven-colored hair highlighted the cover girl features of a woman who could have, in the right hands, rivaled Cindy Crawford, Elle McPherson or Rachel Hunter for top modeling jobs. Sheila felt a sharp pang of jealousy rip through her gut. Any woman in her right mind would kill to look that good.

Nancy Groves, 28: 5 feet 4, 114 pounds; BA, MA, MS ED, doctoral student and instructor in Anglo-Saxon languages at UW, Madison. Submitted doctoral dissertation titled "Fire and Ice: Influences of Pre-Christian Northern European Runic Symbology on Germanic Grammatical Construction." ABD. Orals pending. Blonde. Petite. Contemporary shag haircut. Maybe not as good-looking as her sister, but as cute as a button and as vulnerable-looking as a fragile porcelain doll.

Sheila knew what it was like to grow up the youngest child in a single parent household, and she was surprised to discover a sisterly sympathy for Nancy Groves. Had Nancy's older brother and sister picked on her the way Sheila's brothers had? Was there a hidden mean streak in Thomas or Diane that made growing up as miserable for her as growing up had been for Sheila?

She rolled the driver-side window down an inch and a half, lit the last cigarette in the fresh pack she'd opened at noon, and slid the empty wrapper out the slit at the top of the window.

Fortunately, she still had a full carton of Benson and Hedges squirreled away in a suitcase locked in the trunk. Though she'd have to venture out in the storm to fetch a new pack from the trunk, at least she didn't need to worry about running out of nicotine.

Sheila had given up trying to muster the willpower to quit the cigarette habit entirely, but she was proud she'd managed to cut down in the past year and a half since leaving XIIMI's employ. She'd been up to almost four packs a day while litigating for them on a regular basis, but most days now she did just fine on two—sometimes two and a half—packs of extra-long Benson and Hedges. Someday, she suspected, her nicotine habit would probably kill her. Someday. But not today.

According to the report, Thomas Groves smoked filtered Camels, the purest form of coffin-nails possible. He regularly purchased two cartons a week at a base commissary or PX. Two cartons a week averaged out to almost three packs a day.

Sheila wondered if Ashur had chosen her to seduce Groves because they both smoked two-and-a-half to three packs of cigarettes a day. It was, she knew, the type of thing Ashur would think of. Let Sheila talk Groves out of the land while they're both enjoying a cigarette after a night of wild, passionate, raw, down-and-dirty sex. Fuckin' Phil didn't smoke. She wondered if a man who didn't smoke could appreciate wild, passionate sex—or be wildly passionate about anything.

Someday she'd have to find out what made Ashur tick. Someday. But not today.

Sheila skimmed the rest of the computerized data on Thomas Groves. Her eyes came to a screeching halt halfway down the first page. What's this? Father unknown? Jesus! Wasn't that a polite way of saying the guy's a bastard?

She went back and checked the data on his mother. Ellen never married. Groves was her maiden name. Okay, so she was a liberated woman. How about Diane? Did anyone know the name of Diane's father?

Nope. Father unknown. Christ! What about Nancy? Nancy, too! Jesus! What kind of woman was this Ellen Groves, anyway? Her data sheet was sparse compared to the others in XIIMI's folder. Sheila checked the photocopy of Ellen's birth certificate for the name of her father. Good God! There it was again: Father unknown.

Joanna Groves, Ellen's mother, birthed four children out of wedlock: Cynthia, Carl, Ellen, and Violet. Carl, the second child and only son, was killed in action in Viet Nam during the Tet offensive. Cynthia, the oldest, was still alive, an aging advertising executive for a PR firm in Northern California. Violet was a tenured history professor at a private college in Massachusetts. Like Ellen, neither Violet nor Cynthia ever married. No mention of either having children. Since Ashur had access to XIIMI's huge database of information on practically everyone in the world, Sheila had no doubt the data had been checked and cross-checked.

XIIMI's mainframe acted as a central clearinghouse for the international insurance and credit industries, and scraps of seemingly irrelevant information were routinely correlated from a vast variety of sources: Insurance applications, credit applications, scholarship applications, school records, medical records, even Social Security Administration files. Sheila didn't know how, but Ashur's people had direct access to government computers and routinely downloaded data that was supposed to be restricted. She wasn't at all surprised to discover a hard copy of the National Security Agency's detailed background investigation for Thomas Groves' latest Top Secret Army security clearance. Did that mean someone at the Federal Bureau of Investigation or National Security Agency was on Ashur's payroll? Probably.

Phil had once bragged that XIIMI could access, either through computer records or real-time surveillance, the secret-most fantasies and fears of practically anyone and everyone. As a staff attorney for one of the corporation's subsidiaries, Sheila had learned that XIIMI employed hundreds of private investigators to dig up dirt on corporate competitors. So she wasn't too surprised when Ashur had suggested to her in conspiratorial confidence, "Those that can't be bribed can always be blackmailed." And then he'd shown her how easy it was to blackmail a powerful opponent.

Sheila, at that time, had been unsuccessfully litigating a minor case in Chicago's Dirkson Federal Building before a no-nonsense federal judge named Ellis Powell. Knowing the merits of her arguments were transparently thin and had little precedent in actual law, she'd dutifully reported the judge was certain to rule against XIIMI. In her professional opinion, she'd advised Phil, it would be far cheaper and certainly easier to negotiate an out-of-court settlement than risk losing the case in Powell's courtroom.

Ashur had merely laughed, buzzed his secretary on the intercom, asked Maggie Emmons to bring in the file on Judge Powell, and allowed Sheila to leaf through one of several sets of exceptionally clear color photographs.

Sheila was startled to see pictures of the usually stern-faced judge, spread-eagled on the floor. A completely naked Ellis Powell was being whipped and walked upon by a skinny oriental-looking woman wearing red-lace garterbelt, red stockings, scarlet spike-heeled patent-leather pumps, and nothing else. The judge was smiling in all of the photographs, though Sheila couldn't understand why.

Especially since the oriental appeared to be grinding her patent-leather stiletto heels down hard on Powell's scrotum while whipping his chest raw with a cat-of-nine-tails.

"Judge Powell's greatest fantasy," Ashur explained, "was to have a naked Japanese woman tie him up and walk all over him. XIIMI helped that happen. His greatest fear was to have his wife and children find out. When we told him XIIMI could help that happen, too, he begged us not to. I'm not worried about the way Judge Powell will rule in this case. And you shouldn't be worried, either."

"Jesus, Phil," Sheila stammered, at a loss for words. "You blackmailed a federal judge?"

"Of course."

"I suppose you've got a file on me, too?"

"Naturally. I told you XIIMI keeps files on virtually everyone, didn't I? And I know of no reason to make you an exception. Do you?"

"But I'm on XIIMI's side, Phil. You know I'd never do anything to harm the corporation."

"Of course, you wouldn't. But it never hurts to have a little insurance. After all, XIIMI is in the insurance business. Would you like to see what's in your file, my dear?"

"No, thanks," Sheila had answered, honestly believing at the time she had nothing to hide. Later, however, when she had second thoughts, Ashur steadfastly refused to let her view the contents of her own file.

Had he added something to her file he didn't want her to see? What could he have on her that could possibly matter?

Dozens of times over the past year or two she'd been forced to access XIIMI files on other prominent figures, though few files were as disgusting as Judge Powell's. Compared to Powell and some of the others, the Groves family looked like saints.

"Everyone has their little secrets," Phil had explained. "XIIMI ferrets out those secrets and capitalizes on them. It's done all the time in business, my dear, especially in parts of the world you've been too fortunate to live in. With today's global economy, we use every means at our disposal to remain competitive. It's nothing personal. It's simply good business practice."

If everyone had their little secrets, Ashur appeared to have a few of his own. Shortly after the Powell incident, when Sheila discretely attempted to research his background as her own hole card, she disappointedly drew a blank.

Prior to 1982, it seemed, the refined and sophisticated Philip Ashur that Sheila thought she knew so well, simply didn't exist.

Papers were in place to show he graduated cum laude from Harvard Law School in 1979, but none of the classmates she contacted remembered him at all. His picture didn't appear in Harvard Law School yearbooks, either. Was it possible he could have doctored the records at Harvard to show he'd graduated? Had he even attended Harvard? With Philip Ashur, anything seemed possible.

Evidence also existed he'd studied international law at Cambridge in 1981, and witnesses claimed he actually practiced admiralty law in Hong Kong in the early part of 1989 as a full partner for a law firm Sheila recognized as one of XIIMI's foreign subsidiaries. In 1989 he was promoted to senior vice president of XIIMI's far east operations, responsible for strategic Pacific Rim investments. He earned the company billions by reinvesting in Southeast Asian land and timber at a time when the market was down and land was dirt-cheap. It was a matter of public record that he became XIIMI's youngest President and Chief Executive Officer in 2012, replacing the ailing Theodore Carnes, XIIMI's founder, who remained Chairman of XIIMI's board of directors despite rumors he was dying of cancer.

Ashur's birth date, parentage, and nationality, however, were complete mysteries. Although he obviously held a valid passport from somewhere, Sheila's limited contacts at the U.S. State Department were unable to locate an American passport issued to anyone named Philip Ashur during the past thirty years. A check with the Immigration and Naturalization Service turned up no visa or work permit issued in that name, either. And the Secretary of State's office in Springfield had no record of a driver's license issued to Philip Ashur.

So who was he? When and where was he born? What did he do before going to Cambridge? Who were his parents? And where in the world did he originally come from?

His eyes gave Sheila a clue. Coal black, with just the slightest trace of slant at the corners of the lids. They betrayed some kind of oriental lineage. Not pure oriental, though. Mixed blood. Maybe three or four generations removed.

His hair, a shiny jet-black with a trace of natural curl, might indicate more recent middle-eastern roots to the Ashur family tree. And his year-round tan could easily disguise the swarthy complexion of someone of middle-eastern, or Indian or Pakistani, descent. Iranian, maybe? Or Turkish? That he was tall—an unusual trait for an oriental or Pakistani—obviously derived from his mixed heritage. The aquiline nose and strong jaw were likely Italian or Spanish, but might just as easily be Jewish or Palestinian.

She found herself wondering if he were circumcised. Though Phil occasionally made sexual innuendoes that clearly showed his interest in her was more than simply business, Sheila never let their relationship become physical. She was, after all, in it for the money. If Phil wanted her, he'd have to pay her price.

And Burt Ryan's little girl didn't come cheap.

Nonetheless, she had to fight the constant magnetic attraction she felt every time she was in his presence. The man radiated an animal magnetism so powerful that several times, when she was alone with him, she'd almost lost control.

Her heart would thud in her throat, her hands would quiver, and her knees turn to rubber.

She'd become wet between her legs.

It wasn't only money and power that attracted her to Philip Ashur. It was more. Much much more. Fear was a big part of the fatal attraction, because the man was more dangerous than a loaded gun, or an open flame, or a ticking time bomb. You didn't know when he would go off, rage out of control, or explode. But you felt an uncontrollable urge to touch the flame anyway simply because it was so dangerous, so unpredictable, and so powerful.

If you touched it and survived, you had nothing left to fear.

She'd learned a lot from Philip Ashur about both money and power during the past several years, and she was immensely grateful for minute crumbs of invaluable wisdom he'd thrown her way. She now knew that knowledge was real power. Just as Kabbalists of the middle ages believed that knowing the number of a person's true name gave one power over that person, so did knowing a person's secret desires and fears.

If you knew what someone really wanted or what really scared the pants off them, you could use that knowledge to control them.

So what, she wondered, was his true name? What were Philip Ashur's secret desires? What did he fear?

What was his real reason for wanting this land so badly that he'd promise five million dollars to get it?

She had the feeling that he was hiding a lot more than the names of the investors that wanted to develop Ellen's property. What kind of development would they build in the middle of nowhere that justified a multi-million dollar investment? A resort? A retirement village?

Little secrets. Everyone had them. Philip Ashur had a lot of little secrets. Some of them, Sheila was willing to bet, weren't so little.

More than anything else, she realized, it was his secrets that made the man so goddamned fascinating.

CHAPTER SEVEN

McMichaels reached the junction of County Trunk Double N and State Route 13 shortly after midnight. As he turned south, the north wind carried the faint whine of a four-wheel drive vehicle downshifting to low gear somewhere behind him. Must be a snowplow, he first thought. No one else would be out on a night like this.

Then he remembered Groves had said county road crews wouldn't begin to plow until all the powdery white stuff stopped accumulating. And it certainly hadn't stopped. He eased off the throttle, shifted his weight to keep his balance, and chanced flipping the snowmobile by turning half-way around on the seat to glance over his right shoulder. Though he could barely see two meters behind the red glow of the Ski-Doo's taillight, he should still be able to make out the headlights of another vehicle—if there were another vehicle behind him—reflecting off falling snow for a quarter mile or more.

Either it was too far away to see in this storm, or the driver was running without headlights. That was a crazy thing to do in any weather unless you were a trained operator running covert surveillance on an unsuspecting target.

A sudden blast of icy wind gusted powdery snow in Bob's face and brought to his ears the unmistakable clanking and crunching of a four-wheel drive with chains on all four tires. The sound was now accelerating. If he didn't move fast, the bastards would run him down like someone—quite possibly the same men—had run down a helpless Ellen Groves.

He squeezed the right hand grip to give the Ski-Doo all the gas she could guzzle. Mamma bear growled, stood up on her hind paws, and shot forward at a gallop. Hanging on for dear life as he bounced over four-foot-high snowdrifts, McMichaels widened the distance between himself and his pursuers to more than a mile.

Their heavy four-wheel drive vehicle had to trudge through the thickest parts of the drifts while the lighter, more-mobile Ski-Doo dusted off the powdery tops of drifts like a speedboat cresting waves on a river. He decided to take advantage of his greater mobility and find out just who in hell shadowed him.

As he rounded a tree-lined curve in the two-lane highway that momentarily masked the Ski-Doo's taillights from the men in the truck, he flicked off his own lights, angled off the road into a copse of poplar, killed the motor, and prayed the men in the four-wheel-drive weren't equipped with infrared night vision goggles that could pick up his heat signature.

If they did have night vision gear, it obviously didn't include heat-sensors. The men continued to search for taillights on the highway ahead of them and paid no attention to the half-hidden-by-new-snow snowmobile tracks veering off into the woods. The dark-colored Explorer—silhouetted against an all white background—passed his position. He waited until the SUV was nearly out of sight and yanked the Ski-Doo's rip cord. Mama bear returned to life on the second pull and he eased the snowmobile onto the road. He maintained his distance until he was fairly certain they couldn't see him in their rear-view mirror.

It occurred to him they might be armed and dangerous. Would they be stupid enough to open fire on a moving target? In a blinding snowstorm? Perhaps. If they had automatic weapons. Especially if they were sure he couldn't return fire.

But they had no way of knowing if he were armed or not, and no professional would risk an exchange with a mobile adversary approaching from the rear unless it appeared the only option. High chase gun battles, spectacular as they looked on movie and television screens, made absolutely no sense to trained operatives. The first lesson one learned in this business was to be certain you could take out your target as cleanly as possible before you touched a trigger. Nevertheless, Bob sought to minimize his vulnerability by staying slightly to the left of the center of the Explorer's silhouette, out of clear line of fire of anyone in the passenger seat. The driver couldn't easily turn around to draw a bead while the vehicle was moving forward. The passenger, however, always posed a threat.

If anyone shot at him, it would be the passenger.

Close enough now to confirm there were two men in the front seats, Bob tried to make out the license plates on the back of the Explorer. The numbers had been obscured either by packed snow or deliberately covered with the kind of artificial decoration civilians sprayed on windows or trees to mimic snow at Christmas time.

Like true professionals, they quickly discovered the snowmobile hot on their tail. Brake lights flared brightly as the driver stomped the brake pedal and the Explorer slid to a complete stop.

Bob yanked the handlebars hard to the left. The Ski-Doo veered into the left lane, barely in time to avoid a fatal rear-end collision. He skidded along on the edge of one ski as momentum carried him past the driver's side of the Explorer. He tightened his grip on the handlebars, quickly threw all his weight to starboard, and desperately fought to regain balance.

The machine briefly collided with the SUV's left front fender, sending sparks flying as the hungry bear bit into painted metal, found it unpalatable, and spat it out. Bob cranked the right handgrip a half-turn, heard the snowmobile's rear treads noisily pelt the Explorer's windshield with clumps of snow. The Ski-Doo gained purchase and shot past the front of the vehicle like a roman candle on the Fourth of July. He watched the speedometer climb to thirty-five...forty...forty-five...fifty...fifty-five before easing back on the throttle.

Suddenly, he and the snowmobile were spotlighted in high beams like a rock star on a sound stage. Now that they knew he knew they were there, they felt no need for stealth.

The four-wheel drive gave chase, and a bullet whistled past Bob's right ear.

Farther off to the right, less than a meter from the right ski, another bullet kicked up puffs of snow. He recognized the bark of a nine-millimeter semi-automatic pistol as a third round whizzed over his head.

Taking immediate evasive action, he zigged left, then zagged right, in a random irregular pattern that made an inopportune target. If they picked him off now, it would be purely by luck.

He survived a half-dozen additional near-misses before the snowmobile escaped the effective range of the Explorer's halogen headlights and was temporarily hidden by an artificial barrier of snow and darkness. Though not completely out of range of the passenger's handgun, Bob felt it safe to stop weaving back and forth across both lanes like a drunk. He opened the throttle another quarter turn and charged into the left lane.

Suddenly he saw another pair of headlights burning tiny holes in the almost-solid wall of snow directly in front of him. He was traveling too fast to tell if they were moving toward him at break-neck speed or it was only his own momentum that made it seem like that.

This time when he yanked the handlebars hard to the left to avoid a collision, he felt the Ski-Doo slide out from under him.

He flew through the air like a trapeze artist without a trapeze. He became an olympic highdiver doing a double gainer. The snowmobile flipped over, turned a dozen cartwheels, and buried itself in a drift. Bob came down face-first in another snowdrift twenty feet away from the Ski-Doo, his fall cushioned by powdery white that clogged his mouth and nostrils, and he couldn't catch the elusive breath his abrupt landing forced from his lungs.

For an instant he imagined he'd choke to death.

Then body heat melted the snow in his nose and he was able to lift his head, spit out a mouthful of powder, and gulp fresh air. Fresh air never tasted so good. As he struggled to free his arms and legs from the pile of snow that held him prisoner, he felt the ground shake.

And a brilliant fireball lit up the night and temporarily blinded him.

*   *   *

Sheila dreaded going outside, but she no longer had a choice. Two hours since her last cigarette, she was desperate for a smoke. Waiting out the storm in a rented car wasn't much fun under the most ideal of conditions. And without another cigarette—knowing there was a full carton of Benson and Hedges waiting for her in the trunk—waiting became pure torture.

The sooner she got this over with, the sooner she'd be warm and dry again. Since she never dreamed she'd be caught outdoors in a blinding blizzard, she had power-dressed that morning in a medium-weight navy-blue business suit, silk open-neck white blouse, nylon half-slip, sheer pantyhose, and medium-heeled patent leather pumps. The only coat she'd brought was a lightweight designer raincoat currently draped over the back seat. She mentally kicked herself for being such a fashion-conscious fool.

She did have a pair of wool-blend slacks in her suitcase, and she wished she had them on now. Did she remember to pack a sweater, too? She wasn't sure. Maybe she should bring the entire suitcase from the trunk into the car, just in case there was something else packed inside that could prove useful.

She struggled into the raincoat, buttoned every button including the neck button, and turned up the thin collar to protect the back of her neck and some of her hair. Better get this over with before you lose your nerve, she told herself, jerking the door handle.

She shoved against the cushioned side panel. The door wouldn't open. She tried again. The door wouldn't budge.

"Fuck," she swore aloud, realizing the wind had built a drift almost four feet high against the driver's side of the car.

Tossing her briefcase and the map and the Groves family file folders onto the back seat, Sheila slid across the front seat to try the door on the passenger side. Though reluctant to give more than an inch with each shove, the east-side passenger door finally opened wide enough to worm her way out. Wet snow cascaded through the open door and instantly turned into slush. The snow was almost hip deep on this side where the body of the Lincoln had served as a partial windbreak. Drifts in front and on the other side looked as if they were much too deep to try to navigate. Would she be able to get to the trunk through all this snow? Could she even open the lid if she did? No sense in ruining perfectly good clothes. She removed her pumps and tossed them on the seat. Then she slipped out of her confining skirt and half-slip and tossed them back in the car too. If she were going to climb through snow like an animal, she might as well dress like one. Besides, there was no one out here to see her.

And even if there was, she could care less. Hoisting the hem of her raincoat to her waist, she ventured into the snow. The first step was a real eye-opener, sending chills racing through every bone in her body. Wet pantyhose, she quickly discovered, offered absolutely no help in retaining body heat. Instead, the wet nylon made her flesh crawl with goose pimples as icy wind whipped at her thighs.

"Fuck this," she said into the wind after three agonizing steps toward the trunk. "I don't need anything bad enough to put up with insane wet and cold another goddamn minute."

But it took her almost three minutes to turn around in the waist-deep snow and manage the first step back to the passenger-side door. Drifting snow had already filled in her footprints. She could barely see the car.

A fierce north wind hit her full-force in the face, taking her breath away, making the next step impossible.

A terrible roar assaulted her ears.

She saw, racing toward her across the snow, a dark shape that wasn't tall enough to be a man nor big enough to be a car. The thought occurred to her that it might be a charging bear or some other wild animal whose territory she had inadvertently invaded. Did they still have bears out here in the primitive north woods?

She froze in her tracks.

Suddenly the shape seemed to see her, too. It changed course, leapt into the air, and came crashing down with an ear-splitting *whum-mm-mmmm-p-p-p-h-h!*

Sheila tried to run in the opposite direction, away from the stranded Lincoln and whatever it was that was rolling around in the dark on the other side of the car. But she couldn't lift her legs high enough to clear the tops of the drifts. The best she could do was lunge forward, sink into snow up to her breasts, then flounder forward again. She'd gone no more than ten feet when two glowing eyes appeared to her left, advancing on the Lincoln from the southbound lane of State Route 13. This time she recognized the roar of a heavy automobile engine straining against the inhibiting power of wind and snow.

"Hey!" she yelled, waving her arms, hoping they'd see her in the wash from the approaching headlights. "Over here! Please! Stop! I need help!"

But the car didn't look like it was going to stop for anything.

And then the driver must have seen the Lincoln's snow-dimmed headlights in the center of the road because the vehicle tried to swerve away and grind to a halt at the same time and all the vehicle did was fishtail across both lanes and slam into the Lincoln's grill. As the Explorer catapulted across the Lincoln's roof amid sounds of grinding metal and breaking glass, sparks flew high in the air. A fuel tank, whether the Explorer's or the Lincoln's Sheila didn't know, must have ruptured because suddenly the pungent odor of raw gasoline filled the air.

And then the sky lit up like noon and Sheila was knocked off her feet and thrown into a mound of snow as thousands of flaming shards—some of them pieces of metal and some of them chunks of roasting flesh—peppered the landscape like shrapnel in a war zone.

CHAPTER EIGHT

Had Colonel Jack Delacroix been born in Detroit or Chicago instead of a small backwater town in Quebec, Canada, he might have become a professional basketball player. He may even have become an NBA superstar like Ralph Sampson or Michael Jordan. Instead, Jack Delacroix became an international terrorist.

Maybe if, when a sudden spurt of growth hormone during early puberty sent him skyrocketing over everyone else his own age and even some who were twice his age, the superstitious folks in that backwater parish had simply accepted the boy's rapid development as normal instead of something supernatural, Jack might have lived a near-normal life. But when he discovered his neighbors—even his own parents—all thought him a freak and feared him as an instrument of the devil, he felt he had nothing to lose by proving them right.

Pubescent boys could be vicious. Anyone who looked or acted much differently than them was fair game. Jack's school chums made life hell for him. But Delacroix soon learned he could act twice as cruel. When shunned by classmates, he shunned them back, all the while biding his time and planning how to exact sweet revenge on those who wronged him or made fun of him.

By the time he turned sixteen, he was already a holy terror in his tiny town. If a girl turned him down for a date, Jack would arrange an "accident" that permanently disfigured her face. If a boy refused to share a lunch, that kid soon experienced a mysterious case of painful food poisoning. Though people continued to whisper about Delacroix behind his back, no one ever again dared taunt him to his face.

If he wasn't the devil himself, folks said, then he was certainly in league with the devil.

He enlisted in the Canadian army as soon as he was eligible, and the whole town breathed a lot easier when Delacroix boarded a train and departed. When they heard he was booted out of the army six months later, labeled psychologically unfit for military service, townspeople worried he'd return to torment them again.

But Jack didn't come back. Townspeople weren't at all surprised, however, when an armed contingent of military police showed up to search every square inch of town. The crazy bastard had stealthily entered the home of his former commanding officer and slit the throats of Captain Richard MacKenzie, Mrs. Dolly MacKenzie, eight-year old Molly MacKenzie, and four year old Dickie MacKenzie.

Authorities claimed Delacroix was an egomaniac, a nut case who had left behind his bloody calling card—a hastily scrawled note literally written on one wall with the dried blood of his victims—that boasted, "Compliments of Captain Jack Delacroix."

Although he had never actually progressed beyond the rank of recruit in any regular army anywhere in the world, "Colonel" Jack commanded as many men as most real regimental commanders. He'd written his name in blood all over the world, and his calling card was the jack of spades.

"Colonel" was the misappellation he'd pinned on himself when he passed thirty and felt "Captain" no longer held sufficient status. Someday, he thought, he'd call himself "General" or maybe "Field Marshal." Someday, when the private army he now headed ruled the world, everyone would so fear his name that they'd shit in their pants just thinking about him.

Meanwhile, he was busy. From his headquarters inside a converted machine tool factory on the southeast side of Rockford, Illinois, a mere hour and forty minutes northwest of the towering XIIMI Building that dominated the west bank of Lake Michigan, Colonel Jack directed covert world-wide surveillance and related activities for Philip Ashur and his associates.

His extensive network of current operatives, mostly mercenaries, spanned the entire globe. Some were former CIA or KGB junior officers, caught in agency downsizing after the end of the cold war, professionals who so loved what they did they didn't care who or what they worked for as long as they continued doing what they'd been trained to do. Others were soldiers of fortune, in for a dime or a dollar. A few, like that new kid Walker who shaved his head were certifiable psychos who loved killing people and mutilating corpses.

Delacroix liked Walker, understood him. In many respects, he suspected he and the new kid were a lot alike.

When Walker radioed that he'd lost contact with the other surveillance vehicle—the Explorer tailing an unidentified male who'd left the Groves' property on a snowmobile—Delacroix tried in vain to raise the Explorer with the more sophisticated electronics housed in the command center. Either the storm in northern Wisconsin was somehow interfering with radio reception or the two men in the Explorer had been put out of commission. Neither scenario was good news.

Colonel Jack prided himself on running a tight ship. He didn't tolerate excuses. If the men in the Explorer had screwed up, they'd better be dead or he'd make them wish they were. Meanwhile, he might have a problem that could easily balloon way out of proportion. Ashur had been very explicit in his instructions.

"I want you to shadow everyone who enters or leaves that property. Everyone. Anytime they make a move, day or night, I want to know what they're doing. Is that clear?"

"Perfectly," Delacroix had said. "Piece of cake."

But that was before a goddamned storm—amend that to goddamned blizzard—dumped more than four feet of white powder over the entire surveillance area, obscuring visuals and rendering implanted electronic devices ineffective. Video cameras didn't work very well buried under three-and-a-half feet of wet snow. Ditto, directional listening devices.

Delacroix really didn't want to send an inexperienced kid like Walker to check on the Explorer, but he had no one else close enough to report what might have happened. It was Walker or nobody.

Jack keyed the microphone on the scrambler/descrambler. "Blackbird to Robin One," he called over the powerful radio. "You copy?"

"Robin One," Walker's voice squawked from the speaker. "Read you ten by ten."

"Situation report."

"Snow still coming down like a motherfucker. Can't see a goddamned thing out there."

"Where's your partner?"

"On the grounds, dusting snow off cameras. You want I should call him back?"

"I want him left in place to keep doing what he's doing. You get on the horn and tell him I need a visual of the house. Then get your ass down the road ASAP and reestablish contact with Robin Three. You hear me?"

"I hear."

"Leave this channel open. I want progress reports every two minutes. Got that?"

"Got it."

"Then do it. When you find Robin Three, I'll give you additional instructions. And, Walker, you fuck this up, your ass is mine."

"I won't fuck up, Colonel. You can count on me."

Delacroix hoped for everyone's sake the kid was right.

* * *

As the unexpected concussion knocked Bob flat on his face in the same snowdrift he'd struggled so hard to get out of, his adrenalin-hyped combat-trained mind raced to make sense of what just happened.

In the instant before the stampeding Explorer slammed full force into the stationary Lincoln, he thought he'd glimpsed a lone woman—inappropriately dressed to be outside in this weather—jumping up and down in the snow on the far side of the car, waving both arms in the air like a crazy person. He had no idea who she was or what she might be doing out here in the middle of nowhere, but as close as she'd been to the car when it exploded, he didn't think she'd survived the blast.

He made a mental note to check on her later. His first priority was to check out the two men in the Explorer. If they were still alive, he had to neutralize them before they neutralized him.

Bob pushed himself out of the drift, then fingered the lengths of his arms and legs for signs of fracture. Tomorrow, he knew, he'd be sore all over, covered with bruises from head to toe. But his bones felt intact and he was still alive and, for right now, that was all that mattered.

Navigating through chest-high snowdrifts on foot proved more difficult and time consuming than he had anticipated. Unlike the gritty sand dunes of middle-eastern deserts he'd traversed during the war, the unfamiliar piles of powdery white stuff proved next to impossible. You didn't climb over snowdrifts, he quickly discovered. You had to plow your way through.

He could see by the dying flames that the smoldering Explorer was little more than a burnt-out metal husk. The windows, doors, seats, and roof had been completely blown away when the gas tank and whatever fuel or fumes were trapped in gas lines exploded. Fragments of twisted metal protruded from surrounding snow banks like razor wire littering a no-man's land; shards of shattered glass glittered like thousands of multi-faceted diamonds in the fading light from the burning vehicle.

Part of a human thigh, half-hidden by blood-stained snow a few feet from what was left of the Lincoln's trunk, told him all he needed to know about his pursuers. If one were dead, the other must be too.

Still, he searched surrounding snow banks until he'd located enough of both bodies to be absolutely certain neither man posed a threat.

Then he looked around for what was left of the girl.

He found her buried in a snowdrift off to the side of the road, partially shielded by the massive trunk of an old oak and cushioned by the bushy lower branches of a young pine. Surprisingly, she looked intact.

As Bob pushed snow away from her face, he noticed a fine white mist coming from the woman's nostrils. By some miracle, she was still breathing!

Very carefully now, he ran his fingers over every inch of the woman's body, examining her neck, shoulders, arms, back and legs for injuries. She had no broken bones nor open wounds. So, unless she'd suffered internal injuries that no one but a doctor could diagnose, he felt he could safely pull her from the snow bank and try to revive her.

God, he thought as he uncovered her bare legs from the snow. She wasn't dressed for this weather at all.

He assumed the Lincoln was hers, the car broke down or got stuck in snow, and she'd ventured out to seek help. If she hadn't left the car when she did, she would have burned to a crisp in the collision.

When he had her out of the snow, he visually and manually rechecked the egg-sized bump he'd discovered on the back of her head. The blast must have blown her off her feet, sent her flying, and her head struck the old oak's trunk with considerable force, enough to render her unconscious, maybe even cause a dangerous concussion.

Trained to administer first aid to battlefield casualties, McMichaels recognized the onset of shock: pale complexion, skin cold and clammy. This woman needed expert medical attention as quickly as possible. She also needed warm, dry clothes to prevent lapsing deeper into shock. He had to get her out of this freezing wind before she expired from exposure.

He trudged through the snow looking for something to cover her with, anything that would trap her body heat and stave off hypothermia. He found nothing salvageable in the remains of the Lincoln or the Explorer. But he did locate the Ski-Doo.

Scratched and dented, the machine rested upside down in a big pile of snow a hundred meters or so the other side of the flaming wreckage. Like the girl, the snowmobile appeared intact. Did he dare waste precious minutes trudging all that way through four-foot drifts just to see if the machine still functioned? What if it didn't? There was absolutely no time to waste; the injured girl needed help immediately or she'd die. He decided the snowmobile was the best bet for getting her to shelter quickly, and he felt he had no choice but to go for the Ski-Doo.

Exhausted from fighting his way through the snow, he barely had strength left to maneuver the stalled Ski-Doo out of the drift and back onto its treads.

One ski was badly bent. The rest of the machine seemed reasonably serviceable, though he couldn't be sure. He didn't know what effect a bent ski would have on stability or performance, but he suspected he'd find out soon enough.

Bob turned the choke and yanked the rip-cord. Nothing happened. He pulled the cord again. Then again and again and again and again. Still nothing.

Afraid he'd flood the engine and now totally exhausted—more from the frustration of wasted effort than from the effort itself—he collapsed in the Ski-Doo's saddle and considered alternatives. If he built an igloo out of snow around the girl and himself, then kept his own body tightly pressed against her, would his shared body heat keep her alive?

How long before help arrived? Hours? Days?

Would they both freeze to death in the meantime?

Unlike Groves who carried a Zippo because he smoked, McMichaels had neither a lighter nor matches in his pockets. Trying to start a fire by rubbing two snow-covered sticks together held no appeal. Bob had tried that once when he was thirteen and a Boy Scout collecting merit badges. Despite what the Boy Scout Handbook said, rubbing two sticks together to start a fire hadn't worked. He didn't expect it would work now, either.

His best bet was still to try to start the Ski-Doo. Bob sucked in a deep breath, grabbed the handle of the rip-cord, said a silent prayer, and yanked. This time the engine sputtered.

Encouraged, he tried again. Again the engine sputtered, but it still didn't catch.

"Three times is charm," Bob muttered under his breath. He yanked the rip-cord a third time, and this time the old bear growled to life, sending intermittent black puffs of foul-smelling exhaust shooting through the clogged manifold, displacing globs of packed snow.

He eased the machine around to test its stability with one bent ski, switched on the headlight, circled the smoldering wreckage, and headed for the old oak on the far side of the road. When he reached the girl, he shifted to neutral, left the motor running, quickly dismounted, picked the unconscious girl up in a modified fireman's carry, hefted her dead weight onto the seat with the last of his strength, and managed to wedge his bulk onto the seat beside her. Then he grasped her under the arms, lifted her onto his lap, and held her tightly around the waist as he snapped the Ski-Doo into gear.

Since he didn't know how far it might be to the closest town, or even the nearest farmhouse, he made a command decision to go back the way he had come and take her to the Groves place. There she could thaw out and be more thoroughly examined by a member of her own sex while either Bob or Tom rode the Ski-Doo into town to fetch a doctor.

Conscious of the excessive stress her added weight placed on the broken ski, Bob didn't dare take the snowmobile over twenty miles an hour on the straightaway, ten max on curves. If one of the skis suddenly split in two, he wouldn't want the machine to flip over and break both their necks.

The fierce arctic winds whipped around them, rocking the machine from side to side. When he felt the girl's weight shift slightly, he wrapped his left arm tighter around her waist, pulling her closer, trying to shield her body from the wind with his own. He stopped long enough to transfer the mittens and ski mask to her hands and face, but without a blanket to cover her, there was nothing he could do to keep the fierce wind from leeching precious heat from her bare legs and feet.

He reached the junction with County double N, turned left, and cautiously brought the speedometer back up to twenty. After what seemed like an eternity, he passed the Nelson farm and turned off onto County trunk O. Now, surrounded on both sides by dense pine boughs that absorbed some but not all of the wind's savage onslaught, he could sense the girl's body shivering as if she were inflicted with palsy.

He took that as a good sign. Her body was trying to self-generate heat, and that meant she had the subconscious will to survive.

Bob risked increasing the Ski-Doo's speed to twenty-five, then thirty. The machine vibrated as if it were about to shake apart. The handlebars fought him, and he fought them back.

Not more than fifteen minutes away from shelter, he thought he saw light at the end of the tunnel. Literally. A pair of approaching headlights materialized out of swirling snow approximately a hundred meters or so in front of the Ski-Doo. If Bob could get the driver to stop, the girl could ride the rest of the way to the Groves house in a warm vehicle.

And maybe—just maybe—she might survive.

* * *

Jerry Walker, at nineteen, didn't consider himself lucky to be the youngest member of Colonel Jack's domestic operations team, although others—more experienced hands like Poindexter and

Sawyer—had told him he should. He preferred to think of himself, instead, as extremely talented. Luck had nothing to do with it.

He'd made all the right moves entirely on his own. He'd joined a radical offshoot of the skinhead movement at fourteen, killed his parents when he was sixteen, lived in a survivalist training camp in the hills of Washington state for more than a year before turning eighteen. Recruited into Colonel Jack Delacroix's organization six months ago, he thought he had a right to be proud of his accomplishments.

He was especially proud to have already killed six people entirely with his own hands. Four women and two men. And he'd actively participated in the terminations of two others. Someday, he knew, he'd be credited with more kills than Ted Bundy, that Green River dude, even that crazy queer from Chicago, John Wayne Gacy. Maybe even more than all of them put together. Someday, when truth be told, Jeremiah Walker would be a legend in his own time.

Meanwhile, he was happy to be learning the finer points of being a professional assassin from some of the best in the business: Colonel Jack, the living legend Walker hoped someday to emulate and eventually surpass; Delacroix's second in command, Major Alphonse Scagliano, the best knife man in the world whose only known weakness was a fondness for pretty women, especially young ones; Kevin O'Donnell, a former IRA triggerman and super-sniper who could put a hole through the heart of a mosquito at five hundred clicks; and Mustafa Hussein, an explosives expert who routinely took out passenger planes or whole buildings with home made bombs constructed entirely from common household chemicals, leaving the FBI—or their Israeli intelligence counterparts—no way to trace an explosion back to the source.

Although they all were required to master a variety of common tasks, from clandestine stakeout to full-scale assault on fortified positions, every man on the Colonel's team was valued for his own unique specialty.

Jerry's specialty was clean-up and disposal.

He was responsible for making dead bodies disappear. Not only assigned targets, but also team casualties, should there ever be any. Sometimes his job was as simple as hauling a body away to be dropped off, seemingly, the ends of the earth; plus mopping up spattered blood and policing up spent shells. Sometimes it became as complicated as dismembering the torso, grinding up leftover meat and bones, and burying tiny pieces, piece by piece, at scattered sites around the country.

Sometimes, like with the Groves broad, his orders were to cremate the remains in place and scatter the ashes.

What he really liked best, however, was being tossed a live one. Sometimes he kept it alive long enough to watch its reactions to various torture techniques he'd studied. He learned a lot about human nature from dissecting live specimens. Unfortunately, the live ones were few and far between.

"What's your 20?" Delacroix's voice squawked impatiently from hidden speakers beneath the Dodge Dakota's seat.

"Just passed the eastern edge of the old lady's property line. Can't plow through this stuff at more than ten or fifteen miles an hour. Not without spinning my wheels and fishtailing off the road. Damn light Dodge trucks ain't standardly equipped with four-wheel drives like Jeeps and Explorers."

"You got chains on all four tires, don't you? You got shovels in the cargo bay in case you get stuck. Quit your bellyachin' and get your ass in gear."

"I ain't bellyachin', just tellin' you like it is. Whoa. Wait a second. Wait one goddamn minute. What the hell's that?"

"What's what?" Delacroix's voice squawked impatiently.

Walker squinted his eyes. He thought he'd seen a flash of light a quarter mile ahead, masked by the wall of still-falling snow. Was it just his imagination? No, there it was again.

"There's a light up ahead. Single light, not a pair of headlights. Moving towards me, getting brighter. Could be a vehicle with a headlight out. Can't tell yet."

"Snowmobile," Delacroix said, sounding certain. "Might be the machine Robin One was tailing. Can you confirm?"

"It is a snowmobile," Walker said. "Looks like the same one. You want I should take him?"

"Negative. I want you to find Robin One. Don't do anything until we know who or what knocked Robin One off the air."

"The guy sees me. He's waving me down."

"He wants you to stop?"

"Wasn't he alone when Robin One tailed him from the stakeout? Now he's got someone with him. Looks like he's carting a dead body."

"One of ours?"

"Can't tell. You want I should find out?"

"If it's one of ours, do you know what to do?"

"Salvage, if possible. Dispose, if it's not. Question the driver before termination."

"Good. Leave the mike open. I need to hear what's happening. How are you armed?"

"Nine millimeter Beretta. Serrated hunting knife and Swiss army knife. Garrote. Shotgun and .30-30 hunting rifle with nightscope behind the seat."

Jerry deliberately left out the Saturday night special—an eight shot, .22 calibre automatic—secreted in his right boot. It was his own personal backup weapon, not issued by the organization, and he felt better if no one knew he had it.

"You know the standing orders. No heat. If he knows about us, take him out. If he doesn't know, we don't need complications. You straight on that?"

"Yeah. I'm straight on that."

"Good. Then stop and see what he wants."

*   *   *

The pickup slowed, fishtailed past the snowmobile, and came to a stop. The driver's door opened. A young man the age of an army recruit, wearing a camouflage-patterned parka and waterproofed hiking boots, stepped out into the snow.

"There's been a bad accident," Bob shouted over the wind. "This girl's hurt. We need to get her warm quickly or she'll die from shock and exposure. Can you give us a ride to the nearest house?"

"What kind of accident?" the boy asked.

"Head-on collision. Totaled out both vehicles."

"Anyone else hurt?"

"Driver and passenger of the other vehicle died in the crash. Will you help?"

"Get in," said the boy.

Bob parked the Ski-Doo off the side of the road and killed the motor.

"Lemme give you a hand with her," offered the boy, opening the passenger door of the pick-up.

Together, they manipulated the girl into the truck.

"You've got a shortwave radio?" Bob asked, noticing the antenna mounted behind the cab and sophisticated radio equipment mounted under the seat. "Maybe we can raise someone who can phone a doctor?"

"It don't work too good in the storm," said the boy, climbing into the driver's seat. "All I get is static."

"Top of the line gear. Should be able to get through. Mind if I try?"

"It's my father's truck. Dad don't like no one fiddlin' with his things."

"How about a cell phone? Got a cell phone? We need to call a doctor."

The kid laughed. "No cell towers around here. We're in a dead zone."

"Do you live nearby?" Bob asked, deciding not to push. The important thing was to get the girl warm. He asked the kid to turn up the fan on the heater. Checking the girl's pulse, he rubbed her hands and feet to help restore circulation.

"Came up here from Illinois to do some deer hunting with a few friends," said the boy. "Didn't expect to get caught in no blizzard."

"Do you know where the Groves family lives?"

"I don't know where no one lives. I told you, I'm from Illinois."

"Never mind. Just turn the truck around. The entrance to the Groves home is just up the road. I'll let you know where to turn down the fire lane."

"So tell me about this accident you were in," the boy prompted as he maneuvered the truck forward and backward until turned completely around. "What happened and where'd it happen?"

"Over on the main highway. Two men in a Ford Explorer plowed into this girl's car. Totaled out both vehicles."

"You sure the other guys are dead?"

"I'm sure." His mind flashed on images of scattered body parts. "There wasn't much left of either of them after their vehicle rammed her Lincoln head-on. Both gas tanks blew. Scraps of metal all over the place. Blood and body parts all over, too. Bits and pieces here. Bits and pieces there."

As Bob spoke, he noticed the young man's expression changing. He didn't like what he thought he saw in the kid's eyes. Did he get his rocks off from descriptions of death and mutilation?

"Get the picture?" he almost screamed in the kid's face. "Lots of blood and guts. Is your morbid curiosity satisfied now? Or do you want all the gristly details spelled out?"

"Jesus! I just wanted to know if they was still alive and needed help. You don't need to bite my head off."

"Sorry," Bob said. Maybe it wasn't the kid who'd gone over the edge. Maybe it was him.

He hadn't had a good night's sleep in nearly three days, not since he'd drawn this assignment. Did lack of sleep, combined with the life and death situation he'd just escaped, make him imagine the worst in people?

Bob took a deep breath and forced himself to relax. The worst was over; he'd survived, and he was beginning to think the woman would, too.

Soon they'd be inside a warm house, putting on dry clothes. Soon he could relinquish responsibility for the girl and think about sleep.

"Turn here," he told the kid.

The Dodge Dakota turned onto the fire lane and crawled through deep snow toward the house.

This time the light at the end of the tunnel would mean a fire in the fireplace and people who'd be able to help.

Book II

THE TREE OF LIFE

And when the woman saw that the tree was good for food, and that it was pleasant to the eyes, and a tree to be desired to make one wise, she took of the fruit thereof, and did eat, and gave also unto her husband with her; and he did eat.
--Holy Bible, King James Version, Genesis: 3: 6.

And the Lord God said, Behold, the man is become as one of us, to know good and evil: and now, lest he put forth his hand, and take also of the tree of life, and eat, and live for ever:
Therefore the Lord God sent him forth from the garden of Eden, to till the ground from whence he was taken.
So he drove out the man; and he placed at the east of the garden of Eden Cherubims, and a flaming sword which turned every way, to keep the way of the tree of life.
--Holy Bible, King James Version, Genesis: 3, 22-24.

Remember thee? Ay, thou poor ghost, while memory holds a seat
In this distracted globe.
--Hamlet, I, V, 95-97

CHAPTER NINE

There's nothing new under the sun.

That's what the Preacher wrote millenia ago. If it was true then, it was true now.

Supposedly a scribe of the second son of King David, whose ten tribes formed the northern kingdom of Israel, he also wrote: "For everything under the sun there is a time. A time to be born, and a time to die."

"And a time to be born again," added Diane Groves. "In kinship with wisdom there is immortality. Because of her I shall have immortality, and leave an everlasting remembrance to those who come after me."

While earning her doctorate in philosophy and a companion doctorate of divinity at Harvard, Diane had studied the world's religions in greater depth and far greater detail than any modern practitioner.

But women still weren't welcomed with open arms in the male-dominated disciplines of philosophy and theology, so she settled for a chair in ancient history at the state university after the University of Wisconsin awarded her a third doctorate, this one in history.

Organized religions, in her experience, cared little about truth and even less about wisdom. Their primary concern seemed to be defining social justice: establishing and preserving a social order that leaders could codify into written laws, doling out punishments to anyone who violated codes of conduct. Thou shalt do this. Thou shalt not do that. Thus saieth the Lord.

Didn't people realize how incongruous it was to have one law that said, "Thou shalt not kill," and another law that demanded witches and prostitutes be put to death? Couldn't they see that holy wars—wars waged in the name of a supposedly loving and beneficent father-figure—were blatant violations of the very tenets their religions purported to value?

Tonight Diane Groves would put to the test the truth of her own beliefs. Although she had studied, since earliest childhood, the principles behind the archaic ritual she was about to perform, she was still unsure it would work in the real world.

What were the words her mother used? "If you believe you have the power, then the power is yours. If you don't believe, then heaven can't help you."

Her mother had been a wise woman, one of the few remaining practitioners of what her family referred to as "the old religion." Its tenets predated all known religious systems. Certain elements, however, were integral to human understanding since the beginning of time.

The others here tonight—relatives and close friends of Ellen Groves—were ready and waiting. The cup had passed into Diane's hands, and now she must drink.

She fingered the hem of her gossamer skirt and hefted the translucent gown over her head. Then she fell to her knees to sit on her haunches. As if on cue, the others did the same.

There were twelve, not the usual thirteen, here tonight. Eleven females and only one male. They ranged in age from nearly twelve to eighty-three. Aunt Violet was Sixty-six. Aunt Cynthia was sixty-nine. Roseanne Martindale was thirty-three. Daisy May Martindale, Roseanne's mother, was fifty-seven, and Morgana Martindale, Roseanne's daughter, was fifteen. Neighbor Sara Nelson was only eleven. Deborah Nelson, Sara's mother, was thirty-two. Diane's sister, Nancy, was twenty-eight. Brother Tom, sitting in tonight for Great Aunt Hazel, was thirty-three. 84-year-old Great Aunt Anna was the oldest; second cousin Leander Groves, Anna's granddaughter, was thirty-six. Diane was thirty-one.

All were as naked as the day they were born.

No wind froze their bare flesh here in the heart of the old-growth forest. Concentric circles of seventy-and-eighty-foot-tall pine trees, thick branches intricately interleaved like the weave of a gigantic wicker basket, shielded them not only from prying eyes, but from sub-zero arctic breezes and falling snow. A huge bonfire, blazing bright in an ancient earthen altar in the exact center of the circle, heated frigid air and cast flickering shadows on expectant faces and frail human flesh.

It was a scene as old as humankind itself.

Diane took a deep breath, began a rhythmic chant. The others chimed in. Their melodious utterances seemed to have little meaning as words, certainly nothing modern man would recognize. They were but syllabic sounds: rising and falling tones, pure phonics, metered rhymes, alliterations, onomatopoeia. Sounds such as these precipitated primitive language in man's earliest ancestors. Some neurolinguistic experts suspected such were essential ingredients of all languages, modern and ancient.

This, then, was the mystical incantation, the great hymn of humankind from time immemorial. Rhythmic, flowing, guttural. Primal. Sensuous. Huge conifers that were in their genetic infancy when mankind was in his, responded to the mantra with a mantra of their own.

Or was it only the whisper of winds vibrating treetops like strings of a giant harp?

Diane closed her eyes, concentrated, breathed in through her nose, out through her mouth. Unconsciously, her upper body began to sway—back and forth, back and forth, back and forth—to the rhythm of the chant.

She reached inside herself and, one by one, gently touched each chakra. The flowering energy centers that resided in the very center of her being, blossomed. Lotus petals opened. The power was unleashed.

The sleeping Kundalini, the original serpent of Genesis and the fire-breathing dragon of Celtic and ancient Chinese myths, awakened and uncoiled.

She opened her inner eye, the third eye called the eye of Horus in Egyptian mysteries, that connected with the limbic system in the heart of her brain. She focused on childhood memories of her mother and recalled the songs her mother sang when Diane was still cradled in the waters of the womb.

Now the sounds that flowed from her mouth became recognizable words, although ancient, and those words had meaning. No longer were the vibrating tones merely syllables, simply sounds. They were stanzas of a song. A song her mother had taught her.

The image of her mother as she appeared twenty years ago—young, vibrant, in tune with all of nature—springs full-blown to her mind's eye. This is the Ellen Groves she remembers best. Ma is only forty-four. Diane is eleven.

It is the summer of her menarche, the summer of first blood. Mother and daughter seem closer this year than they've ever been before, or ever will be again. There are no secrets to separate them, nor men's attention to vie for.

The song her mother sings celebrates the mystical bond between mothers and daughters everywhere, a bond that stretches like an uncut umbilical cord all the way back to the first woman, the very first mother. Call her Eve, call her Mary, call her Tiamat, call her Innana, call her Astarte, call her Isis, call her Lilith, call her Shakti, call her Kali, she is one and the same. She has different names and faces, but names are inconsequential to the Great Mother. All that matters is the continuous, unbroken chain of being that unites every woman with every other woman that has ever existed or ever will exist.

Diane feels this unique unity, a sense of perpetual continuity, in her very bones, in her blood, in every fiber of her body, in her essential being. She knows her mother feels it, too.

"I am a part of you," she sings to her mother's image. "I come from you. What you are, I am too."

"You *are* part of me," Ellen confirms, her smile warm, radiant. Comforting. "You came from inside me, from next to my heart. As long as you continue to be, I continue to be."

Mother's song teaches that everything is interconnected: the earth, the moon, the stars. For every effect there is a cause, a relationship. Everything is constantly and continually flowing, shifting, moving, changing according to its own unique pattern of existence. Everything. Both the living and the non-living. And nothing is ever completely destroyed. Nothing ever truly dies. But, in the process of becoming, everything inevitably changes.

"Look at me," says Ellen. "Once I was young and almost as beautiful as you. Now I am older, my figure full. Soon my hair will tinge with grey, my skin begin to wrinkle. Someday I may be very old, my hair turned snow white, breasts sagging to my knees. Such changes are natural, eventual, and inevitable. Someday, when my body outlives its purpose, my spirit will fly free, separate from this physical sheath which keeps it grounded, to soar on the winds like an unfettered hawk. When that time comes, you must take certain steps to ground my spirit to the earth before the sun rises on the fourth day. Then my spirit will roost in these trees. And I will be reborn as a direct descendant of yours. But if I am not rooted to the earth by dawn on the fourth day, my disembodied spirit will soar away on the wind to roost elsewhere. I will eventually be reborn, but where and when the wind will take me is anybody's guess."

"Do you mean our souls live in trees after we die?"

"In trees. Also in birds, in all kinds of plants and animals. But trees are special, because they ground our spirits to a particular place and time. Trees provide spirits a place to roost, and trees help spirits stay connected to the earth."

"Is that why you love trees?"

"I have learned much from trees. Do you know that you can communicate with the spirits of your ancestors by touching wood?"

"Really? How? Will you teach me?"

"Of course. I will teach you to talk to trees, and the trees will teach you to listen to the wind. Now that you have become a woman, there is much you need to know. Are you willing to learn?"

"Oh, yes, mother."

So she taught Diane to talk to trees, and the trees taught her to talk to the wind. And the wind taught her songs to sing. And the songs taught her to remember.

And that was what Diane attempted to do now: to literally remember her mother and materially manifest Ellen within the circle of trees.

Aided by people who knew and often interacted with Ellen Groves when she was alive, people able to remember aspects of her that Diane hadn't experienced, she tried to recall her mother into corporeal form.

Winds howled and shrieked. The bonfire blazed white-hot. Flames and sparks shot skyward like roman candles. A cold gust of wind penetrated the circle and stirred the hairs on the back of Diane's neck. The door between worlds slowly creaked open. But despite their combined efforts to draw Ellen's spirit back into the world of the living, she did not materialize within the circle.

Something or someone was holding her back, inhibiting the alchemical transformation of spirit into matter. Diane knew intuitively she must enter the spirit dimension herself and seek out her mother's essence in the other world. She must personally guide Ma's spirit across the threshold or enlist the aid of a spirit guide to do it. She stepped not into the light but into the darkness of the other world . . .

. . . and teetered on the precipice of a great abyss—a virtual Ein Soph or Wu Chi—that had no beginning and no end, an abyss that had not existed a week ago.

And she sensed this rift between worlds—this nothingness—was growing. If it continued to grow at the same rate, it would consume the spirit world and spill over to the material world within a matter of days.

She could not feel her mother's essence on the far side of the great abyss. If someone or something held Ma's spirit prisoner, it was in a place Diane couldn't reach.

Was there no way to cross this great divide? Where were the spirit guides, the unreborn spirits of ancestors who usually populated this dimension and might show her the way?

Even if Diane were pure spirit—which she was not, her own spirit rooted firmly to her body in the material world—she doubted she would be able to cross the blackness of the abyss and rescue her mother in time.

Her only hope resided in returning to the material world and discovering what had effected this rift between worlds. Then maybe she could act to change it.

As she slipped back into her body, she wondered if all the king's horses and all the king's men could put Humpty Dumpty back together again.

CHAPTER TEN

I got a axe in the truck bed," said the kid when there was no answer to Bob's frantic pounding on the front door. "You want I should break it down?"

"Try turning the knob."

The kid looked disappointed to discover the door wasn't locked. When he turned the knob and shoved the door wide open, Bob quickly carried the girl inside and shouted for Tom and Diane to come help.

"Don't look like nobody's home," said the kid, who'd very reluctantly introduced himself to Bob in the truck only as Jerry. If he was going to be hesitant about placing all his cards face-side-up on the table in front of a stranger, Bob thought it equally prudent to furnish Jerry with information only on a need-to-know basis.

He had a real bad feeling about Jerry. He sensed something violent and ugly lurking just beneath the kid's near normal exterior. But right now Jerry was the only help he had, and he could use all the help he could get.

"There were people here when I left a couple of hours ago," said Bob.

"Ain't nobody here now."

He placed the girl gently on the bare floor in front of the smoldering fire and checked her pulse. "We'll worry about them later. Right now this girl's our primary concern. We've got to get her warm. Toss a fresh log in the fireplace. I'll go hunt up some blankets and be right back."

Carrying the lantern, Bob scoured the house for signs of life while he searched for blankets. He found a home-made quilt in a second floor bedroom. He found blankets, sheets, and towels in a hall closet.

But no Tom or Diane anywhere.

Strange. Their cars were still buried in snow in front of the house. Where could they have gone on foot in this kind of weather? Why would Tom and Diane even leave the house at this time of night?

Jerry had stoked the fire back to life. Shadows danced on the walls as hungry flames licked fresh pine.

"What the hell do you think you're doing?" Bob asked when he saw Jerry remove the girl's ripped pantyhose.

"Gotta get her outta these wet clothes fast.," the kid said. "Get her dry and warm and maybe she'll live."

The kid was right. Bob knelt next to her, lifted her shoulders, and worked her arms free of the raincoat.

"She have any ID?" asked Jerry. "You know who she is?"

Bob searched the pockets on the raincoat and came up empty.

"Designer label on that coat," commented Jerry. "She must be rich. She spent some really big bucks for that label."

"Same for the suit coat," noted Bob. He unbuttoned her blouse, slid the blouse and suitcoat off her naked shoulders and down her arms. The peekaboo bra the girl wore unsnapped in the front.

"No tan lines," said the kid when the bra came off. "She don't get outdoors much."

Bob tried to rub some color into her pale flesh with a terrycloth towel. Jerry worked on her legs. When they'd dried her completely, Bob covered her with the blankets and quilt.

"I'm gonna find the kitchen and heat up some water," said Jerry. "Maybe make some coffee. You want some coffee?"

"Coffee would be great. Go ahead. Take the lantern. I'll stay with the girl."

Bob sat down on the floor next to her. In flickering firelight, her red hair looked like it had caught fire. He tried to blink the illusion away.

"Who are you, lady?" he whispered as if expecting her to reply. "What were you doing on that road in the middle of nowhere? Where were you going in such a hurry that you couldn't wait until the storm let up?"

Now that he was warm and the immediate danger with the serious threat to life and limb over and he and the girl were both still miraculously alive, he let his guard down. The last of the adrenalin that had propelled his body to action drained away like high tides as the moon waned. Lack of sleep, combined with the terrible battering his body had endured when he spilled from the snowmobile and tumbled into the snow, took its inevitable toll.

He fell asleep staring at her face.

*   *   *

"What are you doing in my house?" demanded Diane Groves. "How dare you invade our sanctuary and abuse our hospitality like this?"

The Most Beautiful Girl in the World looked even more beautiful when she was angry.

A whole herd of people trooped through the door. For a brief moment, his mind remained foggy and he was half-certain he was still dreaming. When he saw Tom, he remembered where he was and what brought him here.

"There was an accident on the highway," he hurried to explain. "That girl on the floor is seriously injured. She needs help. I didn't know anywhere else to bring her."

Three of the women immediately knelt next to the comatose girl and threw off blankets and quilt. They carefully examined her from head to toe as expertly as any triage team in a hospital's emergency room. Then, as if they could read each other's minds or had practiced this same routine a thousand times before, they simultaneously aligned the palms of their hands along portions of her anatomy in some kind of meaningful pattern.

Bob thought they must be trying to redirect the flow of energy within the girl's body with their bare hands, but that was a crazy idea. And these ladies didn't look crazy. They looked like they knew exactly what they were doing.

"Massive trauma to head and neck that severely damaged essential neural pathways," said the youngest-looking of the three. "Thank goodness, she possesses a strong spirit still fighting to keep body and soul together. By acting now, we can restore balance."

"Come, sisters and brother," said the eldest of the three. "The time to act is now."

The others quickly gathered around, forming two concentric circles with the girl in the middle. They waved their hands toward the ceiling, reminding Bob of a pentacostal revival meeting. Then, like synchronized swimmers executing choreographed strokes at Olympic games, they plunged their hands downward in unison.

As palms reached naked skin, tiny discharges of static electricity snapped, crackled, and popped like a bowl of breakfast cereal. Color returned to pale flesh. The girl's eyelids fluttered.

"It is done," breathed the oldest-looking of the three. She pressed both palms to the girl's forehead. "It will take time for mind and body to mend, but mend they shall."

"How much time?" asked Diane. She threw the quilt over the girl to cover her nakedness.

"Goodness knows," said the old lady.

"What'd you just do?" asked Jerry as he came into the living room from the kitchen. He'd evidently watched the whole show from the doorway and had removed the wool cap with ear flaps that had covered his head and neck. Jerry's head wasn't just shaved down to stubble like new army recruits in basic but was shaved clean as a cue ball on a billiard table.

"We helped her heal," said the old lady matter-of-factly, squinting to see the boy better in the poor light. "Do you need healing? We can help you, too, my dear. If you wish to be helped, that is."

"I don't need no help," said the boy.

"Oh, pshaw! Everybody needs help. I know I certainly do. Would you be so kind as to help me over to that couch? I'm up long past my bedtime and I'm afraid I've run out of energy. My legs are about to give out."

"Let me help you, Aunt Anna," offered Diane.

"No, thank you, dear. I asked the young man. Let's see what he's made of, shall we?"

She held out her hand to the boy. "Will you help me? Please?"

Jerry slowly came forward from the shadows. "I ain't afraid of you," he said.

"Of course not," said Anna. "Why should a strong young man like you be afraid of anything? Especially a frail old lady like me?"

"You're spooky," said the kid. But he walked over to Anna and offered her his arm.

Anna laughed. She hooked her arm around Jerry's as if they were teenagers off to a high school prom. She leaned against him as he slowly led her to the couch.

"The only bad thing about growing older," she whispered to the boy in conspiratorial undertones as she hobbled, "is that the mind thinks your body can still do all the wonderful things it could do at 20. You're constantly surprised when the body doesn't respond exactly as you expected. But, then, life is full of little surprises, isn't it?"

She sat down on the couch and patted the space next to her, inviting him to sit. "I've told you one of my secrets," she said as she pulled him down next to her on the sofa. "Now you tell me one of yours."

"What is this? Twenty questions? Truth or dare? You wanna play games?"

"A game? Yes, I suppose we are playing games, aren't we? Do you like playing games, Mister...what did you say your name was?"

"Jerry."

"I'm Anna, Jerry." She offered her hand, but he hesitated to take it. "I was 84 on my last birthday. How old were you on your last birthday? Seventeen? Eighteen?"

"Nineteen."

"Nineteen is a nice age."

"I got no complaints."

"You're through with school, Jerry?"

"I been out of school a long time."

"Ah, yes. I remember when I was nineteen. I thought I was through with school, too. I thought I already knew everything, so why bother? It took me another nineteen years to learn I was wrong."

"What's that supposed to mean?"

"It means that when we stop learning, we die. I've managed to live a long time because there's always more I desired to learn. Now take you, for example. You've given me another reason to go on living. I know practically nothing about you, but I want to learn more. So I won't be able to die until I've learned all I can about you. I'm curious. And I sense you're curious about me . . .us . . . too."

"You don't make sense, lady."

"You were curious when you saw what we did for that girl, weren't you? You wondered what those gestures meant, what purpose was served by our little ritual? And I told you, didn't I? We were helping her heal. Would you like to learn to heal like that, Jerry?"

"You one of them religious nuts, like on TV? One of them faith healers?"

"No," she said, softly chuckling as if she'd heard a good joke. "Not like people you see on television. They're polished stage magicians, all show and no substance. Because the people on television possess no magic of their own, they depend on the faith of their flock and a few simple hypnotic suggestions to work illusions, not miracles. If someone believes they can be healed by a stage magician, it is by faith alone that they are healed. We, on the other hand, use the faith of the healer and not the person to be healed to create wellness. Faith is a powerful tool, isn't it, Jerry? Faith can be powerful enough to heal or powerful enough to kill. I have the kind of faith that heals. What kind of faith have you, Jerry?"

"I don't believe in nothin'."

"Everyone believes in something. Don't deceive yourself."

"Not me," he said, jumping to his feet. Obviously nervous, he began to walk away.

"It was nice getting to know you, Jerry," she called after him. "We'll talk again when you're ready."

Jerry stomped into the kitchen, mumbling to himself.

"What did you really do to that girl?" Bob asked Tom, one man to another. "Whatever it was, it worked."

"We shared energy with her."

"I saw sparks leap from your hands. Real sparks. And I smelled smoke, too. It wasn't wood smoke I smelled. I thought you were going to start a fire with your bare hands. How did you do that?"

"The universe is filled with various kinds of energy, and you could say we acted as human lightning rods. We drew and focused a tiny portion of universal energy into ourselves. When we touched the injured girl, that energy discharged into different parts of her body. It's a little like jump-starting the battery of one car with the battery of another. We were the jumper cables."

All around him women were busily removing their wet boots and overcoats. Some of them wore plain housedresses, but more than half wore gossamer gowns similar to the one Diane Groves wore. None seemed self-conscious about appearing half-naked in front of him.

"We're all naked beneath our clothes," Diane Groves said as if she could read his mind. She had come up behind him while he was staring at a cute blonde. "That's my sister Nancy you're undressing with your eyes. The older woman next to her is my Aunt Violet."

"Excuse me for staring. I've been in the army most of my life. I'm used to being around men in various stages of dress. But I'll never get used to seeing women dressed so casually."

"We don't obsess on our bodies the way some people do. We don't dress to hide our physical flaws, nor do we dress to hide or highlight a particular part of our anatomy. We dress simply to feel comfortable and to stay warm."

"Are you warm," his eyes roamed up and down her body, "in that thing?"

"Warm enough."

"Who's your friend?" Tom asked. "Where did you find him?"

"Claims his name's Jerry. I ran into him on the road."

"And the girl was with him?"

"I didn't literally run into him. Well, almost. The girl's car did get run into, but not by either of us. It was accidentally rammed by two men chasing me in a Ford Explorer on Route 13. Fortunately, the girl was outside the Lincoln at the time of the collision. I found her in a snow drift. I think her head impacted with a tree."

"Two men were chasing you?"

"They followed me from here to the highway. When I tried to see who they were, they began shooting. They died when they plowed head-on into the girl's car."

"Who is she?" asked Diane. "Where did she come from?"

"I don't know. She was stranded out on the road. Her car, and everything in it, went up in smoke."

"You did the right thing bringing her here." Her tone was softer, less angry. "The closest hospital is forty miles away. Daisy Martindale works there as a Registered Nurse, and she doesn't think their doctors could have helped even if you'd brought her to the emergency room. Modern medicine is limited in coma cases."

"And Jerry?" Tom asked. "How does he fit into all this?"

"He was driving by in a pickup truck. I flagged him down on the road just this side of State Route 13. When I asked him to help, he did."

"Aunt Anna sensed something in him that's badly out of balance," Diane said. "And I sense he's dangerous. After we thank him for his help, I'm going to insist he leave."

"I'll ask him for a ride to the motel. He was headed in that direction when we met."

"You don't have to leave. You can sleep here, if you'd like."

"With all these half-naked women around? I'd feel more comfortable in a motel."

"We promise not to seduce you," Diane said, and for the first time since they met, Bob saw her smile.

"Let's find your friend," Tom said.

Jerry was in the kitchen nursing a cup of hot tea. "I couldn't find no coffee," he explained. "All I could find was a bunch of herbs. I don't like tea. But it's warm, so I'll drink it if there ain't no coffee."

"Jerry," Bob said, "I want you to meet Tom Groves and his sister, Diane. We're guests in their house."

Jerry shook hands with Tom and nodded to Diane. His gaze focused on Diane's breasts and remained there. Her nipples were shadows beneath the silky fabric, plainly visible to oogling eyes.

Jerry's tongue flicked across his lips like a snake's. He took another sip of tea.

"I really appreciate all your help tonight, Jerry," Bob said. "But I need to ask another favor. Will you drive me to pick up the snowmobile where we left it and then drop me off at a motel on route 13? I want to get to a phone and inform the sheriff's office about the accident."

"Now? You wanna leave now?"

"As soon as you finish your tea."

"Well, I guess I can do that."

"Thanks a lot."

"You want some tea?" Jerry asked Diane, his eyes darting from one breast to the other. "I made a whole kettle of water."

"Where are you staying, Jerry?" asked Tom, taking a seat across from him at the table. "You don't live around here, do you?"

"Some friends have a hunting cabin down the road a piece," he said, fidgeting nervously with his cup. His eyes darted from Diane to Tom and back to her breasts. "I was making a beer run when I saw this guy and the woman come by on a snowmobile. I couldn't just leave them out there to freeze, could I?"

"Of course not," said Diane. "But won't your friends be worried about you? It's taken a long time to go to town for beer, hasn't it?"

"I guess they'll worry about me when the last of the beer runs out." He downed the tea in his cup. "You ready to go?" he asked Bob.

"As soon as I put my coat and gloves on."

"Meet me at the truck. I'll go out and make sure she starts. Wait about ten minutes and I'll have the heater running nice 'n' hot."

They watched Jerry exit. Then they heard a motor turn over.

"I don't trust him," said Tom as soon as the door closed. "Are you sure you want to ride with him?"

"I'll be okay," Bob said. "I know how to watch my back."

"Do you think he was one of the men who murdered Ma?" Diane asked Tom.

"The thought did cross my mind."

"Mine, too," said Bob. He struggled into the parka, put on gloves and stuffed the ski mask into a parka pocket. "What time should I expect you in the morning?" he asked Tom.

"Ten. That'll give the county crews time to clear the roads."

"If the snow stops," Diane added.

"And if it doesn't stop?" asked Bob.

"Then," said Tom, "I'll borrow a Jeep from one of our neighbors and get there as soon as I can."

* * *

"Where the hell have you been?"

The colonel had a right to sound pissed. Jerry had been out of contact for almost two hours. Nothing fried the ass of a control freak like the colonel the way not knowing what might be going on behind his back did.

Jerry had tried to call Delacroix as soon as he returned to the truck, but the radio wouldn't work. He didn't even get static. He had to drive all the way back to the county road before he got a signal, and even then the signal seemed weak and kept breaking up.

"I been inside the house," Walker reported. "I planted six ounces of plastique with a radio receiver wired to the blasting cap inside their kitchen."

"Jesus Christ! Did I tell you to do anything that stupid?"

"I thought you'd be proud of me," Walker said.

"Your orders were to observe the house, not blow it up!" squawked Delacroix's angry voice from the speaker. "Okay. What's done is done. Tell me what you learned."

"Robin One and his partner both got fried to a crisp. Took out their vehicle by running into some broad's car on the state highway. Right now there're fourteen people inside the big house, twelve women and two men. One of the women is the broad from the snowmobile. She's still out cold. She cracked her head on something when Robin One smashed into her car. Bob, the guy that was with her, wants me to drive him to a motel over on route 13. He'll be out here in a minute, so I can't stay on the horn forever."

"A clean up crew was dispatched to the accident site an hour ago," said the colonel. "They're almost finished."

"What do you want me to do with Bob?"

"Drop him off at a motel like he wants. Don't do anything stupid."

"He'll call the cops. Tell them about the accident."

"Let him. They won't find anything to corroborate his story."

"What about the girl?"

"The cops will think she fell off the snowmobile. Went for a ride with her boyfriend and hit a tree in the storm. It's all been arranged."

"I better get back before they see I'm gone. Robin Three signing off."

"Report to the holding area as soon as you've dropped him off. And Walker . . ."

"Yeah?"

"Don't do anything stupid or your ass is mine. I'll bury you so deep that even the devil won't be able to find you."

CHAPTER ELEVEN

When Bob couldn't find the snowmobile where he thought he'd left it, both he and Jerry paced up and down the road for almost half a mile, kicking at snow banks along the north side of the road. The Ski-Doo didn't seem to be buried beneath a snow drift.

"You sure this is where you left it?" Jerry asked for the third time.

"See that little spruce? That's where I left it. Right in front of that spruce."

"Isn't there now."

"No," he admitted. "It's not there now."

"Positive you turned off the motor? Mebbe it kicked into gear and took off on its own. I seen a lawnmower do that once."

"Forget it. Let's just get back in the truck where it's warm. I'll come back tomorrow during daylight."

Bob was absolutely certain he'd killed the motor and he was one-hundred percent sure where he'd left the Ski-Doo. After dozens of army survival courses teaching how to fix position with permanent landmarks, he'd automatically picked three unique landmarks to triangulate the snowmobile's location: the north side of the road, the tiny spruce, and an old oak tree that had been split in two by lightning. If the snowmobile wasn't where he'd left it, then somebody must have moved it.

But who in his right mind would even be out on this desolate country road on a night like tonight? One of the neighbors? Possibly. They may have recognized the Ski-Doo and picked it up. If so, no harm done.

But what if it wasn't one of the neighbors? Who else would be out on this road at this hour? The road still hadn't been plowed, so it wasn't one of the county crews.

Who would steal a snowmobile? Especially one with a damaged runner?

When they reached the intersection with State Route 13, Jerry wanted to know which way to turn.

"Take a right," Bob said. "But about four miles down the road be prepared to detour around a pile of debris."

"That where the accident happened?"

"Yeah. That's where it happened."

Drifting snow had completely covered the Explorer's tracks, and both the highway and surrounding trees looked different from the cab of a pickup truck than from the seat of a snowmobile.

Four miles went by. Then five.

"We should have passed it by now," he said. "We should have seen the wreckage. Where is it?"

"Buried in snow," Jerry said.

They went another mile. Then two. On the left were the cabin courts. A lit neon sign announced vacancies. Jerry pulled into the parking lot and stopped directly in front of a box-like stone building that had "Office" painted on a cedar shingle over the door. The door was locked when Bob tried it, but there was an arrow decal pointing to a doorbell and a small sign that said, "Please ring bell after midnight."

Jerry pushed the doorbell button six or seven times. Two minutes later an old man wearing a brown robe over blue pajamas opened the door.

"You lookin' for a room?" the old man asked, stifling a yawn.

"Yes," said Bob.

"Well, c'mon in then. It's way too cold to stand here with the door wide open. You're in luck, cause I got just two heated cabins left. Indoor plumbing, all the comforts of home. Fifty-two-fifty a night per each. Plus tax. Cash in advance or major credit card."

"I'll take one," Bob said. "My friend's just dropping me off."

He turned to Jerry. "Thanks a lot for all your help tonight." He offered his hand and the kid took it with a surprisingly firm grip.

"Mebbe I'll see you around," Jerry said. Then he hopped in the truck and drove north.

"You got a phone?" Bob asked as he pulled out his wallet and paid cash for the room. "I tried my cell, but there's no reception way out here."

"Got a phone, but it won't do you much good. Lines are down," said the old man, counting the money and writing a receipt. "Went down three days ago when that big wind hit. Wisconsin Power and Light got electricity turned back on yesterday morning, but phone lines ain't fixed yet. I 'spect phone company crews will get to this neck of the woods tomorrow or maybe the day after."

"I need to call the sheriff about an accident. Is there any way to reach the sheriff? CB radio? Cell phone?"

"Nope. Best thing is get a good night's sleep and drive to town tomorrow after the main roads get plowed. You're in cabin number three. Go out the door, turn left, walk past the first two cabins on the right, the third one is yours. Here's the key. You'll find an electric space heater plugged in and running. Heat's set at sixty. Turn the knob a couple clicks to the right and you'll be toasty as a bug in a rug."

As Bob trudged through the snow to the cabin, he had the distinct feeling he was being watched.

But tonight he was much too tired to follow up on his intuition. He decided whoever it was, they weren't going to do anything more than run surveillance.

Maybe tomorrow, after four or five hours of sleep, he'd turn the tables on them and run some surveillance of his own.

CHAPTER TWELVE

"**M**y, how you've changed since the last time I saw you," chortled Philip Ashur when he opened a recently delivered metal box. The severed head of Ellen Groves, packed between chunks of ice, stared up at him from inside. He grabbed the head by the hair, yanked it from the ice-filled box, and transferred it to a metal shelf in one of three commercial deep-freezers he maintained in a special locked room adjacent to his private suite in the XIIMI building.

"But, then," Ashur added as he tossed Ellen's left hand next to the head and slammed the freezer door shut, "so have I."

Four similar trophies resided in the other two freezers: the head and hand of a Tibetan Tulku who had once been Ashur's teacher and guru; the head and right foot of a Sufi dervish; the head, shriveled penis and testicles of a Hawaiian Kahuna, a practitioner of Ho'omana; and the head and bloody heart of a Roman Catholic nun. Each had once stood in his way—in the way of the Great Work—and each had met his or her end at Philip Ashur's explicit direction.

From time to time he liked to pop open a freezer door, look at one of his trophies, and gloat. But taking trophies, he reminded himself lest ego lead him astray, also served a purely practical function. It had absolutely nothing to do with ego gratification.

Each body part captured some vital aspect of a true spiritual adept, and an adept's spirit was forever linked to what remained of the physical body.

The spirit would not be released from its mortal coil until the body itself—the entire body—reached a certain stage of putrefaction. Or unless the body was magically transformed by fire. Until the entire body, which was the temple of the spirit, could be reabsorbed into the prima materia (the first matter, the rich soil or compost from which all life sprung), the immortal spirit was not free to migrate. Without physical transformation, spiritual transformation was impossible.

For dust thou art, and unto dust shalt thou return. *Ars totum requirit hominem.* The art requires the whole man.

Why was it necessary that the body be transformed before the spirit could be reborn? Ashur wished he knew. He did know that the greatest alchemists of history had said it was so, and many had proven it through experimentation. If any had known why, they had failed to commit the secret to writing.

Suspecting this was one of those mysteries passed on only in initiatory whispers between master and pupil, Philip Ashur had combed the world for contemporary alchemists—masters of the mystic arts—who might provide answers. Over the years he'd acquired many of the most important secrets of alchemy, first by collecting rare books, then by rooting out hidden masters and apprenticing himself for a time. Or, if they wouldn't accept him as a student, by torturing them until they revealed their secrets.

Finally he became, himself, a hidden master of the Black Arts. But some secrets still eluded him, and he was painfully aware his knowledge remained incomplete. It wasn't enough for Philip Ashur to know how something worked. He also needed to know why it worked. And until he had all the answers, he felt vulnerable.

When he returned to his office, dawn was still three hours away. The XIIMI building was virtually deserted at his hour. The handful of security guards who patrolled the ground floor were under strict orders not to admit the maintenance crew until six, the clerical staff until seven-thirty. The building didn't officially open for business until nine.

However, Ashur's secret society of world-wide operatives worked around the clock in all corners of the globe. They influenced or controlled money markets, land developments, international commerce and finance, and political actions. Only the U. S. government and the Vatican had more hands in more pies than Philip Ashur. And sometimes he had doubts about the U.S. government.

What he couldn't buy, he stole. Whom he couldn't bribe, he blackmailed. And those very few people or institutions who refused to be influenced by money or threats, like Ellen Groves or some of his former teachers, were easily eliminated, brutally murdered or politically and/or sexually compromised so their reputations were ruined.

Ashur ruled the world from his office in Chicago. And most people didn't even know he existed.

That's the way he wanted it, the way it was meant to be. Real power moved in mysterious ways, and Philip Ashur was and had always been a mystery man. He allowed no one to get close enough to truly know him. To do so would have jeopardized his power and left him vulnerable. He didn't like feeling vulnerable.

He'd trained himself to function at peak efficiency on less than two hours sleep each night, supplemented by occasional power naps and twenty minutes of deep meditation. He hadn't been physically ill since he was seven, and any wound he received naturally healed itself within seventy-two hours.

He spun around in his desk chair to face his computer, checked his e-mail, and replied to half-a-dozen messages that demanded immediate attention. He ordered a shipping magnate in Lebanon to meet with an accident, nothing too serious but just soul-shattering enough to put the fear of God back in his heart. He bought and sold stocks on the London exchange, sold a diamond mine in South Africa, bought a commuter airline in Pakistan, acquired controlling interest in a publishing conglomerate in France, sold land in Malaysia.

None of these things did he physically do himself, of course. He ordered them done. He was the operator. Trusted operatives carried out his directives with promptness and precision. No one who failed him lived to fail him again. He considered himself to be a good and fair master, more than generous in doling out rewards, ruthless in administering punishments.

Ashur was the kind of master mortals had, in the past, worshipped as a god. While he wasn't yet a god, every day he felt more god-like. Someday soon, if not this lifetime then in the next, he believed he would possess the actual powers of a god.

How many lifetimes already had he searched for the elusive key to godhood? The philosopher's stone? The elixir vitae? The Holy Grail?

Though he could vividly recall fourteen of his reincarnations, an achievement in itself few men had truly accomplished, he could not yet recall all.

And that bothered him.

He quickly removed his clothing. He stacked shoes, socks, slacks, wool suitcoat, shirt, tie, and silk underwear neatly on the desktop. He walked to a dimly lit corner of the room where he lit candles and incense. Naked, keeping spine erect but not rigid, he sank to a crosslegged position in the center of an antique Persian rug covering this portion of the office floor.

Aeioummmmmmmmmmmmmmmm," he began. "Aaaaaaaaaaaaaeee-eeeeeeeeeeeeiiiiiiiiiiiiiiooooooooooooooouuuuuuuuuuuuuuummm."

As vibrations emanating, not only from his mouth but from the very center of his being, filled the room and moved outward to conquer the universe, he willed his heart to slow, his internal organs to suspend activity. His body entered hibernation mode. All five senses and nine bodily apertures were hermetically sealed against the outside world. His brainwaves shifted from beta to alpha to theta and remained in theta for twenty minutes, with brief lapses into delta.

The images begin almost immediately. Like standing on the rear platform of a caboose propelled by an antique steam locomotive chugging backwards up a winding track, the journey began ever so slowly. The train gradually picked up steam and speed as internal flames were stoked hotter and hotter, fanned by the breath. As if chunks of primordial coal were being added to an athanor, primal elements heated up, transformed; colors changed from black to yellow to blue to red to white as, one by one, his chakras opened and the five internal energy centers fed the flames of the athanor. Vital elements fused. Earth. Air. Fire. Water. Spirit. The internal cauldron bubbled and boiled. Water became steam became vapor.

Philip Ashur relived his life in reverse. Yesterday, the day before. Last week. Last year. Decades passed before his mind's eye. Although Ashur physically appeared as a man in his early to mid forties, in reality he was much, much older. He viewed his latest birth in 1804, his conception in 1803.

The backward-moving train passed through a tunnel and entered darkness, blacker than the Egyptian earth that covered his grave. Then, like staring directly at a naked light bulb that suddenly snapped on or seeing a sun going nova at the far end of a black hole, Philip Ashur was blinded by the light.

His previous life ended violently in the summer of 1802. He relived, again in reverse, the events leading up to that death. Then back to his birth in 1730. Through the tunnel. Into the light once more. And into another life.

He was reincarnated as a woman. Old, then young, then a child. A fetus. Through the tunnel. Into the light.

A man again. Early seventeenth century. Travels through Europe. the middle-east. Birth in 1605. The tunnel.

He arrived now at his last remembered reincarnation. He was a vizier, a court magician in the court of Suleiman the Magnificent. He studied hermetic philosophy with Paracelsus, letters with Erasmus. He felt his power growing, stronger and stronger. No one knew his real name, and therein resided the greater part of his true power. It was not for glory that he labored; he was but a shadow in the affairs of men. He left behind no writings by which history remembered him, passed on nothing of learned art or craft to disciples. He labored only for himself. He was the most selfish man who ever lived.

He sought out the secrets of the universe, finding hidden clues in the mundane works and obtuse writings of al-Razi, al-Farabi, ibn Sina, ibn Rushid, al-Biruni, al-Ghazali, Albertus Magnus, Duns Scotus. He became a mahdi, a hidden imam, a sufi master, a shaykh. No one knew who was the guiding force behind the moghul empire in India, but Philip Ashur knew. Back to his youth in Byzantium. As a child, he witnessed the fall of Constantinople to the muselman hoards. He was born the son of the widow of a Janissary.

And then the train entered another dark tunnel and the ride abruptly ended.

Philip Ashur remained in darkness for what seemed an eternity.

Then his senses gradually returned, and he was suddenly, shockingly, back in the present, the here and now.

He failed in his quest and could not remember details beyond the beginning of the fifteenth century. What incredible occurrence—what terrible loss of face—created the mental block that even now prohibited entrance to those lives that lay beyond?

Unbalanced by failure, Ashur sought to regain equilibrium. He practiced pranayama, control of the breath. All power comes, say the shastras, from control of pranic energy. First the bellows breath to reheat the fire, snapping the diaphragm 108 times. Then, breathing deeply, he puffed up his chest and refocused his inner eye—the Ajna, the eye of Bohdic insight, the eye of Horus—on the bindu, the point of eternity, the alpha and omega. Finally, practicing alternate nostril pranayama to marry the yin and yang, the female right side with male left side of his brain, Ashur sought to merge his own essence with the essence of God through yogic union.

And encountered yet another barrier.

The familiar features of a face, a face he could never forget, appeared to his mind's eye. "Before you may share the lights of the sun and the moon, my child, first you must master I Ching hexagrams of difficulty and darkness," mouthed the face, reciting verses from the *Guangchengzi*, the ancient Taoist *Book of the Master of Expanded Development*. It was as if Ashur were hearing those words whispered by a man whose head resided in a freezer in the next room.

"You're dead," he screamed at the face in his mind. "I killed you."

"All that lives shall die. And all that dies shall live again."

"Not if I keep you frozen," he told the head. "You taught me the tattva of Hatha Yoga. I know that without the breath, the mind—the intelligence and the consciousness—is useless. Mind without body has no power in this world."

"And do you suppose I taught you all the secrets I learned in 84 lakhs of rebirths? Silly boy! I taught you only what you were capable of understanding, no more and no less. Your beard must be whiter than the pure snows of Mount Meru before you can begin to understand half of what I know."

"Shut up!" screamed Ashur. "Shut up! Shut up! Shut up!"

"And if I don't? What can you do to me that you have not already done? I was beyond the reach of pain when I was alive. Do you think pain can reach me now?"

"I will destroy you! I will squash you like a bug!"

"Go ahead," taunted the head. "Let us see if you have learned anything about siddhis in the years since you were my pupil."

Enraged, Ashur leapt to his feet. He dashed into the next room, threw open the freezer door, and reached for the head of his former guru. If not for a blast of cold air that brought him to his senses, he would have hurled the frozen head against a wall where the skull would have shattered into a thousand pieces.

"That's really what you wanted, wasn't it?" he said to the face he held in his hands. "You wanted me to lose control, didn't you? You tried to trick me into forgetting that your spirit is limited by what remains of the flesh. You thought I'd smash you to pieces and leave you to rot in a corner of the room. But I won't. I'll keep you frozen forever, trapped where you have no power, no siddhis. For you there will never be another birth, and no Great Liberation either."

Philip Ashur locked the head back in the freezer.

Then he returned to his office and began Tai Chi Chuan, the dragon exercises, to still his troubled mind.

CHAPTER THIRTEEN

As soon as Bob and Jerry drove away from the house in a pickup truck, Diane asked Tom to move the injured girl upstairs to Ellen's bedroom. Tom carefully picked her up from the floor, stabilizing her head and neck with his left hand while placing his right hand beneath her knees.

Nancy and Daisy May Martindale followed him with the lantern.

He tucked her gently into Ellen's bed. Then he stepped back and watched Nancy cover her with a cotton blanket and a hand-sewn down-filled comforter.

Daisy May raised the girl's head and shoulders, squeezed open her pale lips. Nancy spoon-fed drops of a concocted herbal medicinal she induced the unconscious girl to swallow.

Tom wished he knew her name. It was ridiculous to keep thinking of this woman—who must surely be close to his own age—as a girl.

But he couldn't help thinking of her that way because there was something so fragile about her, so vulnerable, especially in her comatose condition. She reminded him of a defenseless child.

He wanted to stay with her and take care of her, to shield her from harm and hurt. This feeling, which was dangerously close to compulsion, caught him by surprise.

"I need to speak to everyone downstairs," Diane called. "You, too."

"I'll be down in a minute," he answered, not yet willing to leave. When he was satisfied she would be safe, he reluctantly left her alone in the dark.

Diane requested the gathering to convene around the fireplace. She needed everyone's help to assess an anomaly she had discovered in the spirit world, and she said it was much too important to wait until tomorrow.

"Do you feel it?" she queried each of the women, working her way around the faces in the circle the way she worked her classes of graduate students. "Do you feel the terrible imbalances building up in the aether? I can. I can sense the abyss growing larger, and very soon—maybe not today or even tomorrow—but surely the day after or the day after that it will spill over into this world and begin to devour everything we value."

Tom hadn't cultivated an ability to sense other worlds as these women, but he was sensitive enough to feel a great danger manifesting in the material world. When danger lurked close-by, he could smell it.

"We all feel something," agreed Aunt Violet. "Look outside and see how pranic imbalance affects our weather. But what you see is merely the tip of the iceberg, a spit in the bucket. Tornadoes, earthquakes, floods will follow. Then pestilence and famine. A shift of our planet's magnetic poles. The inevitable destruction of civilization. The loss of countless lives. The end of the world as we know it. We feel it beginning, because it has already begun."

"As above, so below," said Aunt Anna, repeating an ancient hermetic phrase. "A shift of energy in the spirit world affects energy in the material world, and vice versa. Twice before an imbalance in the spirit realm destroyed civilization as we knew it. Twice before we were forced to start over."

"What can we do to restore harmony?" asked Roseanne Martindale. "Is there anything we *can* do?"

"Of course, there is," said Aunt Anna, sitting up straight and alert on the couch. She metamorphosed into a woman half her age. Gone now was the dowager's hump, the sagging flesh.

"Before anything else," she said, "we must return what remains of Ellen to the earth and free her spirit. But that's merely the first step of many. We must find what caused the rift and how. Only then can we take corrective action. By working together, we have a chance to restore harmony to both worlds. But we must hurry. Time is short."

"Let's focus on what we already know," Diane said. "Ma sensed the growing cosmic imbalance three nights ago. She woke Sara and asked her to help. They were headed for the sacred circle when Ma was killed. Sara," Diane looked directly at the sleepy eleven year-old, "what did Ma tell you needed to be done?"

"Just that there was an imbalance that we had to correct right away or something bad would happen."

"Did she say how? What did she want you to do?"

"She wanted me to help her raise energy. She said if we could raise enough energy, we could keep the bad guys from getting a foot in the door."

"Did she say who the bad guys were?"

"The ones who wanted her land."

"Ellen was being pressured to sell," said Aunt Violet. "She told the real estate brokers where to go, but they wouldn't take no for an answer. They kept making offers and she kept rejecting them."

"Do you know who made the offers?" asked Tom.

"Lawyers," sneered Vi. She hated lawyers almost as much as politicians. The fact that most politicians were also lawyers didn't help. Aunt Vi claimed all lawyers and politicians, without exception, were liars and thieves. They used man-made laws to make themselves rich and powerful.

"Who were the brokers and lawyers representing?"

"They never said. I warned Ellen that all lawyers were liars and thieves, but she didn't want to believe me. She invited them in, offered them tea, and tried to make them understand that money didn't matter to her at all. Of course, they thought she was only holding out for more money. They upped the ante and made obscene offers that no normal person could possibly refuse. Ellen not only could refuse, she did. She was the caretaker of the land, and no amount of money would ever tempt her to turn this land over to people who had no respect for living things. How could she have known how little respect for life they truly had?"

"Whoever they are," Diane said, "whoever killed Ma, they know the meaning of taking trophies. As long as they preserve any part of her, they hold her spirit captive and there's no way we can re-member her."

A murmur filled the room as several younger women asked questions of their mentors.

"For those of you who are relatively new to the craft," said Diane, "let me explain how spirit and flesh are intertwined. As you know, spirit is eternal. The material world, however, is temporary. When spirit enters the material world, it becomes temporarily bound or tied to the flesh. Spirit cannot remain in this world for more than a very short time unless it roots to a material object. When spirit does root to a living thing—a plant, a tree, an animal, a person—it can be held captive by the flesh until one of three things happens to free it: spirit becomes adept at loosening the ties that bind it to the flesh, and it is temporarily free to roam at will; a traumatic occurrence separates spirit from flesh and the bonds are temporarily broken; or the flesh is transformed by fire, by certain biological processes, or by putrefaction, and the bonds are permanently broken."

"What's putrefaction?" asked Sara.

"Good question. It means decay. Decay occurs when organic compounds decompose—break down—into baser constituents. This change of state releases energy and, since spirit is intimately related to energy, spirit is also released. When a certain threshold of putrefaction is reached, spirit is no longer bound to the flesh by various intracellular electro-chemical processes that nurture it in the material world. When freed from the body, spirit seeks another home in the material world. Sometimes, when a very strong spirit discovers a body that is already occupied by a weaker spirit, the stronger spirit may be able to take possession of the body and both co-habit one shell, often with disastrous consequences. Sometimes, adepts can raise sufficient energy to guide a spirit to an appropriate home. Living trees make perfect temporary homes for freed spirits. Certain animals, especially birds and cats and reptiles and insects, are also suitable vehicles for free spirits."

"That's why," said Sara, showing off she remembered what Ellen had taught her, "we plant a new tree in the forest near the circle when one of us is born."

"Exactly," said Diane. "Each of us has our own tree near the circle. When we die, the others will raise energy to re-member us. Energy then guides our spirits home to roost in our tree until we are reborn into a new human body conceived specifically to house a particular spirit entity."

"That's what we did for Ellen tonight," said Aunt Vi. "Or tried to do, anyway. But her spirit isn't free. It's still bound to part of her body, and her spirit can neither find a home in the spirit realm nor roost in a tree."

"So whoever took part of her as a trophy," said Tom, "holds her spirit captive."

"Unless, or until, that body part putrefies," said Diane.

"Whoever has her knows enough to keep putrefaction from happening," said Aunt Vi. "Somewhere there's an adept who not only knows the significance of taking a trophy, he also has means to preserve that trophy and hold Ellen's spirit captive indefinitely."

"We must find him," said Aunt Anna. "We must find him and stop him before the rift between the spirit world and the material world grows too big to repair."

"Does he know what damage his actions have already caused?" asked Aunt Vi. "Does he have any idea of the consequences if he continues to disrupt the balance between worlds?"

"Father, forgive them," said Diane, quoting scripture, "for they know not what they do."

"Oh, they know," said Aunt Anna, her words casting a chill over the room as if she had flung open the door to the howling wind. "The person responsible knows exactly what he's doing, and no one or nothing can stop him but us."

CHAPTER FOURTEEN

Sheila saw the light.

It beckoned to her from a distance, and she willingly went toward it with a joy she never thought possible. It was as if she were a child again, and her mother, who died in childbirth, cradled and cuddled her and covered her with kisses. She wanted to go into the light and stay there forever.

Bathed in the light—an energy so pure that it blinded her—every nerve, every muscle, every cell of her body began to reconstitute itself according to explicit instructions from her DNA. Just as undifferentiated stem cells rapidly develop into what nature and a nurturing environment direct them to become in embryo, so do damaged cells repair themselves when supplied with sufficient energy.

Glial cells—microglial cells and astrocytes—rushed to repair damaged neurons. New neurons grew and developed. A hundred million new axons sprouted.

Within minutes, Sheila Ryan was back. Not the old Sheila Ryan, but a new, transformed Sheila that was only now beginning to emerge.

As night turned to day, her body continued to regenerate. And Sheila began to dream.

*　　*　　*

Sun peeked through clouds for the first time in four days. Even the wind, which raged through the night and kept McMichaels from sleeping soundly, was now little more than a whisper.

Bob didn't want to get out from under the heavy down-filled comforter. His body felt like it had been chewed up and spit out, and every time he moved a dozen different aches reminded him he wasn't an 18 or 20 year-old anymore.

He swung his legs out of bed and headed straight for the shower. It took ten whole minutes for the water to heat up, but it was worth the wait. He stood under the steamy spray and let the water ease some of the aches in his neck and shoulders while he inspected dozens of large bruises that had sprouted on his ribs and legs. He saw nothing that wouldn't heal within a week. He stayed in the shower until his skin started to look like a prune, then he toweled himself dry, rinsed his mouth out with water from the sink, and dressed in the same clothes he'd worn the day before.

Bob regretted leaving his suitcase and toilet kit at the Groves house. He'd have to wait to shave, brush his teeth, and change underwear. Since he was out of uniform, shaving wasn't important. And he'd once worn the same underwear six days in a row in Afghanistan. He knew he could survive another day without changing briefs or socks.

When he heard a plow scraping against gravel outside the cabin, he peeked out the window to see an old Jeep Wrangler with a blade attached to the front pushing snow from the parking lot into a big pile at the far end. The old man who had rented the cabin was behind the wheel.

Bob threw on the borrowed parka and stepped outside. The air was crisp and clean. Without the biting wind the temperature seemed bearable.

He hailed the driver and asked the old guy where he could get breakfast.

"My wife's got coffee brewing in the office," the old man said. "But you won't find a restaurant that's open this time of the year until you get all the way into Park Falls. That's a good twenty miles, give or take. Go on in and grab a cup of coffee. Ask Hilda, that's my wife, if she'll whip you up some eggs and bacon."

Hilda, a grey-haired woman about sixty, wore a checkered flannel shirt and jeans. As soon as Bob stepped into the office, she pointed to a 30-cup aluminum coffee maker and Styrofoam cups at the end of the counter. "Help yourself," she said.

"Your husband said you might take pity on a stranded traveler and find some eggs and bacon to tide him over. I'd be happy to pay you."

"Arvin said that, did he? Well, I suppose I could. Bring your coffee around to the kitchen and we'll see what we can find for you to eat. You get caught in that storm last night?"

"Yeah. Do you get this much snow all the time around here?"

"We get three or four big dumps a year, usually starting in mid-December and lasting maybe through March. We might get an inch or two between Halloween and Thanksgiving, maybe even six inches. But no one expected this much snow this early. And the winds! My Lord, we thought the whole place was going to blow away!"

"So this weather is unusual?"

"For this time of year it's practically unheard of. I do remember, when I was a child, walking through drifts that seemed nearly as big.

But I was small and everything seemed big back then. And that was in February. This is still November."

Hilda led Bob into a small kitchen behind the office. While he sat at the table and sipped his coffee, she took a slab of bacon from a refrigerator, cut six strips from the slab, and laid them out to simmer in a cast-iron skillet.

"It started with the winds picking up four days ago," she said. "They howled something awful. Then it started raining, and the rain turned to sleet and hail, then snow. Yesterday morning the temperature dropped, and it started snowing again." She cracked three eggs into the skillet. "By nine o'clock last night, the roads were practically impassable. We probably got only three or four feet of snow, but the winds didn't stop till this morning and some of the drifts out there are six to eight feet deep in places. State highway crews couldn't keep up with it, and county doesn't even try until the snow stops. How'd you get here anyway? You couldn't get very far in a car."

"Someone with a pick-up truck dropped me off."

"Are you visiting friends or relatives in the area?"

"Friends. Do you know the Groves family?"

"I heard about the accident that killed Ellen. Terrible thing to happen to anybody. Everyone's talking about it. It used to be you could cross the road and not worry. Now there's too many people and too many cars. Just last week we had someone going seventy hit a deer. Dragged the deer a good quarter mile before the car stopped. Then they just left the carcass off by the side of the road and drove away. Didn't say boo to nobody. Just left what remained of the carcass to rot and drove off. You think that's what happened to poor Ellen? Thought she was a deer and drove off?"

"I don't know," said Bob. "What do you think?"

"I think it's terrible, is what I think. You want some toast with your eggs? I got some rhubarb jam that goes good on toast."

"Yes, thank you."

"You staying more than one night?" She popped two slices of bread into a toaster.

"I don't know yet."

"We only got twelve cabins, and they all filled up last night. You can keep your room if you want, but don't wait too long to decide. We'll probably fill up tonight, too."

"Do you usually fill up every night?"

"This time of year? No. Most we usually get is one or two hunters during deer season, maybe a tourist or two every now and then. We do a good business in the summer, though. Muskie fishermen, mostly, lots of tourists. Wisconsin is wonderful during the summer and early fall. Arvin and me we bought this place twenty-two years ago. We fell in love with the quiet and the trees and the lakes and the clean air. It's a struggle, though, to make ends meet. Most of the tourists want a Holiday Inn or a Ramada with a swimming pool for the kids and cable tv. All we offer is a clean room to sleep in, a shower, and the smell of pine. Not many people stay more than one night."

"So the storm helped your business?"

"People started stopping yesterday afternoon. Arvin sold the last room about an hour after you checked in."

"Who to?"

"Couple of hunters. They took the cabin next to you. They got that Dodge Ram 3500 parked out there."

Bob went to the window and looked between the drapes. There was a large dark blue Dodge truck in the lot. Packed snow obscured the plates.

A powerful radio antenna was mounted behind the cab.

"Deer hunters?" Bob asked.

"Deer season starts next week," Hilda said. "Lot of hunters come up here early to stake out a stand. Some do a lot of heavy drinking while they're waiting for the season to open."

"Must be good for the local economy."

"Fishing and boating during the summer pays the bills. Tourists from the big cities—Chicago, Milwaukee, Madison, Minneapolis—come here to sightsee and fish all summer long, from Memorial Day to Labor Day. They call this 'God's Country' because it's as close to the natural world as they want to get. But this time of year, when the leaves are off the trees and the north wind bites, only a handful of hunters come up from the cities. Those of us who live and work here year round are grateful for every penny we can get. But at what price? Drunks running around in the woods with loaded guns shooting at anything that moves? Drunks driving back roads at 90 miles an hour? People getting run down when they cross the road? I don't know anymore if it's worth it."

She set the plate of food on the table. "Better eat, or your breakfast will get cold."

Bob sat at the table and cut into the eggs. "Looks and smells wonderful," he said. "You should open a restaurant."

Hilda beamed. "Those are fresh eggs," she said. "From a neighbor's chickens. Bacon comes from the co-op. We have a few acres out back that we use to grow strawberries and raspberries, tomatoes and pumpkins. The rhubarb jam on your toast comes from the patch out back. I do some canning, enough to see us through the winter and a little to sell at the co-op. I wouldn't want to open a restaurant, though."

Arvin came in the front door and walked around to the kitchen. "The boys in cabin number four just left," he said. "You want me to see what kind of mess they made?"

"I'll go check," said Hilda. "You sit and rest. You've been plowin' since sun-up, and you're not as young as you used to be."

"I'm as young as you, Hilda Mae," said the old man.

"Well, I'm not as young as I used to be, either," said Hilda.

"Can I see their cabin?" said Bob. "I'm just curious to see what kind of mess hunters leave behind."

"We'll all go," said Arvin.

They walked across the plowed lot to cabin number four. Hilda reached into her jeans pocket, took out a master key, and unlocked the door.

"Well, I'll be," breathed Arvin.

"I don't believe my eyes," said Hilda. "The room looks ..."

"Unused," said Bob.

"Even the bathroom," Hilda said after glancing in the shower. "The sani-strip across the toilet seat is unbroken, the towels haven't been touched, or the soap unwrapped."

Arvin turned back the bed covers. "Didn't sleep in the bed. No hairs on the pillows."

Bob checked the wastebaskets. Empty.

"Only thing that's been touched is the chairs," Arvin said. "They dragged the chairs over to the window. Then they dragged them back again. See the skid marks on the carpet?"

"All this room needs is a little vacuuming," said Hilda. "I'll tidy up, and it'll be ready to rent."

"Damned unusual for hunters," said Arvin. "Not that I'm complaining, mind you. It's just that I expect they'll use the cabin for a party. Especially the young ones. They're the worst."

"What do you mean by young?" asked Bob.

"Nineteen, twenty, twenty-one. Up to thirty. People over thirty are more respectful of property. When they party, at least they don't trash the place."

"What about those three hunters last year?" said Hilda. "Remember the ones who got sick and threw up all over the bed and carpet? There were these three executives from Chicago," she explained to Bob, "that came up here just to get drunk. They told their wives they were going hunting, but they spent the entire week getting drunker and drunker. Finally, one of them had so much to drink that he threw up, and the others, just as drunk, threw up from the smell. Then they took off in their fancy cars and left the mess for Arvin and me to clean up."

"I forgot about them," admitted Arvin.

"They were all men in their late fifties, for heaven's sake! You'd think they'd know better."

"How old," interjected Bob, "were the two who rented this cabin last night?"

"Early twenties, maybe," said Arvin. "They looked younger, but everyone looks young to me these days."

"How were they dressed?"

"Camouflage parkas. Both had hoods with fur linings. They dressed for the weather like experienced hunters."

"So you didn't get a good look at their faces?"

"No. Why?"

"Because they didn't want you to be able to give me a good description of what they looked like." Bob reached into his pocket for his ID case and showed Arvin and Hilda his military identification. "I've been assigned to investigate the hit and run that killed Ellen Groves near here four days ago. Last night two men followed me and tried to kill me. I suspect the two men who rented this cabin were confederates of the other two. They followed me here and stayed up all night making sure I didn't leave. Could I see their registration records for the room, please?"

"Sure," said Arvin. "Come on over to the office."

"Someone followed you?" asked Hilda as they walked back to the office. "Why?"

"I'm not sure," answered Bob, truthfully.

"Why is the army investigating a hit and run?" Arvin asked.

"Because someone tried to cover up the hit and run. And because Ellen Groves' son is an army officer. I've been assigned to determine if there's a connection."

"Here," said Arvin, handing Bob a 5 x 8 inch card. The guest name was John Jones. The address was just "Chicago, IL."

"No street address? No telephone? Did you get a license number?"

"It was late," said Arvin, apologetically. "I didn't pay any attention to what he put on the card."

"He paid in cash?"

"Yup."

Tom Groves' Ford Focus drove into the lot and parked in front of the office. Tom got out, opened the trunk, and entered with Bob's suitcase.

"Put me down for another night," Bob told Hilda. "I'll be back tonight."

* * *

"Describe the girl," demanded Philip Asher.

"White female, late twenties, red hair," Delacroix reported over the scrambled phone line.

"Sheila Ryan," said Asher.

Delacroix wasn't surprised that Ashur knew her name. He kept his finger on the pulse of the world, knowing more about what was happening than any other man alive. His tentacles spanned the entire globe, and Delacroix knew that the covert intelligence network he ran was only one of many.

If you had enough money, you could buy anyone or anything. And know everything. And everyone. And Ashur certainly had enough money.

"The damage is contained," Delacroix reported. "We've disposed of the vehicles and debris, and the accident site is clean. Colonel McMichaels and Major Groves remain under surveillance. They've been trying to locate the site and the missing snowmobile for the past hour, but they won't find anything."

"Good," said Ashur. "Keep them guessing."

"We can take them out, Make them disappear, or make it look like an accident. Just give the word."

"Not yet. When I do give the word, I want you to handle Groves like you did his mother. It must be sudden. Hit him hard, take him apart, and save the head and hands for me. They must be preserved at all costs. Understand?"

Delacroix thought Ashur's obsession with trophies was an unnecessary complication, but nothing that couldn't be accommodated. And it certainly wasn't unusual. He'd known trophy-takers before, and he knew the value, in certain circumstances, of displaying the severed heads of one's enemies. Many special operations units routinely confirmed targets through DNA, and nearly every army in the world applied forensic science to body parts to confirm kills. Delacroix remembered a unit that collected ears; another that collected fingers. No, it wasn't unusual at all.

What was unusual, though, was Ashur's insistence that the severed head be kept from decaying even a little. They had to get the head on ice within three minutes. That didn't seem like much of a problem with temperatures below freezing. But if a target were taken indoors where normal decomposition began almost immediately, the three-minute rule was essential.

As long as Ashur paid the bills, he called the shots. If he wanted to collect heads, Delacroix would supply all the heads he wanted.

"I understand," replied the Colonel. "When you give the word, I'll put the head and hands on ice."

"Good. Check in again at 1500."

Delacroix switched off the dedicated line.

Then he returned to monitoring the chatter between Chechnyan rebels and Taliban chieftans that originated from somewhere north of Pakistan. Delacroix, like Ashur, had more than one iron in the fire.

CHAPTER FIFTEEN

"They should be right here," McMichaels told Groves. "I can't believe snow simply covered the wreckage. Where are the two vehicles? Where are the body parts? Where the hell did they go?"

"Road crews went through with plows and sand an hour ago," Groves said. "They may have moved the debris."

"But what happened to the two bodies? Maybe they moved the burnt out vehicle chassis. Maybe they sent out a wrecker or a flat bed to haul them away. But what about the body parts?"

"We'll check with the highway department. They'll tell us if they picked up a snowmobile or a burnt-out chassis. And we can check with the sheriff's department about bodies."

"I suspect it won't do much good. They weren't who took away the bodies or the burnt-out hulks and covered up signs that anything unusual happened here last night."

"What do you mean?"

"Look around you, Tom. This place is clean. It's been sanitized by pros. They had a team of experts pick up the pieces and make it look like nothing happened. They have an organization in place capable of responding instantly to any contingency. That means they're well-trained, well-equipped, and in constant communication with command and control. We're talking something big here. Maybe like the KGB or MI-5, The CIA. The FBI. I don't think a small terrorist cell of Islamic extremists—Al Qaeda, what's left of the Iraqi Republican Guard, ISIL or ISIS—or even domestic extremists, like some of the so-called freedom militia, could field the men and material required. These guys are definitely pros."

"The CIA? The FBI? Why would they be involved?"

"They could be involved without knowing. It happens all the time. Someone in covert ops runs a rogue operation. They use agency assets without authorization. No one is ever the wiser. Many officially sanctioned ops require support from unofficial or unsanctioned sources that can be disavowed if the need arises. With everything on a need-to-know basis, the right hand seldom knows what the left hand is doing. You were in Afghanistan, Tom. You saw the way covert ops got things done. You know the same thing happened in Iraq. And in Bosnia. Why not here?"

"Are you saying that the CIA was involved in killing my mother?"

"I'm saying I don't know of many other organizations that have assets in place to pull off something of this magnitude or with such precision. I don't believe the CIA or the FBI are directly involved, but I do think people who were trained by the agency or the bureau or both may be working together to cover up your mother's murder, and I know they've been following my every move since before we left Fort Campbell. Who else would have the capability to pull off something like this?"

"There are people and organizations at work in the world you don't know about. You don't suspect they exist because you aren't willing to believe they do exist. It may not be a government agency doing this."

"Fill me in, Major. If you know something I don't, cue me in right now."

"I only know the basics. You need to talk to my sisters and my aunts. They know a lot more than I."

"Then let's get with it. I want to talk to your sisters and your aunts and get some answers. And I want those answers right now."

CHAPTER SIXTEEN

The Most Beautiful Girl in the World wore cowboy boots.
She also wore faded blue jeans tucked into boot tops, a powder-blue UW sweatshirt with a picture of a badger on the front, and a smile. She seemed honestly glad to see him.

Bob found himself returning the smile. It was the first time he'd felt like smiling in days.

The old house seemed brighter and much friendlier in daylight. Besides the smell of wood smoke that permeated the living room, his nose detected delicious odors coming from the kitchen.

"Lunch'll be ready in an hour," Diane said. "I hope you'll stay and join us."

"I'd like that."

"Then it's settled. Aunt Anna's baking bread and Aunt Cynthia is concocting a humongous kettle of soup. I hope you don't mind plenty of garden vegetables, including mushrooms, garlic, and onions."

"Not at all," said Bob.

"We need to talk," said Tom. "We need to hear what Bob thinks about the people behind Ma's murder. Then we need to share some family secrets we don't normally share."

"With him?" The smile disappeared, and once again she looked at Bob the way an entomologist inspected an insect. "What makes you think he can be trusted?"

"The army trusts him to keep military secrets. And I trust him to watch my back. That means something."

"And what makes you think he's capable of understanding even if we do tell him? Some raised in the arts since birth can't grasp the full import of what's happening. How could an outsider even begin to comprehend?"

"Just what *is* happening?" asked Bob. "Obviously, you know more than you've told me."

"Are you asking as an agent of the government or as someone who's interested in helping us?"

"Both. I do want to help you in any way I can. But I also have a job to do for Uncle Sam. That's my first priority. I need to know if terrorists were involved with your mother's death."

Diane's eyes went out of focus as if she viewed something far away he couldn't see. Then the radiant smile returned, and the Most Beautiful Girl in the World reached out and took his hand and guided him from the foyer toward the living room. "Both of you come with me and help stoke the fire. We'll talk until dinner's ready. Then we can ask the aunts to give you a crash course in magic."

"Magic?" Bob asked.

"What do you know about magic, Bob?" she asked, sitting cross-legged on the floor in front of the fire. She patted the space next to her, inviting him to sit. "Do you believe in magic?"

"Not really," he admitted.

"Well, I do," said Diane, her eyes reflecting the bright glow of the fire's flames. "But whether you believe in magic or not, magic does exist. Not the hocus-pocus of stage magicians, but the magic of the mathematician, the physicist, the chemist. To perform magic, one must first understand the fundamental laws of the universe. Are you familiar with quantum mechanics or Einstein's Unified Field Theory?"

"No."

"In essence, they postulate the total amount of energy and matter in the universe is fixed, a constant. But the forms of energy and matter are not. Energy and matter are constantly changing states, being converted into each other and then back again. Neither can be created nor destroyed but they do change form. Changes in the energy field generates equivalent changes in matter, and changes in matter require changes of energy. Einstein devoted the last half of his life to developing mathematical formulae describing symbolically the interrelationships between matter and energy. He died without realizing his dream, but he got incredibly close."

"E equals mc squared?"

"That's a beginning."

"Magic and mathematics are intimately interrelated," Tom clarified. "So are magnetism, macabre, machine, macramé, magister, magnificent, maiden, mage, make, mama, man, mana, manage, manipulate and a thousand other concept words. They're all ma-words. They're all derived from from Ma, the Great Mother."

"Those who understand magic understand nature is necessarily bi-polar," continued Diane. "It can best be explained in alchemical terms: unification of the feminine and masculine principles generates power; the first principle is feminine—the *ma*teria prima; the second principle is masculine—the *pa*rticulate; and the third principle—the triad or trinity—is the precipitate that emerges from the union of the two, an androgenous composite that embodies both principles. Suffice it to say that the yoga—the union or *ma*rriage—of ma and pa polarities generates energy from matter and matter from energy."

"That's all greek to me," said Bob. "What does anything you just said have to do with your mother's death and the men who killed her?"

"Everything," said Diane. "My mother understood *ma*gic and appreciated the importance of polarities. She willingly accepted personal responsibility for monitoring and maintaining the delicate balance that allows the spirit worlds and material world to co-exist in different dimensions and on separate space-time continua. From this physical place—this very special place on one of the central lay lines connecting heaven and earth—Ma was able to control the flow of energy between worlds. Whenever the spirits of the wind or the trees informed her something was wrong and an imbalance existed, she could usually correct it by reversing polarities.

"She was one of the guardians of the watchtowers," contributed Tom, "a guardian of Magic. She wasn't the only guardian, of course. Ma was one of many."

"I personally know of seven others," said Diane, "four men and three women. They watch and listen at various guardtowers located on lay lines: in the Himalayas, the Andes, along the banks of the Nile, on the Avebury plain in England, a volcano east of New Zealand, a rock formation near northern Finnland, a temple in northern Cambodia, and here within the old-growth forest."

"The eight guardians are hidden masters of the arcane arts," said Tom.

"That sounds crazy," said Bob, "I still don't see why your mother was killed."

"Of course, that sounds crazy," Diane admitted. "It's completely beyond the comprehension of most mortals. They go about their daily lives unaware of powerful forces simultaneously at work all over the world, all over the universe. Ordinary people have no clue. As long as the sun rises every day as it always has in the past, as long as they're alive and well and able to go about their daily business, what I've just told you has no meaning. It simply doesn't compute in their brains."

"But there are some people in the world who do have a clue?"

"Yes. And some who seek to control the power of the universe for their own ends, unscrupulous people who have the knowledge and the will to seize that immense power and bend it and attempt to reshape it. They'll manipulate it until the very fabric of existence breaks asunder from accumulated stress. We—my aunts and I—believe that one or more of those people were behind Ma's murder. Not only did they want her out of the way to possess this land for purposes of their own, they were willing to upset the delicate balance of the universe to acquire ultimate power. That such people exist, I have no doubt. That they'll eventually reveal themselves or we'll be able to uncover them, I have no doubt. What worries me is the damage they do before we find them and put a stop to their insanity. It's up to us to stop them. You, me, Tom, the aunts, the remaining guardians, the good people who are not yet adept but aspiring to become adept. So please join us, Bob. Please help."

"I don't know what to say," said Bob.

"Say only that you'll keep an open mind and consider all possibilities. Listen and learn."

"I didn't believe, either," admitted Tom. "Not at first, anyway. Being male, I wasn't regularly included in the workings of a feminine watchtower. My mother didn't tell me things she told my sisters. It's hard to believe I grew up naïve when all around me the work of a guardian of a watchtower was taking place. But eventually I began to notice things that made me ask questions. Ma never lied to me. Some things, though, she said were woman's work, and those things were revealed only to Diane and Nancy and only tangentially to me. Ma knew the importance of sexual polarities, and she said women's mysteries and men's mysteries were best kept secret from the opposite sex to make each polarity distinctly more powerful when they conjoined. She taught me all she knew of the men's mysteries, and she taught me just enough of the women's mysteries to make them seem intriguing. But there are some things only a man can do, and some only a woman can do. Some things require a union of the male and female to do them."

"That isn't to say," offered Diane, "that men don't have a feminine side. They certainly do. And women have their masculine side. You can learn to increase your feminine energy when it's necessary to do so, Bob. But it won't be easy.

"And, besides," she added as if an afterthought, "I really like your masculine energy. You turn me on. You excite me and frighten me at the same time."

He wasn't certain he'd heard her correctly. Had he truly heard the Most Beautiful Woman in the World say he turned her on?

"Soup's ready," called Aunt Cynthia from the kitchen. "Come and get it while it's hot, boys and girls."

Diane uncoiled her lithe body from lotus, rose effortlessly to her feet, and held out a hand. "You heard the lady, Bob," she said. "Let's eat."

*　　*　　*

Sheila Ryan heard voices.

These weren't only in her head. Unlike the disjointed fever dreams that plagued her throughout the night, these seemed as real as voices of her father and brothers talking about her behind her back when she was a little girl.

Sheila opened her eyes to discover she was surrounded by wood. The ceiling, the walls, the floor were all made of wood. She wondered for a moment if she had died, been buried in a pine box, and this was all she'd see for eternity.

Then she saw sunlight through the frosted glass of an east window, saw snow-encrusted branches of pine trees beyond the window, and she knew she was alive.

But she hurt when she tried to move. She had to pee, but the effort of getting out of bed was too much for her. She'd try to hold it for as long as she could.

Where the hell was she anyway? And how far was it to the goddamn bathroom?

Sheila had no idea where she was or how she got here. The last thing she remembered was stepping out of the car to get cigarettes from the trunk. The only other time she'd experienced a lapse of memory like this was the night she'd graduated from college. She'd celebrated a little too much and woke the next morning in some strange man's bedroom, hungover and feeling like shit. That was the last time she'd allowed herself to get drunk. So how the hell had she wound up here feeling like shit again, this time without drinking a drop?

She tried one more time to get out of bed and discovered her legs just didn't want to move. And to add insult to injury, she discovered she was bare-butt naked beneath the heavy quilt. All right, Sheila, she told herself. Let's think this through. You were stuck in the snow in the middle of nowhere. You got out of your car to get cigarettes. You woke up in a strange place and you're naked as the day you were born. *Just what the hell happened to you?*

And why the fuck won't your legs move?

You weren't drinking, so no one could have slipped you a mickey. You feel like shit, but at least you don't feel like you've been raped.

And why the goddamn hell won't your fucking legs move?

Her arms moved. Barely. Every movement brought a new pain. She clenched and unclenched her fists. Good. The fingers worked okay. She wiggled her toes and saw corresponding movement near the foot of the bed.

A sharp pain shot through her shoulders and neck as she inched her hands down to feel her legs. She dug her fingernails into flesh of her inner thighs and felt appropriate pain between her groin and knees.

She picked up one leg with her hand and moved it slightly to the left. She picked up the other leg and did the same. She continued until she'd scootched both legs to the edge of the bed. She forced her torso erect, gradually lifting her hips until both feet touched the floor. Each movement brought new pains, some excruciating. Still, she persisted. She shoved down on the mattress with both hands while lifting her hips. For a moment she stood erect, full weight on both feet.

But the muscles in her legs refused to support her, and she saw the room suddenly spin as if the rug had been pulled out from beneath her and she tumbled toward the wooden floor. . .

. . .And felt her face flatten against the planks . . .

. . .And the lights went out again.

*   *   *

Tom heard the thump above his head and instantly bolted from his chair. He took the stairs three at a time and was in Ellen's room within a handful of heartbeats.

The girl lay face down on the floor next to the bed. She'd obviously tried to walk and couldn't. He picked her up and placed her gently back on the bed, covered her again with the quilt.

Although fires in both the fireplace and kitchen stove kept the main floor toasty, the house had no modern furnace with ventilation ducts to warm the second floor. Rising heat made the floor feel comfortable, but the air itself wore a distinct chill that demanded covers.

Diane, Bob, Violet, and Nancy came into the room.

"I think she tried to get out of bed too soon," he explained. "She fell and hit her head."

Nancy checked the girl's vital signs and lifted first one eyelid, then the other. "She'll recover. One of us should stay with her, though, in case she wakes up again and tries to move too soon. We can each take two-hour shifts. I'll take the first."

"I'll take the next shift," offered Diane. "Tom, will you relieve me after a couple of hours?"

"Of course," he said. "Bob, would you like in on the rotation?"

"Yeah. I feel kind of responsible for what happened to her. If I hadn't been playing tag with the men in the Explorer, she'd be warm and safe wherever she was heading before the crash. So, yes, I'll take my turn."

"Okay," said Diane, "now that that's settled, we can leave Nancy here to take care of her while we return to the kitchen table and continue our talk. You said someone cleaned up after the accident. You think whoever did it was trained by the government?"

"Yes," said Bob. He and Tom followed Diane from the room and down the stairs. "Maybe not our government, but they use the same methods the CIA uses. So if it isn't someone in the agency, it's someone using agency assets. If it wasn't someone in our government that ordered your mother killed and tried to kill me, it was likely someone trained by our government or an allied government."

Aunt Cynthia, Aunt Violet, and Great-Aunt Anna agreed it would be wise to have someone remain with the girl continuously until she could get around on her own. They each volunteered to do their part. Aunt Cynthia said she would move her featherbed to Ellen's room and sleep on the floor next to the girl's bed overnight.

"She's healing faster than we expected," said Aunt Violet. "Whoever she is, she's a strong woman."

"There's a reason why she's here," Aunt Anna said with certainty. "All of us are here for a reason, you know. There are great forces at work redirecting energies, and she came to this place at this time to be a help to us. In all the years I've been observing nature at work, I've seen people appear when and where they were needed most. There's an old adage that says, 'when the student is ready, the teacher shall appear.' I believe that to be true. "

"It's certainly true," agreed Diane. "But the reason why it's true depends on an individual's powers of perception. Perhaps the teachers were there all along, but the students simply didn't see them until there was a need. Another adage says, 'necessity is the mother of invention.' Humans are great at inventing things to fill their needs. Sometimes we invent explanations to fulfill a psychological need, but the invented explanation bears no relationship to objective truth. We humans are severely limited in our ability to be objective. We should bear that in mind and explore all possibilities."

"Being aware of our limitations is a good thing," said Aunt Anna. "Though we have great power, we cannot know nor do everything. We are neither omniscient nor omnipotent. Over the centuries, however, we have learned much about the way the world works. But there are still some things we do not know, and some things we cannot know."

"What about the other watchtowers?" asked Aunt Vi. "Have you been able to reach any of the other guardians?"

"No," said Anna.

"The rift interferes with our usual means of communication," explained Diane, mostly for Bob's benefit. "Our spirit guides are trapped on the other side, and there's no way for mortals to bridge the gap. Even the mind stuff—the chitta, or whispers of the wind over the waters—has been silenced, and Nancy's dreams are empty and void."

"Have you tried telephoning?" asked Bob.

Diane smiled. "None of the guardians could answer a telephone near any of the watchtowers. Telephones and electricity don't work close to a power vortex because the energy of the vortex affects polarity. Electronic devices need polarity to function. Radio signals are disrupted. There's no way to contact the guardians by telephone or radio."

"Have you considered the possibility," Bob asked, "that the other guardians have been killed like your mother?"

"Impossible," said Aunt Violet. "How could anyone even know about . . . ? Oh, no," she cried, recognizing the possibility for the first time. "No, no, no, no!"

"We didn't even think of it, but of course you're right," said Diane. "Maybe we didn't want to think an adept who could be knowledgeable enough and powerful enough to locate and kill another adept would actually do such a thing. Only a handful of adepts know the exact locations of the watchtowers or the identities of the guardians. If Ma were here, she could name them. We know the general directions of the watchtowers, but none of us knows exactly where they might be physically located."

"Only those who reach the level of an ascended master have such knowledge," Aunt Anna explained. "None of us have achieved that distinction, although several of the women at this table are very close. It takes dedication, sacrifice, and something that borders obsession to master the spiritual challenges of an ascended master. And it takes many lifetimes."

"One must experience and remember a continuous cycle of births and re-births," added Diane, "to achieve the mastery required of a true adept. Do you believe in reincarnation, Bob?"

"No. But I have an open mind. I'm willing to consider all possibilities."

"My mother learned to remember many of her past lives. She once told me she recalled being a man at least twice in recent centuries, and probably a dozen times in the past millennium. But most of her energy was feminine, and the majority of the reincarnations she remembered were female. Because her energy was so strong, she was a natural to assume guardianship of the trees. She felt drawn to this place, to the trees, to the job. In this lifetime, she was born to be a guardian. It was as if she knew that was what she was meant to do with her life, and so she did it."

"Do you remember past lives?"

"Yes. Not as many as my mother. I'm still learning who I am."

"And were you born to become a guardian like your mother?"

"Not in this lifetime. The only person I know who has achieved the cycles of rebirths required to become an ascended master in her current lifetime is Sara Nelson."

"But she's still only a kid! How can she be an ascended master?"

"Her spirit is very old and very wise," said Aunt Anna. "Sara was re-born in this place at this time to be the next guardian of the west watchtower. Four years ago, Ellen began teaching her ways to remember what she had learned in previous lifetimes. It is most unfortunate that Ellen was killed before Sara reached menarche— puberty—when the mind and body achieve the level of maturity necessary. With Ellen to guide her, Sara would have ascended to Grand Master as soon as she reached puberty. Now her future is in doubt, as is the future of all of us."

"Unless we can find who is responsible for this madness and rectify the damage," said Diane. "Are you willing to help us, Bob?"

"If I can, without compromising my mission."

"This *is* your mission, Bob. I see no conflict between your military and your spiritual mission. You were sent to us for a purpose."

"You and Tom are used to working in the world," said Aunt Anna, "and the rest of us are limited in things mundane, especially the machinations of men. Each of us has our niche, our role to play. If you and Tom will gather information in the material world, the rest of us will continue to gather what we can from the spiritual world. We will work on separate planes to discover who is responsible for Ellen's murder and to restore harmony and balance. Your masculine energy is vitally important, and we're grateful the universe sent you to us."

"I'm personally very glad you're here," said Diane, reaching out to gently brush the back of Bob's hand with her fingers. "I'm sorry I acted rude to you last night. My mind was preoccupied with Ma's remembering, and I wasn't able to recognize you."

"I'm curious," said Bob, enjoying the touch of her hand. "What made you change your mind about me?"

"I remember you now. I know who you are and I also know who you have been. I know why you are here in this time and place."

"How could you know me?" Her hand felt wonderfully warm and soft and she didn't try to pull away when his fingers intertwined with hers. "I'm certain we never met before yesterday."

"We've met many times before. I didn't remember you at first. But I do now."

"Remember me? How could you possibly remember me?"

"How could I not? We've often been lovers in past lives. We don't look the same now as we did the last time we met, but appearances can be deceiving. You haven't forgotten. You just haven't remembered yet. But you will. The memories will come back."

"I don't understand." His head was swimming with the intoxication of her nearness, the feel of her hand in his, the intensity of her gaze, the familiar smell of her, the rise and fall of her breasts with each intake and exhale of breath.

"You will," said Diane, squeezing his hand. "Maybe this will help." She leaned forward until her lips met his. The kiss felt good and right and sent electrical currents racing up and down his spine. Her tongue entered his mouth, his tongue danced with hers, and his hand found her breast. He didn't care who might be watching, and he felt her nipple harden at his touch and he he felt himself harden, too.

"You're soul mates," pronounced Aunt Anna, "both drawn to each other through time and space. Not even death can keep you apart. When you touch, magic happens."

Bob looked at the Most Beautiful Woman in the World and she looked back at him, and he knew in his heart it was true.

CHAPTER SEVENTEEN

Philip Ashur drank wine from a human skull as if taking holy communion.

Do this in remembrance of the dead.

Predating the Eucharist by more than 35,000 years, the skull chalice had originally contained sacrificial blood.

This particular trophy held unique meaning for Philip Ashur. The brains once nestled inside were among the first he had eaten. He'd been nourished by sweetmeats in ways ordinary mortals couldn't imagine.

Eating the brains or hearts of those whose knowledge, intelligence, or courage you wished to emulate was an ancient tradition, and Ashur wasn't alone in its practice. Men had once consumed the flesh of bears to gain ferocity, flesh of bulls to grow strong. Didn't it make sense to eat the brains of humans to become smarter and wiser?

Especially the brains of an ascended master?

Other traditions advocated drinking blood to increase vitality, but in this day and age of AIDS, wine was a surer source of vitality.

He raised the skull in mock toast. "This I do in remembrance of you," he said. The skull had once belonged to a man named Kuan Yin-hsi, one of the eight original ascended masters who had pursued immortality. "And where are you now, Master Kuan?" asked Ashur. "Inside me, that's where! You live on only because I live. Without me, you are nothing!"

By ingesting the flesh, he'd also ingested the spirit, capturing its essence forever and making it an integral part of his own DNA. It wasn't until he had eaten his thirteenth victim that he knew he'd made a major mistake.

It had taken several lifetimes to overcome the contamination of spiritual residue, and even today he felt the strong pull of alien spirits directing his body and mind in ways he didn't wish. He sometimes felt as if he were being torn apart by conflicting thoughts and emotions, and he often heard voices in his head. Now that he knew the cause, of course, he could take action to silence those voices. The Great Work must go on without interference.

Communion over, he placed the skull back in the bottom drawer of his desk and returned to the computer. With a few deft keystrokes he sent orders that set in motion the final steps of his master plan. Within hours the last of the guardians would be dead, their spirits in his possession forever, and the Great Work would progress unimpeded.

And then he would transform himself into a god that would live until the end of time. It was easy when you knew how.

And Philip Ashur knew how.

*   *   *

La Curandera lived, and would soon die, in *el fin del mundo*, literally the end of the earth.

She had always thought this place was the closest to heaven she could get on earth, and the closest she ever wanted to get to hell.

The Patagonian Andes were a strange marriage of fire and ice, with hundreds of active volcanoes and dozens of moving glacial ice sheets. It was a place where the wind was never silent.

La Curandera was descended from a long line of Mapuche Indian healers and shamans. She had been a curandera in all past lives she remembered, and she would be a curandera or bruha in future incarnations.

If there were future incarnations.

For four nights and three days now there had been whispers on the wind: whispers of death and dying, of doom and destruction. She had heard it in the condor's call, in the fierce wind whistling through towering mountain peaks of the *Torres del Paine*, in the frigid temperatures that remained well into mid-November when the southern hemisphere's lengthening daylight should already have transformed the countryside.

Evil was coming, and the healer had prepared for its arrival as best she could.

Like most of the other guardians, La Curandera believed evil did indeed exist, and sometimes it took physical form. In a universe of polar opposites, how could there be good without evil? All of life—all of existence—was a divine dance that required partners.

La Curandera was not afraid to use her powers—both light and dark—to achieve balance. She had made the journey many times into darkness, and she knew well the darkness that lived in her own soul.

But, always, she returned to the light.

She called her familiars and gave them their instructions: the condor would watch from above, the serpents from below. They would report any intrusion onto the sacred mountain. Four pumas were also sent to patrol the mountain paths. They were told to kill anyone who approached the sacred circle.

When she had done all she could do, she went into the sacred circle and removed her clothing.

She was still sitting there, naked, when the twelve men came to kill her.

*   *   *

Jerry jumped.

There were six parachutists in each of two rented Cessna Citation Excel corporate jets, flying at 41,000 feet and 465 miles per hour, and one of the men sitting next to him had quipped that they were crazy to jump out of a perfectly good airplane flying that high and that fast.

But each of them jumped on their marks, free-falling into clouds that covered the snow-bound Andean peaks, counting down until it was time to release their chutes.

"One hundred and twenty," Jerry announced into the wind and threw out his pilot chute. As the wind caught the pilot, the bridle pulled taut, the pin holding the main chute dislodged, and the deployment bag released a fabric canopy from the back pack one stow at a time until the ram-air canopy was fully inflated. He knew the parachute had fully deployed when his torso was yanked upwards and his descent suddenly slowed. He pulled on one control line and then the other until he positioned himself over where he thought the jump zone should be.

Jerry was glad to finally be out of airplanes. He had flown from Hayward, Wisconsin, to Greater Rockford Airport in northern Illinois where he joined Scagliano and the rest of the team and picked up his gear. Colonel Jack spent fifteen minutes briefing them on the mission, and then they were airborne again, stopping four times for refueling before reaching their objective.

Jerry was getting tired of killing little old ladies. When was the Colonel going to give him a real target, something worthy of his specialized skills? Diane Groves, perhaps. Or her younger sister. He would love to do either or both of them.

As he dropped below the clouds, he was struck by the breathtaking beauty of the Andean continental divide. It was unlike anything he had seen before. Smoke rose from two active volcanoes whose crater-centers were bubbling masses of bright yellow and reddish-orange molten lava. To the east and north, tree-shrouded valleys surrounded bright-blue crystal-clear lakes fed by melting mountain glaciers, and to the south lay steaming geysers sending intermittent spumes of water high into the air.

"What the hell is this place, anyway?" he asked aloud. The landscape looked as alien as the moon.

Jerry spotted two of his team off to the left. He tugged on a control line to correct his descent, angling the air-foil canopy to swing left. Suddenly, icy wind gusts caught the canopy and blew him off course. He fought desperately to regain control, but to no avail. The winds were much too strong. He watched in horror as a gust blew one of his teammates into a craggy out-cropping of naked granite. The man's body bounced off solid rock and went slack in the harness. Directionless, his ram-air canopy bobbed around in the wind until another fierce gust carried the limp body miles off course. Finally, the chute disappeared from sight.

He pulled down hard on both control lines. As camber increased and the air-foil canopy flared, Jerry's body swung forward. Changing the angle of attack deflected the wind, decreased forward speed, and allowed the chute to descend straight down. Maintaining trim, he came down within twenty meters of the drop zone.

Five minutes later, he was on the ground and unbuckling his harness. He waited for the last of the team to land, then hauled the deflated chute, backpack, and harness over to where the others had piled their equipment. Scagliano, wearing a camouflage-patterned baseball cap instead of his usual broad-brimmed black hat, began issuing orders.

They broke up into four teams. Each team had three men. Jerry was assigned to a two-man team. The dead man would have been part of his team.

After the mission was accomplished, he'd be assigned to find the missing man's body and clean up loose ends.

Scagliano distributed maps that had been digitally constructed from photo composites. The photos had been taken by aerial reconnaissance flights over the area, based on coordinates the Colonel had supplied, and the digital images were overlaid with grid coordinates. Significant landmarks had been identified and labeled. In the middle of the map was a blurred area that didn't photograph. That's where, Scagliano told them, they'd find the target.

The drop zone was less than two kilometers from the target herself. They were near the base of the mountain. Now all they had to do was get to the top.

Tall pines had rooted in the volcanic soil. Surrounding mountain peaks appeared ice-capped and barren at this altitude, but the mountain where the old lady lived was still an active volcano that generated enough heat and steam to hold glaciers at bay.

The ascent was treacherous and steep, but not difficult for men in good physical condition. Previous eruptions of the volcano had deposited two inches of ash over beds of hardened lava and cinders, and each step the men took sent small clouds of grayish ash into the air.

Now they were above the treeline, and the landscape literally looked as barren as the surface of the moon. Any trees that had once stood here lay buried under rock and ash.

"First landmark," announced Scagliano, pointing to a huge rock structure that materialized from the clouds and steam.

A giant stone face and torso, carved from the lava bed, stood like a sentinel at the foot of the cone surrounding the crater. It faced away from the mountain as if looking at something or for something.

"I seen pictures of that face before," said Jerry's teammate. "Only it wasn't pictures of here. It was Easter Island."

"Ain't that supposed to be near Tahiti, or someplace like that?" asked Jerry.

"Yeah," his teammate agreed. "In the middle of the Pacific Ocean. So how the hell did that thing get here on a mountain top in South America? I swear, it looks exactly like those stone faces on Easter Island."

"There's more than just that one," said a man from another team. "I seen the map the old man's got." Scagliano, the mission leader, was called "the old man" out of respect. "There are four faces on this side of the mountain and four on the other. They must mean somethin' to somebody."

"You ain't scared, are ya?" asked Jerry. "Worried they'll put the hoodoo on you like in those mummy movies?"

"No. I ain't scared. But I like to know what I'm getting' into, so I can plan a way out if things go sour."

"Don't worry about it," said Jerry. "The Colonel's got it all planned for us. We go in, we take care of business, and we get out. We call for the choppers and all of us go home."

"I know what the battle plan says. What I can't understand is why they had to send twelve of us to take care of one old lady."

"Forget about it. Just do your job."

"Knock it off back there," ordered Scagliano. "We don't know how far sound carries up here."

"So what's an old lady gonna do if she hears us?" whispered Jerry's teammate. "Run? Where could she go up here that we wouldn't find her?"

Suddenly, two of the men in a forward team fell to the ground, wrestling with snarling black shapes that seemed to materialize out of nowhere. The third member of the forward team got off a short burst of automatic rife fire before he, too, fell victim.

"Black tigers," someone shouted as the other teams opened fire. Two of the shapes seemed to explode in sprays of blood and guts. The third animal leapt away and somehow disappeared before anyone could nail it.

Another man fell to the ground as a fourth black shape appeared. This time, Jerry was ready. He emptied a full magazine into the big cat. Jerry's teammate picked off yet another puma while Jerry was reloading.

They were down to seven men now, having lost four to the cats and one to the wind. Scagliano reassigned them, three men to each of two teams, with himself as odd man out. They reloaded, salvaged what they could from their fallen comrades, and quickly moved on. There was no doubt the old woman knew they were coming. The time for stealth was gone.

Overhead, huge vulture-like birds circled as if waiting to scavenge carrion as soon as those still living moved on. Jerry wondered whether the birds would choose to feast first on the fallen men or the cats. Not that it mattered. They were both dead. Maybe the birds would make his job easier when he returned later to clean up the mess.

They were nearly to the summit, and Jerry could just barely make out a human form through sulfurous vapors rising from the crater's mouth. It looked like a woman, the target, and she was sitting incredibly still, as if oblivious to the seven armed men and the previous sounds of gunfire. Surely, she must be aware that death was coming for her. Why didn't she get up and run? Why did she appear so damn calm?

Suddenly, from fissures in the volcanic rock, hundreds of tiny slithering things emerged, covering his boots, crawling up his legs, heading for his groin.

"Snakes!" yelled one teammate, firing off a burst at the ground. The bullets ricocheted off the basalt and filled the air like flies.

"They're not poisonous!" shouted Scagliano. "There are no poisonous snakes in Chile. Brush them off and keep going!"

All around him now men were writhing in a weird St. Vitus dance, swatting at their legs, twisting and squirming, leaping and running. One man tripped and fell. Within seconds, swarms of writhing, crawling things filled the man's nostrils and gaping mouth and stifled his screams.

Scagliano ended the guy's anguish with one carefully placed round.

"Move, goddamit!" Scagliano ordered. "Outrun the damn things!"

Jerry brushed at his pants as he ran. All but one of the snakes fell off. Finally, he stopped running, plucked the last snake from his pants leg, and ground its head beneath his boot heel. The crunching sound was eminently satisfying.

Now there were only six men left to complete the mission. Half had been lost getting this far. Overhead, giant birds circled, waiting to feed on death. Today, they would feast well.

Three condors made wide loops around the top of the mountain, looking more like airplanes than birds. There was something distinctly purposeful about their flight that made Jerry uncomfortable.

When they attacked, they soared like Japanese dive bombers on WWII suicide missions. With a ten-foot wingspan and red eyes that glowed like burning embers, the flesh-eating birds of prey swooped down at more than 40 miles an hour, talons outstretched.

Three of Jerry's comrades fell before anyone could react. With incredible accuracy, talons and beaks connected with face and eyes, tearing, ripping, gorging.

Jerry swung his rifle into position and picked off one of the birds before it flew away. Scagliano and the remaining team member took out the other two.

Condors circling overhead scattered to the four winds. Jerry waited, his eyes and rifle trained on the sky. They'd soon be back. Death drew them like bears to honey.

Scagliano took out a knife and briefly knelt next to each of his fallen men. Whatever pain they may have felt was mercifully gone now. He wiped the blade clean on the sleeve of one of the deceased. Then he stood and motioned Jerry and the other man forward.

If the woman had moved, Jerry hadn't noticed. She still sat in the same spot he'd first seen her. She looked incredibly tall for a woman. Maybe not as tall as Delacroix, but taller than any of the three men who approached her. Even sitting cross-legged, the top of her head was level with Scagliano's shoulders.

And she didn't look old anymore. Mid-thirties, maybe. Trim, well-muscled. Beautiful.

She was as naked as a Playboy centerfold.

Jerry felt a stirring in his groin. Taking this woman apart would be pure pleasure.

She looked straight at them, unblinking. Scagliano raised his rifle and aimed at the center of her chest. A tiny red dot appeared between her breasts. The sound of the rifle echoed from the surrounding mountaintops.

The impact of the 5.56-millimeter bullet striking flesh and bone should have knocked her over like a bowling pin, but didn't. She remained sitting as she had before, spine erect, head held high.

Scagliano fired two more rounds, one into each nipple as if they were bulls-eyes. Two more red dots appeared, but she still sat as before, tall, defiant, a smile crossing her lips.

"Die, damn you!" shouted Scagliano, emptying his magazine into her torso.

But she didn't die.

"Take her out. Shoot the witch!"

Jerry and his teammate both emptied their weapons. Her body became peppered with red blotches like a child with chicken pox.

The first red dots in the center of her chest disappeared. Before Jerry had ejected the empty magazine, inserted a full new 30-round mag, and slammed the charging handle forward to chamber a round, all remaining spots faded as if her flesh healed without leaving a single scar.

Earth beneath Jerry's feet buckled and heaved, and vile noxious gasses spewed from the crater to sear his eyes as if both eyeballs had been coated with sulfuric acid. He couldn't breathe. His lungs felt like they would surely explode. He lost his balance and fell to the ground as the earth opened up around him, cracks large enough to swallow a man running everywhere as gas and steam and smoke filled the air and a rain of fiery cinders pelted his back and threatened to set his fire-retardant jumpsuit aflame.

He knew he had to get out of there, but how? If he turned tail and ran, Scagliano would cut him down in his tracks.

The fissures in the earth grew larger—huge rifts too big to step across in some places—and the smoke became so thick that he lost sight of Scagliano and the other man entirely. All he could see now was the figure of the woman—tall, majestic—no longer sitting but standing with her legs apart and her arms uplifted, her long black hair shimmering with an eerie glow.

And then the volcano erupted.

And the mountain blew apart.

And the chunk of rock Jerry was on flew off into space carrying the mortal remains of Jerry Walker with it.

CHAPTER EIGHTEEN

Sheila opened her eyes and beheld the face of an angel.

The woman was incredibly beautiful, possessing not just physical beauty, which she certainly had in abundance, but a strange kind of beauty which Sheila tried to identify but couldn't.

There was something hauntingly familiar about that face that stirred long-forgotten memories. Sheila had seen that inner beauty before. There was something familiar about the physical features of that face, too, that Sheila knew she should recognize.

"I'm Diane Groves," the angel said, holding a glass of water to Sheila's lips and letting her drink. "Do you remember who you are?"

"Where am I? How did I get here?"

"This is my mother's house in northern Wisconsin. You were injured in a highway accident during a snowstorm. Do you remember that?"

Sheila tried to think. She was Burt Ryan's little girl, the poor little nobody from the south side of Chicago. But how did she get to Wisconsin? And how did she get to be all grown up?

"I'm Sheila," she said. "You asked my name. My name is Sheila Ryan."

"Where are you from, Sheila?"

"Chicago." That much she did remember.

"What are you doing up here in the north woods?"

"I don't know. I can't remember. There's a lot I can't remember."

"That's okay. It'll come back to you."

"I was in an accident? Was anybody hurt?"

"You were. I don't think anybody else was with you. The other car and driver can't be found. My brother and his friend are talking with the sheriff today. They want the sheriff to search for that other car."

"Oh."

"Are you okay? How do you feel?"

"I've got to pee."

"Don't get out of bed. I'll bring you a pan."

"I can get up."

"You can sit up, but you don't need to get out of bed. We all pee in a pan here in the winter. We don't have indoor plumbing, and it's much too cold to go to the outhouse. So we keep a small pan next to the bed. Here," she plucked a ceramic bowl from the floor and handed it to Sheila. "I'll leave you alone to conduct business. When you're done, I'll take the pan outside and empty it."

Diane returned in a few minutes with a sweatshirt and jeans in her hands. "These were my mother's. They should fit you. After you get dressed, we'll look for some shoes. We washed your underwear, but your bra and panties are still drying in front of the fire."

"Thank you," Sheila said.

"You're most welcome."

*   *   *

Bob and Tom visited the sheriff's office at the county seat and talked about Ellen's murder and then about the accident on route 13.

The sheriff agreed to send investigators to look for debris from the accident, but this was the first anyone had reported it and none of the county crews had mentioned anything about debris on or near the highway.

Ellen's disappearance was still classified as suspicious and not as a homicide. The sheriff had no corpse and no forensic evidence that proved she was indeed dead, and only the uncorroborated eyewitness testimony of an eleven year old girl indicated otherwise. A girl that age, said the sheriff, was prone to fantasy, and this particular girl was known to have experienced "visions." That made Sara's version of Ellen's disappearance suspicious. For all the sheriff knew, Ellen Groves could be alive and well and vacationing in Florida. Lots of folks went south this time of year. Officially, she was a "missing person, whereabouts unknown." No real evidence existed that she had been murdered.

With deer season about to open, the county had filled with non-residents, most of them from downstate or from surrounding states like Illinois, Indiana, Iowa, and Minnesota. It was impossible to question all the strangers in town, much less all the strangers county-wide.

The Ellen Groves case would have to stay on the back burner for weeks, maybe longer. If she didn't turn up by Christmas, the case would become the sheriff's number one priority. But right now he had neither the time nor the staff to follow up on Ellen's disappearance.

Bob asked the sheriff for permission to hook up his laptop to the department internet, and the sheriff let him use an interrogation room to provide privacy. Bob logged on, checked his e-mail, browsed through the daily intelligence briefs he'd missed, and sent the following report to the Deputy Director of Defense Intelligence Services:

CONFIDENTIAL

In accordance with the special instructions contained in DA Special Orders dated 17 November, I have determined that an organized surveillance of Major Thomas Groves and his family has been put in place by parties unknown. Surveillance techniques have been employed that are consistent with current established G2 procedures. Unless another branch or agency of the US has been assigned dual oversight, international involvement should be considered. Follow up reports will be sent daily no later than 1500 hours Zulu. If reports are delayed more than 24 hours, assume this mission has been compromised.

ROBERT S. MCMICHAELS
LTC, IN, US

He sent the following e-mail to a friend at Fort Hood, Texas:

Larry,

I need you to cover my back. I'm TDY for DIA and there may be other operations in play. Can you monitor all traffic with reference to Groves, Thomas A., or any other reference to the name Groves in or out of Wisconsin? Also, please inform of any large scale unsanctioned operations in Midwest continental US, irrespective of component.

Bob

After leaving the sheriff's office, they visited the Nelson farm and talked with Sara. He found her to be an unusually bright eleven year old, keenly observant, but normal in every other way. If Sara Nelson was an ascended master, she surely didn't show it.

But, then, Bob didn't know what an ascended master was supposed to look like. An old man with a long grey beard? A Hindu swami with a turban? A Christ figure wearing a white robe and sandals? How the hell could a little girl be an ascended master?

Sara reiterated what she'd told the sheriff. There were six vehicles, two men to each. Some were in pick-up trucks, and some rode jeep-like SUVs. One of them was real tall and skinny. He was the boss because the other men did what he told them. The front vehicle, a black pick-up, hit Ellen while she was crossing the road. Ellen knew they were coming, and she had ordered Sara to run and hide. Sara could run faster, and she made it across the road and into the woods before the men in the trucks saw her.

Bob asked how Ellen had known the men were coming to kill her. "Because," Sara told him, "she had second sight. She knew things before they happened, but her visions came only when she was meditating. Reason blocked her from seeing. It often gets in the way, you know. That's why men don't have second sight. They're too logical."

"Do you have second sight?"

"Sometimes. Little kids—boys, too—all do. Only most of us lose it when we're six or seven. Some grown-ups get it back, especially girls when they reach adolescence. My mom says it's because of hormones."

"I see," said Bob. "But you're not quite an adolescent yet, and you've got second sight?"

"I had to work really hard to get it back. Ellen showed me how. It doesn't work all the time. Just sometimes."

"But your second sight will get better once you're an adolescent?"

"Yes. I know it will."

"How do you think those men knew Ellen had left her house?"

"She said they'd been watching her for weeks. They couldn't touch her if she remained at home, but the moment she crossed the road she became fair game. I think they had cameras and drones. They knew she crossed O to visit me. They waited for her to head back towards the woods. Then they ran over her."

He asked if it would be all right to come back later and ask more questions, and she agreed to talk with him again. As he and Tom were about to leave the Nelson farm, Sara began crying. She said she knew the men who had killed Ellen would come after her and try to kill her, too. Those men didn't know what she knew, but when they found out they would come to kill her.

"We won't let them, honey," Bob said.

"Promise?"

"We promise."

She smiled then, and he saw something in her smile that told him she expected him to keep that promise. He swore to himself that he would.

Sara's smile was the same kind of trusting smile his own eleven year old daughter had given him when he had promised he would still love her and protect her even after her mother and he were divorced. "I'll be there when you need me," he'd promised his daughter. "I'll always be there for you."

If he hadn't been able to keep his promise to his own daughter, he wondered, how did he expect to keep a promise to this girl he barely knew?

*   *   *

This is nice, thought Burt Ryan's little girl as she sat in front of the fire and spooned soup from a bowl into her hungry mouth. *Peaceful and nice.*

Sheila couldn't remember the last time she'd felt so contented. The fact that there was a lot she couldn't remember didn't seem to bother her.

I am exactly where I'm supposed to be, she thought. *Nothing else matters.*

When Diane had introduced her to Nancy, Anna, and Violet, that same feeling of familiarity Sheila felt when she first saw Diane's face returned to her again, stronger than ever. It was as if she'd been looking for these people all her life, and now she'd found them!

The other women—Aunt Anna, especially—treated her like a long lost relative. When the old woman hugged her, Sheila felt indescribable warmth.

"Welcome," Anna told her. "We really mean that. You are welcome here."

Sheila felt like the prodigal daughter returned home.

Don't be silly, another part of her mind said. *You've never been here before. You've never met these people before. You don't really belong here.*

But everything felt so right, so good. She didn't want the feeling to ever end.

"Tom and Bob are back from town," Nancy announced. Two car doors slammed near the house. She heard the front door open and close. A moment later, Diane led two men into the room and introduced them to Sheila.

It was immediately obvious that something special was going on between Bob and Diane. They kept sneaking little glances at each other whenever they thought no one was looking.

When Sheila was introduced to Tom, he took her tiny hand in his massive maw with unexpected gentleness for a man.

I know you, she thought. *Where do I know you from?*

When he finally released her hand, she still felt a connection. *It's as if we're still holding hands*, she thought. *What in the world is happening to me?*

Her head was spinning. Or was it the world that was spinning? Did it matter which?

"You look like you need to lie down again," said Aunt Violet. "Are you feeling all right?"

"I'll be fine. I'm just a little light headed."

"You're still healing, dear. You've had a traumatic experience that will take time to overcome. Take deep breaths. Let the healing energies of the universe guide you to wholeness and wellness."

Sheila took a deep breath. The pain she'd felt earlier in her lungs was gone, and it didn't hurt at all to expand her ribs.

"I am feeling better," she said after several deep breaths.

"Bob was the one who found you and brought you here last night," said Diane. "You would've died if he hadn't acted quickly. We're all grateful to him for doing the right thing."

"Thank you, Bob," Sheila said. "And thank you all for taking me in and making me feel like part of the family."

"What about your real family?" asked Tom. "Won't they be worried about you? Is there someone we should notify? Husband? Fiancé? Friends?"

"I don't think so. I've tried to remember, but I can't recall very much. I know that my mother died shortly after I was born, and my father died when I was in college. I know my brothers are both married, and I don't have much to do with them anymore. I think if I were married, I'd remember. But I don't."

"Where were you going when you got stranded by the snowstorm?" Bob asked.

"I'm sorry. I don't remember that, either. An hour ago, I didn't remember graduating from high school. Now I remember graduating and going on to college. So my memory is returning, but it's coming back slowly."

"You think you live in Chicago? Do you know the address?"

"I remember growing up in Chicago and going to the University of Illinois and then to DePaul law school. I do think I still live in Chicago, but I don't know where."

"Do you remember when you were born?"

Sheila told him her birth date. Bob took a pen and small notebook out of his pocket and made a few notes. "I'll ask the sheriff to run a license check on your name and DOB. He should be able to obtain your address from driver's license records. This afternoon we filed an initial report with the sheriff about your accident. So far, however, there's no news about your car or the vehicle that hit you. It seems both disappeared into thin air."

"How can that be?"

"We think someone cleaned up the evidence during the night. We checked with road crews that plowed this morning, and they claimed they saw no evidence of an accident. Last night I saw debris scattered everywhere. This morning, it's all gone."

"I don't understand."

"Neither do we," said Tom. "That's why we need your help. As of right now, Bob and you are the only known witnesses to what happened last night. He's new to the area, and he thinks he remembers the exact location where the accident happened. But it would be really helpful if you could remember where you were going and where you had stopped. Maybe, if the two of you could put your heads together, we'd have a better idea of where to search for wreckage. If we still don't find anything, we'll know someone deliberately cleaned up the accident site without reporting it. Then, maybe, we'll convince the sheriff the same people who killed my mother were involved in your accident."

"Your mother was killed? What happened?"

"Someone ran her down on the county road right outside this property. They did it deliberately. Then they set her body on fire and cleaned up the mess as if nothing happened."

"How terrible!"

"We think," said Bob, "that the same people who killed Ellen Groves were also involved in cleaning up your accident. But the sheriff has nothing to follow up with at this point."

"I wish I could help. But I don't remember anything about the accident or where I was going."

"You will, dear," said Aunt Anna. "Give it time. Sooner or later your memory will return better than ever."

"You really think so?"

"I know so," said Aunt Anna, smiling. "Just you wait and see."

BOOK III

"There was a man of the Pharisees, named Nicodemus, a ruler of the Jews: The same came to Jesus by night, and said unto him, Rabbi, we know that thou art a teacher come from God: for no man can do these miracles that thou doest, except God be with him. Jesus answered and said unto him, Verily, verily, I say unto thee, Except a man be born again, he cannot see the kingdom of God. Nicodemus saith unto him, How can a man be born when he is old? Can he enter the second time into his mother's womb and be born? Jesus answered, Verily, verily I say unto thee, Except a man be born of water and of the Spirit, he cannot enter into the kingdom of God. That which is born of the flesh is flesh; and that which is born of the spirit is spirit, Marvel not that I said unto thee, Ye must be born again, The wind bloweth where it listeth, and thou hearest the sound thereof, but canst not tell whence it cometh, and whether it goeth: so is every one that is born of the Spirit."

--*Holy Bible, Gospel of St. John: 3, 1-8.* King James Version.

The Moving Finger writes; and, having writ,
Moves on: nor all thy Piety nor Wit,
Shall lure it back to cancel half a Line,
Nor all thy Tears wash out a Word of it.
But helpless pieces in the game He plays,
Upon this chequer-board of Nights and Days,
He hither and thither moves, and checks... and slays,
Then one by one, back in the Closet lays.
And, as the Cock crew, those who stood before
The Tavern shouted— "Open then the Door!
You know how little time we have to stay,
And once departed, may return no more."
A Book of Verses underneath the Bough,
A Jug of Wine, a Loaf of Bread—and Thou,
Beside me singing in the Wilderness,
And oh, Wilderness is Paradise enow.
If chance supplied a loaf of white bread,
Two casks of wine and a leg of mutton,
In the corner of a garden with a tulip-cheeked girl,
There'd be enjoyment no Sultan could outdo.
Myself when young did eagerly frequent
Doctor and Saint, and heard great Argument
About it and about: but evermore
Came out of the same Door as in I went.
With them the Seed of Wisdom did I sow,
And with my own hand labour'd it to grow:
And this was all the Harvest that I reap'd—
"I came like Water, and like Wind I go."
Into this Universe, and why not knowing,
Nor whence, like Water willy-nilly flowing:
And out of it, as Wind along the Waste,
I know not whither, willy-nilly blowing.
And that inverted Bowl we call The Sky,
Whereunder crawling coop't we live and die,
Lift not thy hands to It for help—for It
Rolls impotently on as Thou or I.

--*Ghiyāth ad-Dīn Abu'l-Fath ʿUmar ibn Ibrāhīm al-Khayyām
Nīshāpūrī. Rubaiyat of Omar Khayyam, translated by Edward Fitz-
gerald*

CHAPTER NINETEEN

Jack Delacroix analyzed Landsat satellite photos of the Patagonian Andes that contained before and after shots. Now you see the top of the mountain. Now you don't. Where, oh where, did the top of the mountain go? Twelve good operatives gone, and a mess made of the mission. Delacroix was angry.

But he was afraid when he reported this failure to Ashur, Philip would be much, much angrier. He'd only seen Ashur angry once before, and it wasn't a pretty sight. Heads had literally rolled.

When a man had as much power and money as Ashur, failure was never an option. Temporary disappointments, yes. But failure was totally unacceptable.

So Delacroix had to find a way to turn this failure into a temporary disappointment. And the only way he thought to do that would be to locate the head of the woman, regardless of its current condition, and present the remains to Ashur.

Ten teams had been dispatched to the region immediately following the explosion. The evacuation team with two UH-1A helicopters were already in place on the Argentinean coast, and additional search and rescue teams had been rushed down from Santiago, Buenos Aires, Peru, and Honduras to report on the scene and look for survivors. He had a dozen planes in the air and fifty men on the ground. What more could he do?

If there were anything remaining of the woman, his men would find it. They'd better. Or he would have their heads in place of hers to send to Ashur on a silver platter. Delacroix had no idea why preserving the heads was so important, but he'd known plenty of other men in positions of power who had collected heads, too, and the idea of collecting trophies didn't bother him. Others had been satisfied with more conventional trophies, like the sidearms or sabers or favorite shotguns of their enemies. One, he remembered, wanted to marry the wife of his deceased opponent and adopt the guy's kids as a kind of trophy. Most, however, were happy with disposing of their enemies.

But Philip Ashur was obsessed with body parts: heads, fingers, genitals, certain internal organs like hearts. Delacroix had helped his boss collect everything from eyeballs to testicles. This was the first time he'd failed to deliver.

He looked again at the before and after photos of Patagonia. He didn't hold out much hope for finding anything salvageable in the aftermath of the volcano's violent explosion.

If anything had survived the blast, it was buried beneath rivers of molten lava and tons of fiery ash.

*   *   *

Jerry Walker was blind.

The crushing pain in his left leg and hip were unbearable, but what bothered him most was not being able to see.

Walker had always depended on his eyes for primary sensory input. He supplemented visual images with sounds, but sounds by themselves weren't enough for him. He wanted to see life, not just hear and feel and smell and taste it. Seeing was believing, and Jerry didn't believe anything he couldn't see. He didn't want to believe he was blind, but his eyes told him it was so.

When he tried to raise a hand to feel if his eyes were physically present, the hand didn't move. Not even the fingers. He couldn't even wiggle a single finger! Or a single toe! He couldn't move a muscle in his entire body. If he wasn't already dead, he soon would be.

Jerry couldn't tell if he was breathing or not. He couldn't feel his chest rising and falling, and he couldn't hear any inhales or exhales. The only clue he had that he was still alive was the excruciating pain radiating down his left leg.

The pain kept bringing him back to conscious awareness, and he couldn't escape. It held his attention like nothing else ever had or could. He speculated he might be dead and simply not know it yet. Maybe the pain was from the devil sticking a pitchfork into his leg and twisting, the way Jerry had liked to twist a knife in the most sensitive parts of his own victims to watch them squirm. He had lost all sense of time. All he could see was darkness, and days may have passed or merely minutes, an eternity or only a few fleeting seconds. He could feel nothing except the constant pain radiating into his groin and stomach and shooting down his leg like flashes of lightning. And the pain went on and on and on. There was nothing he could do to stop it or lessen it.

Pain was his sole companion in the darkness, and he was scared he would go insane if it went away and he was left with nothing.

"Do you need healing?" asked a voice in his mind.

Oh, great, he thought. *Now I'm hearing voices. I'm hallucinating.*

"I don't need no help," his mind said.

"Everyone needs help," said the voice.

He didn't reply. Maybe if he ignored the voice, it would leave him alone.

"I can make the pain go away." The whisper inside his head was seductive. It was a woman's voice, and it sounded familiar. Perhaps a little like his mother when he was a very small child and he still believed she loved him and could protect him. Back when life was good. Long before Jerry Walker had become disillusioned and killed his father and his mother and burned their bodies.

"I don't want the pain to go away," he said before he could stop himself. "It's my only friend. I'm afraid that if the pain goes away I'll die."

"Then you can keep the pain, if you want. And you can let me be your friend, too."

"I don't need no friends. I sure as hell don't need a friend like you."

"Oh, but you do need me, Jerry. You can't do anything without my help."

"How did you know my name?"

"I'm inside your mind, Jerry. I know everything about you."

Everything? If she did know everything about him, then why was she willing to help him? Didn't she know what he had done to his parents? To the others? Did she know what he would do again if he had the chance?

"What's the catch?" Jerry demanded. "There's gotta be a catch. People don't do nothin' for me unless I do somethin' for them first."

"What can you possibly do for me, Jerry? In fact, in your present condition, what can you possibly do at all?"

He didn't know, but there had to be a catch. There was always a catch.

"There is no catch, but there will be an exchange. The exchange may change you in ways no one can predict. Are you a gambler, Jerry?"

"What do you mean?"

"Are you willing to take a chance?"

Jerry didn't know what the voice was talking about. Take a chance? Take a chance on what?

"On living," replied the voice. "On becoming truly alive for the very first time."

Don't trust her, said that part of him that had trusted his mother and been disappointed in the results. Don't trust anyone.

"I can make you see again. This is your last chance, Jerry. Do you want to be healed, yes or no?"

Yes, Jerry's mind shouted. *Yes, I want so see again. Yes, I want to be healed! Yes, I want to live!*

"Then focus on the pain, Jerry. Pay attention to the pain as it spreads throughout your body. Feel the pain, and know what it means to be truly alive."

As Jerry's attention was drawn once again to the pain in his leg, the sensation radiated up through his spine as spasm after spasm of sharp, gut-wrenching misery wracked every nerve and muscle and fiber of his broken body. He shook, he convulsed; he wished a thousand times he had died.

And then, maybe he did die. Because the pain suddenly went away and his eyes snapped open.

Floating in the air in front of his face was the last image he remembered having seen: the woman he had come to kill, standing tall, naked, incredibly beautiful. Her arms were upstretched to the sky.

It seemed for a moment that she held in the palm of one hand the crescent moon, silvery-cold, and in the other hand the blazing red-hot sun.

And then the scene faded, and he heard the sound of helicopters beating the air.

And the drip, drip, drip of his own blood.

*   *   *

They found the broken body of Jeremiah Walker cradled in the branches of a pine tree some six kilometers southeast of the volcano. According to preliminary medical reports, Walker had suffered a crushed pelvis, multiple fractures of both arms and both legs, and a punctured lung. He'd lost a lot of blood from shattered bones that had shredded his skin, and he'd been crazy with pain before medics filled him full of narcotics that made him sleep.

All the hair on his head—including eyebrows and eyelashes—had been burned completely off. The flesh on his forehead had actually boiled in some places, and the rest of his face looked as well-done as a butter-basted turkey on Thanksgiving.

How Jeremiah Walker survived the volcano's blast was anybody's guess. The kid should have been killed instantly, and it was a miracle he still lived. After a brief stop in Panama to tend to his wounds and set the fractures, he'd be flown to Rockford for interrogation and debriefing.

Assuming, that is, that he didn't die enroute.

Ashur hadn't called yet for a report, and for that Delacroix was extremely grateful. He needed time to prepare a defense. Maybe talking to Walker would provide the Colonel a way out. Search and rescue teams were still looking for body parts. They had fanned out in concentric circles from what remained of the volcano's crater, and ground crews were beating the bushes while chopper crews flew low-level recon. If there were anything left to find, they'd find it. But Delacroix wasn't counting on another miracle.

Meanwhile, he had other work to do that would keep him busy and his mind off the consequences of failure. Almost literally at the opposite end of the globe to Patagonia, Lappland stretched across international boundaries to occupy parts of Norway, Sweden, Finland, and Russia. For tens of thousands of years, the Saami people, like their Komsa cousins for countless centuries before them, had followed meandering reindeer herds across the frozen tundra. The man Ashur wanted killed next was a Fjeld Saami, and he looked and acted a lot like the popular American version of Santa Claus.

His name was Biegolmai Davvii. He had long white hair and a beard. He was a giant of a man, nearly seven feet tall and three hundred pounds. His own people called him "Grandfather Winter" and treated him with respect. No one knew how old Biegolmei was. Some said he was older than the hills.

Although Ashur provided a description and locale—the man would likely be found in a reindeer hut near the Tornetrask river between Karesuando and Kiruna—there was no picture of him available nor satellite photos of the area. So how hard would it be to find a seven-foot tall giant? Surely, no harder than finding Ellen Groves and La Curandera.

Complicating matters was the lack of available daylight. Biegolmai lived north of the Arctic Circle in the land of the Midnight Sun. Unfortunately, it was now late November, and the sun had virtually disappeared from that part of the world. With less than one hour of daylight each day, aerial surveillance was practically impossible.

Delacroix dispatched seven of his best European operatives, veterans of cold war espionage and covert operations, to find the man and kill him. "Bring me the head of Santa Claus," he ordered. "And if you see Rudolph, bring me his head, too."

Biegolmai's family were reindeer herders, following the animals up into the mountains during the summer, returning to pasture along the rivers in the winter. But the old man no longer followed the herds, preferring to remain close to the Seita—an ancient artificial rock formation not far from the town of Karesuando, near the Swedish border with Finland. Local legends claimed this so-called Seita possessed magical powers, and some historians had speculated that the Seita—and other man-made rock formations like it in Sweden and Norway—had been the scenes of bloody ritual sacrifices 11,000 years ago, around the end of the last ice age.

Jack Delacroix didn't believe in magic, but he knew from experience how stubborn superstitious people could be in clinging to their beliefs. They easily became obsessed with icons like the Seita, or the Kabaa in Saudi Arabia or the Shiva lingam in India, and they would give their lives to protect a stupid piece of rock.

Biegolmai believed he was the guardian of the rock, just as Ellen Groves had believed she was guardian of the trees. "Find the rock," Delacroix directed his operatives, "and you will find the man. Take him out quickly and cleanly. Don't get close enough to engage in hand-to-hand combat. He's big enough to tear you apart with his bare hands."

Delacroix was busy monitoring communications between his men in Sweden when an excited XIIMI doctor in Panama phoned to report on Walker's condition.

"It's the strangest thing I've ever seen," said the doctor. "This man should have died hours ago either from loss of blood or from extensive internal injuries such as punctured lungs, crushed spleen, ruptured intestines, or fourth-degree burns over his entire body. It's a miracle he's still alive. But the biggest miracle is that he appears to be healing at a phenomenal rate, healing from the inside out. You can actually watch tissues regenerate. I've never seen cellular activity like this before, and the closest I can compare it to is in-utero fetal development or maybe a salamander growing a new tail. I've had him in an MRI and the scans are unbelievable. Nothing about this kid is normal. What happened to him?"

"He was mountain climbing in the Andes," said Delacroix. "A nearby volcano exploded and blew him off the mountain."

"I don't see how a volcanic eruption could account for such radical cellular changes. There must be something else that happened to him."

"Will he live, doctor?" asked Delacroix. "That's the bottom line. Will he live, and will he regain consciousness?"

"Yes, he'll live. And he's already conscious."

"Then send him to me, and I'll find out what happened to him."

CHAPTER TWENTY

W hen Bob returned to his cabin, Hilda stopped him to say phone service was restored. Although there was no phone in his cabin, he was welcome to use the one in the office anytime he wanted.

Bob dropped his suitcase on the bed in the cabin and took his laptop to the office. After connecting the internal modem to the phone line, he punched in the access codes. Then he checked his e-mail.

A message from the office of the Deputy Chief of Staff for Intelligence confirmed that no other sanctioned operation was in play in the area at this time, and any organized intelligence operation should be investigated and reported. Bob was authorized to request additional resources to determine the source of any alien-directed operation. DIA had asked the FBI, CIA, and Department of Homeland Security for support. Bob was given an official case number to reference when requesting assistance from other government agencies.

The second e-mail was from his friend at Fort Hood. Larry Palmer had conducted a remote search of computers at the military personnel center at Fort Knox and the military records center in Saint Louis. There had been two recent downloads by civilian contractors with need-to-know clearances of Major Groves' complete service record and details of security background checks. Larry was bothered by the fact that unauthorized civilians had been granted access to classified personnel data, and he had tried to discover who provided access. There was no record of authorization for either of these particular contractors, but both of them were subsidiaries of yet another government contractor, XIIMI.

The parent company had installed security upgrades to the main personnel computers during the past year, and XIIMI still retained access privileges to the core computers. Another subsidiary had installed the firewalls at the Fort Knox records center of the Human Resources Command. Not only did XIIMI have direct access, it also owned the source code. It could go anywhere in the interlinked computer systems of the federal government without anyone knowing it had been there, and the only trace left behind would be the destination IP of the data flow.

But what really worried Larry most was the download of data from Robert McMichaels' personnel file just yesterday. "Someone wanted to know all about you, my friend," Larry had written. "They got your entire file, including National Agency background checks. If there's a birth-mark on your butt, they know about it."

Bob did a Google search for XIIMI. There were more than eleven hundred hits, and he wondered why he'd never heard of them before. As he scanned the first page of entries, the answer quickly became obvious.

They were an umbrella company for diversified world-wide investments, and many of its acquired subsidiaries were household names. One was a player in international finance, owning or controlling hundreds of banks and insurance companies in various parts of the world. Another branch of XIIMI specialized in computer programming and systems security for industry and governments. Yet another specialized in providing satellite television, cable tv, and broadband internet access in dozens of states and in countries around the world. They also owned several hotel and resort chains, and they operated franchises for hundreds of others.

They owned companies that owned companies that owned companies. It was rumored that they owned a third of downtown Chicago through blind real estate trusts, and their commercial real estate holdings worldwide was mind-boggling. They controlled oil, gas, mineral, and timber rights in many undeveloped countries, and they owned ship lines, trucking firms, and charter airlines.

Although the Board of Directors included well-known names in politics and business, the company was privately owned. You couldn't buy XIIMI stock on the stock exchange.

Their corporate headquarters had relocated from Hong Kong to Chicago's Magnificent Mile in 1997, shortly before the British turned political control of Hong Kong over to Communist China. The new corporate office building was now a distinctive landmark of Chicago's lakefront, towering over the city like a giant among dwarfs. Although XIIMI owned and operated the building, it wasn't generally known as the XIIMI Building. Instead, it bore the logo of a well-known subsidiary.

It appeared they tried hard to keep a low profile. Ordinary people had no clue there was a hidden puppeteer pulling the stings that made the dummy dance. XIIMI remained secluded in shadows while hiding in plain sight.

While public attention was focused on high-profile subsidiaries, the parent company's global positioning maneuvers proceeded virtually undetected.

Just how big were they? No one really knew. Only the tip of the iceberg was visible, and the tip seemed small and insignificant.

The Chairman of the Board was Theodore Carnes, a reclusive billionaire business magazines had compared to Howard Hughes or Rupert Murdock. Carnes began collecting corporations back in the 1930s, buying up nearly bankrupt businesses for pennies on the dollar, and turning them into profitable enterprises. When World War II came along, he had positioned himself to make a fortune from government contracts. After the war, he helped rebuild industry in Germany and Japan. He was an early pioneer of oil exploration in the South China Seas, and he began acquiring land in the Far East, including China, Viet Nam, Cambodia, Thailand, Burma, Australia, New Zealand, and Korea.

Carnes became a rabid anti-communist after Mao nationalized his holdings in China. It was rumored he'd been a major contributor to the political campaigns of Richard M. Nixon and Senator Joseph McCarthy and even George W. Bush. Some speculators suggested he was primarily responsible for America's involvement in defending South Korea and Viet Nam against communist takeovers during the 1950s, 1960s, and early 1970s. There were additional speculations he helped fund covert CIA operations at the request of Alan Dulles, and one web site tried to link Carnes with CIA operations up to the present day.

Almost all of the eleven hundred mentions on the web credited Carnes as founder of the corporate giant. Although he continued to be listed as the Chairman of the Board, it had long been rumored he suffered from terminal cancer or even Alzheimer's because he hadn't been seen in public since the British relinquished control of Hong Kong in 1997. There was even speculation he'd died and the company he'd created simply carried on his draconian policies as if he were still alive.

He'd be well over a hundred if he remained alive.

There was no mention on the web of who currently ran the company. XIIMI had no corporate web site, and none of the private company's annual reports were available for public scrutiny.

He linked into the NSA main computer and ran a keyword search. XIIMI was not only a major contractor with the U. S. government, it also did business with nearly every other government in the world. Bob found references to classified files he was unable to access. Why couldn't he? He possessed the highest level of clearance possible. Had someone suddenly decided he had no right to know anything more about XIIMI?

Encountering blocks to further queries, Bob logged off the NSA mainframe. At least now he had an idea what he was dealing with, but there were still plenty of unanswered questions. Who ran XIIMI now? Was it still Carnes? Or was someone else calling the shots? And why was XIIMI, a gigantic multinational conglomerate, interested in the Groves family?

Despite everything Diane Groves had told him, he simply couldn't believe that a circle of trees in northern Wisconsin could be so critically important to the way the world worked that powerful men would murder people to acquire them. All the talk about guardians and universal energy centers sounded like a bad plot for a low-budget film. There had to be something more. What wasn't he seeing?

Bob knew he shouldn't let his attraction to Diane Groves cloud his reasoning. He was trying hard to look at this whole thing logically, but the pieces of this puzzle didn't fit together neatly. Not yet. A lot of pieces were still missing and he needed to locate them before he could grasp the big picture. He decided he required more detailed information and sent off a series of e-mails to people he knew in various branches of the service, people he'd worked with before and who owed him favors.

Bob had kept in touch with many of the men he'd served with over the years, and he knew several that were currently serving in positions that could access the information he needed. He sent each of them personalized requests to dig up everything they could find on XIIMI.

Then he sent an e-mail to a reserve lieutenant colonel who lived in Chicago and asked him to reconnoiter the XIIMI corporate headquarters building.

Bob logged off and powered down. He thanked Hilda and Arvin for the use of their phone line, and he asked if he could use the line again in the morning.

Hilda said, "Sure. Come by for breakfast and I'll fix you some of my fabulous blueberry pancakes."

After returning to his cabin, he sat on the bed and made notes for his detailed report to DIA. He divided notes into two sections: Facts and Speculations. Under facts, he included the murder of Ellen Groves witnessed by Sara Nelson. He added organized surveillance by trained operatives, including pursuit by two men who opened fire when they discovered that he'd made them tailing the snowmobile. The two men died when their vehicle collided with Sheila Ryan's parked vehicle. However, all evidence had been expertly removed within hours, indicating prior planning and organization of considerable sophistication.

Under speculation, he included XIIMI.

He wondered if XIIMI operatives were watching the cabin. He got up, turned off the lights, waited five minutes, then walked to the window and peeked out between the curtains. There were at least a dozen pick-up trucks and SUVs in the parking lot. Any one of them could belong to a surveillance team. He scanned the other cabins for activity. Two cabins had lights on, and the rest were dark and looked deserted. He eliminated the two with lights and scanned each of the others, watching the curtains for movement. After twenty minutes, he detected slight movement in the blackout curtain of the cabin opposite his.

They were watching.

He made his way back to the bed in the dark. He unzipped his suitcase, felt through his clothes until he found what he wanted. Wrapped inside a folded t-shirt was a 9-mm Beretta M9. He removed the weapon from the t-shirt, felt around in the suitcase until he found two pairs of socks containing loaded magazines. He inserted one magazine into the weapon, pulled back the slide to chamber a round, and slowly eased the hammer home. He slid the spare magazine into a pants pocket.

Bob lay on the bed with the weapon beside his right hand. He would remain fully clothed, ready to react should they come for him.

He lay there in the dark listening for sounds.

After an hour, he fell asleep.

*   *   *

Gunther Weiss had been a double agent during the cold war. Employed by the East German Ministry for State Security (MfS) as an intelligence analyst, his real job had been to spy and assassinate for the First Chief Directorate of the KGB. He had successfully carried out assassinations of high-profile communist defectors to the west, and he was highly prized by his handlers in the KGB.

After the fall of the Berlin Wall, Gunther's MfS job had ended, and the once-regular paychecks from the KGB became few and far between. In 1999, he was recruited by an ex-KGB officer to work for XIIMI at triple his former monthly income. He jumped at the chance to continue his work, and he became an industrial spy in the emerging European economic community.

Now he found himself far from his comfortable home in the new united Berlin. His cover was a skiing holiday to Kiruna in northern Sweden, and he had flown SAS into Stockholm and Luftfartsverket to the Kiruna municipal airport. The total travel time was just over three hours, including the transfer in Stockholm.

He waited four hours for the rest of his team to arrive. They rented a car at the airport and drove eastward, through the villages of Vittangi, Lannavaara, and Soppero. They left the car just north of Soppero, picked up weapons and supplies at the pre-arranged drop point, and followed ski trails northeast toward Karesuando.

Like many cross-county skiers who traveled to Lappland to take advantage of snow cover from October through April, the seven enjoyed crisp arctic air and the opportunity to stretch their muscles over dozens of kilometers of unbroken ski trails.

The two Americans on the team had trained at Fort Drum in upstate New York as part of the Tenth Mountain Division. One of them had seen action in Iraq. The other had been in Afghanistan. Both were expert skiers and trained in hand-to-hand combat and air-assault.

The others were Czech, Italian, Austrian, and Hungarian.

Night came early in the far north, and the entire landscape took on a greenish-blue haze as the Aurora Borealis danced in the sky. They were close now, within two or three kilometers of the Tornetrask. Gunther checked his compass. They were right on target.

They had been told they would find the old man in a reindeer-fur covered hut called a goahti. Similar in design to a native American sweat lodge, the goahti consisted of reindeer hides stretched over pine poles, with a firepit in the middle of the floor and a smoke hole in the ceiling. Though outside temperatures may drop well below zero, the inside of the goahti remained relatively warm and comfortable.

The particular goahti they were looking for was supposedly near a big pile of rocks that stood out in stark relief to the frozen tundra. Someone, a long time ago, had moved a bunch of granite boulders to mark this particular site. All they had to do was find the boulders, and they would find the man.

The Italian motioned to the north. There, along the banks of the river, were a dozen reindeer-hide huts with smoke streaming skyward from smokeholes in the roofs. Nearby, a herd of forty to fifty reindeer grazed on shrubs along the riverbank.

"I thought he was supposed to be alone," one of the Americans said.

"I don't see the rocks," said the Italian.

"We're too far west yet," suggested Gunther. "Follow the river east."

They skied eastward another two kilometers looking for the Seita. Gunther checked his compass again. The Seita should be around here someplace. How could they miss a big pile of standing stones?

"What's the matter?" asked one of the Americans.

"I can't get an accurate compass reading," Gunther said.

"Did you correct for declination? At this longitude and latitude, it should be 5 degrees east."

"I did. But the damn compass is off. From back there," he pointed, "this way is north. From here," he pointed 90 degrees to his right, "that way is north."

"Lemme see," said the American, skiing over to Gunther. He took the compass and moved away. After taking a reading, he came back, took another reading, and handed back the compass. "Must be a magnetic anomaly," he said, shaking his head. "Happens sometimes. Places around Carn Angli in Wales make a compass practically useless. Same thing happens around volcanoes. Supposed to have something to do with fluctuations in the earth's magnetic core."

"Why don't we have GPS?" asked the Austrian. "It's reliable and doesn't depend on magnetism."

"This was a rush job," said Gunther. "The colonel ordered us here with the equipment we had in place."

"Okay," said the American. "We're here. Let's make the best of it. The compass worked fine until we got close to the target. That means he's got to be around here. We found the river. Let's split up and look for the bastard. We've all got cell phones. If you haven't already done so, turn off your ringers and set your phones to vibrate. First team to spot the old geezer calls the other team. Everyone got all the numbers pre-programmed in?"

Everyone nodded assent. Gunther took out his cell phone and checked it.

"No carrier," he said. "We're too far from any tower to get a signal."

"Then we do it the old fashioned way," said the American. "When we locate the target, we send a runner to fetch the other team. Everyone straight on that?"

"We're straight," said Gunther. "Pick three men and I'll take the other two. Find him, fix him, but don't finish him until your backup arrives."

"Roger that," said the American. He picked the other American, the Italian, and the Hungarian. Gunther got the Austrian and the Czech.

The American headed northwest, toward the mountains. Gunther and his team went southeast, following the river. Six hours later, after combing both sides of the river in both directions, they met again near the twelve goahti of the siida, or village.

"He ain't here," reported the American. "We checked every hut, and none of the people looked like him."

"Maybe he was hiding," said Gunther.

"No place to hide in a deerskin tipi. Most of the men are close to 6 feet tall, but no one much over that. And no one looked like Santa Claus."

"What about the Seita? Did you see any big rocks?"

"No, Did you?"

"This is crazy," said Gunther. "The Colonel told me he had it on very good authority that the target was camped next to the Seita. According to the archeological survey and my map, there should be nine granite boulders right here. Or maybe over there, where that birch stands. I tell you, I made all the necessary corrections for magnetic declination. The compass was working until we got to this immediate area. Those rocks have got to be around here somewhere. Standing stones weigh tons. People can't simply move them."

"People moved them from someplace else to here in the first place," said the American. "Thousands of years ago, without heavy equipment to help, people supposedly moved nine granite boulders all the way down from distant mountains to here. And then they stacked them up on top of each other, the biggest on the bottom, to make a kind of pyramid. I don't know how they did it, but they did. So maybe they moved them again."

"Impossible!" said Gunther. "Those rocks are here someplace."

"Whatever," said the American. "But I sure don't see them. So what do we do now?"

"Now," said Gunther, "you keep looking. Spread out and go over everything again and again until you find the goddamned pile of rocks and Mr. Santa Fucking Claus. Then you take care of him and box up the head for the Colonel."

"And what are you going to do?" asked the American.

"I," said Gunther, "am going back until I can get a good signal on my cell phone. Then I'm going to call the Colonel and tell him there'll be a slight delay."

"He ain't gonna like it," said the American.

"No," said Gunther. "He isn't going to. But he'd like it a lot less if I didn't report in. So I'm going to tell him the situation. Maybe he can see something we can't."

CHAPTER TWENTY-ONE

Dan Wilson was a senior programmer-analyst for the XIIMI subsidiary that contracted to program computer systems and networks for businesses and governments. Dan had written code for many of the computers that defense and other security agencies used to compile and store data.

He was a loyal U.S. citizen, born in the USA, educated at UCLA and Stanford, and held a top secret crypto security clearance as an employee of a government contractor. He'd never been arrested nor convicted of a crime because he had never deliberately perpetrated any crime.

But, then, Dan didn't consider spying on other people's computers a crime.

He'd been a hacker since age eleven. Getting in and out of computers without anyone's knowledge was a fine art he'd perfected over a decade and a half of practice. He loved what he did, and he did what he loved.

Dan was a natural with numbers, and he had attained almost perfect scores on the math portions of both the SAT and the GRE. At age 27 he held dual doctorates in higher mathematics and cognitive science. XIIMI paid him half a million dollars a year just to play with computers, and they paid him a bonus for special jobs that came up two or three times a year.

One of those special jobs was to monitor inquiries into XIIMI's businesses. With nearly unlimited computing power at his disposal, he set up a system to infiltrate major search engines and report downloads of data that included XIIMI's name and other parameters related to current operations. Dan had included DIA, NSA, and CIA mainframes in his program.

When multiple systems reported activity from the same IP, his curiosity was aroused. He ran a spyware program he'd developed to track incoming and outgoing activity from that IP. He downloaded half-a-dozen e-mails from Robert McMichaels to recipients all over the country.

As instructed, Dan immediately locked McMichaels out of NSA and CIA main frames. Then he dutifully forwarded McMichaels' internet history and copies of his e-mails to Jack Delacroix and to the XIIMI corporate offices in Chicago. What XIIMI or Delacroix did with that information, he didn't give a shit and didn't want to know. All he wanted was bigger and better toys to play with. As long as XIIMI gave him everything he asked for, he was happy.

Let's see now, what was it he wanted that he didn't already have? He had no idea, but he'd think about it until he discovered something. He returned to the online game he was playing with other hackers, and within moments Dan Wilson was back in cyberspace having a ball.

*   *   *

Delacroix couldn't believe his bad luck. Not only had his best men botched two very important missions, but that army buddy of Groves was poking his nose where it didn't belong.

Any minute now, Ashur could call. "Where are the heads I ordered?" he'd ask, and the Colonel would have to say he had no clue. In the intelligence business, admitting you didn't know was the same as admitting you were useless.

Everyone could be replaced, and he knew very well that people who outlived their usefulness couldn't be left alive to vend their wares to a competitor. This wasn't just a job, it was a profession. Only in this profession, there were no golden parachutes.

No parachutes and no safety nets. When you fell from grace, you plunged to your death. Delacroix had no illusions. His power depended on his value to Philip Ashur, and he was valuable only as long as he carried out his instructions expertly and efficiently.

And secretly.

Delacroix nervously glanced at a clock. The plane carrying Jeremiah Walker should be landing any minute, and it was only a ten minute drive from the Chicago-Rockford International Airport to the old factory building.

After finally talking to Gunther Weiss, he'd phoned an operative in Denmark and arranged air drop of a Global Positioning System, seven pairs of night vision goggles, seven hand-held walkie-talkies, and an ultra-high frequency short-wave transmitter/receiver. He expected to be able to communicate with Weiss by radio within the hour. There might still be time to pull a rabbit out of the hat before Ashur phoned.

He ordered the comm operator to page him when Weiss radioed. Then he walked down the steel steps that connected the second floor communications center with the ground floor operations staging area.

Ten minutes later, the van arrived. Jerry Walker—no longer looking like the kid who'd left here less than two days ago—got out of the passenger seat and walked across the cement floor without crutches.

He was smiling, and he had a healthy tan as if returning from a restful vacation on a tropical beach instead of death's door.

*　*　*

Biegolmai Davvii watched from his perch atop the birch tree. However, this was no ordinary birch. It was the shaman's tree—a branch of the World Tree—by means of which he could ascend into the spirit realm.

There were nine steps to becoming a shaman. There were nine steps on the Seita, and nine notches cut into the World Tree. There were were nine scars on Biegolmai's body, too, each wound inflicted by a master shaman, symbols of the steps he had completed to become an ascended master.

The birch and the Seita were one and the same. The men below couldn't see that, of course. Nor could they see Biegolmai as he walked between worlds.

But he could see them.

From the World Tree, he also viewed La Curandera walking in the spirit world. She had climbed another branch of the World Tree to position her spirit between worlds when the bad men came to kill her.

She had even chosen to shield one of the bad men, cradling his body instead of her own in the protection of her tree, and restoring his spirit to the same mortal coil. She had persuaded him to allow her to cohabit his body because her physical self had been destroyed by fire.

Biegolmai had danced the dance of ecstasy around the Seita for nine hours, beating upon his shaman's drum with fingers that had a mind of their own. His painted hoop drum was made from the skin of a sacred animal stretched over a wooden frame and decorated with runes and sacred symbols.

As he beat upon the skin, the frame resonated. Its vibrations reverberated through every corner of the universe, the continuous rhythm of the drum transforming the Seita into the Cosmic Tree, physically altering the molecular structure of rock in a quantum shift.

His physical body also altered. It became tiny and light as a feather. To mortals, he appeared a raven roosting in the branches of a scrawny birch.

As an aircraft droned overhead, Biegolmai saw men look to the sky. A cargo parachute deployed, barely visible in the blue-green flickering northern lights.

Two of the men skied. Twenty minutes later, they reappeared with boxes of electronics: a radio, walkie-talkies, night-vision goggles, and a small, hand-held device that looked something like a miniature computer.

After a few minutes, they resumed their search for Biegolmai and the Seita, searching for what was right under their noses. They split up and followed the river in opposite directions. None of their expensive electronics worked, and they couldn't understand why. But Biegolmai knew. He knew many things.

He wasn't about to tell those stupid men any of the things he knew.

*   *   *

Walker's story didn't change. He was certain the woman and the rest of the team were dead, blown up by the explosion and buried under rivers of molten lava.

He had no explanation for his own amazing recovery. His arms and legs and skin had healed overnight. He said he had no idea how it happened, but he wasn't going to look a gift horse in the mouth. Delacroix grilled him for well over an hour. The kid didn't know anything more than the Colonel, or if he did, he wasn't telling. Delacroix ordered an injection of sodium pentothal, and he ordered Walker to sit still while a medic administered the injection. Under the influence of truth serum, Walker recalled the excruciating pain he had felt as the expanding gasses of the volcano hit his body and carried it into the air. He could recall nothing but pain until he awoke in the hospital in Panama.

Gone was the rebellious teenager with seemingly uncontrollable rage seething just below the surface. In its place was a calm and a clarity that implied a maturity far beyond his nineteen years.

The kid wasn't a kid anymore.

Delacroix knew that trauma could do that to a person. He had seen it happen in combat to men who survived near-death experiences, especially when their comrades had perished and they alone had survived.

It was a kind of acceptance of one's mortality that men who had never faced death couldn't understand. Jerry Walker looked and acted like a man who knew he was living on borrowed time.

But there was something else, too, that contributed to the uneasy feeling the Colonel had about the kid. The hair on Walker's head and his beard—he now had a full head of hair and a beard—were as white as hair of a ninety-year old man.

Before Delacroix could decide what to do about Walker, the comm operator interrupted with an urgent message.

There was a call on the secure line with XIIMI. Philip Ashur was on the line, asking for Delacroix, demanding to speak with him.

The Colonel's time had just run out.

CHAPTER TWENTY-TWO

D iane, Nancy, Aunt Anna, and Aunt Violet allowed their spirits to detach from their bodies.

All four women were adept, but none was yet an ascended master. There were limits to where they could go and what they could do. Aunt Anna, the most developed of the four, had ascended the eighth step on the Cosmic Mountain, the eighth notch cut into the World Tree. Diane was at the seventh level; Nancy, the fifth; and Aunt Vi, only the third. Sara Nelson had climbed all nine steps in a previous incarnation, and Ellen had identified Sara as her successor. Once she reached puberty, the memories of her previous lives would be available to her again. Until then, she was no help.

The four had learned to walk between worlds for brief periods, and Aunt Anna had the ability to recall lives between lives in detail. But the spirit world had changed dramatically since she had last been a resident.

Plus, the abyss had grown so large that nothing in the spirit world could cross over. Nor could anything of the physical world reach now-trapped spirits on the other side. Those grounded in the physical world—the walkers between worlds—could only climb the World Tree half-way.

Because none of them had the power to ascend the tree by herself, they combined their spirits in hopes of reaching the top. Diane, Nancy, and Violet had given themselves completely to Anna, and their co-mingled spirits had the temporary power to penetrate the mist and communicate with spirits currently connected to the tree. Though it was Anna's spirit, the others were present, too. What one saw and heard, so did they all.

Half-way up the World Tree they met Biegolmai.

"Grandfather," said Anna, "what is happening to the spirit world? We desire to cross, but cannot. Why is that?"

"Granddaughters, the very fabric of the universe is at risk. Five of the eight current guardians have been killed, and the spirits of former guardians are held captive in the physical world. Even as we speak, men seek to do the same to me."

"Who would do such a thing?"

"One," said Biegolmai, "who seeks power over all else. There has always been one—the hidden one—who seeks to become immortal, one who holds all others and all things in total disregard, one who would destroy to gain absolute power. This is he who has disrupted the flow of energy for his own ends, creating the abyss. As long as that abyss exists, no spirit may cross. The cycles of birth and rebirth will end. The old ways will be forgotten, and no one else but he will know how to stir or still the winds. This one would destroy all of us and hold our spirits captive in the flesh. So long as I sing the Jojk, so long as I hold the drum, neither he nor his confederates may harm me. But I am an old man, and I grow tired."

"What can we do? How can we help?"

"Find the hidden one and stop him."

"How do we find him? How will we recognize him when we do find him?"

"He has walked among you in past incarnations. You may recognize him when you meet again."

"But how will we find him?" asked the combined spirit, feeling the bond of union unraveling and the physical world pulling their spirits back.

"He will find you," said the spirit of Biegolmai, his fading words little more than whispers on the wind.

Diane, Nancy, Anna, and Violet returned to their separate bodies. Their temporary union worked for but a short time. If they were to journey again to the World Tree, they would need the combined spirit of more than just the four of them.

They now knew that an older spirit, sufficiently ancient to be an adept, had created the present crisis for his own purposes.

And it was someone they had met before in past lives. Perhaps, if they went deep inside and explored their past lives, they'd discover a way to identify him.

Each began her own personal journey back in time, reliving previous existences. They looked for similarities between those men and women they encountered in one life and people they encountered in another. The man they were looking for might even have been a woman in a past life. There was no way to tell what he or she would look like.

Although every human spirit had the potential to experience multiple rebirths, few chose the path of pain that led to multiple reincarnations and, eventually, to enlightenment.

Sometimes, after only one or two incarnations, a freed spirit opted to remain sequestered in the spirit world for as long as possible. Others, unable or unwilling to remember lessons of their past lives, repeated the cycles of birth and rebirth without progressing to higher levels of consciousness. A very few elected to return again and again to the physical world to help others become enlightened or to protect the vulnerable during their spiritual journeys. They became healers, shamans, bodhisattvas, priests, physicians, philosophers, physicists, pundits, policemen, or poets. Some became soldiers.

And an elite few eventually became guardians.

There were far too many hedonistic types, addicted to the pleasures of the flesh, who came back solely to re-experience the joys of physical interactions. They were totally unconcerned with spiritual enlightenment and never became adept.

And then there were those spirits who followed the paths of power, the so-called left-hand paths, seeking to amass the ultimate knowledge which would give them control of other sentient beings and power over inanimate objects.

True adepts preferred complete anonymity, doing his or her work in secret. An incarnated magus deliberately shunned the spotlight, working magic during dark of night when the eyes of ordinary mortals were tightly closed and the doors between worlds were easily opened. The science of magic was an occult science—secret and hidden.

As Diane, Violet, Anna, and Nancy revisited their past lives and searched for clues from the people, places, and things they had encountered, Philip Ashur felt their presence in his own past lives.

Ashur had finally broken through the block of remembrance, finding himself in Cairo shortly after the turn of the first millennium. He was a student at the Dar al-Hikmah, the Abode of Learning, where the dawa—the fraternity of those personally called by Allah—initiated Ismailites into the nine mysteries of the Seventh Imam.

When al-Muiz al-Din, Caliph of the Fatimites, and his brilliant general Gawhar, who built a new Shiite city along the banks of the Nile just north of Fustat-Misr named the city, Gawhar called it al-Qahirah or Cairo. Al-Qahirah meant "the victorious" in Arabic. It was also the Arabic name for the planet Mars, because Mars was in the ascendant when the workmen began the walls of the palace and the mosque of al-Azhar.

Al-Hakim, the grandson of al-Muiz, became successor to the Fatimite Caliphate of Cairo upon the death of al-Aziz. He also became the recognized leader of all Ismaili Shiites, followers of Fatima, daughter of the Prophet and wife of Hazrat Ali, cousin of the Prophet.

Fatimid Shiites believed that the Prophet Mohammad had personally designated Ali to be his successor, and all future succession to Imam thereafter depended on nass, or designation, by the Imam of the Time.

Ismailis referred to themselves as al-dawat al-hadiyah, the rightly-guided dawa. Besides believing in the succession of Ali and the uninterrupted succession of divinely chosen and divinely inspired Imams, they also believed in hidden esoteric knowledge. Though much knowledge could be found in the almost 200,000 volumes housed in the royal caliphal library which al-Hakim generously shared with scholars he assembled from all over the world, true knowledge of the hierarchy of cosmic principles could only be gained by proceeding through the nine steps of initiation.

It was a quest for knowledge, wisdom, and understanding that had brought these outstanding scholars to this place at this time. For here resided the spirit of the Seventh Imam—the Hidden Imam—who walked anonymously among mortals and was said to perform miracles.

There were separate Assemblies of Wisdom for men and women at the Abode of Learning, of course, in homr of Fatima. The mysteries were essentially the same for both sexes. The assembled scholars, any one of which could be the secret embodiment of the Hidden Imam, came from all corners of the world.

Famous names included ibn al-Haitham, Masawaih al-Mardini, Abu Ali al-Hassan ibn Abdallah ibn Sina, Abu-l-Hasan, Ali ibn Radwan ibn Ali ibn Ja'far, al-Misri ibn Yunus, and Abu-Raihan Mohammed ibn Ahmed al-Biruni, as well as high-paid administrators, generals, and physicians of the royal court.

There were nine degrees of initiation, or steps of transformation. The first taught science, mathematics, logic, language and literature. Students were also expected to learn Islamic law, analyzing the literal and symbolic meanings of the arabic text of the Holy Quran.

By the time of the first initiation, students' heads were swimming with knowledge. The purpose of the initiation, however, was to throw doubt on all that they had learned. Knowledge, the instructors argued, was never enough. Nor was belief. Truth lay hidden beyond faith, beyond reason.

Truth was only manifest through action.

The act of initiation, the first step toward creating personal truth through action and interaction, was learning that the world was created and was constantly being recreated by means of movement and sound, the act of creation itself. The second step was to imitate exactly the divinely-inspired actions and words of the teachers.

The third step included the power to name Names. Through concentration and absorption, the aspirant acquired the magical powers of invocation and evocation. For it was only by calling upon the Names that one gained power over all of creation.

The fourth step was to remember and repeat the divine Names and all the attributes of the Seven Imams. For it was whispered that prior to the creation of the universe, the divine Names yearned to be known. With a sigh of compassion for the Names, God—whose true name was Allah—caused each to be manifested. Thus, the universe was created, and the universe continued to be recreated each moment the divine Names were remembered by the heart and spoken to the wind.

This act of remembrance and repetition created alternating waves of expansion and contraction of consciousness that reverberated throughout the universe until union with the divine could be achieved. The initiate became a Possessor of the Heart. For it is by the heart that the Names are remembered.

During the fifth step, the true Names and attributes of the Seven Mystical Law-Givers, the seven mystical helpers, and the Imam of the Time were revealed.

The sixth step taught the power of words. Words could create, and words could destroy.

The seventh step revealed the First Great Secret: Everything in creation was related. Every action generated a reaction. The key was to act and not react, to take control and exert power over others. Knowing in advance how others would react to your actions gave you power over them in all things.

The eighth step taught that all beliefs were false. Good and evil, right and wrong, did not exist. Beliefs were merely distractions designed to enslave the believer, and what really mattered—after all was said and done—was power over things and power over people.

So the ninth step—the step into power—was the action itself. It was through action that the Lord of the Time—the Hidden Imam— moved men like pawns on a chessboard.

The final initiation required the aspirant to vow to act as his personal Lord—the Lord of the Time—commanded. To act without thought, without hesitation. Once the initiate had carried out the directed act, he or she was admonished to never betray any of the secrets entrusted to him. Then he was awarded a new Name. He was now one of the "Assasseen," which meant "Guardians of the Secrets."

The man who would someday become Philip Ashur completed all nine steps in under two years. His name then was Hassan, the son of Ali Shabbah, and he left Cairo to put into practice all he had learned.

His personal motto became: Nothing is true; everything is permitted.

Many years later, the name "assassin" would become synonymous with al-Hassan ibn Shabbah. It would be rumored that Hassan had used hashish to mold men who came to study under him—the new assassins—to his will. That was a lie, of course. Hassan had spread many lies about himself and his organization to protect the true secrets, part of the Doctrine of Intelligent Dissimulation he had learned at the Abode of Learning in Cairo.

It wasn't until shortly before his death at the age of 90 that Hassan ibn Shabbah, the Old Man of the Mountain, sensed the presence of the others—four men and four women—who had also studied at Cairo and who could see through his lies.

He died while searching for them.

CHAPTER TWENTY-THREE

"I s there a tree?" asked Ashur as soon as Delacroix told him the team in Sweden had failed to locate Biegolmai Davvii or the Seita.

Delacroix didn't know what he meant. "A tree?" he asked. "Did you say tree?"

"Ask Weiss if he sees a tree. If he sees a tree, tell him to cut it down."

Ashur remained on the line while Delacroix radioed the team in northern Sweden. "There are lots of trees," said Weiss. Reception was terrible. The signal kept breaking up. "What kind of tree should we look for?"

"A lone tree. A tree that is not part of any forest," said Ashur after Delacroix relayed the question. "The man's a damn tree-hugger like the Groves women. If he's walking between worlds, his spirit is tied to a rock or to a tree. Tell your men if they can't find the rock, to chop down the tree and they'll find the Seita and the target."

When Delacroix relayed the information, Weiss replied that he didn't have an axe.

"Get one. Get a goddamned axe and chop down the goddamned tree."

Weiss was silent for a moment. Then he said, "Roger that."

"Now tell me about McMichaels," Ashur demanded when Delacroix got back on the phone. "How did he learn about us?"

"He's an intelligence analyst. And he's smart."

"He's too smart. Kill him."

"Are you sure you want to do that? He's DIA. If we take him out, there'll be an investigation."

"Then find a way to compromise him. You have his file. Find his weakness. Make him back off. If he won't play ball, find a way to discredit him and make him have an accident that looks like his own negligence. Don't fail me again, Delacroix. You know what you need to do, so get it done."

Delacroix hung up the phone. He returned to the interrogation room.

"I have an assignment for you," he told Walker. "I'm sending you back to Wisconsin to have a talk with an old friend."

* * *

Diane felt the presence of the same man in each of her previous lives. He was there but not there, hidden behind the scenes.

His psychic signature was unique. Although his life force increased with each incarnation, he did not walk between worlds. Wherever his spirit went when it left his body, it was not to trees or birds or rocks. Nor did his spirit enter the spirit realm where it might be refined and cleansed.

She began to suspect that this man chose to stay earthbound between lives, a discarnate entity that took possession of another person's body. Either he displaced the resident spirit or held it prisoner. That person could do nothing but watch his own body act without his volition. After a discarnate entity used up its host, it simply discarded that body and entered another.

Instead of walking between worlds, discarnate entities walked into another person's body and took over his life. The possessing spirit could then continue to work in the physical world and have a direct effect on events. The advantages of choosing such a path were obvious: one could continue to control people and events over multiple normal lifespans, directly influencing politics and institutions in ways no one else could. What was left undone at the end of one person's lifetime could be completed without any loss of continuity in another person's, because the consciousness and personality of the primary operator remained unbroken.

Of course, the cycles of birth and rebirth would periodically claim even an earthbound entity, usually though accident, and each time the cycle reclaimed him, he would be reborn as a child who had to learn to remember his past lives all over again.

How much more advanced was this man than anyone else? Did the path he had chosen really make a big difference?

Diane thought she finally understood what was happening to the spirit world. This man, whoever he was, had no need for the spirit realm. Perhaps he felt threatened by it and those who entered it and returned with new knowledge and new strength. Had he deliberately created the abyss to prevent others from communicating with the spirits of their ancestors? Did he seek ultimate knowledge and power while preventing others from achieving spiritual growth and advancement during lives between lives?

Though she didn't know what the man looked like in physical form today, Diane now knew how she could identify him if she found him.

Time was running out. And she had to find him fast if she hoped to stop his evil plan from succeeding.

CHAPTER TWENTY-FOUR

Bob rolled out of bed and hit the floor running.

He'd been awakened five minutes earlier by the crunching sounds boots make breaking through the icy crust atop snowdrifts in sub-zero weather. The crisp night air magnified the sounds, and he knew there were two pair of heavy boots advancing toward his cabin from different directions.

Prone on the bed and facing the door, he assumed a two-handed firing position with the muzzle of the Beretta aimed twenty inches above the floor. When they came in, they'd likely come in low. If they didn't, he'd take out their knees.

When he heard them scrambling away in opposite directions, he knew they weren't planning on entering his cabin. He had to get out fast. Either they'd set a timer, lit a fuse, or were about to use a radio-controlled detonator. As he barged through the door running for his life, he caught the pungent odor of propane gas.

Propane fueled water heaters that provided hot showers, and Bob had noticed separate liquid propane tanks attached to the rear of each cabin. Propane was highly combustible. If someone torched the tank and all that liquid propane ignited at once, the resulting inferno could easily consume the cabin and everyone and everything in it.

Instead of running across the parking lot where he would make an easy target for anyone with a weapon, he dodged to his left and ran into shadows behind the cabin where massive snowdrifts slowed him down but afforded excellent cover. If the men watching from their cabin or from a vehicle on the far side of the parking lot blinked, they might have missed his mad dash out the door and around the side of the building.

And even if they'd seen him, they couldn't get a clear shot at him.

He ran as fast as his legs would carry him through waist-high snow. He was thirty yards away when the building burst into flames, and he dropped into a drift and covered himself with snow before the inferno could reach him.

He heard Arvin shout to Hilda that the water in the garden hose he was using to put out the fire froze as soon as it hit the air.

Hilda shouted back that she had called the sheriff and the volunteer fire department.

Arvin told her to get everyone out of the other cabins. The wind had picked up and the fire was already spreading to the roof of the cabin to the south. The whole place'd go up in flames any second now.

Bob heard other shouts—men's voices—and vehicles starting and moving out of the parking lot. A car horn blared. More shouts. Ten minutes later, he heard sirens in the distance.

No one came for him. Either the men who had set the blaze left, or they were watching from a safe distance. For all he knew, they were sitting in their vehicles with high-powered rifles aimed in his direction.

Two sheriff's deputies were first to arrive. Not long after, a fire engine pulled in with a water tanker in tow. Bob raised his head enough to see that two of the cabins were a total loss, and a third was belching smoke and flames. The formerly white landscape was peppered with soot and ashes, Puddles of melted snow were beginning to crust over with thin films of ice.

The deputies evacuated the owners and guests to the highway while firemen set to work extinguishing the flames. Within an hour, it was all over. The fires were out, and Bob emerged from the snowdrift and went to talk with the sheriff.

*   *   *

Sheila dreamed about Tom Groves. In one dream, he was a Roman Catholic priest and she a parishioner hopelessly in love with the man wearing collar and cassock. In another dream, he was a wounded soldier and she was a hospital nurse who cared for him. In yet another, their roles were reversed: she was the man who went off to war, and he was the woman who waited faithfully for her to return.

In one particularly memorable dream, she was a witch. He was a druid. Both were burned at the stake when an itinerant Irish Bishop roused the community against them. Sheila thought the bishop looked and acted like a much older Philip Ashur.

Each time she awoke from another dream, she discovered Tom Groves sitting beside the bed. He would smile at her, she would smile at him, and she would go back to sleep. Once or twice she awoke to find him asleep in his chair. He was the only man she had ever met who made her feel she didn't need to prove herself. It was as if he accepted her for who she was, loving her unequivocally and without hesitation.

Not like her rotten father who had never loved her, despite everything she had tried to do to earn his love. Tom was nothing like her father, that good for nothing drunken bastard who had used her and abused her, nor like either of her older brothers who had teased her and taunted her and tormented her relentlessly. No, Tom was different.

She dreamed of ancient days when she was a Queen and he was captain of her armies. They both looked different then. But at heart, they were the same.

Tom Groves had always been the man of her dreams.

As she dreamed, her spirit left her body and traveled. At one time she lived as a tree, tall, majestic, peering down from eighty feet or more. Another time she became a bird, observing the affairs of men from great heights that offered unique perspectives.

When she awoke, she knew who she was. To ground herself in the here and now, she asked Tom for a cigarette.

"You must be feeling better." He lit a filtered Camel and handed it to her.

"Physically, I feel fine. But mentally and emotionally, I'm a mess. I didn't come here to help you. I came here to cheat you out of your land."

Tom lit a cigarette of his own and waited for her to elaborate.

"Three days ago I was a successful practicing attorney in Chicago. One of my clients, a large corporation that said they wanted to remain anonymous, asked me to come here to negotiate the purchase of your land. They were willing to pay me an unusually large sum. My commission, of course, would be dependant on how little you could be persuaded to accept."

"This land doesn't belong to us," said Tom. "We're only the caretakers here. We could never sell it, because we don't own it."

"But you *do* own it, Tom, all 1800 acres. It's legally registered in your mother's name. I checked title and tax records. Unless your mother left a will no one knows about, the land passes on equally, by law, to any surviving children upon her death. You and your sisters will each inherit a third after probate. My job was to convince one of you to sell. Then the land would need to be liquidated and the proceeds distributed as part of the estate."

"How did you plan to do that?"

"By driving a wedge between you and your siblings. Divide and conquer. I've done it before. In fact, I'm really quite good at it."

"Why are you telling me this?"

"Because I owe you my life. Not only did you and your family take me in when I was seriously injured, you helped me heal and made me a stronger person. I owe you, and I always pay my debts."

"Is that the only reason?"

"No. I feel an attachment to you. And to your family. It's as if I've known you all my life. I've never met you before, yet I feel like I know you better than I know myself. Does that make any sense? I'm not sure it does to me."

"Yes, it makes perfect sense. We feel the same way about you, Sheila. You're like one of the family. You belong here."

"I've been having dreams about you, Tom." She blushed as she asked, "Have you ever dreamed about me?"

"Yes. I've dreamt of you all my life."

"Really?"

"Yes."

"You've never married. Have you, Tom?"

"No."

"Me, neither. Why not? Why aren't either of us married? And don't tell me you never had the time to get married because that's the lie I usually use. "

"I was waiting for the right person." Tom's shyness seemed to evaporate. He smiled at her as if he were about to share a precious secret. "I've waited all my life for *you*, Sheila Ryan. Not just someone like you, but you. I knew someday I'd find you, or you'd find me, that you'd come back into my life again. And now it's finally happened. You're here and I'm here. And I'm glad."

"It sounds crazy," Sheila said, "but I feel the same way. I've been waiting for you, too, only I didn't know it before I saw you yesterday. When I met you yesterday, it was like . . . like . . . like I've known you all my life. I think I've carried a part of you around inside of me forever."

Tom snuffed out his cigarette in an ashtray. Then he reached out, took her cigarette, and stubbed it out, too.

They looked into each other's eyes for what seemed like an eternity before she pulled him onto the bed and slowly undressed him. She was already naked. They explored each other's spirits through the flesh.

And as male and female united, magic happened.

And it felt grand and glorious and was a gift from the gods.

*   *   *

As Jerry flew to Hayward aboard a private jet, he peered down at the snow-covered trees with a fresh perspective.

Everything looked radically different

When the old Jeremiah Walker perished in Patagonia, the new Jerry was reborn in a tree. It was as if his eyes were opened and he could see—really see—for the first time because what he saw now was not what he'd seen two days ago. Everything looked clearer, sharper, brighter, more in-focus than ever before. Even people looked different now. He no longer saw them as bloody strings of nerves, muscle, fat, and fecal matter to take apart and dispose of. Now they were vibrant, vibrating, complete entities with a purpose and a place, and he saw himself as having a place among them.

And he could see connections between all things, between the living and the dead, between the animate and the inanimate, the sun and the moon, the earth and the stars. He knew he was no longer separate, alone. He was an integral part of a great chain of being that possessed direction and purpose.

The old Jeremiah Walker knew nothing at all of love. At nineteen, he'd never had a girlfriend, never been on a date, never kissed a girl. Though he'd never experienced normal intercourse, he was intimately familiar with female anatomy. Twice since joining the Colonel's crew, he'd had the pleasure of taking women apart while they were still alive, and he had spent extra time exploring their most sensitive parts while they pleaded and begged for their lives. But he had never loved nor been in love.

The reason he had never loved was no one had ever loved him. He'd grown up fearing his father, a man who had regularly beaten both his wife and son for no reason. No reason other than that he could because one tried to stop him.

Jerry learned from his father that women were useless objects to be kept in their place. His father claimed he'd screwed Jerry's mother during a moment of human weakness, when he was too drunk to know any better, and she had screwed up his life ever since.

He'd been brought up believing his birth was one big mistake, something both of his parents regretted to their dying day. When he was fourteen, he corrected their mistake. He shot his mother to put her out of her misery, then shot his father to stop the incessant hammering of the old man's fists. Jerry burned their pitiful house to the ground with his parents still in it.

He was placed in a succession of foster homes until he turned eighteen.

He never made the same mistakes his father had because he never allowed himself to get close enough to a live woman to be tempted. He'd never kissed a woman, never allowed a woman to kiss or fondle him, and he sure as hell had never put his thing inside a woman to get her pregnant.

But now he saw women differently. They did have their place, and it wasn't what his father had said. Although Jerry had never been inside a woman, a woman had been inside him. He could feel her inside him still, and for the first time in his life he felt whole and complete.

High winds buffeted the fuselage as if the airplane were being battered by his father's giant fists. Despite high winds, the experienced ex-military pilot made a final approach to the snow-covered landing field. He dropped the nose and compensated for wind sheer by increasing rpms. The small plane bounced and skidded sideways until it came to an abrupt stop.

Steve Miller waited on the tarmac in a black GMC Sierra pick-up. He was 23, an ex-Army ranger who'd seen combat in Afghanistan, and a decent guy who thought he was employed by a covert branch of the U. S. government. Steve had been recruited by a man he'd known to be a CIA operative in Kabul.

"We think we got him," he said as Jerry climbed into the truck. "We burned his cabin. We think he was inside when the cabin blew."

"Take me there," Jerry ordered. "If he's alive, I have a message for him from the Colonel. If he's dead, I'll ID the body for you."

Steve drove. As they headed toward highway 13, he kept sneaking glances at Jerry's face. "There's something different about you, Walker. I can't put my finger on exactly what. You look different, you sound different, too. You're the same guy, but you've changed."

Walker removed his stocking cap.

"Jesus Christ! What the hell happened to your hair?"

Walker turned the rearview mirror and stared at his reflection. His once-shaven head possessed hair that had not only turned pure white, it had grown at a phenomenal rate. There were six inches layered on top of his head, and his sideburns and beard were half an inch thick.

"I guess I did change," he said, rubbing the stubble on his chin. "It looks like I've finally grown up."

CHAPTER TWENTY-FIVE

Susie McMichaels loved chatting with friends after school. Ever since her father—her real father, not either of her step-fathers—sent her a personal laptop for her birthday, she'd looked forward to rushing home to chat online. No one hung around hallway lockers like they used to.

Today she beat her brother home, and she had the whole house to herself. She grabbed a diet Dr. Pepper from the fridge, kicked off her shoes, and went directly to her computer without passing go and without collecting two hundred dollars.

Suzie booted up and immediately logged onto Facebook to see who else was online and available to chat.

So engrossed in reading and replying to messages, she didn't hear either her brother get home from school or her mother arrive home from work. She totally ignored her mother's first two calls to supper. It wasn't until she heard adult footsteps on the hall carpet outside her room that she realized she was in big trouble.

Donna stormed into Susie's room and yanked the computer's plug completely out of the wall socket. "I'll teach you!" she raged as she grabbed the laptop off the tiny desk, raised it above her head, and sent it crashing loudly to the floor. The screen shattered into shards of broken plastic. Donna kicked it with the toe of her shoe and stomped on it with her heel. "I'll teach you to ignore me!"

Susie cowered as a clenched fist hovered in front of her nose like a hammer. "Nobody ignores me! Do you understand? Nobody ignores me!"

Donna stormed from the room as fast as she'd entered and left Susie there alone, crying, shaking with fear. The message was perfectly clear: Although this time the computer had suffered the damage, the next time Susie herself would be the sole target of her mother's rage.

She collapsed atop her bed, sobbing. This was so unfair!

Her mother ruined the computer, a gift from her father. It was as if Donna had deliberately resented him so much she looked for an excuse—any excuse—to destroy his gift.

Susie stayed in her room, waiting for her mom to come back for a second round of shouting. It didn't happen, and she began to suspect Donna intended to let her brood on an empty stomach. Shortly after nine, she heard her mother tell thirteen-year-old Sean that it was past his bedtime. Sean knew better than to argue, and Susie heard her brother's footsteps in the hall as he went to his room and prepared for bed.

Not long after that, she heard the back door open and close. Waiting just long enough to be certain her mother had left the house, Susie risked a quick raid on the refrigerator. She piled three pieces of Swiss atop a slice of whole-wheat bread, added a slice of tomato, and grabbed a Mountain Dew. Then she returned to her own room and wolfed down the sandwich.

An hour later, she had cried herself to sleep.

She was totally unaware when two burly men wearing ski masks stealthily entered her bedroom. She barely noticed the pinprick on the side of her neck that injected enough Ketamine to knock out an elephant.

The men wrapped her limp body in an oriental carpet and carried her out to a nondescript van parked on the street two houses away. Then they went back into the house for her brother.

Sean McMichaels felt a tiny sting on his neck like a mosquito or maybe a spider bite, and he slapped the air as he tried to wake up. He felt woozy, light-headed. The room spun and turned upside down just like the world had that day last summer when he'd spent his entire month's allowance on sugary cotton candy and stomach-churning carnival rides.

He sensed someone stood next to his bed, and he tried to turn to see whether it was his mother or his sister. But it became too much of a bother to keep his eyes open.

Strong hands grabbed his shoulders. Another pair took hold of his ankles. As if in a dream, he tried to squirm away or scream. But none of the muscles in his body wanted to work.

The boy barely fit inside a carpet. At thirteen, Sean was three-inches taller than his sister.

The two men carried their package to the van and shoved Sean inside. One of them climbed into the back where a third stood guard. The other closed the rear doors, joined a fourth waiting in the front seat of the van, buckled his own seat belt, and signaled the driver to start off down the street as if they were in no particular hurry.

Within minutes they were speeding northeast on the Thornton Freeway. They were already half-way across Arkansas before Donna McMichaels Waterson reported her children missing.

* * *

"I'm looking for Bob McMichaels," Jerry told the sheriff's deputy. "He's a friend of mine."

"Your name?" asked the deputy.

"Jerry. Jerry Walker. Is he okay?"

The deputy made Jerry wait behind a yellow plastic crime scene tape stretched across the entrance to the cabin court parking lot. He moved away, spoke into a hand-held radio, waited for a response, and motioned Jerry inside the perimeter.

"He says he knows you. He's inside the office with the sheriff. You can go on in."

"Is he okay?"

"Go in and see for yourself."

The sun was just peeking through the trees to the east as Jerry walked across the debris-strewn parking lot. Two of the cabins had been completely destroyed by fire, and two others were so badly damaged that they needed to be torn down.

The office itself had been spared, although the place reeked of smoke.

Bob sat nursing a cup of coffee at a kitchen table, surrounded by an old man, a gray-haired woman, the sheriff, and several firemen. The old woman looked like she'd been crying.

"You okay? I heard there was a fire. I came to see if I could help."

"I'm still thawing out," Bob said. "But I'll be fine once I warm up. The real damage was to Hilda and Arvin's property."

"What happened?"

"Someone wanted me out of the way. They torched my cabin in the middle of the night when they thought I was asleep."

"Someone deliberately tried to murder you?"

"Yeah. They tried, but they didn't succeed."

"I'm glad you're okay. Do you know who tried to kill you?"

"No. I heard them, but I didn't see them."

"Do you think it was the same ones who tried to kill you the other night?"

"What do you know about that?" demanded the sheriff.

"Only what Bob told me. I almost ran into him and some half-frozen woman during the big snowstorm the other night. He said some guys tried to shoot him and plowed into the woman's car while they were chasing him. He asked me to give him and the woman a ride to a nearby house, which I did. Later, I gave him a ride to this motel. That's all I know."

"That so?" the sheriff asked Bob.

"Pretty much. Jerry and I looked for the wreckage of the woman's car and the vehicle the men were driving, but we couldn't find anything in the storm."

"Where you from?" the sheriff asked Jerry. "You don't live around here, do you?"

"I came up from Illinois to hunt deer with some friends."

"Then you won't mind showing me your hunting license. You do have a license, don't you?"

He handed a real Wisconsin hunting license to the sheriff. The Colonel believed in establishing viable covers for operatives in the field. Jerry had been supplied with Wisconsin hunting licenses, Illinois driver's licenses, and valid insurance cards.

"Thank you, Mr. Walker," said the sheriff, returning the license.

"I borrowed a warm truck from a hunting buddy," Jerry told Bob. "When you're ready to leave, I can give you a ride anyplace you want to go."

"Tom Groves is picking me up at noon."

"We can save him a trip. Let me drive you to his place. It's on my way. Besides, I need to talk to you about something."

"Okay, then. Give me a couple of minutes to finish my coffee and wash up. I'll meet you at the truck."

Jerry walked back to the truck and called Steve on a satellite phone the Colonel had given him that worked because it didn't depend on nearby cell phone towers. Steve had joined two other men in a tail vehicle where they could watch from a safe distance, and Steve picked up on the first ring.

"He's alive. You missed him with the fire."

"That guy has more lives than a cat."

"I'm driving him back to the Groves place. Once I deliver the Colonel's message, I've blown my cover. "

"We're on you."

"Are the packages secured?"

"We have them. "

"Keep them safe. I'll pass this phone to McMichaels so he can verify we have the packages and negotiate an exchange. I'll stay with him until the exchange is complete."

"We'll stay on you."

"Here he comes. I'll be in touch."

Bob ducked under yellow police tape and climbed into the truck. "You look different," he said. "And you sound different. What happened to change you?"

"It's a long story," Jerry said, turning the truck around to head up SR 13 toward the county turn-off. "I don't understand everything yet."

"You said you wanted to talk. Go ahead, I'm listening."

"I know you don't trust me," Jerry said. "I also know you think I'm connected with the men who tried to kill you. Well, you're right. I am connected with the men who tried to kill you."

"Why are you telling me this?" Bob's right hand slipped into one of the pockets of his parka.

"I was sent to tell you that people I work for hold your children hostage. They took Susan and Sean from their Texas home sometime during the night."

"You bastard!" Bob's hand came out of the pocket filled with gunmetal. He flicked the safety off.

"Shooting me won't get your kids back," Jerry said calmly. "I'm just the messenger. And right now I'm your only hope of getting those kids back alive and safe. So put the gun away. We've still got a lot to talk about."

"What do you want?"

"What I want and what the people who have your kids want aren't the same. You probably noticed I've changed a bit in the past few days. Well, I've changed a lot, and I'm still changing. Last week, I wouldn't have given a rat's ass if your kids lived or died. Now I want to see you get your kids back safe and sound."

"Keep talking," said Bob, lowering the pistol but not putting it away.

"There's a satellite phone in the glove box. Take it and keep it turned on. When the phone rings, answer it. The person on the other end will give you the details of conducting an exchange."

Bob opened the glove box and found the phone.

"It connects directly via satellite. They have the number and they'll call when they're ready to talk. Meanwhile, there's nothing you can do but wait."

"Who are they?" Bob asked. "You know them. Can they be trusted?"

"They're a big organization. The man running this operation is a guy named Delacroix. We call him the Colonel. If you back off and do what he tells you, you might get your kids back. But I wouldn't bank on it. The Colonel doesn't like loose ends."

"Where will I find this Colonel Delacroix?"

"He's got a headquarters just over the border in Illinois. Runs international ops out of an old factory building, tied in with government and commercial interests in every part of the world. Lots of high-tech stuff for command and control. Don't even think about trying to get to him. He's got an army at his beck and call, and he'll know you're coming before you even get close."

"Why me? Why go after my kids to get at me?"

"The Colonel likes to keep a low profile, and you've been asking too many questions. He has to stop you from asking the wrong questions of the wrong people. Since you won't just roll over and die, he has to find some way to induce you to back off before you attract too much attention."

"There're not just coving up the killing of Ellen Groves?"

"No. They've got 24/7 surveillance on the house and the people in it. They've been watching the place for weeks and they're still watching."

"Why?"

"I used to think it was stupid to hang around just watching. I thought it was stupid to kill the old woman, too. But now I know there's more involved than you or I imagined, and we have to do something to stop this insanity before it's too late."

"You sound like Aunt Anna," said Bob.

"I'll take that as a compliment."

"Then you have changed." Bob shoved the gun back inside a parka pocket. "What the hell happened to change that cocky kid into a grown man who can accept compliments?"

"I died," said Jerry.

"You what?"

"I died. And then I was reborn."

"You got religion?"

Jerry chuckled. "Something like that. Only it's not the standard go to church and get converted kind of religion. I was touched by an angel—a real angel, not some beatific man or woman wearing wings. Or, maybe she did have wings, I don't know because I couldn't see. All I do know is I was hurting so bad I wanted to die, and then this angel's voice said she could take my pain away if I let her, and I let her. I've been changing every day since. It sounds crazy when I tell it, but that's what really happened. It's like I'm not alone anymore. She's still with me, inside me, healing me and helping me to be a better person. That really does sound crazy, doesn't it? But it's true."

Jerry turned off Highway 13 onto the county trunk.

"The reason you couldn't find your snowmobile or the two wrecked cars is because the Colonel mobilized half-a-dozen clean-up crews to dispose of the evidence."

"How many people does he have in place up here?"

"Too many to try to take out. Unless we had a whole army and even then I'm not sure we'd win. There are three men in a Jeep Eagle on our tail. Another six are on surveillance around the entrance to the Groves property. Maybe a dozen teams at the base camp. All total I'd guess forty to sixty men, well-trained and heavily armed."

"And who pays for all that? Where's the money come from?"

"Beats me. I never worried about the money part."

"How do you get paid?"

"I get a check once a month mailed to my Rockford post office box from a company in Florida. It's a real company that does travel and tours. I'm supposed to be a travel expediter, whatever that means."

"Ever heard of a company named XIIMI?"

"No."

"Neither had I until yesterday. I'll bet you a month's pay that XIIMI is the money behind your travel company."

The phone Bob held in his hand rang. He pressed the answer button and raised the phone to his ear. "I'm listening," he said.

"We have something of yours," said a male voice. "Two somethings."

"I know what you mean."

"Good. This is what we expect in exchange, and it's non-negotiable. Do you understand?"

"I understand."

"You will file a voice report with G2 that you have determined Ellen Groves was accidentally run over by a hunter. The driver panicked and disposed of the body when he discovered he'd hit a woman and not a deer. You found no evidence of any kind of conspiracy. You are closing your investigation. You are also requesting that your previously approved leave be reinstated. Tell them you have already picked up your children and will file a detailed report when you return from vacation. Is that clear?"

"Yes."

"When we're assured you've complied, we'll arrange for your children to join you on vacation. Use the phone you now hold—and only this phone—to complete all transactions. Is that clear?"

"Yes."

"We'll be in touch." The caller ended the transmission.

Bob left the phone on standby and placed it carefully in his breast pocket. "They want me to file a false report," he said.

"Do it. They'll monitor your e-mails and phone calls, so don't try to trick them. What's a false report compared to the lives of your children?"

Bob dialed the G2 operations center at the Pentagon Annex, selected the appropriate option, entered his ID and password, and recorded his report. He also requested that his leave be reinstated, effective immediately. He stated that he and his children would be vacationing for the next two weeks, and he would file a detailed report when he returned to duty at the end of his leave.

As soon as he ended the call, the phone rang again. It was the same voice on the other end.

"Keep the phone with you. We'll make arrangements for exchange when we're ready."

"I did my part. When can I ...?"

The line went dead.

"What now?" he asked Jerry.

"Now we talk to Aunt Anna. We have a lot to do if we're going to get your kids back alive and save the world in the process."

CHAPTER TWENTY-SIX

Weiss swung the axe and felt vibrations in both his arms as steel connected with something that felt more like rock than wood. The tree shuddered and shook but neither split nor fell. The thin birch—a miserable excuse for a tree—should have fallen from the first blow.

But still it stood.

As the men watched in awe, the gash in the wood began to disappear. Within seconds, any evidence that the tree had been struck was gone. Weiss raised the axe again and whacked the side of the trunk in the same place. Within seconds, the tree had healed itself.

"Son of a bitch!" said the American.

"You want to try?" asked Weiss, offering the axe to the American.

The American took a step back, hefted the woodsman's axe above his shoulder, and put his entire weight into the swing. This time the trunk cracked.

Before the tree could work its healing magic, the American swung the axe again. The crack widened, and the tree threatened to topple.

As the American hefted the axe one more time, a bolt of lightning arced through the night sky. Multiple prongs of radiant energy struck both the blade of the axe and the tree trunk simultaneously. The axe blade melted, and the tree disappeared.

In place of the tree, there stood a scattered pile of rocks.

Only one man—the Italian—noticed a big black bird, a huge raven with outstretched wings, leave a heartbeat before the lightning flashed. The raven swooped off to the north.

"We found the Seita," said Weiss.

"But where's Santa Claus?" asked the American.

"On his way to the North Pole," said the Italian, only half in jest.

* * *

Biegolmai felt his hold on the World Tree loosen with each successive blow. He was an old man, and he was tired. In the old days, he could have chanted Jojks for three days and three nights non-stop.

But the old days were gone, and so was the energy that youth possessed and old men did not.

Though he had lived through many previous lifetimes, each incarnation ended exactly the same way. Just at the time one's mental acuity peaked, the body's physical vitality ebbed. The Great Work took its inevitable toll, and it seemed as if nature would never allow one person to know how to do and to be able to do at the same time.

Biegolmai Davvii had spent years—lifetimes—honing mind, body, and spirit to perfect synchronicity. For one brief, shining moment during each incarnation, he came very close to being what he knew he was meant to become.

And then his body began to fail him. It happened every time, regular as clockwork. No matter how much he managed to learn in a succession of lifetimes, the flesh always failed.

Oh, he knew ways to repair the body when it was injured or sick. And he knew ways to prolong the inevitable deterioration of the body for years and even decades. But the day inevitably came when the body didn't respond the way it was supposed to. Some cell in connective tissue broke down or died; the mitochondria malfunctioned and one nerve cell out of ten billion failed to fire when stimulated; or cells failed to regenerate fast enough to replace cells that had decayed. It was nature's way of telling you it was time to move on. Biegolmai knew the end of this life was just around the corner.

But not yet. Not tonight.

"I have miles to go before I sleep," he repeated to himself as he winged over the top of the world. He hadn't been to Wisconsin in ages. He prayed that he was up to the long journey.

*　　*　　*

Lokesvara Sailendravarman paddled a small boat down the Tonle Sap—the Great Lake of central Cambodia—and traversed one hundred and ninety-two miles, all the way from the village of Siem Reap down to the capital of Phnom Penh, in less than twenty hours.

He boarded a commuter flight at Pochentong airport, arrived in Hanoi just in time to connect with the weekly Aeroflot jet to Moscow, caught a British Airways jet from Moscow to London, and arrived at Chicago's O'Hare on an American Airlines 763. The flight from Heathrow to O'Hare took slightly more than nine hours.

After passing through customs, the Buddhist monk rented a dark blue Toyota Prius at the airport's international terminal, drove to a clothing store in nearby Schiller Park, quickly purchased suitable clothes and shoes and a warm winter overcoat and a broad-brimmed hat to cover his shaved head. He exchanged his conspicuous orange robes and sandals for street clothes in the store's dressing room.

Within half an hour, he was northbound on I-90 heading for Wisconsin in the Prius.

Lokesvara Sailendravarman had once been the humblest of monks at the ancient Hindu and Buddhist temples near Ankor Wat in northern Cambodia, and now he served those same temples as an esteemed Lama whom it was said embodied the reincarnated spirit of a Bodhisattva named Manjusri. During the Pol Pot regime, he had convinced the Khmer Rouge they had nothing to fear from a humble monk who loved his fellow man and showed compassion to all. He proved it by feeding them and tending to their wounds and even praying for them. He was allowed to live amongst them, working side-by-side with the common folk who farmed the fertile flood plain around the Great Lake, and they allowed him to teach the dharma to children and novitiates at local temples.

Lokesvara became known, over time, as the guardian of the land, and it was said that he possessed great powers of protection and prosperity.

During the monsoon season, when flood rivers of the Meikong caused the Tonle Sap river to reverse and swell the great lake to nearly twice its size, local residents believed Lokesvara had intervened with the spirits to provide a good harvest. Lately, however, the ancient ecosystem showed signs of weakness as a direct result of commercial timbering enterprises in various parts of the Meikong.

Many of the old-growth forests that were essential to protecting the watershed had already vanished, and the future of Tonle Sap and the lifestyles of millions of people in southeast asia were now threatened.

Then, two nights ago when seven of the eight guardians of the watchtowers were attacked and five of those seven were no longer able to communicate, Lokesvara knew he would be targeted, too. It was only a matter of time.

So he left the safety of the temples and the simple life of study and contemplation, and Lokesvara Sailendravarman—also known as Manjusri Bodhisattva—once again returned to the real world to battle the forces of evil.

While paddling down the Tonle Sap to Phnom Penh in a dugout carved from the trunk of a single tree, Lokesvara's spirit connected with the World Tree. He shared his thoughts with Biegolmai and La Curandera, and they agreed to meet in person and combine their powers at the site of one of the few remaining old-growth forests, a place in northern Wisconsin Lokesvara knew well.

CHAPTER TWENTY-SEVEN

Ashur viewed the recent trophies he'd collected. With five of the eight guardians out of the way, what could the three remaining do that'd make a difference? It would take four or more adepts—spiritually progressed to the brink of godhood—to stop the destruction of the spirit world. Two had to be male, two female, to balance polarity.

Of the remaining three guardians, assuming La Curandera had survived, two were male and one female. Unless a hidden female guardian existed somewhere he didn't know about, his manipulations were irreversible.

But the empty spaces in the freezers reminded Ashur his collection was incomplete. He wanted those missing heads so badly he could actually taste it.

All his life, and in all remembered previous lives before this, he'd felt a burning need to possess knowledge and power. These trophies represented the greatest knowledge and power available, and he was three short of having it all. That there could be one person left anywhere who knew more or could do more than he, was more of an abomination to Philip Ashur than eating pork was to devout Muslims or orthodox Jews.

Ashur had to acquire the heads of Biegolmai Davvii and Lokesvara Sailendravarman to complete his collection. Although he could accept the fact that La Curandera's flesh had been annihilated by the volcano's eruption, it still galled him that nothing remained to prove his superiority. Her death was a hollow victory without a trophy to add to his collection.

But, with the abyss blocking the way to the spirit realm, there was no place for her spirit to go, and so he had won, after all. Within 72 hours of her death, her spirit would be scattered by the winds.

Unless she found a new abode within the physical body of another spirit who was willing to share its vehicle.

Everything in existence had a resident spirit, including rocks and water, fire and air. It was difficult, but not impossible, to share a vehicle with pure elemental spirits. It was easier to share with living things.

Trees and birds were preferred by wandering spirits, because the spirits of trees and birds were usually willing to share, and trees and birds offered superior perspectives to the surrounding world than rocks, insects, or cows.

One could always take possession of a human vehicle, of course, provided the subject was willing to allow possession or unable to put up a fight. Ashur had never lowered himself to refuge in anything but another human, having possessed hundreds of unsuspecting people during interims between rebirths. But tree-huggers found such actions so reprehensible that none of the guardians would ever think of possessing the body of another human unless that person specifically asked. Guardians preferred to return to the spirit world between lives, and that's what they would attempt to do now. Only now that the way to the spirit world was blocked by the abyss, their spirits would perish. Their brilliant flames would wink out like starlight entering a black hole or candles snuffed by an ill wind.

Ashur concentrated all his energy on Biegolmai and Lokesvara. Now that they had been warned they were his next targets, they would be difficult to find.

He locked his trophies away, and entered the sanctum sanctorum of his inner office. There, he lit incense, removed his clothing, and entered trance.

Somewhere in the world were the spirits of the remaining guardians, and Philip Ashur would search until he found them.

*   *   *

Aunt Anna welcomed Jerry with open arms.

Diane was surprised to see him return Anna's hug. She was even more surprised when he removed his cap and revealed his new growth of snow-white hair.

"I've brought a mutual friend with me. She's come to help. Soon, two others will also join us, Biegolmai and Lokesvara."

"The last of the guardians," explained Aunt Anna. "Jerry has brought the spirit of La Curandera to us in his person. Biegolmai and Lokesvara are still alive and on their way here. The rest of the guardians, like Ellen, have been killed and their spirits held captive on this side of the rift."

"You have La Curandera with you?" asked Diane. "Where?"

Jerry tapped his heart. "Inside me. When she brought me back from the dead, she became a part of me." He related what happened in South America, the volcano's explosion, La Curandera's promise to take the pain away. "I allowed her spirit to enter my body, and she changed not only my broken body but also my mind. I see things very differently now than I used to. I'm no longer the man I once was."

Then he told them about the kidnapping of Bob's children.

"Oh, no," said Diane, rushing to Bob, hugging him tight. "What can we do to get your children back?"

"We wait," said Bob. "That's all we can do."

"Let us help," offered Aunt Anna.

"I appreciate your support. But this is something I'd better do alone."

"Don't be a fool," said Jerry. "They'll kill you *and* your children. You know they can't let you live with all you know about them."

"What else can we do?"

"When you go to get your children, allow us go with you in spirit," said Aunt Anna. "We may be able to protect you, or at least warn you of imminent danger."

"I don't see how you can protect me."

"Oh, Bob," Diane said, "just agree. Say you want us to go with you in spirit." She put a hand on his chest. "You do want me with you, don't you? I can go with you, if you ask me. I can go anywhere you go."

"I don't want you to get hurt."

"You still don't understand. My body will stay here where it'll be perfectly safe. But my spirit can accompany you, if you agree. I want to be with you. Do you want me with you?"

"She can't help you unless you ask for her help," said Aunt Anna. "We all want to help. But we can do little without your permission."

"Of course, I want your help," said Bob.

"Good," said Diane. "Then I can go with you in spirit?"

"In spirit," said Bob.

"And the rest of us?" asked Aunt Anna. "Can we go with you too, in spirit? Do we have your permission to help?"

"Yes," said Bob. "You can go with in spirit."

"Then," said Aunt Anna, "when the time comes, you will have our help."

"Ask, and it shall be given unto you," said Jerry.

Sheila and Tom came down the stairs from the second floor, their faces flushed.

"I saved you a trip," said Jerry. "I picked Bob up at the motel."

"What the fuck happened to you?" asked Tom. "Your hair, your face, everything about you is different. You look like you've been to hell and back."

"In a sense, I have." He offered Tom his hand. "I'm not the same person you met a few days ago." After shaking hands with Tom, he offered his hand to Sheila. "I'm glad to see you up and walking."

"Do I know you?" asked Sheila.

"We met the night of your accident. You weren't looking as healthy then as you do now. I'm glad to see you've recovered. By the way, my name's Jerry."

"I'm Sheila."

"Take good care of her, Tom. She's really very special. You've been looking for each other a long time. I'm glad you found each other again."

"How do you know that, Jerry?" asked Tom. "The other night Sheila was unconscious. How do you know so much all of a sudden?"

"La Curandera helped me to remember my past lives. You and I soldiered together twice that I remember, and Sheila was part of your life in both incarnations."

"You really have changed," said Tom, amazed. "How did you meet La Curandera?"

Jerry told him everything, including his own part in Ellen's murder.

"Do you know who ordered the attacks on the guardians?"

"My orders came from Jack Delacroix. I don't know who he takes his orders from, but it's somebody who knew or obtained the identities and locations of all eight guardians. Only an ascended master would know."

"Or someone who acquired the knowledge of a master without ascending himself," said Aunt Anna.

The north wind brought the sound of gunfire. "Hunters," Diane said. "Deer season opened today."

"That's automatic weapons fire," said Jerry. "Hunters don't use fully automatic weapons."

He joined Tom and Bob as they rushed outside. Diane, Nancy, and Anna followed. Violet and Sheila stayed inside the house.

More rapid-fire bursts sounded from the direction of the road. "Delacroix's men?" asked Bob, and Jerry nodded.

"They're not shooting at us," said Bob.

"Look!" said Diane, pointing at the sky.

A magnificent bird with a wing-span of nearly four feet sailed into view above the tree tops at the far edge of the forest. It was the biggest raven any of them had ever seen.

"Why are they taking pot shots at a bird?" asked Bob. "They're giving away their position by wasting ammo on birds."

The raven swooped down between the trees as another burst of automatic rifle fire ripped branches from the taller pines. Showers of pine needles, splinters, and snow cascaded down.

"The Colonel figures you already know about his men, so he's not concerned about giving away his position," said Jerry. "But he wants that crow awfully bad."

The majestic bird danced among the trees, swerving in and out as if he were taunting the hunters to waste lead. Another hail of bullets took off additional tree tops as the raven dipped out of sight.

"Did they get him?" asked Tom. "I don't see him."

"There!" pointed Jerry. "He's all right!"

The black spot grew in size as it approached, coming straight in toward the house like a 737 lining up along a runway, dropping its tailfeathers and stretching out its talons. Below the treeline now, it was out of sight of the riflemen on the road and the sound of gunfire abruptly ceased.

With its wings stretched out on both sides like open arms, the bird touched down on snow. In the blink of an eye, the raven disappeared.

In its place, stood an old man whose long, white beard was even whiter than the snow.

Santa Claus arrived early this year.

*   *   *

Ashur located Biegolmai soaring over Canada. It was obvious where he was heading. Ashur would tend to him later. There was still plenty of time.

Lokesvara, too, was on the move. Ashur managed to track him from Cambodia to Viet Nam. But the Buddhist monk entered meditation and separated spirit from body. Ashur wasted valuable time tracking his spirit while his body flew in the opposite direction.

By the time Ashur realized the trick, it was too late to track Lokesvara and still be able to stop Biegolmai from reaching Wisconsin. Ashur returned to his own body, allowed precious minutes to lapse while reacclimatizing himself to the here and now, and when he called Delacroix to order the men stationed near the Groves property to shoot down any large black birds flying overhead, Delacroix wasted additional minutes asking for clarification.

In retrospect, Ashur realized how crazy the order sounded to an ordinary mortal. "Shoot every damn blackbird in sight. Just do it, Delacroix. Don't ask why." Finally, Delacroix realized that Ashur was serious.

When he returned to tracking Lokesvara, the monk had managed to mask his trail so Ashur again followed false leads. It wasn't difficult for an adept to do. Simply visit battle sites where the restless disembodied spirits of men killed during war lingered. Some spirits—the spirits of soldiers killed in battle or persons unexpectedly killed or murdered before their time—never advanced, never went on to the spirit realm. They remained tied to the land they had fought over or the places where they died.

In parts of Viet Nam, for example, where many people had died suddenly and senselessly, restless spirits abounded. To try to follow the trail of one spirit through such chaos was impossible. By the time he muddled through the chaos and picked up Lokesvara's trail again, the old man's spirit had already reunited with his body in America. Ashur returned to his own body. He now knew where Lokesvara was heading.

Did he have time to stop him from getting there?

CHAPTER TWENTY-EIGHT

The cell phone in Bob's pocket rang.

"Your children are waiting for you," said the voice on the line. Bob could barely hear due to static. Something interfered with the signal, but he cranked the volume and listened intently.

"These are your instructions: leave now. Walker will drive you. Turn left on the county trunk and continue northwest until we tell you to turn. Someone will be following you. When we're certain you've complied with all our instructions, we'll call to provide additional directions. Is that understood?"

"Yes," said Bob.

"Then leave now. We expect to see you on the road within five minutes."

Bob put the phone in his pocket and grabbed his parka and gloves. "Jerry, you're the designated driver. We're to turn left on the county trunk within five minutes. They'll phone with additional instructions."

"Good luck," said Tom. "Watch your back."

Diane kissed Bob on the cheek. "I'll be with you in spirit. So will Nancy, Anna, and Violet."

Bob and Jerry rushed to the truck. They were northbound on the county trunk four minutes later, and a Dodge Ram pulled onto the road behind them and followed at a discrete distance.

"I recognize the guys tailing us," Jerry said. "They'll hand us off to another team as soon as they've made certain no one else is following."

"They sure make it difficult for us to contact anyone," said Bob.

"These people don't want witnesses. They'll string you along for awhile until they're assured there won't be any. Then they'll reel you in and kill you."

"What about my children?"

"They'll kill them, too."

"So this is just a wild goose chase? A set up? They have no intention of letting me see my children?"

"Oh, they'll let you see your children. They went to great lengths to make it look like you abandoned your post here to go to Texas to kidnap them. Their aim is not only to get you out of the way, but to discredit anything you may have said. It's called plausible deniability, and they've set up a scenario that'll make you look like a divorced father who went off the deep end and made up all kinds of wild stories before you took the lives of your children, plus your own. They've used similar tactics before. Works like a charm."

"Then you think my kids are still alive?"

"Sure. They'll want you to be there when they kill your kids. Not only does it look good at autopsy that your children died just before you did, but there are hardasses who work for the Colonel who want to see the helpless look on your own face as you watch them die."

"You used to be like that, didn't you?"

"Yes. I used to be like that."

Jerry said it so matter-of-factly that Bob didn't know what to think. It was as if he had accepted what he'd been was necessary to become the man he was now.

The phone in Bob's pocket rang.

"Turn right at the next intersection," said the voice. Bob relayed the message, and Jerry turned right at the crossroads.

Five minutes later, the phone rang again. "Slow down. After you go over the next bridge, you'll see a gravel road on the left. Turn left onto that gravel road. Your children are waiting for you just around the bend."

"This is it," said Jerry, turning onto the gravel road. "Are you still armed?"

Bob showed him the Beretta. "Are you?"

"I have this," said Jerry, reaching under the seat for a tire iron. "It will have to do. I lost my back-up piece in South America."

"Why do I feel like Daniel going into the lion's den?"

Jerry smiled. "When we get out of the truck, I'll take the men in the vehicle behind us. You worry about getting to your kids."

As they rounded the bend in the road, they saw two Ford vans and a pick-up truck parked in a clearing near a frozen creek. An old house trailer, rusted and with half the windows broken out, sat at the edge of the clearing close to the trees. Any other time, Bob would have considered this an idyllic setting. Far from the nearest town and hidden from the road by pine and birch, the place provided complete privacy for hunters or fishermen looking for a getaway from civilization and its discontents. The thick blanket of snow was punctuated with deer tracks, and the caws of crows sounded from the trees.

The skies had become overcast. There was a storm brewing off to the west, and the change in air pressure was palpable. The air was not as crisp and clean as it had seemed only an hour ago. The atmosphere had become oppressive, as if something bad was about to happen.

Jerry stopped the Sierra in the middle of the road, blocking the view of the men trailing them. The truck would afford some protection against small arms, but Jerry and Bob both knew heavy automatic weapons could cut through the thin metal of the truck body like a hot knife slicing butter. The men who had fired on the raven had demonstrated they possessed fully automatic weapons and that they knew how to use them. The truck was nothing more than a minor obstacle, but it might afford Bob some concealment as he moved forward into the lion's den.

As soon as he knew where his children were, he could make his move.

The Dodge Dakota that had replaced the Ram as a tail car came to a stop ten meters behind the Sierra. Jerry opened the driver's door and walked back to the Dakota as if to talk to the men.

Or to join them. Bob still wasn't certain which way Jerry would turn when the chips were down. He opened his door and stepped outside into the freezing cold. His children were being held in one of the vans or in the run-down trailer, but he had no clue which. As he took a step forward, the phone in his pocket rang.

"Keep your hands in plain sight," said the voice on the phone. "Walk to the trailer. Your children are inside."

Bob began walking toward the trailer. He knew he was walking into a deathtrap, but he had no choice. He was willing to die to save his children. He kept his hands away from the pocket with the Beretta. He wouldn't dare fire until he knew where Sean and Susie were held. He couldn't risk accidentally hitting either of them.

"Your children are in the second van," Diane's voice seemed to whisper inside his mind. "Your children are not in the trailer. Please do not go near that trailer."

Bob looked at the tracks in the snow. As his eyes darted back and forth between the trailer and the parked vehicles, he was able to visualize the men who had made those tracks.

There were two men from the pick-up and two from the first van—but no children—inside the trailer. All four carried side arms, and one had a 30-30 deer rifle with sniper scope. Another held a 12 gauge shotgun. Two of the men carried tasers that were capable of shocking a man unconscious.

Bob didn't know how he knew those details, but he certainly did. It was as if he had actually seen the men inside the trailer, rather than inferring their presence from their footprints in the snow. He also knew that there were four men inside the second van with his children. Susan and Sean were partially sedated. They were semi-conscious, but they couldn't move or speak because their sympathetic motor neurons had been chemically neutralized with a derivative—a kissing cousin—of curare.

Behind him, there were two men in the tail car and another four waiting in trucks back at the highway.

Bob continued walking toward the trailer. If he were going to make an end run for the second van, he would have to do it soon.

"Do it now," Diane whispered in his mind. "They don't expect it, and you can take them by surprise."

Bob made his move. Decades of infantry training, daily exercise that moved muscles, bone, and sinew through their full ranges of motion, and the will to save his children from certain death all kicked in and took over. He no longer had to think about what he was doing. He just did it.

The Beretta was in his hand now, pumping deadly fire at the trailer with an incredible accuracy that pinned down all four men inside so they couldn't get off a single shot. The man with the hunting rifle took a round in his shoulder when he tried to raise the rifle over a windowsill, and another man fell with a bullet between his eyes.

The rear door of the second van exploded open, and the men inside used Bob's two children as human shields as they aimed automatic weapons straight at him and opened fire. He dropped to the ground and rolled as a hail of bullets bit into the snow all around him, kicking up a wall of white that masked his whereabouts as he reloaded the empty Beretta. With a few well-practiced movements, he ejected the empty magazine, slammed a fresh one home, released the slide to chamber the first round, and got off two quick shots as he leapt to his feet and rushed the van.

Two of the men were down, one dead and the other writhing on the floor of the van with a gut wound. Bob fired at the man behind Susan, and the man's head exploded like a ripe pumpkin.

The fourth man, seeing unstoppable death rapidly approaching, jerked Sean upright in front of him, shoved the smoking barrel of his Uzi against the boy's right temple, and grinned defiantly at Bob as his finger squeezed the trigger.

The roar in the van was deafening as Bob's entire world literally turned upside down in an instant.

*   *   *

Jerry sidled over to the Dakota and greeted the men inside.

"I did my part," he said, standing next to the driver's door. "This time the bastard won't get away."

The two men nodded assent. The driver, a man named Earl, held a .380 magnum, a Walther Bodyguard with integrated laser sights, in his right hand. The passenger, a man whose name Jerry couldn't recall, had a pump shotgun—a Kel-Tec KSG Bullpup—across his lap. Their job was to make sure Bob didn't run.

These men were professionals, and Jerry's casual conversation certainly wasn't going to distract their attention from the target. They had both of the truck's windows rolled down half-way. If Bob made a wrong move, they were prepared to raise their weapons and take him out.

Jerry tried another ploy. "Hey," he said. "The wind's picking up, and it's getting cold out here. Slide over and let me get out of the wind."

Earl gave him a look that implied he was out of his mind to even suggest such a thing.

The sound of small arms fire jerked both men alert, but Jerry's distraction had been enough to make them take their eyes off the target. As Earl raised his weapon and leaned out the window, Jerry swung the tire iron at his face, driving the cartilage of his nose up into his brain.

The other guy already had the barrel of the shotgun out the passenger window, but he couldn't maneuver the weapon around to fire at Jerry before Jerry's fingers reached the .380 that had fallen from his companion's hand.

He fired two rounds into the middle of the second man's chest. The holes made horrible sucking sounds as the guy tried to catch a last breath while drowning in blood.

Jerry walked around the truck and retrieved the shotgun. Then he ran toward the van to add his firepower to Bob's Beretta.

A sudden gust of wind swept him off his feet and sent him flying. The wind had come out of nowhere as if a tornado touched down and sucked up everything in sight.

Jerry saw the two vans and the pick-up truck swirl around in the air along with the house trailer.

Then, as suddenly as it had come, the wind simply dissipated, spitting out onto the ground the trailer, the pick-up, the vans, and a battered and bruised Jerry Walker.

He fought off the dizziness and nausea that followed being tossed around in the air like a rag doll. He'd lost the shotgun and the pistol and one shoe.

Bob McMichaels lay motionless on the ground near the battered vans. Jerry could see he was still breathing, but there was no way to tell from this distance how badly he might be hurt.

Bob's children lay on the ground near the bodies of two of Delacroix's gunmen. Neither of the gunmen appeared to be breathing.

Jerry scrambled to his feet and limped over to the girl. She was breathing but looked drugged. Her limbs acted loose and limp, but nothing appeared broken.

The boy had fallen face down four or five yards from his sister. Jerry rolled him over, expecting the worst. The boy, too, was breathing, and frozen vapor from his breath formed a thin cloud around his mouth and nose.

Jerry looked around for the rest of the Colonel's men. When he was certain there were no more left alive, he returned to Bob and the children.

One by one, he carried the three unconscious bodies to the Sierra and crammed them into the cab. Then he started the truck and turned the heat up as high as it would go.

Knowing that there would be at least one more vehicle watching the site, he walked back and combed the area for weapons. He found Bob's Beretta, the .380 Walther, and a 9 mm Glock 19. There were eight rounds left in the Beretta, four in the .380, and a full 15 in the Glock. He shoved the Glock in a pants pocket, the Beretta in a pocket of his parka, and carried the Walther in his right hand. He also found his missing shoe.

When he got back to the truck, Bob was beginning to stir.

"You're all right," Jerry said. "Your kids are okay. We won round one."

Bob opened his eyes and looked around, surprised to find himself in the truck with Susan and Sean squeezed into the seat next to him. Both kids wore identical camouflage parkas, similar to the hunting jackets the Colonel's men had worn. Bob touched their faces, checked their pulse rates, and tried to revive them.

"They're still doped up," Jerry said. "But I don't think they've been hurt."

"What the hell happened? The last I remember, some asshole was about to blow Sean's head off."

"A big wind came up all of a sudden."

"A wind? I have a wind to thank for saving my kids' lives?"

"Funny how things work out. This time it was a big wind that blew everything away. Last time it was a volcano. That makes twice this week that I've fallen out of the sky and lived to tell about it. Why are we still alive and the other guys aren't? Ever wonder about such things? I never used to, but I do now."

"It was Diane," said Bob, remembering the sweet sound of her voice inside his head. "She promised to be with us in spirit, and she was. Aunt Anna and Aunt Violet were, too. I don't know how, but somehow they made that wind when we needed it most."

"Then let's hope they're still with us." Jerry turned the Sierra around and maneuvered past the overturned Dodge Dakota. "If I know the Colonel, he's got at least one back-up team watching the road." He handed the Beretta to Bob. "There's eight rounds left. Make them count."

Bob ejected the magazine, counted the rounds, replaced the magazine, checked the round in the chamber and assessed the smooth operation of the slide. The weapon was serviceable.

They rounded the bend in the road. Now they could see there was nothing between them and the highway. But both men knew they would be most vulnerable when they turned onto the highway, and that was where the back-up team would be waiting for them. Bob recalled the vision of two men in a Dodge Ram 3500 watching the entrance to the highway from the other side of the bridge. Now he also saw, as if looking down at the highway from the height of one of the towering trees, a second vehicle—a black Chevrolet Silverado—on the east side of the entrance.

When they emerged from the side road, they would be sandwiched between two teams and caught in a deadly crossfire. If they turned right, they'd be driving straight into the Ram's field of fire with the Silverado coming from behind them. If they turned left, they'd have to pass the Silverado with the Ram behind them. Either way, they'd be sitting ducks.

"Go left," Diane's voice whispered inside his mind. "They expect you to turn right and go back the way you came."

"Turn left," Bob told Jerry and quickly pushed both children as far down in the cramped seat as he could. Then he rolled his window all the way down to allow a clear field of fire. "As soon as you hit the highway, floor it. We're outgunned, so we've got to try to outrun them."

"You saw 'em?"

"Diane showed me. There are two gunmen in a truck just outside the entrance, another two in a Dodge down by the bridge. I think they're the ones who followed us from the house. It looks like the same Dodge."

They reached the highway. Jerry didn't hesitate. Instead of slowing to make a heft turn, he hit the gas. The Sierra shot forward to fishtail across both lanes when he yanked the wheel hard to the left. All four tires kicked up loose gravel from the far shoulder before the Sierra gained traction and recovered from the spin. He kept the pedal to the metal and both hands gripping the steering wheel. He wore a smile on his face that said he was having more fun than a barrel of monkeys.

They sped past the black Silverado that was parked with its motor running sixteen meters from the side road entrance. They saw the surprised driver open his window to fire.

But they were already doing sixty miles an hour when the first shot missed, and they were doing eighty when the Silverado made a U-turn to pursue them. Rapidly moving targets were incredibly hard to hit.

Bob looked over his shoulder to see the Silverado accelerate behind them, followed by the Dodge Ram.

"Any idea where this road goes?" asked Jerry.

"No clue," said Bob.

They whipped around curves at close to a hundred miles an hour. Jerry pushed the speedometer beyond its readable limit on straightaways. Fortunately, traffic was light. The few cars that passed in the opposite direction were momentary blurs that disappeared as quickly as they appeared.

Then the unthinkable happened. A slow-moving county maintenance truck pulled onto the highway ahead of them in their lane at the same time two cars approached from the east in the opposite lane.

Jerry slammed on the brakes and the Sierra fishtailed, threatening to flip over. Bob grabbed Susan and Sean and hugged them tight as the Sierra spun out of control, slid off the road, and slammed into a snow-filled ditch that cushioned the impact.

The Silverado couldn't stop in time, plowing into the back of the county truck at over a hundred miles an hour. The pick-up folded like an accordion as the top of the cab sheered off and flew back at the oncoming Dodge Ram like a discarded piece of cardboard sailing on the wind.

The driver of the Ram—someone Jerry had identified earlier as a man named Steve—swerved into the left lane and barely avoided a head-on collision with a Toyota Celica. Steve expertly maneuvered the pick-up around the accident site and kept driving until he was out of sight.

"You okay?" Jerry asked, unbuckling his seat belt.

Sean and Susan had landed on top of Bob and trapped him against the passenger door. Snow had barreled through the open passenger window and showered them with layers of white. Bob gently brushed away the snow and pushed both children back onto the seat. Sean's lip was bleeding where a tooth had nicked the flesh, but otherwise he appeared unhurt. Susan's body was loose and limp like a wet dishrag, but she was breathing normally.

"We're all okay," Bob said. "How about you?"

"Sprained my wrist holding onto the damn wheel," Jerry muttered. "But I think I'll live."

A crowd was gathering on the road, and the county worker who'd been driving the truck called down to them. "I've radioed for an ambulance. Stay where you are until the sheriff gets here."

"Do you want to stick around and talk to the sheriff?" Jerry asked.

"I have a duty to report what's happened," Bob said. "But first I want my kids to see a doctor. Once a doctor verifies they were drugged, we'll have all the evidence we need to prove a conspiracy."

"They'll find a way to discredit you, say you drugged your own kids because they didn't want to go with you. And how do you know you'll be able to protect them in a hospital? The Colonel'll find some way to get to the doctors, or maybe a nurse or an orderly. And what happens if the sheriff sticks you in jail for attempted kidnapping? Or for causing an accident that killed two men?"

"I'll tell him what happened. I'll take him to see the corpses back at the clearing. He'll believe me then."

"Don't bet on it. The Colonel's likely got a clean-up crew already sanitizing that place. The sheriff won't find anything there to confirm your story. Instead, he'll find something that'll frame you right into jail. Remember, Delacroix wants everything you say discredited."

"What do you suggest we do?"

"First, let's see if this heap will start. It got banged up enough to kill the motor." Jerry turned the key and the Sierra sputtered and dieseled, but wouldn't turn over. He tried again. Still nothing. Jerry tried once more and this time the engine purred.

"Then we shove it into four-wheel drive. If we get enough traction, we'll climb out of this hole and hit the highway."

All four tires dug into the snow and eventually found solid ground. Jerry eased out of the ditch in front of the disabled county plow. He stopped just long enough to shift out of four-wheel drive. Behind them came shouts: "Hey! Stop!"

Somewhere, off in the distance, sirens sounded.

Jerry drove straight east for two miles, until he came to a county crossroad. He turned off the highway.

"They'll be waiting for us at the Groves place," Jerry said. "I don't think we want to go back there now. It's too big a risk."

"You've got to risk it," said Diane's voice inside Bob's head. "We need you. Both of you. Please hurry."

"Why?" Bob asked aloud. Jerry looked at him quizzically.

"We need Jerry because he has the spirit of La Curandera residing in him. And we need you—*I* need you—to provide the male energy that adds power and balance to my female energy."

"I need to get my children to a doctor," Bob said.

"Bring them here. We can do for them what doctors cannot. Trust me, Bob. Please."

"I do trust you," he said. "But you have to help us. We don't know where we are. Can you guide us home?"

"Follow the birds," she said.

"Who you talkin' to?" Jerry asked. "You sure you didn't hit your head? It sounds like you're praying. You know, like you're talking to God and He's answering back."

"Diane says if we follow the birds, we'll find our way home."

"What birds?"

"Those birds." Bob pointed to three hawks swooping and gliding like ballet dancers in Swan Lake.

"I'll be damned!" said Jerry as one of the hawks swooped in front of the truck.

One would fly off for awhile, then come back. When they arrived at an intersection, all three hawks lined up to show which way to go. When they flew to the right, Jerry turned right. When the birds flew left, he turned left.

Forty minutes later, they reached the county trunk and the hawks flew higher in the sky, making great circles.

"There are six vehicles and thirteen men," Diane whispered to his mind. "They have the firebreak blocked. You can't drive through them, so park the truck where I show you. I'll guide you through the woods on foot."

"We'll have to walk in," Bob told Jerry. "I'll carry Sean, you carry Susan. When the birds show us where to stop, pull off to the side of the road."

All three hawks landed. "This must be the place," said Jerry. He pulled completely off, slipped the Sierra into 4-wheel drive, and parked behind a stand of spruce. "They'll have to look hard to find it. That'll buy us some time if they're patrolling this stretch of road."

As Bob picked up his son, he noticed the boy trying to open his eyes. "I don't know if you can hear me, Sean," he said. "I'm going to carry you to a place that's warm and safe. Don't try to speak until we get inside the house. All right. Here we go."

Bob followed the birds, and Jerry picked up Susan and followed into waist-high snow. As they got deeper into the woods, snow cover diminished.

Both men carried their loads in a modified fireman's carry. Sean weighed maybe a hundred and thirty pounds, slightly more than a full infantry pack. Though it had been a while since Bob hiked through woods with a full load on his back, he remembered what he needed to do to shoulder the weight so he wouldn't easily tire.

Jerry, although younger and with a slightly lighter load, asked to rest after five hundred yards of trekking through snow. While they rested, the birds impatiently circled overhead.

Both children were beginning to snap out of their drug-induced stupors. Susan's eyes remained open for longer periods of time now, and Bob was fairly certain she recognized him as her father. When he kissed a finger and touched it to her forehead, a single tear formed in the corner of one eye.

If they lived through this, Bob promised himself he'd find some way to make it up to his children. He would become a real father, an important part of the rest of their lives. He would never allow them to be put in harm's way again.

"They must live their own lives," said Diane's voice. "And you must live yours. You must never stand in the way of their spiritual growth."

"I won't stand in their way. I just want to protect them."

"Then teach them what you know. Teach them to protect themselves. Life is full of dangers, and you won't be able to prevent the challenges they'll face. It will be enough for them to know that they can call upon you when they need you."

"I'll be there for them."

"You were today."

"I couldn't have done it without you. Thank you."

"Thank you for asking for my help and for allowing me to be with you."

"We make a good team."

"We do indeed. We always have."

The hawks grew restless. It was time to push on. He signaled to Jerry. Then he knelt in front of Sean, grabbed the teenager's arms, and hefted the boy onto his back. When he saw Jerry had Susan mounted in a similar fashion, he resumed walking. Sean seemed lighter somehow, and Bob remembered the old commercials for Father Flannagan's Boys Town: "He's not heavy, Father. He's my brother."

Bob changed the words into: "He's not heavy, Father. He's my son."

As they approached the house, they heard gunfire from the direction of the road. Not just random shots but sustained fire.

"Go inside the house and tell them to send help," Diane's voice sounded inside his mind. "The last of the guardians has been shot."

All three hawks took off for the road like attack planes on a strafing run.

Bob bent at the waist, shifted Sean's weight higher up on his back, and ran for the house.

Book IV

"Two are better than one; because they have a good reward for their labour.
For if they fall, the one will lift up his fellow; but woe to him that is alone when he falleth; for he hath not another to help him up.
Again, if two lie together, then they have heat; but how can one be warm alone?
And if one prevail against him, two shall withstand him; and a threefold cord is not quickly broken."

--Ecclesiastes 4, 9-12. Holy Bible, King James Version.

"And all things, whatsoever ye shall ask in prayer, believing, ye shall receive."

--Gospel of St. Matthew 21: 22. Holy Bible, King James Version.

CHAPTER TWENTY-NINE

The amount of activity in the command center was unprecedented. Although the men and women who worked for Delacroix were used to carrying out multiple operations simultaneously, this was the first time they were ordered to work with a sword literally hanging over their heads.

The Colonel made it crystal clear death was far preferable to failure. Not only had they failed six times to take out assigned targets, one of their very own—one who knew their secrets—had turned traitor and was now considered a target. Anyone else who failed to carry out the mission would likewise be considered a traitor and dealt with accordingly.

Clean-up crews had already sanitized the clearing where nine of the Colonel's top men lost their lives. The two others that died on the highway had been fitted with cover stories. No one would believe what really happened. All tangible evidence had been swept away or covered up. Their families would receive hefty insurance benefits from legitimate companies. Death certificates would show they died in traffic accidents. Funeral homes would certify cremation of remains. XIIMI's Human Resources staff would be busy for days handling all the paperwork and actively searching for suitable replacements to fill vacancies.

Meanwhile, the Colonel ordered a shift in priorities. Instead of concentrating solely on Walker and McMichaels, the men in the field were to locate and stop an oriental approaching the Groves property from the east. It was imperative that the man in the Prius be killed, his head and hands retrieved, kept refrigerated, and delivered to the Colonel ASAP.

The Colonel himself sat at a control console where he was in direct communication with his lieutenants. When the call finally came that a Prius containing a man who fit the description of the target was less than half a mile from the entrance, Delacroix gave the order to open fire. "Kill him. Kill him now."

He put the radio on overhead speakers. Everyone in the command center heard the sounds of gunfire and sundry chatter from men in the field, all of whom possessed commo gear.

Because they were under orders to retrieve recognizable body parts, field operatives employed limited firepower. The idea was to stop the vehicle with well-placed rounds, not totally destroy it and its occupant.

"We hit the guy!" came the call that elated everyone in the control room. "He's down."

"The vehicle isn't slowing," came another voice. "We nailed the driver, but the damn car keeps going like a fucking rabbit on Energizers!"

"Take out a tire," commanded Delacroix.

More gunfire. Four or five pops.

Then a scream.

"Where the hell did that come from?" asked one of the lieutenants. "Oh, shit!"

"What's happening," demanded Delacroix, his voice calm but firm. "Identify yourself, then tell me what you see."

"This is Fox Six, Sir," came the voice from the speakers. "I'm in a truck a hundred meters from the target. A bird just dive-bombed one of my men and took out his eyes. His face is slashed to ribbons. Oh, shit! Another man just went down."

"A bird?" asked an incredulous Delacroix. "Another fucking bird? What's with all the fucking birds today?"

More pops. Several in rapid succession.

"They came out of nowhere," said the voice of Fox Six. "Three birds at once. They just dropped out of the sky, hit our men, and then they were gone."

"What about the target vehicle? Did you stop it?"

"It's still rolling. We took out the tires, but it's rolling on rims. We got the entrance blocked. It won't get past us. We got men all over the place. Oh, shit! Here come the birds again!"

"Listen to me," shouted Delacroix. "You must stop that vehicle. That's a direct order. Stop that vehicle and cut up the man inside. Do you understand? I don't care about any damn birds. Just stop that vehicle and bring me the head of the man inside the motherfucking car."

"Roger that," said Fox Six.

The overhead speakers erupted in loud static. Delacroix switched bands to contact men who were enroute from the rest camp. "Fox Nine, how do you read?"

"Fox nine here. I read you five by."

"What's your twenty?"

"Fifteen minutes to target."

"Make it ten," ordered Delacroix.

When he switched back to the main channel, there was nothing but static coming from the speakers. He failed to raise any of the six vehicles with radios. Why didn't anyone answer? What the hell had happened up there?

"Get me a chopper," Delacroix ordered. "Have it ready to take off in fifteen minutes. Route all incoming radio traffic to the chopper as soon as I'm aboard."

"What shall I tell the pilot is your destination?" asked the comm chief?

"Tell him I'm going to northern Wisconsin to hunt heads," said Delacroix. "Tell him to pack a dezen ice chests. I aim to bring back a bunch of human heads, and maybe a few dead birds, too."

*   *   *

Bob entered the house and discovered Diane, Anna, and Violet sitting erect on the floor in front of the fire. Their eyes were closed, and he would have thought they were dead if he hadn't noticed the rhythmic rise and fall of breasts and shoulders with each intake and exhale of breath. All three women were completely naked. Nancy and Sheila were also sitting on the floor. But they remained dressed. Their eyes met his as he entered.

Also sitting on the floor, fully dressed and holding a round drum with brightly painted images of birds and trees and reindeer decorating the circumference, was an old man who looked like a giant Santa Claus. His eyes were closed, but his fingers tapped rhythmically on the drumhead as his giant's body swayed back and forth like a pendulum.

Tom was in the kitchen, putting on parka and mittens.

"Diane needs help," Bob said. He put Sean into a chair he moved from the kitchen table to in front of the cooking stove. Jerry gently placed Susan in one of the other kitchen chairs.

"I heard lots of gunshots," Tom said. "I was going out to investigate. Coming with me?"

"I'll stay with the kids," said Jerry. "We'll be okay now we're inside where it's warm."

"Diane said the last of the guardians has been shot," Bob told Tom. "She wanted me to ask you to send help."

"Nancy," Tom said as he and Bob crossed the living room on their way to the front door. "Diane needs our help."

"I heard," Nancy said, already unbuttoning her shirt. "You go. I'll be there in a few seconds."

Nancy dropped her jeans and pulled off her panties. She wasn't wearing a bra or shoes. She slipped her socks off and slid to the floor.

"What can I do to help, Tom?" asked Sheila. "I want to help."

"Stay here and guard their physical bodies. Keep the home fires burning until we get back." He kissed Sheila on the cheek and opened the door.

*   *   *

Sheila watched in fascination as Nancy entered trance. It looked so easy, and she wanted to try it, too. She was sure she could feel the passing of Nancy's spirit when it left her body.

Jerry was already removing his clothes as he came in from the kitchen.

"What are you doing?" she demanded, shying away from the half-naked young man. "Put your clothes back on!"

"Diane needs help," he said. He took his place in the circle. "La Curandera can help, but she's trapped inside my body. I'm going to release her spirit."

"And you have to be naked to do that?"

"No," answered Jerry, sounding impatient. "It can be done while wearing clothes, but it takes longer. Diane needs help now."

Sheila watched as Jerry closed his eyes, shutting out sensations from the outside world, going deep within the core of his being. The muscles of his face went slack, his breathing slowed, he looked like a corpse. Once again, Sheila sensed a spirit leaving the room.

Sheila Ryan was left alone with five naked human bodies, plus two teenagers in the kitchen, all of whom appeared more dead than alive.

*   *   *

Diane perched on the branch of a tree and surveyed the carnage. Fourteen men had fallen prey to the hawks' deadly attack. Male bodies were scattered everywhere, and the snow was bright red and strewn with entrails.

The Prius had come to a complete halt, wedged between two of the pick-up trucks that blocked the firebreak's entrance. The windshield and the window on the driver's side were little more than shards of jagged glass. The hood and doors were pock-marked with bullet holes.

"Is he sill alive?" whispered Aunt Anna in Diane's mind. Diane looked up to see Anna's hawk circling the scene.

"Barely. I sense his spirit still linked to living flesh."

"I see Tom and Bob driving from the house in Tom's Focus," said Aunt Violet. "They should be here within a minute or two."

"There are six vehicles approaching from the west," said Aunt Anna. "They'll be here in four minutes."

Diane willed her spirit to leave the hawk, and the next instant she was nestled inside Bob's body. "Listen carefully," she whispered to his mind. "There are more men coming. You will have less than two minutes to get Lokesvara from the Prius and into Tom's car. Drive up to the trucks that block the road, walk quickly around them to the Prius, and pull the man you find there out. Don't waste time trying to stop his bleeding. Just get him back to the house as quickly as possible."

Diane didn't wait for Bob to reply. She was back in the hawk, soaring above the trees, headed straight for the convoy of trucks and SUVs. Anna and Violet were close beside her, flying like a squadron of fighter plans in tight formation.

A fourth hawk joined their formation, and Diane acknowledged Nancy's presence with a tip of her wing.

Diane led the attack by diving directly at the lead vehicle, talons outstretched as if to claw through the windshield. An instant before impact, she sailed to the side and allowed the Jeep Wrangler to pass. The driver hadn't blinked. He didn't try to swerve out of the way, barely slowed at all, and hadn't panicked.

Anna had better luck with the third vehicle in line. The Ford Explorer swerved to the other lane, and the driver lost control of the wheel. The Explorer skidded off the pavement, hit a snow bank, and flipped over. The vehicles following were forced to slow, but they didn't stop.

Nancy made a run at the fourth vehicle, a Ford E-350 van. Either Nancy hadn't yet learned to navigate as a hawk or she had made a deliberate decision to smash into the van's windshield, because she came in much too low and much too fast to avoid a collision.

Diane winced at the sound. The broken carcass of the bird sent spider-web cracks racing across the windshield. The driver couldn't see the road ahead, slammed on his brakes without thinking, and caused a three car pile-up. The Ford F-250 pickup that was following the E-350 Econoline plowed into the back end, and a Dodge Ram 3500 rammed into the rear of the F-250.

If Nancy had deliberately sacrificed her bird, she may have been able to get her spirit out in time. If she had miscalculated, her spirit would have been trapped inside the body of the bird when it died. Nancy would have died, too.

Diane didn't have time to think about that now. There were still two vehicles remaining. They raced around the wrecks. If those vehicles arrived before Tom and Bob moved Lokesvara from the Prius to the Focus, Nancy's sacrifice would have been in vain.

The three hawks tried to catch up to the speeding cars before the bad men reached the firebreak, but Diane knew they were already too late.

*   *   *

Bob tried not to be distracted by the carnage all around him, but he couldn't help feeling he'd entered a war zone. The metallic odor of blood, combined with the stink of urine and feces that always accompanied sudden and violent death, blotted out the sweet smell of the pines.

The front of the Prius was pock-marked with bullet holes, and the windshield and two of the windows were practically non-existent. The driver's door was sprung, and the bullet-ridden body of the driver had partially fallen out of the car.

Tom picked up the driver and carried him to the Focus. Bob opened a rear door. Tom lowered the body onto the back seat.

A hard-covered Jeep Wrangler squealed to a halt less than 500 meters away, and two men with automatic weapons jumped out and began firing. A second vehicle pulled up behind the first, and two more men deployed with weapons.

Both Bob and Tom ducked behind one of the abandoned trucks. Bob passed the Glock 19 to Tom, and began returning fire with his Beretta.

What happened next couldn't actually happen. It must have been a mirage. Air directly above the Jeep Wrangler began to shimmer the way superheated air above deserted highways or desert sands does on very hot days. Only this wasn't the desert, and the day was far from hot. The men shooting at them kept firing, oblivious to what manifested.

A giant bird appeared from nowhere. One minute it wasn't there, and the next it was. Nearly four feet long, solid jet black with a bald brown head and glowing red eyes, its head was devoid of plumage. Bob thought it looked like an ugly wild turkey, except for the prominent beak, which was hooked and eagle-like. There was also a fur-like collar of white feathers around its neck. And it had talons the size of bear claws.

This wasn't just an oversized Andean condor that was completely out-of-place in northern Wisconsin woods. This was the harbinger of death.

With both wings outstretched more than ten feet and its eight talons fully extended, the bird descended, ripping one man's head completely off. It smashed another gunman hard against a tree with a casual slap of one wing.

The first men never saw their ends coming. The others did. They fired at the bird, but their bullets had zero effect.

The huge condor turned on them. It picked up one by digging talons into the guy's neck and carried him off into the sky. The remaining men watched in horror as the bird circled high in the air, its helpless victim dangling lifeless beneath those massive wings. Then the bird dropped its prey straight down on top of the remaining men before they could get out of the way.

As quickly as it had begun, it was over. The air shimmied again, and then the bird simply disappeared.

"Let's get this guy back to the house," said Tom. "He's in bad shape."

"Did you just see what I saw?" asked Bob.

"I don't know what I saw," said Tom. "It happened too fast. C'mon. Let's get out of here while we can."

* * *

Sheila watched the women return to life. One by one, spirit rejoined flesh. Nancy was the first. Her breathing became more rapid. Color came back to her face. The muscles in her arms began to twitch, and her eyes popped open.

She was already dressed when Jerry began to stir. Bullet holes that had appeared in his naked body were starting to fade. Sheila had worried when his torso jerked dozens of times, and pencil-eraser-sized holes appeared in his chest, abdomen, and arms. Blood had seeped from the wounds before they began to seal themselves.

Violet, Anna, and Diane returned at the same time. Diane looked around for her sister, and she smiled when she saw Nancy standing next to Sheila.

Bob and Tom entered the front door carrying a bullet-riddled body. They placed the bleeding man gently on the bare floor in front of the fire.

Anna, Violet, Nancy, Diane, and Jerry immediately joined hands. Tom, too, entered the circle and offered his hand. The old man, who had been softly drumming all the time that Diane, Anna, and Violet had been gone, changed his tune. Now he banged loudly on the hoop drum. *BOOM-da-da. BOOM-da-da. BOOM-da-da.*

They chanted rhythmically in a foreign language. Although it sounded vaguely like a Gregorian chant, Sheila knew from her Catholic upbringing they weren't singing in Latin.

She felt a charge of static electricity build gradually in the room, the thing that sometimes happened when leather soles rubbed wool carpets in wintertime, the same thing that recently happened when her fingers accidentally came into contact with Ashur's. The air crackled with electricity, and the tiny hairs on the back of her neck and on her forearms stood straight up like iron filings pulled toward a magnet. She shivered, not from the cold, but from the expectation of what was about to happen.

Tiny sparks, not unlike miniature lightning bolts, leapt from assembled hands. The infused energy coursed through the injured man like a blood transfusion. A halo of bluish-green light formed around his entire body, encasing him from head to toe the way a cocoon encased a chrysalis during metamorphosis.

The drumming and chanting continued for what seemed like hours. Sheila and Bob watched as the light in the room grew brighter and brighter, became as intense as the glow of a full moon on a clear night. Now the chanting intensified, as did the drumming. Louder. Faster. Building to crescendo.

When the chanting and drumming ceased, the glow continued unabated.

The group moved into the kitchen, and repeated the entire cycle with Bob's children. Then they dispersed, and the green glow diminished.

While Diane, Anna, Violet, and Jerry dressed, Bob and Tom moved the unconscious man, then the children, upstairs to beds.

Diane hugged Nancy. "I feared I'd lost you," she said. "What you did was so very foolish."

"But necessary. It was the only way I could think of to keep those men from killing Lokesvara. Besides, if I had died, you know I'd come back."

"But not immediately. And we need you with us now."

"What's done is done," said Aunt Anna. "Now we must prepare. More men will come. Next time they will not be stopped by the wards and boundaries established to keep them away. They will attack the house and everyone in it. We no longer have power to stop them."

"Is there nothing we can do without Lokesvara to aid us?' Nancy asked.

"To re-establish polarity," answered Diane, "we need guardian spirits at all four cardinal directions: Biegolmai at the north, La Curandera at the south, Lokesvara at the east, and Aunt Anna, who is not yet a guardian but the closest we have, here at the west. If the rest of us combine our powers to aid Aunt Anna, it might be enough. But we need Lokesvara to complete the circle."

"Meanwhile," Aunt Violet said, "our powers grow weaker while our adversary grows stronger. He has closed off access to the spirit world. We're limited to working on the physical plane. Soon we'll be helpless to stop him."

"How much time do we have?" asked Diane.

"Less than three days. If we do not re-establish polarity within sixty hours, the door to the spirit world will be sealed."

"What's so bad about that?" asked Sheila.

"This world will become overrun with restless spirits," said Violet. "And restless spirits can be vile, mean, and nasty until cleansed."

"Spirits who return to the spirit realms find peace," explained Anna, "They become rejuvenated, invigorated, eager to be reborn. Before they return to this world, they have forgotten the travails of past lives. They come back refreshed."

"It's impossible to explain," said Diane. "The closest we can come to realizing that experience in this world is through the practice of yoga."

"And sex," said Aunt Anna. "Don't forget sex. Sex between two lovers can be a spiritual experience."

"Yes," agreed Diane, "sex, like yoga, unites polarities. Sex between soul mates is a spiritual unification, a wholeness, that transcends time and space."

"If spirits can't cross over and they remain earthbound discarnates more than three days," said Anna, "they naturally seek ways to join with someone else, to take possession of another person's body. Anyone who is vulnerable—anyone who is lonely or depressed or whose immune system is compromised, anyone who takes certain prescription medications, uses illicit drugs, or consumes alcohol, anyone who has sex or masterbates or has sexual fantasies or sexual dreams, or dreams of any kind—may find one or more entities has walked in to possess his or her body. Multiple spirits that are not kindred spirits but occupy the same body drive all the occupants crazy."

"It's not a world you or I would want to live in," said Violet.

"But it's the world we'll have," said Diane, "unless we can reestablish polarities. There must be a male and a female guardian at opposite poles before the door between worlds will open. Biegolmai will be the north, La Curandera the south. Lokesvara will be the east, and we will be the west."

"It will take all of us to work this miracle," said Aunt Anna. "You must help also, Sheila. And so must Tom. And Bob."

"If Anna, Violet, Nancy, Diane, and Sheila combine their feminine energy, and Tom and Bob activate their feminine side," said Jerry, "perhaps it will be enough. We won't know until we try."

"And we can't try until Lokesvara regains consciousness," said Anna. "That may take some time."

"How long?" asked Sheila.

"We don't know. It could take a day. Perhaps longer."

"And what if it doesn't work?"

"Then," answered Diane, "were out of time, and not all the king's horses nor all the king's men can put Humpty Dumpty together again."

* * *

Delacroix had to fly around the property, not over it, because the pilot said there was something down there that affected the instruments, some kind of electro-magnetic fluctuation that made the gauges and meters go crazy. "It's like there's a high-tension power grid running through those trees, only I don't see any wires. Maybe wires are buried underground."

Coming in from the east, Delacroix couldn't see the devastation until the helicopter crested the last of the trees to set down on the road a few meters from the firebreak. Two experienced clean-up crews had already begun their back-breaking work, and fifteen of the sixteen bodies had been packed away into the back of a Ryder rental. The Jeep Wrangler was being winched onto a flat-bed. The two pick-ups and the pock-marked Prius were all that remained unsecured.

Delacroix was silent as two men carried the last of the human remains to the back of the Ryder. It was evident his men had put up a good fight, but it hadn't been good enough. Sixteen men were dead, and the enemy had escaped without a single fatality.

How could that be? Delacroix was aware there were forces at work here that he couldn't explain nor comprehend, but his men had been well-trained, well-armed, and well-equipped. They had superior numbers and superior firepower. They should have prevailed.

He thought for a moment about confronting Ashur directly and getting to the truth, but he realized that would only mean his own death. He suspected Ashur had a dozen other paramilitary organizations at his disposal. If he asked the wrong questions, he would disappear without a trace.

Delacroix looked down the firebreak and knew he'd have to go down there himself if he wanted answers. He found one of his lieutenants who had survived the crash on the road. The man confirmed that three birds attacked their convoy, and one of the birds flew into the windshield of a moving vehicle to cause the three-car pile-up at the firebreak entrance.

Counting the men on the clean-up detail, Delacroix had only thirty left. Two were assigned to drive the Ryder rental and the flat-bed. That left twenty-eight men to launch a frontal attack against the house.

He ordered his remaining lieutenants to organize three teams with automatic weapons. They would begin the march down the firebreak in exactly ninety minutes. He would lead them. This time nothing would stop them.

The Colonel checked his own sidearm, a modified U.S. Army .45 caliber Browning automatic with laser sights. He had a back-up .32 Colt revolver strapped to his ankle above his combat boots. He borrowed an AR-15 from one of the men, tightened the sights, aimed at a tree, and fired one round. The bullet hit the tree low and to the left. He didn't have time to properly zero the weapon by firing three three-round shot groups. He'd simply use Kentucky windage to compensate, now that he knew how the sights were set.

Walking five hundred meters down the firebreak, he reconnoitered the terrain. As long as he stepped in tire tracks, snow drifts weren't a problem. He turned back before he came in sight of the house. Now he knew all he needed to know. There were no impediments to block their advance, and they could march two abreast in the tire tracks. A column of twos was less vulnerable to snipers, should the enemy position someone in the woods to try to pick them off. One column could break off to deal with the sniper, while the other advanced on the objective.

While the Colonel waited for his men to assemble, he took stock of remaining weapons and ammunition. They had two rocket-propelled grenade launchers and a dozen rockets. Every man would carry his own automatic rifle and forty-five extra rounds, fifteen rounds to each of three extra magazines. That should be more than enough firepower to flush a hand-full of civilians from an old wood-frame house.

Besides, he had an ace up his sleeve he'd play when the time was right. Walker had placed a radio-controlled incendiary device in the kitchen of the house on the night of his first visit, and the Colonel had an UHF radio transmitter in his pocket that would work up to 200 meters from any receiver-detonator. Assuming the kid knew what he was doing when he assembled the explosives, the blast should take out the whole back half of the house and everyone in it.

Some of the men were milling around. A few were smoking cigarettes. Most were seasoned combat troops who knew what to expect.

Some of them wouldn't make it back, and Delacroix tried to guess which of them would be first to fall. Would it be that tall, skinny kid? Or maybe the ex-marine? One of his two remaining lieutenants? There was something intoxicating about putting yourself in harm's way, and that was why these men had chosen this line of work. They were all chronic risk-takers who bet their lives in the biggest game around. Winning meant God looked favorably upon you today, and He had personally picked you over someone else to keep alive.

For today, anyway.

Playing the God's-On-My-Side game was like playing Russian roulette. If you played it long enough, sooner or later you'd lose. It was, after all, a game of chance, of probability. Your number was bound to come up, the single round in the chamber with your name on it would face the firing pin. Gods were fickle. Sometimes they choose the other side instead of yours.

Delacroix didn't believe in any god. He believed in superior firepower, strict discipline, and rigorous training.

And he believed in the element of surprise.

What you didn't know could indeed hurt you, especially on the battlefield. He had always relied on superior intelligence to provide the winning edge. Superior intelligence combined with good command and control was what won battles.

The goal of the commander was to control what happened in combat. A good commander anticipated every contingency. He worked hard to make sure there were no surprises that might compromise his battle plan. Conversely, the good commander always surprised the enemy with an unexpected maneuver, a secret weapon, or the quisling in the enemy's camp.

Delacroix touched the radio-transmitter in his pocket for luck. The bomb in the kitchen of the Groves house was the unexpected maneuver, the secret weapon, and the quisling in the midst all rolled up into one.

*   *   *

Sheila felt self-conscious being naked. She knew she shouldn't be self-conscious about exposing her body, but she couldn't help herself. All of these people, with the possible exception of Biegolmai, had seen her naked before. Bob, too, looked self-conscious being naked. He had a superb physique for someone his age, and she couldn't help but admire his bulging pecs and biceps, his tight butt, his runner's quads and hamstrings. Though there was nothing sexual about what they were doing, she felt slightly aroused.

Diane talked them through the process, step by step. First, they sat on the floor with their legs crossed, their heads high and backs straight. Then they closed their eyes.

"Focus on the breath," instructed Diane. "Breathe deeply, and pay attention to the breath as it enters and exits the body."

Sheila felt her other senses shut down as she re-directed her attention to inhales and exhales, and without visual stimuli to distract her, her mind began to turn inward as if it had a mind of its own. She became aware of her heartbeat. *Thuh-thump. Thuh-thump.* As she returned her attention to the breath, she noticed her heartbeat noticeably slowing, becoming stronger and more regular. Between breaths and heartbeats, her mind jumped. First one image, then another, and yet more came unbidden to the theatre of her mind. Faster and faster they came until they became a blur of colors and flashing lights.

Diane walked them through the panoply of pranayama exercises: the bellows breath, alternate nostril breathing, and the suspension of breath. They learned to control the mind chatter—the citta of their monkey brains—that rippled the waters of the mind like an unruly west wind playing on the surface.

Suddenly, long forgotten memories returned. Sheila knew what to do next even before Diane instructed her to do it. Her mind freed itself from her body and her spirit soared.

Diane showed them how to seek refuge in the trees. Trees, too, had spirits, and they were welcoming to visitors, but you had to ask a tree's permission to roost. Next they learned to fly with the birds. Some birds had highly developed spirits, and a few had even been human in past lives. Some, especially ravens and hawks, welcomed company. But you still had to ask permission before joining your spirit with theirs.

When Diane invited Bob and Sheila to enter her own mind and share her thoughts, Sheila was surprised by the intimacy she experienced as her own consciousness merged with Diane's. Not only did she have instant access to all of Diane's memories, thoughts, and feelings, but she had access to Bob's memories, thoughts, and feelings, too. And she knew they had access to hers. She accepted them for who they were, despite their faults. And they accepted her.

At first, it was all too overwhelming to comprehend. It was as if she had three different minds, each wanting to take her in a different direction. But there were commonalities—parallels—in each of their lives that made it easier for her to identify with Diane and Bob. Just as she had been raised without a mother, they had grown up without fathers. All three had worked their way through college, concentrating on studies to the exclusion of relationships with other people. They had continued that same drive in their careers. It was as if they had known, deep down in their centers, that this day would come and they needed to prepare for it.

As her consciousness reacclimatized to the here and now, Sheila heard Bob ask the question she dreaded: "XIIMI sent you here?"

"Yes," she said, feeling ashamed of the original motives that brought her here. "They sent me to convince Tom to sell the property."

"You know the man who runs XIIMI? You've met him?"

"Yes. His name is Philip Ashur."

"That's the person we're looking for," Bob excitedly told Diane. "He's the one behind all this. He knew about the special relationship Tom has with Sheila, and that's why he chose her. He banked on Sheila being able to seduce Tom and talk him into selling. But Ashur couldn't know she'd get in an accident, be healed, and remember her past lives. His plan was spoiled by a freak accident."

"Where will we find this man called Philip Ashur?" asked Aunt Anna.

"In Chicago," said Sheila. "He's the CEO of XIIMI. His office is on Michigan Avenue, near the lake."

"Then that's where we'll find Ellen," said Anna. "He will have her remains, plus parts of the other Guardians, in his keeping. Once we reestablish polarity, we must locate their remains and free their spirits."

"Getting to Philip Ashur won't be easy," said Sheila. "The building has security on every floor. And the only way to reach Phil's offices is by private elevator."

"Once we have polarity again," said Anna, "one man—even an adept like Philip Ashur—won't be able to stop us."

Biegolmai suddenly stopped drumming. He had been drumming so long that no one really noticed the soft THUP-thup-thup of his fingers on the drumhead until the familiar rhythm ceased.

The old man raised his white-haired head to look at Aunt Anna as if he were looking through her.

"They come," he said. His heavy accent made it sound like he had said, "Day kump."

"How many?" Bob asked.

"Too many," said the old man.

Bob and Tom ran for the door to take up defensive positions around the house. Everyone else took off their clothes and gathered around Beigolmai on the floor in front of the fire.

*   *   *

Delacroix led the march himself. Two long columns, fourteen men in each, followed the tire tracks leading to the house. All wore woodland-patterned camouflage hunting parkas and similar colored wool baseball caps with earflaps. Each man carried an automatic rifle in gloved hands, and their exhaled breaths formed frozen clouds in front of their faces.

He'd briefed his men on their objective before the march began. "Kill everyone you see," he'd told them. "Everyone on the property is an enemy. Leave no one alive. Take no prisoners. If you see an old man who looks like Santa Claus, bring me his head."

Privately, Delacroix had instructed his lieutenants to cut off the heads and hands of all the males. After the battle was over, they would box the heads and fly them back to Illinois for identification and preservation.

As the Colonel rounded the next bend, he saw the clearing for the first time and felt a fresh rush of adrenalin course through his veins. There, surrounded by eighty-foot trees, stood the lone house, a big two-story wooden box, painted white, with cedar shingles on the roof and wood smoke curling from a stone chimney.

It looked so homey and vulnerable that he wanted to laugh. Taking the house should be a piece of cake. There were three cars parked near the front door. Two were completely snow-bound. Only the Ford Focus looked drivable. About twenty paces behind the house stood a wooden shed that was not quite a barn, but looked a bit bigger than a two-car garage. Delacroix deployed half his men to a frontal assault on the house, while the other half were directed around behind the shed to the rear of the building. It was a classic pincers movement that cut off all escape routes at the same time it forced the occupants to defend in two directions at once.

When all his men were in place, he'd give the order to fire at will. The wooden house, and anyone inside, would be drilled with holes in no time. Before Delacroix could give the order, however, a flock of birds flew out of the trees like javelins shot from catapults. They came straight at the men who were advancing on the house, causing pandemonium in the ranks. Two of his men fell, their faces torn off by talons. The others scattered, trying unsuccessfully to run in knee-deep snow.

The same thing happened to the group heading for the rear of the building as the birds circled and hit the second column from behind. Delacroix counted six birds—hawks or eagles, he couldn't tell—diving at his men like F-16s.

He raised his rifle, tracked a bird, and squeezed the trigger. All of his rounds went low and to the left, missing the target. He drew a bead on another bird, aiming high and right to compensate for windage.

Suddenly, a fire erupted in his left shoulder as he was spun half-way around by the impact of a pistol shot. Some son of a bitch had shot him from close range, probably from cover behind the parked cars. With his left arm dangling uselessly at his side, Delacroix raised the rifle with one hand and fired a burst at the cars. Snow flew in the air and windows shattered.

A second pistol round caught him in his right knee, knocking him off his feet and into the snow.

"Goddamn it!" he swore and pulled the Browning from its holster. He raised himself up with his right elbow and emptied a full magazine, this time at the Ford Focus.

Though he couldn't see his own men, he could certainly hear them. One or two must have gotten off a few shots before they screamed in agony, because he still heard occasional pops. But there were more screams than shots fired, and most of the single rounds sounded like they came from a Glock or a Beretta.

This had gone all wrong in a matter of minutes, and Delacroix's mind was reeling with pain and confusion. Pain was something he knew how to live with, but confusion was foreign to him. He felt an ugly darkness descend on him as his wounds bled out on the ground, and he tried to fight off encroaching despair with reason and willpower.

Where could those birds have come from? They didn't act like ordinary birds that would've turned tail at the first sounds of shots. No, these were trained birds that had been well-coached in the hunt.

Who had trained them to do such a thing? He had seen with his own eyes half his men ripped to shreds by trained attack birds! What the fuck was going on here? He ejected the empty magazine and shoved a new one into place. Once again he elbowed himself up over the snow to fire at the gunman he was certain was hiding behind one of the cars. This time he held his fire, pending visual identification of a live target.

None of his men were still standing, and all the birds had disappeared back into the trees. Delacroix's eyes scanned the horizon for movement, caught a blur out of the corner of his eye. As he rapid fired six times at the figure that fired once at him before darting behind the shed, someone else opened fire at him from the other direction.

Jesus, he thought. I'm caught in a cross-fire.

They were good, these two. Worthy opponents trained in cover and concealment. Delacroix couldn't get a decent fix on either of them, but they had him pinned down in the open. They could afford to wait it out until he bled to death from his wounds.

Delacroix holstered his weapon and used his good hand to reach into his pocket. He pulled out the radio transmitter, aimed it at the back of the house, and pushed the button. Nothing happened. He pushed the button again. Still nothing happened. Something was interfering with the radio signal.

He crawled backward through the snow. He tried the transmitter again, Still nothing. He crawled back more, pressed the button again. Still nothing happened. He continued crawling backward until he reached the end of the transmitter's range. He tried the button one last time.

The entire back of the house blew out toward the shed, sending splinters and tongues of fire leaping into the air.

As the man hiding behind the cars broke cover and ran for the house, Delacroix picked up the AR-15 and emptied his magazine.

Then, using the rifle as a crutch, he limped back up the firebreak as fast as his injured leg would allow.

*   *   *

Bullets kicked up snow all around him as Bob ran for the house. He felt a round burn the skin on his left hip as it passed through his parka, but he didn't stop. His kids were in that house, and the house was on fire.

He pushed through the door and raced past the stunned group of people picking themselves up from the floor in front of the fireplace. Clouds of thick smoke enveloped the stairway as he leapt up the stairs three at a time.

Susan and Sean were in the front bedroom, and they had survived the blast. Knowing he couldn't carry both, Bob grabbed the semi-conscious Susan, slung her over his back, and carried her downstairs and out the door.

He dropped Susan in the snow and raced back into the burning building to get his son. A half-dressed Jerry had beat him up the stairs, and the kid was battling both smoke and flames to get to Lokesvara. It looked like a losing battle, but Jerry plunged fearlessly into the fray.

Bob's eyes were burning from the smoke, but he got Sean out of the room before fire reached that corner of the second floor. Flames were licking at the stairs as he hauled his son to safety.

Diane and Sheila were helping Anna and Violet dress. Nancy and Tom came out the door carrying coats and gloves. Biegolmai looked stunned, but his gnarled fingers continued to tap their ceaseless rhythm on the magical drum.

Flames leapt from the roof, raining sparks down on the group of half-naked people as they backed farther from the maelstrom. The whole house was engulfed now, and portions of the roof were falling inward.

"Jerry's still in there!" Bob shouted to Tom. "Isn't there anything we can do?"

Tom tried to go back inside, but it seemed as if the smoke and heat stopped him half-way through the doorway.

As Tom stepped aside, Jerry emerged carrying the unconscious body of Lokesvara Sailendravarman. Both men were badly burned, but they were alive.

Just then, the roof collapsed completely. The walls pushed out, and the entire building fell in on itself.

Leaving them out in the cold with no place left to go.

CHAPTER THIRTY

A shur was in Egypt again. This time he was in ancient Egypt, long before the Upper and Lower Kingdoms were united and the land wasn't called Egypt but al-Khem, the black earth, the prima matera that gave birth to alchemy and to much of modern civilization.

In this life, Philip Ashur was a servant of Seth, ruler of the arid Upper Kingdom, the southern half of the Nile Valley. Seth's brother, Osiris, ruled the fertile Lower Kingdom. They were the archetypal Cain and Abel, sibling rivals who warred to prove the favor of the gods. Both lusted after their sister, Isis, the proverbial mother and giver of all life.

For Isis was the Nile, the magic waters that nourished the lands of both kingdoms. Without her, there would be no life and no civilization.

And no magic.

Once, long ago, there were actual people named Seth and Osiris— and Isis and Nephthys, and Horus, too—that had lived and died. They may or may not have been related to each other, though it was likely that direct blood ties existed between all of the Naqada peoples living along the River Nile, especially members of the royal families. If they weren't siblings, they were probably cousins.

Today, there was a man that had assumed the title and throne of Seth, and another that personified Osiris. These were living men who emulated the gods, but who were not yet gods themselves.

And there was a woman—a real woman—who called herself Isis, and who sat on a golden throne between the two lands and was said to be an embodiment of the spirit of the goddess. She was the mistress of He-Ka, and her title was Weret-Hekau, Great of Magic, for she alone of all beings knew the true names of the gods. He-Ka was the magic of the Nile, and no one knew He-Ka like Isis.

Seth, Ashur's master in this time, desirous to conquer the Lower Kingdom in order to unite the two under one rule and become the supreme god of both, first had to subdue Isis and the women warriors and magicians of the Middle Kingdom who stood in his way.

Likewise, Osiris, desiring to conquer the Upper Kingdom, first had to subdue, or woo, Isis.

Ashur, a learned traveler who journeyed to the valley of the Nile to increase his knowledge, already knew the Harappan and Dravidian mysteries of Mohenjo Daro. He had studied long and well in the valley of the Indus, and before that in the valley of the Yang-tse. He was well-versed in the black arts, and he knew how to transform base metals into gold.

He had heard that the people of the Nile knew how to change from humans into hawks. And he had heard they knew the secrets of rebirth and eternal life. Ashur had come to Egypt to learn those secrets and steal the power of He-Ka.

But those secrets were closely held by a small group of women fanatically devoted to Isis, and Ashur was not welcome in their presence. Not only was he a foreigner, but he was also male. And devotees of the Isis mysteries were said to do terrible things to men.

Except once each month when the moon was completely hidden. Then, and only then, were men allowed to visit the Isle of Isis. There, on an island in the heart of the Nile, the women would offer the men intoxicating brews: beer made from the finest hops and grains; aphrodisiacs made of roots, spices, and bark of the yohimbine tree; wormwood soaked in distilled pure-grain alcohol; honey mixed with the juice of poppies.

And then the women would allow themselves to be seduced.

Men from both the Upper and Lower Kingdoms would make monthly pilgrimages to the Isle, setting aside their petty squabbles and weapons for a night of wild debauchery. Sometimes a man might be allowed to stay yet another night, but never more than three. When the crescent moon reappeared, all men disappeared. The crescent moon became a symbol of renewed hostility between the peoples of the Nile.

Any man found on the island became, or so it was rumored, food for pet crocodiles or various kinds of giant cats or hooded cobras or trained hunting hawks that the followers of Isis penned near their temple's gate to guard against unwanted intrusions of men.

Actually, Ashur had been told, any man found on the isle after the moon returned was allowed to live. But live as a eunuch, not a real man, for it was only his male member that was fed to crocodiles.

Unlike the Lower Kingdom that viewed all foreigners with suspicion, the Kingdom of Seth welcomed an influx of new people and new ideas. Ashur was accepted as a valued addition to the assemblage of sorcerers that advised the King, and he was given the vestments of Thoth and the title of Sesh, or scribe. After a year-long initiation, he had access to the inner mysteries of the dark.

For Seth was the defender of the sun-god Ra in the underworld, and the followers of Seth were taught ways to navigate in total darkness. In this land between the Tropic and the equator, night and day were equals, and those who could see in both daylight and darkness had tactical advantage over those who could not. Ashur learned to love the night.

Much of his study involved contemplating the heavens. Each of the gods had his or her own star, and Ashur paid particular attention to Septit, called Sothis by the Greeks, the star that would later become known as the dog-star, Sirius. This was the star that gave birth to the gods, and it was the personal star of Isis. Septit was written in the holy language of the scribes as a half-circle above a five pointed star, followed by an isosceles triangle.

The rising of Septit on June 21, the evening of the summer solstice, marked the beginning of the new year in the Egyptian calendar, a time of great celebration. It was one of the rare times of the year that the temple of Isis on the sacred island at the heart of the Nile was open to all, men and women, royalty and commoner, and the Great Queen herself participated personally in the rites. On this night, sometime between midnight and the rising of the sun, the Queen of Heaven would pick a consort that would, the gods willing, father her first-born child.

The morning of June 22 was especially auspicious in this, the three thousandth, three hundredth, and thirty-third year before the birth of Jesus in Nazareth. According to Ashur's calculations, the positions of Sirius, Orion, and Scorpio, combined with the concordance of Venus, Jupiter, Mars, and Mercury—plus the first sliver of a new-born crescent moon—made dawn on this day the dawn of a new era. It marked the end of women's rule of magic and the beginning of male domination over the female. For shortly after midnight on the night of the twenty-first and the morn of the twenty-second of June, Isis would conceive a son who would unite the two kingdoms.

Ashur knew that Seth planned to make the journey to the island to court Isis, and he expected Osiris to be there, too. When the two unarmed adversaries met, they would have to pretend—at least for one night—to act civilized like siblings.

Whichever man Isis chose as consort would become the most powerful man in all Egypt, at least until their son became king. For it was written that the son of Isis would unite the two kingdoms and wear the combined crowns of Upper and Lower Egypt.

Ashur conceived a plan to get Osiris out of the way so that Seth would be the father of Isis' child. He bribed a scribe in the court of Osiris, exchanging forbidden knowledge for the physical measurements of the current Lord of Lower Egypt. Then he built an ornate sarcophagus to the exact measurements of Osiris' body, ensuring the box would fit the man like a glove.

For it was written that he who knows the measure of a man—either the number that defines the true name of his spirit or the exact physical measure of his earthly form—holds power over him.

Ashur went to his master and instructed Seth how to flatter his brother into the sarcophagus. If his plan worked, he would become the new High Priest of all Egypt, and the secret of eternal life would be his.

On the fourteenth day of June, Philip Ashur and seventy-two loyal servants of Seth accompanied the Dark Lord and the sarcophagus on the journey down the Nile. It took them seven days and six nights to arrive at the island.

They were welcomed to the feast by bare-breasted, perfumed, and face-painted initiates of Isis, young girls trained in the art of seduction. Any man who succumbed to their wiles would know great pleasure, and it was certain many of these girls would become pregnant even before night came and the great rite began.

Every one of these girls had, herself, been conceived on the Isle. None knew her own father, for men were not allowed to remain on the island, and each of the girls' natural mothers had indulged multiple sex partners on nights of the new moon and during solstice festivals. These were called children of the gods, and they had been raised to devote their lives to serving the gods.

Seth and his companions steadfastly refused the girls' offers of personal comfort. They could wait to indulge their passions, preserving their vital energy for later. Though the girls expressed disappointment, they were trained to respect the wishes of the gods.

For every man who entered here today was to be treated as a deity. The girls truly believed that on these special days the gods themselves descended from heaven, taking possession of the bodies of the men and women that walked the island.

It was easy, even for Philip Ashur, to believe this time and place special to the gods. As they had approached the island, he had sensed incredible energy building around them, as if all the energy of the universe were now focused on a single vortex, and that vortex was here. Something magical was about to happen, and Ashur would be at the center of it.

Common to the esoteric lore of all great civilizations, he'd learned from earlier studies at Mohenjo-Daro, was the idea that vortices shifted as polarities changed. The gateways to other worlds were constantly moving from one place to another, not only here on earth but in all the star systems of all the galaxies in the entire universe. As above, so below: all things were connected. All things were in motion. All things were constantly changing. Revolving. Evolving. As the heavens moved, so did the vortices.

In this time, 3,333 years before the birth of Christ, a vortex between worlds was physically located here in Egypt, at this particular place in the heart of the Nile, this place of polar unification. The unseen forces that drew the great male and female energies together were ripe with potentiality.

There were three temples on the island: the temple of Isis, the temple of Nephthys, and the temple of Hathor. All three goddesses represented separate aspects—generations—of the same life force: Isis was the maiden; Nephthys, the mistress and seducer; Hathor, the mother and crone.

As women progressed through the cycles of life, they worshipped in different temples, depending on their needs. The birth house was the temple of Hathor, for example, and women who were with child went there to be nourished by the Great Mother goddess. Hathor had many names. She was also known as Hat-Hor and Het-Hert. She was often seen in the shape of a cow, or as a sycamore tree. She was also goddess of song and dance and was present at all Egyptian festivals as the mistress of music, movement, beauty, and intoxication.

Amentet was another name for Hathor. It was said Amentet, in the aspect of a hawk perched in a sycamore tree, welcomed spirits to the afterlife with fresh bread and beer.

The temple of Hathor was set apart from the twin temples of Isis and Nephthys. It was both the birth house and the death house. It was where young women went when it was time to give birth. And it was where old women went when it was time to die.

Nephthys, twin sister of Isis, represented the dark and wild side of the goddess. Her temple, the western half of the temple of Isis itself, was lined with dozens of dark and secluded alcoves for seduction and lovemaking. The two halves were separated by a great hall where the merrymakers gathered and all feasts took place.

The temple of Isis faced the east, and the outer court was open to the stars and the morning sun.

Two important rites would be performed during the festival: the Great Rite in the temple of Nephthys during the seventh and eighth hours of the night (1-2 AM); and the Rite of Coming into the Day in the temple of Isis during the twelfth hour of the night (5-6 AM). Nephthys was the goddess of the night, and Isis was the goddess of the day. Each had her special time and place.

242 · PAUL DALE ANDERSON

The real women who had assumed the roles of the goddesses in this lifetime looked like true sisters, although Ashur knew that may merely be an illusion fostered by similarities in cosmetics and costumes. Hathor, Nephthys, and Isis all looked the same to him, and even native-born Egyptians had difficulty telling them apart.

But there were differences, mostly subtle; and Ashur soon recognized the unique personalities of Ellen Groves, Sheila Ryan, and Diane Groves emerge from the temporal beings that contained eternal spirits choosing rebirth in this time and place. He'd encountered their spirits before in his travels, and he wasn't surprised to meet them again here in this auspicious time and place.

They feasted together in the great hall during the second hour of the night, the Hour of She Who Knows How to Protect Her Consort. Ashur and the 72 co-conspirators he had brought with him supped with Seth near the southern end of the huge hall, while Osiris and his retinue dined on the opposite side. There were forty-two groups of men between them, plus hundreds of serving girls and dancers. It was impossible to move around the room without bumping into someone's half-naked body.

All the serving girls and exotic dancers were bare-breasted, as was the custom. The serving girls wore beaded belts around their slim waists, and their bare pubes were shrouded only by tantalizing veils of multi-colored beads that jingled like tiny bells as they moved around the room. Men, too were bare beneath their kilts and from their kilts up, except for the elaborate mantles decorating their upper chests and shoulders. All those present at the table, men and women alike, were provided perfumed cones of ox tallow and myrrh to wear on their heads. As the cones slowly melted from body heat, the heady scents of myrrh and musk coated the hair and masked body odors better than any 21st century deodorant.

The priestesses, seated on raised platforms on the west side of the hall, wore plain sheaths of the finest white cotton linen that clung to the shape of their bodies. Conical breasts peaked out between two thin shoulder straps that held the sheath up but did little or nothing to cover bare flesh beneath. There were nine priestesses, three for each of the goddesses. They ranged in age from early teens to late twenties.

Midway through the feast, the three goddesses made grand appearances in physical form, entering from behind a veil on the east side of the hall, preceded by twelve-year-old virgins shaking sistrums in unison. First came Hathor, Lady of the House. Then came Nephthys, Lady of the Night. Finally, Isis, Lady of the Morning, appeared through the veil.

They were magnificent in their splendor. All three were freshly bathed and shaved, every hair removed from their flawless bodies as part of an elaborate ritual of preparation, and their bare skin sparkled with rich oils, refined fragrances, and tiny flakes of pure gold. Their eyelids and painted-on eyebrows glowed with brightly-painted colors that sparkled and glittered like jewels: Hathor black, Nephthys red, and Isis green. They wore slitted sheath dresses, tied immediately below the breasts with a sacred knot called the tyet, revealing their hairless limbs and sexual centers as they walked or sat upon their thrones.

The throne of Isis, flanked by the thrones of Hathor and Nephthys, was in the middle of a raised platform. The thrones, elaborately carved wooden chairs inlaid with precious gold, silver, and lapis lazuli, were placed on a three-foot-high platform of painted baked clay, and the floor and sides of the platform were decorated with symbols of the women's mysteries and paintings of reeds and trees and birds. Everyone in the audience, therefore, was forced to look upwards as each goddess took her seat on the raised platform. Everyone was expected to look up to the Goddesses, and so they did.

Each woman wore a unique crown on her shaved head, symbolic of her dominion. Hathor—Ellen Groves—sported the head and spread wings of a vulture wrought in silver; Nephthys—Sheila Ryan—a golden falcon; and Isis—Diane Groves—a hawk, its eyes inlaid with brilliant red rubies. Hathor's necklace was silver, inlaid with precious stones. Nephthys wore a collar of pure gold, and Isis had above her breasts a golden mantle layered with hammered silver, lapis lazuli, amethyst, jade, and inlaid rubies.

Between each woman's breasts lay a golden ankh—the symbol of life and the eternal life-force—dangling from a hammered-gold chain fastened around their necks.

Ashur could feel sexual tension on the Isle rising to a fevered pitch. Even one such as he, trained in the secrets of polarity, was not immune to its subtle effects, especially when three of the most beautiful and desirable women in the world had entered the feast to seek consorts. Everyone expected that three lucky men would intimately partner with a living goddess from midnight to dawn, and every man present wanted to be one of the lucky three.

Ashur sneered at the foolish belief that fathering a child— especially fathering a child bore by the living embodiment of a goddess—would assure one's immortality. Of all those present in this room, he alone—with the possible exception of the three women on the raised platform—knew the true paths to immortality. Fathering a child was not one of them.

The rituals tonight that celebrated the recurring cycles of nature—the cycles of birth, death, and rebirth—represented but one small part of the Mysteries of Isis. Though the Egyptians knew every spirit was inherently immortal, they recognized the body that housed the spirit as mortal and subject to decay. It was said the Mysteries of Isis, a vast storehouse of arcane lore collected by middle-eastern and African women over countless millennia, taught how to assure the vehicle of birth and rebirth would be one the initiate freely chose. If one could somehow plan in advance where and how she'd be reincarnated, then one could leave signs for her spirit to recognize—a kind of déjà vu—in the next life.

Rather than start over as a blank slate, one could pick up practically where she or he left off in a previous life.

Later tonight, while others were fornicating, Ashur planned to steal away to underground crypts beneath the temple. The seven underground crypts contained not only vast storehouses of knowledge, they were also the place of initiation into the Mysteries of Isis. To navigate the crypts, one needed a guide.

No one but priestesses of the goddesses, and their female initiates, possessed a clue where the secret entrances were located. Ashur devised a plan that would get him in and provide him the precious time he needed to study the Mysteries. In a vial in a tiny pocket sewn within his kilt, he'd secreted a minute amount of pure soma, obtained at great cost from a Dravidian sorcerer in Mohenjo Daro. Soma was more than merely a powerful aphrodisiac. When mixed with alcohol, it was the ideal date rape drug of the fourth millennium BC.

Anyone ingesting soma did everything you asked them to do, and they remembered nothing afterwards.

An induced hypnotic somnambulism with post-hypnotic amnesia.

Ashur needed to select one of the priestesses and get her to accept a drink. Since there were nine priestesses, three for each of the goddesses, finding one susceptible to his wiles and charms should be no problem.

As the feast progressed, many male guests displayed obvious signs of intoxication. Some of the men staggered from the banquet hall with dancers or servant girls, adjourning to dark alcoves for private interludes. Open flirtation between the sexes was not only permitted, it was encouraged.

Before the night was over, everyone was expected to have coupled with someone, sometimes several someones.

Ashur made his move. His target was a priestess of Hathor, a woman in her late twenties. She was older than most of the other priestesses, though no less beautiful.

Other men had approached the younger priestesses, but none had offered this formidable-looking lady a drink. His timing was impeccable. The woman was obviously wondering if she would have to spend the night alone, an unappealing prospect for the priestess of a fertility goddess.

"I bring the Lady a drink from the far-away lands of the Indus valley," said Ashur, offering her a chalice filled with wine and laced with soma. "It is said this drink enhances wisdom and understanding. I offer it most humbly to one who is already wiser than I."

"I have been to the valley of the Tigris and the Euphrates," said the priestess. "And I have seen the isle of Cyprus. But the valley of the Indus is beyond the mountains, too far to travel by bark or charriot. I welcome a taste of their culture."

Ashur watched the lady test the drink with her tongue. "It is sweet like honey," she said, pleasantly surprised. She took a deeper drought. "I adore the taste."

"I thought you would," said Ashur. "If it pleases the lady to meet me after the midnight hour, I will share more of the secrets of the Indus in private."

Her eyes sparkled as she agreed to meet him in one of the alcoves. "Tonight you are mine, in body and spirit," said Ashur, implanting the first post-hypnotic command that bound her to his will until the effects of the drug wore off. "No other man may have you. We shall meet at midnight and share secrets."

"At midnight," she whispered. "In the third alcove."

He left the chalice in the woman's manicured hands and returned to his seat at Seth's table. "You chose well, Sorcerer," said Seth. "She is Hathor's high priestess, keeper of women's secrets. Her name is Purple Lotus Flower. She is said to be most passionate when you bite her left ear."

"I will remember that, my Lord."

"It is time to begin the games," said Seth. He sent his envoy to Osiris with a proposition. In an alcove on the west side of the island, near the banks of the Nile, stood a beautiful bejeweled sarcophagus, crafted of the finest Lebanese cedars, inscribed with the symbols of resurrection and eternal life. This was Seth's gift to anyone who perfectly fit into the sarcophagus. If any man at Osiris' table fit the sarcophagus exactly, he could take it home.

They waited until several men had left to try. Then, one, by one, Seth's henchmen went to stand watch at the sarcophagus. When Osiris heard that many men had tried but none fit the sarcophagus, it peaked his royal curiosity. He wanted to try the sarcophagus himself.

It would be, Ashur knew, a perfect fit for the Lord of the North, and he would sink into the plush lining to find himself trapped inside.

But Osiris showed kingly restraint. It wasn't until he had first let all his men try it on for size that he finally went to see this amazing sarcophagus for himself. He left his men to drink and flirt with the dancing girls. He got tipsily to his feet and staggered toward the alcoves.

Seth and Ashur followed. When they arrived at the alcove containing the sarcophagus, Osiris was openly admiring the beauty of the carved wood and the lavishly painted symbols.

"We have craftsmen in the north who can do much better," boasted the Lord of the Lower Kingdom, obviously enamored by the excellent craftsmanship. "Nevertheless, it is a fine piece of work."

"It is yours, brother, if it fits you," said Seth.

"Why do you not keep it for yourself?"

"I have gained some weight," said Seth, rubbing his belly. "Perhaps too much beer and not enough exercise. It no longer fits me."

"Ptah!" spat Osiris. "I run every day. You should run, too, brother. A king must stay in shape if he wishes to stay in power."

"That is good advice, brother of mine. Perhaps in the morning, if you are not too worn out from a night of lovemaking, you and I could have a race."

"I can make love all night long and still beat you in a footrace," bragged Osiris.

"Then we shall race in the morning. Meanwhile, let us see if you can fit into the sarcophagus, brother. Perhaps, you also have gained weight."

"I am as fit as a teen-ager," said Osiris. "Watch and know what a true king looks like on the day of his resurrection."

Osiris backed into the sarcophagus and crossed his forearms over his chest. As his form nestled perfectly into the fine linen lining, a smirk crossed his face. "See?" he said. "It is a perfect fit. The sarcophagus is mine."

"Indeed," said Seth, signaling to the four men who held the lid. They slammed the lid on the coffin while six others hammered nails into the wood. Still others brought pitch to seal it shut, cutting off air from entering. The curses and screams from within, muffled by linen glued to the inside of the sarcophagus cover, ceased completely after a minute or two.

"Cut the body into fourteen pieces," ordered Seth. "Throw all but one into the Nile. Save his cock that I might keep a trophy in remembrance of victory. For it is written that one's enemy cannot enter the afterlife so long as any part of his body remains a trophy. Have the embalmers wrap his penis in the finest linens, preserve the flesh forever with myrrh and pungent spices, and seal it in an earthen jar with the air removed. Let no corruption touch this trophy for ten thousand years."

The 72 men went about their work while Seth and Ashur returned to their seats in the great hall. "Is it true, my Lord," asked Ashur after Seth was seated, "that embalming a man's vital part will keep his spirit from entering the afterlife?"

"Of course, it's true," said Seth, sipping a tincture of wormwood and quickly washing the bitter taste down with beer. "Why else would kings take such elaborate measures to ensure their predecessors are embalmed and mummified? It's not because kings are nice guys and wish their predecessors well in the afterlife. Uh uh. It's really because we're afraid their spirits will come back to challenge our authority. Embalming preserves the body and traps the spirit inside."

"Such a thing is possible?"

"Ask your lady when you meet her tonight. As high priestess of Hat-Hor, Purple Lotus Flower can tell you more about the resurrection of the ka and the ba than can I. It is said that only she, and the priestesses of the three temples, know the true secret of the ba. It is also said that your lady and her friends can send their spirits into birds, and that the hawk of Horus is sometimes possessed by the spirit of Hathor, or Isis, or Nephthys. But enough of this talk. Let us drink and make merry. For tonight I will bed the Lady Isis, and—the gods willing—make a child that will someday rule the two kingdoms."

Ashur glanced in Purple Lotus Flower's direction and found her looking at him with a strange mixture of lust and devotion in her eyes, eyes no longer able to focus. Many of the guests had already paired up with girls and left the banquet hall. Ashur knew it was time to claim his own prize. He stood up and walked across the room with a smile on his face and anticipation in his heart.

Suddenly, he found himself back in his own body in the XIIMI building in Chicago, and his link with the past was but a fading memory.

The emergency telephone that connected XIIMI with Delacroix's field operations was ringing off the hook.

CHAPTER THIRTY-ONE

They built a fire in the sacred circle and huddled together for strength and warmth. Susan and Sean were finally awake. Susan regained consciousness first, rubbing sleep from tear-filled eyes. She was startled to find herself outside in snow-covered woods. Only the familiar face of her father kept her from totally freaking out.

"You're okay, honey," Bob reassured her. "You and Sean are with me."

"Where's mom?" She looked around but didn't see her mother. "How did we get here? I don't remember."

"What's the last thing you do remember?"

"Mom went out. I was in my bed. I think I fell asleep. How did I get here?"

"It's a long story, and I promise to tell you all I know. But, first, I want to check on your brother. Can you stand up?"

She tried her legs. She was unsteady at first, but she managed to stand and walk without difficulty. Sean was already sitting up and looking around when Susie and Bob sat next to him.

"Hi, Dad," said Sean. "Mom said you weren't coming."

"I couldn't go to visit you, so you came to visit me. I'm glad to see you, son. How do you feel?"

"Light headed. And I'm hungry."

"Me, too," said Susan.

"We'll get you something to eat as soon as we can."

"Where are we?" asked the boy. "I see snow! Are we going camping or skiing?"

"We're in Wisconsin. Right now we're camping. I promised to take you camping, didn't I?"

"You always promised to take us camping. This is the first time you ever did."

"Who are all these people?" asked Susan.

"Friends," said Bob. He motioned Diane to come over. "Diane Groves, this is my daughter Susan, and this is my son Sean." Diane hugged each of the children and asked them how they felt. "Hungry," said Sean.

"My sister Nancy went to the Nelson farm to fetch food and blankets," said Diane. "She'll be back within an hour or so. Can you wait that long?"

"I guess," said Sean.

Bob introduced Sheila and Tom to the children, then Anna, Violet, and Jerry. When Sean saw Biegolmai, he asked the old man where Rudolph was.

"I left the reindeer at the North Pole," said the shaman with a twinkle in his eye. "They have to graze and rest until solstice. I made this trip all by myself."

"Solstice?" asked Sean.

"Christmas," said Bob. "Solstice is another word for Christmas."

"Where I come from, "said Biegolmai, "we call it Yuletide. The sun all but disappears for three days before and three days after the solstice. The morning of the 25th of December is the first full dawn. We celebrate by dancing around big outdoor bon fires that light up the sky all night, and we greet the sun when the first glimmer of sunlight appears on the horizon. We have a good time. You must come visit us some solstice."

"You aren't really Santa, are you?" Sean asked suspiciously.

"What do you think?" asked Biegolmai.

"I don't believe in Santa," said Sean. "He's just a lie parents made up to get kids to act good because all kids want presents at Christmas."

"Let me tell you a story," said Biegolmai. "It's a true story, not like lies you've been told about Saint Nicholas. Once upon a time, in a land far away, there lived an old man. He looked a lot like me, but he couldn't possibly have been me because this story takes place long ago, long before either you or I were born. This old man's job was to make sure the sun rose every morning. It wasn't a hard job, once you knew what to do. The only hard part was learning all the things that had to be done to keep the earth in its orbit around the sun, all the other planets and moons in their proper orbits, and just the right balance of light and dark, north and south, east and west, male and female positioned throughout the universe. He studied long and hard for many years, and eventually he came to know what needed to be done. But by then he was a very, very old man, and he found he could no longer do everything himself. So he trained someone to help him, someone younger who could carry on after he died. And the old man did die, and the helper eventually grew old himself and had to train a new helper to help him. And then the first helper died, and the second helper grew old and so he trained a third helper. And this tradition has carried on since the beginning of time up to this very day. Do you know how I know this is a true story?"

"No," said Sean. "How?"

"Because I saw the sun rise this morning. And I knew that if the sun rose as it was supposed to, then someone was still on the job. Somewhere there was a helper doing what helpers do, and all was right with the world. But suppose, just suppose, that something bad happened to the current helper and he died before he could train a new helper to carry on. What do you think would happen? Would the sun still rise?"

"That's silly. The sun would still rise in the morning. Nothing would change."

"Are you sure?"

Sean looked a little nervous. There was something about the question that struck deep at his inner core, casting doubt. Finally, he said, "Yes, I'm sure."

"Well," said Biegolmai, "it's just a story. Stories don't have to be true. But, like the story of Santa Claus, there may be some part of truth hidden within. Much of what we believe is based on half-truths. Stories that have been around for a long time have tiny kernels of truth embedded somewhere. It's often difficult to sort out what's true and what isn't—to sort the chaff from the grain. Because the story of Santa Claus has been around for a very long time, there must be some truth to it. What that truth is, I can't say. That is something you must learn for yourself."

"You talk funny," said Sean.

The old man laughed. "English is not my native language."

"No," said Sean. "I mean, you talk funny like some of my teachers in school."

The old man laughed again. "I like you, Sean. You listen to your teachers, do you?"

"When I can understand what they say. Sometimes they say things I don't understand."

"He's only thirteen," said Susan. "He doesn't understand a lot."

"And how old are you?" asked Biegolmai.

"I'm fifteen."

"You have learned much in the two years since you were thirteen, haven't you? So, too, will your brother learn much. I envy both of you. You still have the joy of learning, of experiencing and experimenting, without the awesome responsibility of having to put your learning to work. But today you, too, must become helpers, and we may ask you to do things beyond your current understanding. We will not lie to you, but we may not be able to explain everything to your satisfaction."

"You want to involve my kids in this?" asked Bob. "Why?"

"They are here, and they are already involved. Is it not better that they know what we are doing?"

"What *are* you doing?" asked Susan. "And why are we here?"

"We are going to save the world," said Biegolmai. "And you are here to help. Are you willing to help insure the sun will rise again tomorrow?"

"You gotta be putting us on!" said Sean.

"No," said Bob. "I don't think he is. You might as well both sit down by the fire, and I'll try to explain what's happened to you and what we need to do."

Bob began with the kidnapping, explaining that the men who had abducted them had also drugged them. That was why they couldn't remember anything that happened the last few days. He told them about the gun battles, not only the firefight when he rescued them, but also the recent battle at the house. Both children said they had a hard time believing they could have gone through all that without remembering anything. Biegolmai pointed out that if they couldn't even remember how they got all the way from Texas to Wisconsin, why did they find it so difficult to believe they weren't able to remember people kidnapping them, drugging them, shooting at them, and trying to blow them up with a bomb?

As Bob continued to explain all that had happened since the death of Ellen Groves, Susie started crying. Diane put her arms around the girl and tried to comfort her, but she wouldn't stop crying. Her whole world had been turned upside down, and she didn't know what else to do but cry.

Sean, on the other hand, was intrigued. He expressed disappointment that he couldn't remember any of the details of the kidnapping or the high-speed chase. He said he looked forward to helping in the next gunbattle, and he asked his father to show him how to shoot a gun.

When Jerry suggested that Sean might want to help him gather up weapons from the fallen attackers back at the house, Sean eagerly agreed. Bob protested he was too young to see such carnage, but Jerry and Biegolmai both insisted that Sean help them collect weapons.

"He needs to know death is real," said Biegolmai. "Unless he learns this lesson now, until he sees death for himself, he cannot understand the true value of life. Or the value of death nor the value of rebirth. At thirteen, a boy feels invulnerable. But in the hours to come, he may face death himself. Do you think he—or any of us—is out of danger? If you do, please think again."

"Remember the first time you witnessed death in combat?" asked Jerry. "It made you realize you, too, could die. After that, you knew you had to kill or be killed. Sean needs to confront death before he has to make the decision himself, or he'll think it's all just a game. That's what it was like for me. The first time I killed, it was like a game. Bang! I win, you lose. Game over for you, but I get to go on to the next level. It never occurred to me death was real and I could die, too."

Bob relented and let Sean go with the two men. Susan finally quit sobbing, but she had a look on her face of total disbelief. All this must seem a bad nightmare to her, and he suspected his daughter expected to wake up any moment and find herself back home in her own bed.

Lokesvara was still unconscious, but his wounds were rapidly healing. Diane said he should recover within a matter of hours.

"Will he awaken in time to help stop the abyss from spilling over into this world? And will he be strong enough to make a difference?"

"Even with all of us pooling energy," she said, "it may not be enough. We need at least four guardians to reverse polarities and set things right. Our best hope is to free a spirit Ashur holds hostage. If we go where he's keeping their remains and release even one of the five guardians, we could then invite that spirit into our bodies and restore polarity."

"Do you think Ashur will attack us again?"

"Of course, he will. Isn't that why Jerry and Biegolmai are gathering up guns and ammunition?"

"Maybe we should attack him first," Bob said. "Watch Susie for a few minutes, will you? I'm going to find Tom and see if any vehicle is drivable."

"You're going to Chicago to confront Ashur? Are you sure he's there?"

"You said yourself we don't stand a chance unless we free one or more of the guardians he holds hostage. Time is running out, and I don't know if we'll ever get another chance."

"I want to go with. Take me with you. Please."

"No, love," he kissed her. "I'll need Tom because he's a trained combat officer, Sheila because she knows Ashur and how to find him, and Jerry because he knows how the enemy operates. But you're needed here."

"Then let me go with you in spirit. I can help. Really, I can."

"Yes, of course. I always want you with me in spirit. Can you do the same thing you did last time? There's no problem with distance? It's more than six hundred miles to Chicago."

"As long as I have your permission, I can accompany you anywhere."

"Good. We won't have any other way to communicate, no radios or telephones, no e-mails or instant messenger. When we find what's left of your mother, we'll need you to tell us exactly what to do."

"I'm not sure what to do. I'll have to talk to Aunt Anna and Aunt Violet. It won't be enough to just take possession of the remains. You'll need to find a way to transform them, break them down into their essential elements. I know fire works best. If there's enough heat, the transformation is instantaneous."

"Then what happens?"

"Since a guardian's spirit has already progressed through the requisite cycles of rebirths, her spirit may come back immediately in any form it chooses. There's no wandering of the wasteland waiting for spirit guides. The guardian *is* a spirit guide."

"Then," said Bob, "all we need do is locate your mother's remains and burn them?"

"If the fire is sufficiently hot to transform the remains to ash. Scatter the ash to the winds and the guardian's spirit will be free."

"And any one of the guardians will do? It doesn't have to be a male or a female?

"Pure spirit is androgynous, both male and female. In alchemy, the androgyne is the precipitate of polarity. It encompasses both male and female energies. Spirit takes the form of the gender needed to create balance."

"Then," Bob said, "we have five chances to make this work. All we need do is locate the remains of the five guardians and burn any one of them."

"I'll stay with Susie while you and Tom find a car. Hurry. We have less than ten hours to reverse polarity. Twelve hours from now the abyss will spill over into the material world and the spirit world will be lost to us forever."

* * *

Delacroix was completely exhausted by the time he reached the helicopter. His left arm was useless, and his right leg wasn't much better. He managed to stem the flow of blood with a tourniquet around the thigh above his fractured right knee, and a pressure bandage pressed against the punctured flesh of his left shoulder. Nevertheless, he felt lucky. If that bullet had been two inches lower, he wouldn't be around to worry about anything.

But the long trek and the loss of blood had taken their inevitable toll, and he needed the pilot's help to drag his bloody body into the metal bird and belt him into the co-pilot's seat. They were airborne within minutes.

Delacroix got on the horn and ordered the comm chief to immediately alert all available personnel. "Have anyone not assigned to a critical mission redeployed to the Wisconsin project. Call Weiss and his team in from Europe. I want massive firepower assembled and ready to move when I get there. And have a doctor on the helipad when we land. Tell the doctor his patient needs sutures, two pints of O positive blood, and a knee brace."

He debated calling Ashur and breaking the bad news. He knew Ashur had access to resources that might turn the tide of battle, but reporting another failure was tantamount to Delacroix signing his own death warrant. Ashur wanted results, and now he'd failed to deliver the desired results three times in a row, he was expendable.

The only way he could redeem himself was to bring Ashur the heads of Biegolmai and Lokesvara, and that meant he had to go back to Wisconsin yet today and launch another attack. If he were successful, all would be forgiven.

If he failed, he was a dead man.

Sharp pains in his shoulder and knee helped him focus on the operational requirements of another fray. This time he'd go in with enough firepower to wipe them all off the map, and he would ensure his men were armored to survive attacks from freaky birds. He got on the radio again and talked with his logistics people. He ordered six transport helicopters, heat-seeking surface-to-air shoulder-fired missile launchers, pyrotechnics, enough weapons and ammunition to outfit an army, and Kevlar body armor with face shields and night-vision goggles for every man. When the logistics officer protested that it would be impossible to procure everything in the requisite time-frame, Delacroix ordered the man to find a way to make it happen before the chopper touched down or face the consequences. "I don't care if you have to beg, borrow, and steal to get it. Just get it!" he ordered.

"When we reach Rockford," he told the pilot, "set down on the helipad at the factory long enough for me to get out. Then I want you to proceed to the airport and fuel up. Check the bird over good, and be ready for another mission in an hour."

"We going back to the same place in Wisconsin?" asked the pilot. It was the first time he had asked any questions. It bothered Delacroix that the man, trained to follow orders without questioning, would dare to ask instead of waiting to be told.

"Yeah," said Delacroix. "Why?"

"I have to file a flight plan with the FAA. This is a commercial chopper flying in civilian airspace. It ain't like in the military where you can fly anywhere without prior clearance."

"Fuck the FAA!" said Delacroix.

The pilot didn't say another word until they were past Janesville, following the Rock River Valley southward. Then he spoke softly into his headset, coordinating landing instructions with the comm center at the factory, verifying weather conditions over Rockford. He switched bands and talked with the air traffic people at Chicago-Rockford International Airport, indicating he would land there in twenty minutes for refueling. Then he switched back and chatted with the comm center.

Delacroix dozed off. He'd lost a lot of blood, and his eyes didn't want to stay open.

Changes in the sound of rotors woke him from a restless sleep. The chopper swung to the east, lined up with Harrison Avenue, and slowed, beginning a gradual descent to the reinforced roof of the old factory.

Four men waited on the roof, waving the copter in. It seemed strange to see grass on the ground instead of snow. Delacroix felt for a moment as if he had just returned to civilization from a third world country.

He recognized two of the men on the rooftop now, his operations chief and one of the Americans he'd sent to Europe to get Biegolmai. The other two men he didn't recognize, and he assumed one of them was the doctor he'd ordered.

The pilot spoke softly into his comm set, informing the operations team he was setting down only long enough for his passenger to disembark. He briefly glanced at Delacroix, then returned his attention to the chopper's gauges and controls as he set the bird smoothly down on the rooftop.

He motioned to Delacroix that it was safe to unbuckle his seat harness, but he kept both hands on the controls and made no move to help the Colonel out of the helicopter. Two of the men on the rooftop approached the passenger side and yanked the door open. Delacroix felt excruciating pain shoot through his shoulder as the two grabbed his arms and effortlessly lifted him from his seat.

The last thing "Colonel" Jack Delacroix saw was the helicopter lifting off as the American ex-ranger placed an automatic pistol against his temple and scattered his brains to the four winds.

CHAPTER THIRTY-TWO

It was bad enough the Colonel failed to acquire La Curandera, but allowing Biegolmai and Lokesvara to slip through was unforgivable.

Unfortunately, there wasn't enough time to bring the necessary replacements into position before now. Delacroix not only twice failed to kill Lokesvara and Biegolmai, he also twice failed to eliminate McMichaels.

He had exhausted Ashur's patience and sealed his own fate.

The last straw was a brief telephone call from the American ex-ranger that Ashur had sent to Rockford to keep an eye on Delacroix, reporting the Colonel lost all his men and suffered severe personal wounds in a last abortive attempt at killing Lokesvara, Biegolmai, and McMichaels,

"In your opinion," asked Ashur, "can Delacroix complete the mission in his current physical condition?"

"No, Sir."

"Do you think you're capable of replacing him and completing the mission?"

"Yes, Sir."

"Then kill him. Shoot Delacroix the minute you see him. Do it publicly. Make sure everyone understands the price of failure."

Like any well-run organization, XIIMI rewarded performance and punished incompetence. It was the modern chief executive's duty to cultivate healthy competition in the ranks and periodically cull the herd.

The American's name was William Carter, and he was both ambitious and ruthless. Unlike Delacroix, Carter had been a junior staff officer—a real captain—in the U. S. Army in Iraq, but that was before he got caught abusing his position by torturing prisoners of war. Carter claimed he was only following orders, and his commanding officer was court-martialed when other members of his unit substantiated his claim. Nevertheless, he was given a written reprimand and transferred to the Army Reserve, a dead-end for a career army officer. Carter resigned his commission, went back to Iraq as an employee of a civilian contractor where he was subsequently recruited by a XIIMI subsidiary.

He was bold, innovative, and results-oriented. His co-workers called him "Wild Bill," and he came to Ashur's personal attention as one of six possible replacements for the Colonel. When Scagliano and O'Donnell were unexpectedly killed in Chile, he advanced to the top of the list.

And when Weiss phoned Asher with an after-action report on the debacle in Sweden, he confirmed Carter's leadership ability. "He's a bit too aggressive for my tastes," Weiss said. "But he knows how to get the job done, and that's what counts."

"Send him to me. Put him on the next flight to O'Hare. I'll book a suite for him at the Hyatt, and he and I can have a private chat."

While Delacroix was still in Wisconsin fighting for his life, Ashur briefed Carter on command and control. He made it crystal clear he had to prove capable of following orders explicitly. The first test was to observe and report but do nothing until Ashur ordered.

"I need to know you'll do whatever I ask when I ask it. I cannot and will not tolerate failure, nor can I nor will I tolerate rogue action. I give the orders, and I expect you to carry them out exactly as directed. Do you understand me?"

"Yes, Sir!" said Carter.

"Then go to Rockford and wait for my orders. I'll have a car and driver outside this hotel in one hour, and when you get to the factory, the comm chief will show you what you need to know. There's a direct line between the factory and my office. I expect you to call me if Delacroix fails to complete his current mission. When you call, I'll tell you what I want done. Is that clear?"

"Yes, Sir!"

"If Delacroix successfully completes his assignment, you will take no action and wait for further orders. If I order you to take Delacroix out, will you do it?"

"Yes, Sir!"

"If I tell you to do nothing, will you obey?"

"Yes, Sir!"

"Good. Then we understand each other. Do you have any questions?"

"No, Sir."

Ashur was satisfied he'd picked the right man. Carter was sharp. He knew he'd eventually get Delacroix's job. If it took a little longer, he could afford to be patient. If it happened sooner, rather than later, he was ready.

When Ashur returned to his office, he immediately phoned the comm chief and told him that Carter was being assigned second in command to replace Scagliano. Ashur asked the comm chief to keep him informed of the situation. Certain there was nothing more he could do at the moment, he locked himself inside his office, removed all his clothing, and regressed himself back to ancient Egypt in search of the secret of immortality.

And he'd been right on the verge of putting the final piece into the puzzle when the sound of the telephone brought him back to the here and now. Whatever knowledge gained from his tryst with Purple Lotus Flower was lost to him. There was no time to go back again; he had to move forward.

He could feel his personal power increasing exponentially as cosmic forces continued to shift. Without guardians to balance polarity at key energy centers around the globe, each of the vortices between worlds had slowly shut down. Only one vortex, centered in a circle of ancient trees in northern Wisconsin, remained active. Even if he did nothing, the last vortex would self-implode from entropy within seventy-two hours.

When Carter phoned to report Delacroix's remains had been disposed of, Ashur immediately ordered him to follow through with Delacroix's plans. "The comm chief will brief you on the status of ongoing operations. I want you to fly as many men as you need to Wisconsin and do whatever it takes to secure that property."

"Why don't we just burn them out?" suggested Carter. "We could set a few good fires. We could solve the entire problem without losing any more men."

"Do not," snapped Ashur, "burn them! I repeat: do not burn them! I want you to bring me their heads. If their bodies are completely destroyed by fire, it won't end the problem and may complicate things. Burn what remains after you've severed the heads, but I need those heads. Do you understand me? Bring me those heads! Don't fail me, Carter. Bring me those heads!"

"Yes, Sir!" said Carter.

"Do you think if it was as simple as just burning them out that I wouldn't have ordered that long ago? And forget about an aerial assault. There are parts of that land you can't fly over because your instruments won't work and your engines will cut out if you fly too low. The only way in is through the firebreak. You can drive in nearly as far as the house, but motorized vehicles won't work beyond a certain point. Neither will your communication devices. Take my word for it, there's a section of that property that can only be accessed on foot. That section also garbles radio signals and plays havoc with electronic instruments. Don't try anything fancy. Just go in there as infantry, shoot every bastard you see, and bring me their heads!"

"Yes, Sir!"

Ashur checked his watch. "You have twelve hours to complete this mission. What's the latest intel from the site?"

"We have none."

"What?"

"Delacroix took every man in with him, and they're all dead."

"You mean no one's watching the entrance?"

"Not at the moment."

"Then get some people out there right away. I want to know every time anyone goes in or out."

"Yes, Sir."

"Call me back when you have people in place. I'll expect a full report as soon as you have something to report."

Ashur slammed down the phone without waiting for Carter to say "Yes, Sir" again. Obviously, Carter didn't understand the whole situation. Someday, maybe, Ashur would fill the man in.

Meanwhile, he had a world-wide business to run. There were deals to be made, people to be persuaded, and lots of work to be done.

CHAPTER THIRTY-THREE

Bob found a perfectly serviceable GMC Yukon SLE 1500 4x4 parked, with the keys in the ignition, on the side of the road twenty feet west of the entrance to the firebreak. There were several other vehicles also parked along the side of the road, and he could see no one guarding any of them. In fact, he could see no one anywhere. When he got into the driver's seat of the Yukon and started the engine, he half-expected someone would materialize out of the woods and try to stop him. But nobody did.

Obviously, these vehicles belonged to the men who had attacked the house and whose bodies now lay scattered on the ground at the opposite end of the firebreak. At least one of those men had escaped death and made it all the way back up the firebreak, judging from the trail of blood he'd found in the snow. He'd followed that trail to where it ended abruptly at the county trunk. The wounded man had gotten into a waiting car or a helicopter, and his bloody trail simply disappeared at the edge of the plowed highway.

The Yukon purred to life, and he was delighted to see it still held more than half a tank of gas. As he eased the four-wheel-drive down the firebreak, he felt the heater kick in and was toasty warm before he reached the still-smoldering burnt-out husk of a house.

When he saw Jerry and Sean helping Biegolmai collect weapons and ammunition, he honked the horn. Sean came running, and Jerry followed. Biegolmai looked up, then returned to his work.

"Come on in and get warm," Bob called to them as he opened the passenger door. Sean slid onto the seat next to him, and Jerry climbed into the back.

"Are we going home now?" asked Sean hopefully.

"Not yet. Daddy's got to make sure it's safe for you to return home before I take you there. In the meantime, I want you to stay here and take care of your sister. Can you do that?"

"I guess. I'm not a child anymore, you know."

"No, you're definitely not a child. In many parts of the world men your age are carrying weapons and defending what they believe in. I'm going to depend on you to defend your sister. There are things I wish

I'd taught you, but you'll have to learn most of 'em on your own. When this is over, we'll spend lots of time together and I'll teach you."

"Promise?"

"Yes," said Bob, hugging his son close. "I promise."

Sean looked at his father as if he wanted to believe him, but a string of previously broken promises stood in the way.

"Now," said Bob, "I want you to promise me something. Promise me you'll take care of your sister. Don't be too proud to ask others for help. Diane and Biegolmai will give you a hand, if you ask."

"What about Jerry?"

"Jerry is going with me." he looked over his right shoulder at Jerry in the back seat. "What's the weapons situation look like?"

"We've got two dozen sidearms and a dozen semi-automatic rifles, two shotguns, and plenty of ammunition." Jerry patted his packed pockets. "I'm loaded for bear."

"We'll each take two pistols and a rifle. It'll be you, me, Tom, and Sheila. We should leave in twenty minutes. Right now there's no one guarding the entrance. If we're lucky, we'll be on the highway before they send reinforcements. If we're not lucky, we'll have to fight our way out of here."

"Here," said Jerry, handing Bob two 9 mm handguns. He reached into another pocket and brought out four loaded magazines.

Bob took the weapons. He placed one in his right parka pocket and handed the other 9 mm pistol butt-first to Sean.

"This," warned Bob, "is not a toy. It's a nine millimeter Sig-Sauer P-226, and it'll blast a hole in a man nearly half an inch wide. Don't ever point a gun—loaded or unloaded—at anything unless you intent to kill what the gun's pointing at. Always keep the muzzle pointed toward the ground or the sky until you're ready to shoot." Bob showed Sean how to move the safety on and off with one finger. Then he talked the boy through loading and unloading the magazine, and chambering the first round.

"Always keep a round chambered. When you fire the chambered round, the recoil sends the slide to the rear, ejecting spent brass and chambering the next round. Because nine millimeter recoil is significant, I recommend a two-handed stance. Step out of the car, and I'll show you how to fire the weapon."

Bob found a half-burned plank from the front porch of the house that would make a suitable target. He judged the distance to be about fifty feet from where they stood. "Watch," he told Sean as he extended his arm in a one-handed stance. "Notice I have my body turned to offer my opponent the smallest profile possible. I'll snap off the safety and bring the weapon down until the front and rear sights are aligned on the target." He squeezed the trigger and his hand jumped nearly an inch from the recoil.

"The two-handed stance offers your opponent a bigger target, but it minimizes the recoil and provides a better chance of hitting what you aim at. Always make sure your feet are spread a comfortable distance apart to provide adequate stability. Rest your weight equally over the heels and balls of both feet, and don't lock your knees." He assumed a two-handed firing position and squeezed off a second round.

"Now you try it," he said, snapping the safety back on.

Sean raised the Sig-Sauer. He seemed surprised at how heavy the loaded weapon was and how difficult it seemed to keep the sights level. He squeezed the trigger, but nothing happened.

"You forgot to flip the safety off," said Bob. "Try it again, and this time take the safety off before you aim."

Embarrassed by the oversight, Sean flicked the safety off and raised the weapon with one hand. As he brought the sights down on the target, he squeezed the trigger and almost fell backwards from the recoil.

"That round went high and wide," said Bob. "Take a two-handed stance, and try it again."

This time the round clipped the edge of the wooden board in the upper right corner.

"You're getting it," said Bob. "Try again."

Sean fired three more rounds, increasing in confidence with each shot that found its mark. Bob showed the boy how to get into other firing positions, dropping into prone or kneeling, then rolling for cover.

"Remember to keep your muzzle pointed in the direction of your target at all times. If you can't locate your target, point the muzzle toward the sky until you do. Never fire until you've identified your target."

"Even if someone is shooting at you, don't return fire until you're certain of your target," added Jerry. "You'll only waste ammunition and give away your position."

"This is for real, isn't it, Dad?" asked Sean, the realization that someone might want to kill him finally sinking in.

"It is for real. If you have to fire that weapon at a person, shoot to kill."

"Because," added Jerry, "the other guy will certainly be shooting to kill you. Don't hesitate. If you do, you're dead."

Bob showed Sean how to reload, how to clear a jam or misfire, and how to keep the pistol clean in the field. "We don't have cleaning solvent or oil, and no brushes or rods. As long as you keep the weapon dry and clear of dust and dirt, you'll be fine. Someday, I'll show you how to field strip and break it down for cleaning. But for now, you know all you need to know."

"Can I practice some more?" Sean asked.

"If Jerry will stay here with you while I go fetch Tom and Sheila. We haven't got much time."

"Go ahead, " Jerry offered. "I'll give Sean a few pointers while you get us ready to go."

Bob found Sheila and Tom and told them he'd meet them at the car in ten minutes. Then he went to say his goodbyes to Diane and Susie.

"I don't want you to go," cried Susie, clinging to her father. "I want you to stay here with me and Sean."

"I don't want to go, honey." He held his daughter close and let her sob out her fears on his shoulder. "I'll be back as soon as I can. Meanwhile, I need you to take care of your brother. Remember when you were a little girl and you learned to watch out for your littler brother? Well, now I want you to be a big girl and watch out for Sean the way you always have. Can you do that for me?"

Susie dried her eyes on her sleeve. "Why do you always have to go away?" she asked.

"To keep the world safe so you can grow up in it."

"Why does it have to be you? Why can't someone else keep the world safe?"

Bob looked at his daughter and tried to find the right words. "There *are* others doing their part, honey, but it takes a lot of people all working together to keep the world safe. It's a really big job. You have to do your part, too, you know. You have to take care of your brother. If I know both you and your brother are taking care of each other, then I can do what I have to without worrying about you every minute."

Susie thought about that. "You really have to go?" she asked.

"Yes. I really have to go."

Susie relaxed her grip on her father. "When will you be back?"

"Tomorrow," he said. "Or the day after tomorrow at the latest."

"Really?"

"Really," he promised.

CHAPTER THIRTY-FOUR

Sheila hadn't thought about a cigarette for days, not only because she didn't have any, which she didn't, but she didn't want or need them any longer.

Smoking in a car was a ritual she'd practiced religiously since her teens. Back then, it had been the "in" thing to do, and even after smoking became socially unacceptable, lighting up in the sanctity of one's own vehicle still seemed an inalienable right.

Smoking cigarettes was a power trip. Holding fire in her hand was symbolic of exerting control over one of the most powerful forces in nature.

People feared what they didn't understand. Those who pushed to ban smoking did so because they feared fire.

As a corporate attorney, she became an expert at using laws to control those she intended to exploit. According to Ashur, no one did it better than Burt Ryan's little girl.

Aunt Anna claimed Ashur had to be a very old soul, a spirit with many lifetimes under his belt. Instead of progressing to the spirit realm between incarnations, he remained in the physical world by taking possession of weaker-willed individuals, enabling his consciousness to continue, virtually uninterrupted, for longer periods than anyone else on the planet.

Biegolmai speculated Ashur had accumulated vast storehouses of knowledge, but his perspective was badly skewed. He was the archetype of selfishness and had no intention of sharing what he learned. Such a warped spirit probably viewed polarity as a threat.

Sheila tried to recall everything she could remember about Phil. The man had appeared practically out of nowhere. His personal life, if he had one, was a closely-guarded secret. It was said that Theodore Carnes hand-picked him to head the XIIMI empire, and then Carnes disappeared as if he'd ceased to exist.

What she knew about XIIMI's vast holdings she'd learned representing them in court. Besides insurance, real estate, and investment banking, they were into communications, transportation, travel, and hospitality. They owned radio, television, motion picture, and print media. They owned satellites and internet service providers. Some of the biggest hotels and resorts in the world were owned and operated by their subsidiaries, and several well-known restaurant chains, liquor labels, and grocery and drug store chains were XIIMI acquisitions. Even the designer shoes Sheila liked to wear were produced in a factory they owned in Indonesia, and the apartment she rented in Chicago was owned by a XIIMI land trust.

Ordinary people were unaware that almost two out of every ten dollars they spent went into a company that XIIMI financed, supplied, or controlled. Why did a man who already owned so much desire even more?

She was ashamed to admit she knew the answer to that question. Burt Ryan's little girl knew what it was like to have next to nothing, and when she finally began acquiring things for herself—little things at first, like brand-new underwear and clothes; bigger things later, like a nice pen and leather briefcase—she was afraid she would lose them. When her father found out she had a job that paid real money, he had taken all she'd saved away from her. He'd threatened to beat her until she handed it over, and when she refused, he carried out his threat. "You live in my house and eat my food," he'd told her, pounding with his massive fists where bruises wouldn't be visible. "Any money you make is mine."

Not only did he take her cash and waste it on booze and lottery tickets, he made her share the nice things she had already bought with her two older brothers. They took her fountain pen and briefcase, and she considered herself lucky they didn't take her clothes and underwear, too.

She didn't tell her father when she found a second job. Though she continued to pay him to leave her alone until she turned eighteen and moved out of the house, she still managed to tuck away enough to pay the security deposit and first month's rent on a cockroach-infested studio apartment in Uptown. When she left, she didn't bother to say goodbye.

But she'd always worried he'd find out about the money and take it all from her. Even today, with Burt Ryan dead and buried for eight whole years, she feared he would find a way to take everything from her. Fear was a powerful motivator.

It seemed obvious to Sheila that something similar had happened to Phil. Maybe not in this lifetime, but in a previous one. More was better, especially when you expected to lose some of it. The more you had, the more you could afford to lose.

Imagine a man who amassed incredible wealth and knowledge, and then lost it all, had it all taken away from him. Perhaps he'd been a king, and his kingdom had been invaded and he'd been unable to stop it from happening. Or perhaps he had been a scholar, his books confiscated and burned. Sheila could imagine how he must have felt.

Now imagine a man who spends his whole lifetime acquiring wealth and knowledge, and who knows he'll lose it all when he dies and will have to start over again from scratch in the next life. What if such a man were able to stick around and continue to affect the world even after he had died?

If Anna and Biegolmai were correct, Ashur accomplished exactly that. He'd learned how to keep his spirit in the world after he died. Normally, spirits couldn't wait to detach from the body after death. It sometimes took up to three days for a spirit to be completely freed of the flesh, and the spirit world beckoned to them and pulled at them relentlessly. Eventually, the freed spirit moved on to reside in the spirit realm until it became time to be reincarnated again. With reincarnation came forgetfulness, and what had been learned in one life had to be relearned in the next. Though everything learned in previous lives could be recalled in the present, the process of remembering was extremely difficult—if not impossible—without expert help.

Diane had said it was the mark of an ascended master to be able to recall all of one's past lives. When ascended masters were reincarnated, they devoted each new incarnation to helping other spirits remember.

A few devoted their lives to being guardians.

Sheila was far from an expert in spiritual matters. Her Catholic upbringing made her think of ascended masters as a lot like saints or angels. Despite all she'd seen and heard in the past few days, she couldn't even begin to understand why things worked the way they did. One moment, the concept of spirit was crystal clear to her, and the next moment it was amorphous and impossible to fathom. On one hand, it made perfect sense to her. On the other, it seemed insane.

Then she looked at Tom, sitting in the seat next to her, and she knew in her heart that she had loved him forever. She also knew that, even if they died, they would meet again someday.

Or would they? If Ashur had closed the doors to the spiritual realm, what happened to spirits now when the body died and the spirit had nowhere to go?

If she understood correctly what Diane had told her, spirits were pure energy. Though there were multiple realms—sometimes called "worlds" or "dimensions" or "planes"—that co-existed in the universe, the totality of energy and matter in all of them combined was a fixed amount, a constant. The universe was kept in balance by subtle shifts in energy between them, and that delicate balance was maintained by increasing or decreasing polarity at key points between dimensions. It was the job of the guardians to balance polarity, and the right combination of male and female energy was what allowed spirits to cross over.

Without guardians to balance the flow of energy between dimensions, would spirits be forever trapped on one side or the other?

It was almost too much for Sheila to think about. But the more she thought about it, the more she realized how important it was to find the trapped souls of the missing guardians and release them.

It was as if something in her own spirit recognized the inherent wrongness of Ashur's actions, something inside her that knew instinctively what needed to be done to set things right. She didn't yet know what cards she'd need to play in this game. But all the cards had been dealt, and she had anteed up, and the stakes were much too high for anyone to back out now.

*   *   *

Carter had twelve men, all he could get on such short notice. He planned to personally lead them to victory.

Three helicopters took off from the roof of the factory about an hour before dark, and they were loaded with weapons, ammunition, and high-tech gear to support them during night operations. Carter expected to wrap up in time to be home for breakfast.

Flying nap-of-the-earth, the choppers followed Interstate 90 north. Somewhere between Baraboo and Necedah, much like ships passing in the night, they flew directly over a GMC Yukon that was southbound to Chicago. Lost in their own thoughts, neither the passengers in the Yukon nor the battle-ready men in the helicopters paid the least bit of attention to the other.

Wild Bill Carter had always wanted to act like a general, and soon he'd have his chance. Tonight he would prove himself worthy to succeed the Colonel. Tomorrow, he would take his rightful place in the command center, directing world-wide operations.

It never occurred to him that, because of his own actions this very night, tomorrow might never come.

CHAPTER THIRTY-FIVE

Diane worried about her sister. Nancy set off through the woods for the Nelson farm more than five hours ago and hadn't yet returned. The snow was deep in places, and it was more than a mile's walk each way, but Nancy should have been back by now. Something must have happened to delay her, and Diane feared the worst.

Although they knew these woods well from their childhood, it had been years since they'd trudged through the thick undergrowth. Nancy could have tripped and broken a leg. Perhaps she tried to cross the creek that ran near the edge of the property line and fell through the ice. Worse, she might have walked into some sort of trap set by the men who were watching, and she could have been captured or killed.

Diane sent Sean and Susie to gather more firewood. Then she went to check on Lokesvara where he lay near the bonfire.

"He's healing nicely," said Aunt Anna. "All the bullet wounds have closed completely, and his lungs and internal organs have regenerated. He should be conscious soon."

"Have you heard from Nancy?"

"No, dear," said Anna. Aunt Violet, standing next to Anna, shook her head, indicating she hadn't heard from Nancy, either.

"I think we should look for her," said Diane.

She sat down in front of the fire and stared at the glowing embers. As her eyes drifted out of focus, her spirit detached from her body and flew to the trees. Within moments, she was seeing clearly again, this time through the sharp eyes of a hawk perched on one of the highest branches.

Nancy and six other women were slowly working their way through the snow and woods, a quarter mile from the sacred circle. Two of the women carried blankets in their outstretched arms, and the others carried picnic baskets filled with food and hot cider. Obviously, Nancy had taken the time to call together the entire circle of Ellen's friends.

Satisfied that Nancy was well, Diane was about to detach from the hawk when eagle-like eyes detected blinking lights far to the south. They were too high in the sky to be anything other than aircraft.

As the hawk flew from its perch to circle to the south, Diane could just barely make out three distinct shapes. There were indeed three aircraft coming this way, and they were getting closer by the minute.

She swooped back around and flew down toward Nancy and the women in the woods. Nancy looked up, saw the hawk, and waved.

Hurry! Diane urged her sister. *Move faster! Time is running out!*

*   *   *

Jerry, too, felt the urgency. He increased the Yukon's speed to eighty-five, then ninety.

Traffic doubled as they approached Madison, the state capital. Jerry expertly weaved in and out of various lanes, passing trucks and cars as if they were standing still.

Clouds began spitting heavy snow north of the Dells, and now winds picked up as even darker storm clouds rolled in from the west. Snow came down in earnest, piled up on the pavement, and gusts spread drifts across the roadway. The Yukon's wipers couldn't keep up with the onslaught.

When Jerry couldn't see three feet in front of the windshield, he slowed to eighty.

That's when he heard the siren.

Flashing lights appeared in his rear-view mirror as a Wisconsin State Patrol car materialized from the side of the road. Jerry thought about gunning the engine and making a run for it, then thought better of trying to get away in this kind of weather. He slowed down and pulled off to the right, coming to a full stop in the middle of a snowbank.

"Let me handle this," said Bob. "I've got a government get out of jail free card."

A young trooper, probably no more than a rookie, approached with an oversized flashlight in his left hand and his right hand resting on the butt of a holstered pistol. Jerry rolled down the window, and the cop beamed the flashlight directly into Jerry's eyes.

"Twenty-five over the limit is a felony in Wisconsin," said the officer. "You're under arrest for reckless endangerment. Please step out of the vehicle."

"I'm a military officer on official business," said Bob. "It's a matter vital to national security that we get to Chicago as soon as possible."

"Can you prove it?" said the cop. Bob passed his orders and ID to Jerry, and Jerry passed them out the open window to the state trooper.

"Please stay in the vehicle," ordered the trooper. Jerry watched the man battle valiantly against the fierce winds and driving snow to finally reach the warmth of the patrol car.

"Too bad it isn't Seifert," said Tom.

"Who's Seifert?" asked Jerry.

"A state patrolman who stopped us on the way up to Ma's. Bob was driving a bit too fast for Trooper Seifert's tastes."

"That was quick," said Jerry. "Cop's coming right back, and he doesn't look happy. He's armed with a shotgun. That's getting awful serious about a routine traffic stop."

"Don't nobody move," said the cop when Jerry rolled down the window again.

"What's the problem, officer?" asked Bob.

"Your orders have been rescinded. You're wanted on a federal warrant for kidnapping your kids and taking them across state lines. What did you do with them? I don't see them in the van." The patrolman raised the shotgun. "Very slowly, open all doors and everyone step out of the vehicle."

Jerry pushed the button on the arm rest that unlocked the doors. Then he pulled up on the door lever as if complying, but instead he shoved the door wide open and sprung like a cat. He grabbed the shotgun and swung the barrel at the trooper's forehead hard enough to render the man unconscious.

"Let's move," he said, slamming the door and cranking the motor. "He's got backup on the way. We want off the Interstate at the first exit."

"Exit coming up," said Bob. "Dane County Hwy V, Exit 126."

Jerry turned east on the snow-packed county road. He dropped the transmission into 4-wheel drive high speed for extra traction and maximum power. "Tom, do you know how to get to Chicago on back roads?"

"Head south and east. We want to find US 12. You should hit County N in a few miles, then turn right and head south. N should take us to 12. And 12 goes all the way to Chicago."

Snow continued to accumulate, and Jerry had difficulty seeing the edge of the road. The best he could do was crawl along at 30 miles an hour.

"Maybe it wasn't such a good idea to get on a back road," said Bob.

"Did we have a choice?" asked Tom.

"It never even occurred to me that Delacroix set me up for a kidnapping charge. After we rescued Sean and Susie, I forgot I'd been forced to tell the DIA I was taking my kids on vacation."

"That's the way the Colonel works," said Jerry. "He planned to make it look like you went crazy, drugged your kids, kidnapped them, took them to woods in northern Wisconsin, then killed them both before committing suicide. Even if you escaped alive, he'd make it look like you were guilty or crazy. No one would believe anything you told them. He figured he had you by the short hairs."

"Forget about him," said Tom. "Philip Ashur is the honcho who gives Delacroix orders. If we take out Ashur, the whole organization will crumble."

"Even if we get to Phil and manage to kill him, what good will it do?" asked Sheila. "Won't he just take possession of another body and come back to haunt us?"

"Not if we take his head as a trophy," said Tom. "And it doesn't have to be his head. Any part of his body will do. If we keep any piece of his body from transforming, his spirit can't migrate."

"Hunters mount heads of animals," said Jerry. "Cavemen once drew pictures on walls for the same reason. Native Americans donned animal masks and draped themselves with animal pelts because they thought it gave them power over the spirits of those animals."

"Is that why women value fur coats?" asked Sheila. "Mink or fox or rabbit?"

"Could be."

"Some people believe," said Tom, "that consuming the blood or flesh of an animal adds its spirit to yours and makes you powerful. Many religions have feast days where people congregate to share the flesh of fatted calves. Just think about the sacrament of Holy Communion in the Christian Church. Congregants ritually consume the flesh and blood of Christ to acquire the Holy Spirit, and they sing about power in the blood."

"If you kill it and eat it, then its power becomes yours?" Sheila shuddered. "I think I just became a vegetarian."

"Acquiring Ashur's head is secondary to finding the guardians and freeing their spirits," said Tom. "Once we release Ma and the others, killing Ashur is icing on the cake."

"I just had a horrible thought," said Sheila. "What if Ashur has eaten them? What if he's preserved their flesh inside himself?"

"Then," said Tom, "we're screwed."

CHAPTER THIRTY-SIX

P hilip Ashur opened each freezer door to be certain. The guardians were precisely where he'd left them. It was crazy to think they'd moved on their own. Visions he'd had of trophies conspiring against him must have been illusions, but they seemed so real. He needed to be certain the trophies remained inside the freezers. Had his mind been playing tricks on him again? Or had Guru Rimpoche played the trick?

It was from that ancient Tibetan Tulku, Ashur's one-time teacher, that he had extracted the secret of Pho-wa, the act of conscious dying or the transference of consciousness at the time of death. Tulku Guru Rimpoche had mastered Lung-gom, and he could send his spirit to any part of the universe at will. He practiced Tum-mo, and his body could generate psychic heat to melt even the ice outside hermitage caves in the Meili Snow Mountains connecting Tibet with China. He was a master of the Bar-do, the disembodied state between life and death, and was said to have transcended samsara, suffering caused by wants and desires of the body. Rimpoche had lived many lives and was dangerous even when dead.

Forty-two years ago, Philip Ashur had traveled to Bhutan and then to eastern Tibet to be initiated into the secrets of the Pho-wa. It was there, during seven long years of study and practice, that he learned of the Gongter, or hidden mind treasure. And it was there that he met Ellen Groves and Lokesvara Sailendravarman in their current incarnations.

Ellen was only twenty-two. She was the most beautiful woman Philip Ashur had ever seen. She was tiny compared to him, barely more than five feet tall, blonde-haired and blue-eyed. He knew he had to have her the moment he saw her.

Lokesvara Sailendravarman was tall for an oriental. He was already a Buddhist monk wearing a traditional red robe with yellow sash draped over one shoulder and tied to his waist in sacred knots, and he wore sandals made from braided straw and shredded woven bamboo to protect bare feet. Ashur had hated the man the moment they met.

They were the only three initiates of Pho-wa this cycle, and they lived and studied together in ancient caves carved out of solid rock by fast-running water from melting glaciers over many millennia.

"The body is more than a mere vehicle that can be driven by the spirit, as a bicycle or automobile can be propelled by muscles," taught Tulku Guru Rimpoche. "The body is the tool through which one may achieve enlightenment and liberation."

All four—Ashur, Ellen, Lokesvara, and Guru—sat naked in lotus. The ambient air temperature even inside the cave was well below zero. Ashur's teeth chattered, goose-bumps speckled his bare flesh, and he shivered incessantly. He felt certain he'd freeze to death.

"First," taught the Guru, "you must learn to subdue the body to overcome samsara, the terrible suffering all flesh is heir to. You must overcome your fears of illness, of aging, and of dying. Fear of losing keeps your soul imprisoned. You must rid yourself of all possessions—gold, jewels, family, friends, even a precious possession like the human body—to gain enlightenment. Here you will use the body in ways yet unimaginable to you. We begin with control of the breath, for as the breath enters and leaves the body, so is the body reborn with each intake and dies with every exhale. All sentient beings, male or female, are born with an allotted number of breaths. Learn to slow the breath, and life can be extended almost indefinitely."

They practiced meditation and various breathing exercises called "pranayama." They learned to alternate breaths between nostrils. They learned to fire up the Dan-tien—the alchemical athenar, an internal furnace near the body's exact center—with the bellows breath. Thus, they sat naked in harsh Himalayan winters and melted snow and ice with body heat.

They learned other things, too. They learned to leave the body and travel vast distances in spirit form, able to witness events in the present and the past. They learned to recall past lives. They learned who they were and what they had done. They learned to inhabit other bodies, including animals such as cats and birds and snakes. And each received a spirit guide to teach them about the spirit realm and the lives between lives.

Ashur yearned to explore the marvelous body of Ellen Groves, for he felt drawn to this woman like iron to a magnet. She became a constant distraction that interfered with his studies. Ellen seemed receptive to his bold advances, perhaps even encouraged him. They coupled in nearby caves when they had time and opportunity.

Before their second year together ended, she left the caves and returned to America because she was ripe with child. Ashur forgot about her until much later.

He stayed with Guru Rimpoche and Lokesvara and continued his studies. After seven years, he left the cave and took up residence in Hong Kong. It was in Hong Kong that he met Theodore Carnes.

*   *   *

Wild Bill swore he wouldn't make the same mistakes his predecessor made. Each of his men wore body armor and were all issued face shields, night vision goggles, automatic weapons, and at least one sidearm. They were well-equipped, highly-trained professional soldiers. Most of them had served in Iraq or Afghanistan, and they'd continued in their chosen profession after leaving government service. They were combat-seasoned troops any commander would be proud to have.

He directed a team of three to circle through the woods and approach what remained of the house from the other side. He led two teams down the firebreak and kept one team in reserve. The reserve team had pyrotechnics and grenade launchers, and they were prepared to torch the woods and everyone in it if frontal and flanking assaults failed.

Carter was aggravated he couldn't get satellite photos of the property, but for some inexplicable reason there was nothing but a blur on photos where the woods and house should have been. Likewise, communications gear failed to function adequately, if at all. So, too, did night vision goggles prove useless. He felt blind, deaf, and dumb. This was something like out of the dark ages, and he had to learn to cope without eyes in the sky or microphones and headphones or infra-red optics that kept him in constant contact with his men and the tactical situation.

Nothing happened for the first hundred meters or so. Then all hell broke loose.

Hawks, nearly half a dozen of them, swooped down and attacked the necks of mercenaries in the advancing column. Carter whirled around to find men behind him pumping blood onto the new-fallen snow. Others were firing blindly at shadows that kept coming at them again and again, along with snow and wind, knocking them off their feet and ripping off face shields to pluck out eyes. Both columns shrunk to a handful of men still standing, and most of those were wounded.

Talons hit Carter in the face, tore off his goggles and face shield, and barely missed his eyes. Both cheeks were streaming blood, and his nose was bent out of shape. Pain, unlike anything he had ever felt before, hit him like a ton of bricks. If he lived, he would be horribly scarred for the rest of his life.

Anger took control of him and he raised the M4 and fired bursts at the sky until the rifle bolt locked to the rear. He released the magazine and replaced it with another, slapped the charging handle with the heel of his hand, and fired again. But the moon was obscured by clouds, the air filled with snow driven by arctic-like winds, and he couldn't see beyond the tip of his bloodied and broken nose.

"Pyrotechnics!" he shouted into the wind. "Light up the sky, god-dammit! I need pyro and I need it now!"

He heard the "phuttttt" of a launcher sending white phosphorous projectiles into the clouds. Suddenly, the night sky lit up like the fourth of July. Now he could see hawks circling overhead, diving down at anyone still standing.

He raised his weapon and fired.

But if he could see the hawks, they could also see him. They dived down with talons extended, and this time they hit his eyes and ripped them out. Now he really was blind, blood streaming out of empty eye sockets, drenching his field jacket and quickly turning cold.

The last thing Bill Carter knew was darkness, despite the continued launch of pyrotechnics from the reserve team. He was dead before he hit the ground.

*　　*　　*

Fire raged in the woods. Whipped by high winds, flames spread from tree to tree. Only the blanket of snow on the topmost branches kept the fire from consuming the entire forest in a matter of minutes.

Diane, in the form of a hawk, followed the trail of pyrotechnics back to the source. There were four men, two loading canisters into the backs of metal tubes that the other two held on shoulders. She signaled Nancy to follow, and both hawks dove at men loading the launchers. Diane ripped out the eyes of one man while Nancy skewered the other.

The remaining two dropped the long metal tubes to reach for sidearms. Both hawks circled and dove again. Diane hit her target squarely in the face with outstretched talons, tearing skin off the man's forehead and digging bottom talons into his eyes. She was still tearing away skin when she heard the gunshot.

Nancy's bird slammed into the snow three feet in front of where her target still stood.

Diane released her prey and furiously flapped her wings. As she took off she saw the other man take aim at her bird which was perfectly silhouetted against flaming trees to the east. She heard the second gunshot at the same instant she banked west, and the round whizzed by and tore only a single feather from the tip of one wing. The man fired twice more, but those rounds also missed.

Now she was behind him, coming out of the dark north, hidden behind waves of snow being driven by the northwest wind, and she dove for his exposed neck and connected with bare flesh. One talon ripped out his carotid artery, slitting his throat as neatly as a butcher opened pigs in a slaughterhouse with a sharpened blade. The man dropped his gun and grabbed at the hole in his neck. It was a futile effort to stanch spurting streams of lifeblood pumped out in the final spasms of a frantically beating heart. When the man who'd killed Nancy finally fell to both knees and collapsed into the snow like a limp sack of shit, Diane landed on his face to peck out his dead eyes with her beak.

This time she knew Nancy was dead. Really, really, really and truly dead. Her spirit had been trapped inside the bird's body when it died, and her spirit was unable to return to her own back at the circle because the fragile link that tied her to her body was broken. Nancy's tree, the tree that had been planted on the day Nancy was born, had burned up in the fire and her spirit had no place to roost.

Diane flew over the battlefield one more time to make certain there were no more men left alive. Then she released the hawk she inhabited and returned to her own body that sat naked in front of the bonfire.

Nancy's naked body lay limp on the ground. The bullet caught her completely by surprise. She hadn't been able to return her spirit before it died. Nancy's body was now nothing but an empty shell.

Diane dressed, walked back past the house and then up the fire trail to where the dead hawk lay. She picked up the bird and carried it back to the fire, placing the carcass on top of a burning log. The damp feathers smoked, caught fire, and Diane watched in silence as fire consumed the hawk and released Nancy's spirit.

At last Nancy's spirit was free, but it had nowhere to go. It couldn't go to the pure land on the other side because the door between worlds was shut.

Where Nancy's spirit went, Diane had no way of knowing. All she knew was that her sister was gone, and she wouldn't be back in this lifetime.

Nancy's human body had already begun to decay. Diane would ask Biegolmai and Lokesvara to help her burn the remains when the two returned to their own bodies.

But right now both of those men, plus Aunt Anna, Aunt Violet, and the Martindales, were busy utilizing their own spirits to put out the fires still raging in the old growth forest. Mrs. Nelson had returned home to her neighboring farm before the fire began, taking Sara, Sean, and Susie with her.

The winds began to die down, and she had no doubt it was due to the combined efforts of Biegolmai, Lokesvara, Anna, Violet, and the Martindales. Snow continued to drop out of the clouds, and billows of steam and smoke rose over the forest as the fires were snuffed out one by one. Enough of the old-growth trees remained to provide protection to the land, and out of the ashes would someday arise a new forest, stronger than ever.

But Diane's heart had already turned to stone. In the last week she had lost her mother, her only sister, their family home, and many of the trees that had been her friends forever. Her brother, Tom, was still alive, but he was about to put himself in mortal danger, as much or greater than she and Nancy had just been in. Nancy hadn't survived. If anything happened to Tom or Bob, Diane wouldn't be able to forgive herself.

She stripped out of her clothes again and sat down in front of the fire.

Taking care of Nancy's body could wait. First, she had to look after Tom and Bob. She detached from her own body, found her hawk again, and winged south to help her brother.

*   *   *

They bogged down in the snow. Even with a powerful 320 horsepower V8 and four-wheel drive, the Yukon couldn't move very far or very fast when the driver couldn't discern the edge of the road.

"How much farther to US 12?" Jerry asked.

"Can we make another four miles?"

"We'll have to crawl."

"Crawling is better than sitting still."

Jerry pushed the Yukon forward at 3 miles an hour. Twice he slid off the road, and twice he got back on. Finally, they reached a plowed US 12 and turned east.

Forty-five to fifty miles an hour seemed the best they could manage with drifting snow. They passed a sign that said Chicago was 157 miles ahead, slightly more than 4 hours at their current speed, and they drove another ten miles before anyone spoke.

"I hate to give up this vehicle," said Jerry. "But we better find something else. The cops have make and plates. If every cop in the state isn't already out looking for us, they will be soon."

"What do you propose?" asked Bob.

"Steal something. What's the next town?"

"Fort Atkinson," said Tom. "US 12 takes us right through the center of the city."

"Then we'll go car shopping in Fort Atkinson. Any requests?"

"Four-wheel drive," said Bob.

"Good heater," said Sheila.

"More than one seat," said Tom. "I don't want all four of us to be packed into the front of a pick-up truck like sardines."

They cruised around Fort Atkinson looking for a vehicle with keys in the ignition. Bob spotted a recent model Subaru Forester, all-wheel drive, with a front seat and a back seat and chains on the rear tires, parked at a gas station and convenience store. The owner had left it running while he or she ran into the store.

They were on US 12 and heading east to Chicago again in less than 18 minutes. The winds had died down, and what little snow still drifted earthward from the sky danced in the headlights like frolicking fairies.

They passed the Elkhorn exit before spotting the roadblock. There were four squad cars, with MARS lights strobing red and blue, parked along both sides of the eastbound lanes. Cars had to slow down and pass one-at-a-time through a gauntlet of armed cops.

"Think they're looking for us?" asked Jerry.

"Bank on it," said Tom.

"Not much we can do. There's no place to turn off, and there are cars ahead and behind us. Let's hope they're looking for the Yukon and not a stolen Forester."

Jerry slowed to twenty miles an hour and kept moving forward. The cops weren't stopping any of the cars, just noting make, model, and license plate numbers. One of the sheriff's deputies standing along the side of the road peered into each car as it passed the checkpoint, but he waved the Forester on through.

"Wheeeee-ewwwww!" whistled Jerry as he accelerated away from the checkpoint. "It's a good thing we switched when we did. They were looking for the Yukon."

"And for two missing kids," said Bob. "That's why the deputy peeked inside. When he didn't see any kids, he waved us on."

"How much farther to the Windy City?" asked Jerry.

"Little more than 90 miles," said Tom.

"Now that we're south of the heavy snow, we can do 65. That puts us in Chicago in an hour and a half."

"Make that more like two and a half hours," said Sheila. "You never know what Chicago expressways will be like."

"Where do we find this Philip Ashur?"

"North Michigan Avenue, downtown near the lake. When we get close, I'll direct you."

"How do we want to do this?" asked Bob. "If Ashur's expecting us, he'll have armed guards all over the XIIMI building."

"There's only one way up to his offices on the 76th floor," said Sheila. "And that's his private elevator. You need to know an access code to get the elevator to go all the way up."

"Shit," said Tom. "I guess we're out of luck."

"Not necessarily," said Sheila. "Because, unless Phil changed them in the last day or two, I know the codes to get his private elevator to go all the way up to the boardroom and his private office on the 76th floor."

Book V

Hog Butcher for the World,
Tool Maker, Stacker of Wheat,
Player with Railroads and the Nation's Freight Handler;
Stormy, husky, brawling,
City of the Big Shoulders:
They tell me you are wicked and I believe them, for I have seen your painted
women under the gas lamps luring the farm boys.
And they tell me you are crooked and I answer: Yes, it is true I have seen the
gunman kill and go free to kill again.
And they tell me you are brutal and my reply is: On the faces of women and
children I have seen the marks of wanton hunger.
And having answered so I turn once more to those who sneer at this my city,
and I give them back the sneer and say to them:
Come and show me another city with lifted head singing so proud to be alive
and coarse and strong and cunning.
Flinging magnetic curses amid the toil of piling job on job, here is a tall bold
slugger set vivid against the little soft cities;
Fierce as a dog with tongue lapping for action, cunning as a savage pitted
against the wilderness,
Bareheaded,
Shoveling,
Wrecking,
Planning,
Building, breaking, rebuilding,
Under the smoke, dust all over his mouth, laughing with white teeth,
Under the terrible burden of destiny laughing as a young man laughs,
Laughing even as an ignorant fighter laughs who has never lost a battle,
Bragging and laughing that under his wrist is the pulse, and under his ribs the
heart of the people, Laughing!
Laughing the stormy, husky, brawling laughter of Youth, half-naked, sweat-
ing, proud to be Hog Butcher, Tool Maker, Stacker of Wheat, Player with
Railroads and Freight Handler to the Nation.
---*Carl Sandburg. Chicago Poems. New York: Henry Holt and Company, 1916*

CHAPTER THIRTY-SEVEN

When Carter didn't report back in a timely manner, Ashur called the comm chief in Rockford and asked for an update. The chief had heard nothing from Carter or his men, and he sounded worried. Helicopters dropped them and their equipment near the entrance to the target's property hours ago, then flew to Hayward for refueling. They were still waiting at the Hayward airport for him to request a pick up.

Ashur concluded he'd failed, and Lokesvara and Biegolmai remained alive. He wasn't worried, because two male guardians could do little to interfere with his plans without at least two female adepts to balance polarity, but it was still aggravating. It felt like a slap in his face that he didn't have their heads to add to his collection, and he didn't like to leave loose ends lying around that might someday trip him up or bite him in the butt.

Ted Carnes was another of those loose ends that might bite Phil's butt. He knew immediately when he met Carnes in 1989 the man was no ordinary mortal.

He had the distinct feeling they'd met someplace before, but he was unable to recall where or when.

Carnes was one of the richest men in the world, and his money and power extended to nearly every military and political action in every part of the globe. He was the master puppeteer—the hidden Imam—who pulled the strings of politicians and assassins from behind a curtain of secrecy, a translucent black veil that masked his movements and kept him from the limelight. Rumors abounded that Carnes was the Devil incarnate, and Ashur soon discovered those rumors weren't very far from the truth.

Although Carnes appeared forty years older than Ashur, he possessed a certain charisma that drew people to him like excrement drew flies. Both men were tall, over six feet, and both displayed that lean and hungry look Julius Caesar considered dangerous. Carnes was better dressed and more expensively tailored than Ashur when they first met, but that would soon change. Phil was nothing if not a fast learner. If clothes made the man, there was no place better than Hong Kong for a sartorial remake.

They were like two male cats who suddenly discovered a rival inside marked territory, and they sniffed each other out while pussyfooting in circles, hissing and growling, with fangs occasionally bared and claws half-extended.

Carnes could have killed Ashur then and there when he'd had the perfect opportunity and power to do so, but he acted too intrigued by the younger man to do that yet. Instead, Theodore Carnes surprised Philip Ashur by inviting him to dinner at the exclusive club in the heart of Hong Kong where he was an esteemed member and had his own private dining area.

Both men wanted to know what the other knew, and Ashur cautiously accepted Carnes' olive branch. Despite the repulsion of like polarities, Adepts were known to seek out other Adepts in every incarnation.

"Where do I remember you from?" asked Ashur after the waiter had brought a bottle of expensive wine and accepted their orders for Roast Prime Rib of Beef, the specialty of the house.

"Were you ever in Egypt?" asked Carnes.

"Yes. Were you?"

"Yes. When were *you*?"

"Only once that I remember. A thousand or so years ago."

"I was there then. I remember you as my student at Cairo's Academy. Is that correct?"

"Yes. Who are you exactly?"

"A force to be reckoned with. I also remember you as a sorcerer of Seth. Do you remember that?"

"No," said Ashur.

"I was Seth."

"I knew I recognized you," said Ashur. "But I couldn't recall from where."

"Recognition memory is different than recall. You knew I looked familiar. Were you unable to recall the details?"

"Like déjà vu, I recognized you. But I can't remember the context of where or when."

"I remember you well, my sorcerer," said Carnes. "Let me refresh your memory. What did you learn from Purple Lotus Flower that allows you to be here now in this time and place as am I? Did she take you into the underworld and introduce you to the nature of true magic? Did you die the little death? Did she steal your life force, or did you steal hers?"

"I don't know what you're talking about."

"Sure, you do. Did she show you the secret of Ma-at?"

"I really don't know what you're talking about."

"You would lie to the man who slept with Isis and fathered Horus? Isis never revealed her closely-guarded secrets to me or to any man. But you stole them from Purple Lotus Flower, didn't you? Then you disappeared from Egypt without telling me. You may be the only man living who knows the secret of Ma-at. I want to know it, too, so I might live forever."

"What will you give me to learn the secret?"

"Anything. Name your price."

"Then I want everything. I want your money, your power, your influence. I want the corporations you own, all the gold squirreled away in Swiss bank accounts, everything you own in this life. Agreed?"

"No," said Carnes. "That is too much to ask."

"Too much to ask for the power to control your own ka and ba through all eternity? I don't think so."

"Half. I'll give you half of all the corporate entities, and half of all I have in Swiss accounts. You can have half, no more than that."

"Fifty-one percent. You will give me immediate control of the corporations, stick around long enough to make the transition seem orderly, and then you'll bow out and enjoy a good life some place where you will live forever. Agreed?"

"Agreed," said Carnes without hesitation.

"Then, let's seal the deal with a toast." He hefted his wine glass. "L'chaim. To life."

"To life," said Carnes and touched glasses. The ring of pure crystal meeting pure crystal sent vibrations scurrying through the air.

Although Ashur hadn't yet remembered the secret of immortality he'd stolen from Hathor's temple, he did know how to take possession of another body.

Theodore Carnes remained alive today in a new body with a new identity, thanks to arcane knowledge he'd acquired in Hong Kong. He still had all the money he needed to live a very, very long and happy life. He maintained a low profile and stayed away from politics and out of Ashur's way. He'd just married an eighteen-year old girl, and they now lived in a private villa near Geneva, Switzerland.

But Carnes was a loose end, and Philip Ashur hated loose ends.

He sent an order to Weiss in Berlin who called together the same team, minus the American named Carter, employed to locate Biegolmai in northern Sweden. It was a little more than eleven hundred kilometers from Berlin to Geneva, slightly more than ten hours by train. Weiss requested 12 Heckler and Koch MP5SD submachine guns in 5.56 and five thousand rounds of 5.56-millimeter ammunition be available on their arrival in Switzerland. The H & K MP5SD had built in-silencers and flash suppressors, and Weiss considered it the most accurate submachine gun currently on the market. He also requested three Audi A8 sedans be at the train station.

Their target went by the name of Johannes Burkholdt, and he looked 31 years old. He lived in a house in Pinchat, a suburb south of Geneva. The house had been built in 1917, during the First World War, on 2300 square meters of wooded land. An Olympic-sized outdoor swimming pool and Italian-terrazzoed cabana had been added to the back of the house in the 1950s. That property had been purchased in 1989 by Theodore Carnes, and Carnes had deeded the property to Burkholdt.

It would take the team less than an hour to drive south from the Cornavin train station in central Geneva to Burkholdt's house in the suburb.

As soon as the team assembled in Berlin, they would be on their way. By tomorrow, at this time, the head of Johannes Burkholdt that contained the spirit of Theodore Carnes, aka Seth, should be on ice inside a private jet bound for Chicago's O'Hare International Airport.

* * *

It hadn't snowed at all in Chicago, and traffic on the Edens and Kennedy Expressways was practically non-existent at 4:00 AM. The Subaru breezed into town at a legal 55 miles per hour. Sheila told Jerry to take the Ohio Street exit and head all the way east to Michigan Avenue and then turn left. If he reached Lake Shore Drive, he'd gone too far.

They found self-parking in a municipal garage two blocks from the XIIMI building, and they left the Subaru in a stall on the third deck. They took an elevator to the ground level and walked one block north and one block east.

"I'm here with you, my love," spoke Diane's voice inside Bob's mind. He looked up and saw a lone hawk circling the shoreline of Lake Michigan.

"Can you see inside this building?" he asked the voice in his mind. "Do you know how many people are inside and where they're located?"

A few minutes later, she reported. "Four armed men on the first floor. Two are seated at a desk in the lobby, and two are positioned near the elevators. I see only one other person in the building, and he's sitting at a computer on the top floor."

"That's got to be Ashur. Keep an eye on him for us, will you?"

"Say please."

"Please."

Executing the plan they'd worked out in the car on their way to Chicago, Sheila and Jerry entered the lobby and occupied the guards while Tom and Bob took both from behind, rendering them unconscious with quick blows to the side of the head. Then they took out the men watching the elevators so they could use Ashur's private elevator and Sheila's access codes to get to the 76th floor.

Sheila found the private elevator and entered the codes she remembered into a keypad next to the elevator door. The door refused to open. She tried again, and still the door remained tightly closed.

"Third time's charm," said Bob, as Sheila tried one more time. But the elevator door refused to budge.

"Ashur must have changed codes," said Sheila.

Diane's voice sounded inside Bob's head. "There's a parade of police cars on Michigan Avenue, lights flashing but no sirens. A dozen additional cop cars are only blocks away, and more are coming your way on the outer drive."

"Get out of here now!" he shouted. "It's a trap."

They ran out the front doors and Diane guided them in the opposite direction of the cop cars, keeping them informed of the dragnet spreading to ensnare the entire near north side. Cops were stopping traffic and checking through parking garages.

"Phil must have cameras in the lobby," said Sheila. "He phoned the cops even before we took out the guards. The bastard knew our every move."

"What do we do now?" asked Tom. "We're running out of time."

"We keep running," said Jerry. "If the cops catch us, we're as good as dead. Ashur'll find ways to reach each of us in jail. And even if we live long enough to tell our fantastic stories, who'll believe us? He's a pillar of the community, and we're wanted fugitives. We have to keep running until we find a way back inside that building and up to the top floor."

"Where to now?" Bob asked Diane.

"To the lake," her voice answered. "Go under Lake Shore Drive and get on the bike path. Jog north along the lake."

Fifteen minutes later they were jogging north on the bike path that paralleled the shoreline. Jerry suddenly stopped dead in his tracks. His body went rigid. Then he began convulsing.

By the time the others stopped running and turned back to help him, the convulsions had ended. Jerry looked around like he was lost.

"She's gone," he said. "La Curandera is gone. She left me."

"Where did she go?" asked Bob.

"She went home," Jerry's voice sounded shallow and forlorn. "Aunt Anna called her back to Wisconsin."

"Why?" asked Tom. "Why did Anna call La Curandera back to Wisconsin now?"

"Because Sara Nelson is bleeding. She just started her first period. And you know what that means, don't you?"

"Yes," said Tom. "I do. We have another female Ascended Master to give polarity to the directions. Biegolmai to the north, Lokesvara to the east, La Curandera to the south, and Sara Nelson to the west. We're back in business, and we can make magic happen."

*   *   *

Ashur knew the minute it happened. Another Ascended Master appeared, and her presence caught him completely unawares.

She'd ruin everything he'd worked so long and so hard to accomplish. He had to kill her and take her head before she joined with the others.

If he wanted to become like unto a god and possess all the attributes and powers of a god himself, he had to keep this newest female guardian from balancing the watchtowers that kept his male energy in check.

Her very existence posed a threat. He hadn't worried because even if La Curandera's spirit had survived the erupting volcano in Chile, one female Ascended Master wasn't enough. One female didn't add sufficient polarity to balance the directions. It took two: two females and two males working in tandem, working in harmony. One, even the most powerful Ascended Master, did nothing by herself.

But two—assuming La Curnadera's spirit found another host to remain grounded—made all the difference in the world. Ashur's magic would be useless in a balanced universe.

He'd learned that secret—one of the many sacred secrets of Ma-at—from Purple Lotus Flower three millennia ago.

Now that Sara Nelson, the reincarnation of Purple Lotus Flower, remembered all her past lives, so did Ashur.

It was from Purple Lotus Flower he'd learned his true name. She said he was the embodiment of Thoth, and the number of his name was 666. He was called Hermes in Greece, where they thought him a god. Thoth, or Hermes, was said to be Three Times Great because he embodied three aspects that made him great.

Ancient Egyptians, long before the births of Isis and Osiris, believed Thoth was born not of the union of man and woman but was self-begotten. He was also said to be the only male who knew the secrets of Ma-at.

He was sometimes referred to as the Lord of Ma-at because he knew the secrets of alchemy and the methods of transformation of matter into energy and back again.

Matter and magic were ma-words and the high priestess of Ma-at knew the power of ma-words. She had shared the secret with Thoth, and he devised a system to record words that would preserve secret knowledge for more than merely one lifetime.

He knew what the gods knew, and he was like unto a god and he desired to become a god himself.

Without female energy to balance the new extremes of his male energy, the spiritual realm was shutting down. He saw that as a good thing, because he didn't need the spiritual realm like those other poor fools, the mere mortals and the tree huggers. He was at home in the physical realm and in a male body, and he knew ways to keep his consciousness alive forever by taking possession of others.

If balance were restored, however, his powers would be diminished. His male energy would be held in check. He'd never become omniscient and omnipotent like a god.

No one remained in place in Wisconsin to kill Sara and take trophies. Weiss was on assignment in Switzerland, and Carter and Delacroix and their troops had been eliminated. Although he hated to dirty his own hands, Philip Ashur would have to do this job himself and he'd have to use magic if he were to be successful.

Magic was a ma-word, and he knew the secrets of magic because he had stolen those secrets from Purple Lotus Flower who used the power of words to cast spells. But to utilize magic in the real world, he would need to tap into what little remained of his feminine self because only women could work true magic in this world or any other.

So Philip Ashur tried to remember the times he had been born a woman. There weren't many, and he could count them on the fingers of both hands. Perhaps there were enough to generate what magic he needed to destroy a tiny farm in northern Wisconsin, kill all the occupants, sever their heads, and leave the severed heads to freeze in the sub-zero temperatures. He had to try, because it was his only chance.

He began chanting.

"Aeiouwoooommmmmaaaaaaaaaaauuuuuuuuuu-ummmmmmmmm!

CHAPTER THIRTY-EIGHT

Susie McMichaels helped Sara Nelson adjust to the trauma of womanhood. Sara, of course, knew all about the price of being a woman from previous lives, and Ellen Groves and Sara's mother had prepared her well for this day they knew would eventually come. The flood of memories was more overwhelming than the sudden onset of menstruation because Sara had suddenly become an Ascended Master who could recall everything she had learned from every life she had ever lived, and there had been many, many lives.

There was power in the blood.

She said that she had been known by other names in the past: Sa-Ra, Kwan Yin, Ta-ra, Kubaba, Cybele, Freyja, Purple Lotus Flower, and many more. She also said there was a man who wanted to kill her and cut off her head as he had done before in ancient Egypt. She said this crazed man would use magic to try to kill everyone he found at the Nelson house, and Sara urged Susie to alert everyone in the house while she went to talk with Aunt Anna. She said she would have to use some of her new-found powers to leave her body and become a bird and fly next door to Ellen's sacred circle in the woods, and then her body went slack as she released her spirit to fly away to become one with a bird roosting in a tree outside her bedroom window.

Susie warned her brother and implored him to run and tell Mrs. Nelson and everyone else he could find that they were in immediate danger and had to get out of the house right now. Susie stayed behind to watch over Sara's vacant body during the short time the 11-year-old was gone. When Sara returned, she said they had to leave now, or it would be too late.

They were both downstairs next to the back door getting into their heavy coats and overshoes when the big wind hit, ripping the roof from the house and collapsing the chimney. Sara shoved Susie out the door before three of the walls caved in from the second icy blast of hurricane-force wind.

Sean and Mrs. Nelson were already running for the woods, and the rest of the family had also cleared the grounds, escaped across the highway, and were now hiding in the trees on the far side of the road. But Sara and Susie still had to cross the highway before they could find protection from the high winds. Another blast of fierce frigid cold hit Susie in the face and knocked her to the ground.

She struggled to get up, but her arms and legs didn't want to work. It was as if the winds had glued her to the pavement and held her down, face pressed against the pavement, while the cold seeped into her bones and stole her strength.

She felt Sara on top of her, shielding her from the winds, and Sara's body was warm and wonderful and filled with life-force. Some of that special life-force must have seeped into Susie, because she felt Sara lift her from the ground and the two girls practically flew across the road despite intense winds that pursued them and tried to knock them down. Susie was filled with incredible energy, transfused with vitality. Her feet finally touched down on the other side of County Trunk O where the woods began. The winds diminished to shrill shrieks. She thought the winds sounded like a spoiled child wailing in Walmart when his parents told him they wouldn't buy an expensive new toy.

She looked back across the road to where the Nelson house was scattered rubble, and she was amazed that she was still alive. Nothing remained of the century-old farmhouse, the barn, nor the silo but broken bricks and splintered wood.

"Hurry," said Sara, as the 11-year-old bent to pick up a forked stick that had broken off one of the tall trees. "We won't be safe until we reach the circle."

Sara led the group—Susie, Sean, Mrs. Nelson, Mr. Nelson, and her brothers and sister—through the woods toward the old-growth part of the forest. Susie could see that some of the old trees looked badly scorched, and some had even been burned all the way to the ground. Terrible heat had recently separated bark from wood, and many of the trees looked naked and vulnerable. Even the snow that had fallen through the branches had melted, and the ground beneath the trees was muddy and marshy and mucky and sucked at their overshoes with sounds that seemed almost obscene.

Without any warning, cracks appeared in the mud ahead of them and snakes—hundreds of snakes of all kinds including timber rattlers and cottonmouths, massasauga swamp rattlers, and even hooded cobras—came out of hibernation and prepared to strike at passersby. Their tails buzzed, their necks craned, their hoods flared. The way to the sacred circle was blocked by deadly venomous reptiles that slowly advanced, and the trail writhed with twisted hissing shapes and colorful coils of certain death.

Sara stepped forward. She held the forked stick in her outstretched right hand, and she parted the sea of serpents as easily as Moses had parted the Red Sea in the Book of Exodus. It was as if the snakes were afraid of the stick—or afraid of Sara—and they scattered off into the woods where they would either burrow down into the ground or die from the cold. Even now they seemed sluggish, and the powerful energy they had exuded just moments ago vanished as Sara approached them with the forked-end of the stick.

She said a few words in a language Susie didn't recognize, and the hooded cobras that had taken a stand seemed to hiss back to her in the same language. Then they collapsed their hoods and lowered their heads and slithered away into the underbrush.

"We're not safe yet," said Sara as she began walking forward holding the stick in front of her. "Follow in my footsteps and we'll see what happens when we cross the creek. If there's a trap, it will wait for us there."

"I hope we won't have to swim across the creek," said Sean. "I never learned to swim. My dad promised he'd teach me, but he never had time."

"Don't worry," said Sara. "When we cross the creek, I'll teach you to walk on water."

"You can do that?" asked Susie. "You can walk on water?"

"Yes," said Sara. "And so can you."

*   *   *

Sheila felt the winds pick up over the lake as the air pressure drastically dropped. And as high-pressure areas far to the northwest sucked energy from the warmer waters to the east, waves battered the shore with the force of a thousand giant sledgehammers, pounding cement breakwaters with enough power to crack the concrete and send geysers of water spraying high into the air. All four were already drenched to the bone, and now incoming waves threatened to engulf the four friends and sweep them from the bike path like a giant fist clearing clutter off a tabletop.

Tom tried to shelter Sheila from the onslaught with his own body, but he was battered and buffeted by the incessant waves until he fell to the ground and nearly floated away in the waters that flooded the shoreline.

"Enough!" commanded Sheila as she raised her hands against the wind. Though it never worked in the past, she knew instinctively their only hope lay in her magical ability to control the winds and thus the waves. It wasn't just her own life she was fighting for now, but the lives of Tom and Bob and Jerry and the lives of countless Chicagoans that would be lost if those waves crossed Lake Shore Drive. Ashur was safe in his 76th floor tower overlooking the lake, but all the people on lower floors and in basement apartments along the whole north shore were threatened by the high waters that cascaded over broken breakwaters and tore away the shoreline.

"You do have the power," whispered Diane in her mind. Diane's hawk had sought shelter from the winds under an overhang on one of the taller buildings, and now her spirit watched over the lakefront from a perch seventy stories up. "Want it to happen, expect it to happen, watch it happen."

Sheila's hands began to vibrate as she pushed back at the wind. She felt power surge through her body as she sucked feminine energy from the earth beneath her feet and drew masculine power from the skies above. As those energies married in the center of her being, sparks flew from her fingers and lightning flashed down from dark clouds to electrify the lake. The winds began to howl and shriek like nothing she'd ever heard before.

And now she pushed back at the howling winds and the high waves with renewed confidence, holding the water at bay as she soothed the wind with words. She spoke in a language she didn't understand but the sounds seemed natural and right and she knew she was speaking in tongues and the power of the spirit was upon her and she shook and convulsed as though a thousand orgasms coursed through her body all at once and threatened to tear her apart. Burt Ryan's little girl had the power of the gods at her fingertips, and she felt like the most powerful person on the planet because, at that very moment, the power was hers.

Slowly, the winds abated. As waves rolled back out to the lake, they were swallowed up by hundreds of whitecaps that still swelled but no longer advanced beyond the shattered breakwaters. The winds calmed, and so did the waters.

Sheila lowered her hands. Remaining power drained away, returning to the earth from whence it had come. Lightning stopped flashing in the heavens, and dark clouds parted like window curtains thrown open at dawn.

Streams of early morning sunshine danced on the lake and turned the bluish-green waters of Lake Michigan into pure gold as the sun rose once again in the east and gave birth to a new day.

*   *   *

Ashur was furious. Something or someone had stolen much of his power. Female energy had been unleashed to counter his male onslaught and that made him madder than hell. Not only had he failed to reach Sara Nelson in time, but something much closer to home had sucked away at his strength and made him impotent.

Ashur went to the other room where he kept his trophies in the freezer, threw open the doors, and jerked out the head of Guru Rimpoche. "You did this, didn't you?" he shouted. "I don't know how you did it, but I know you're responsible."

"No one but you are responsible for your own actions," spoke the Guru inside Ashur's mind.

Ashur threw the frozen head against the wall where it shattered to a thousand tiny pieces. When he realized what he had done, he picked up as many of the pieces as he could find and shoved them back inside the freezer.

He returned to his office, removed his clothes, and sat in lotus on the bare floor. He had one chance left. If he could stop Sara Nelson from crossing the creek and reaching the sacred circle, he could still prevent balance from being restored and regain his powers quickly and easily. Once again he tapped into the energy of his female side and sent magic northward. This time he called wolves to help, and hundreds of hungry wolves answered his call. Sara and her companions would be surprised. Before they could reach grandmother's house, a pack of big bad wolves would rip them apart and gobble up the pieces. All but the heads, of course. The heads would remain frozen in the snow until Ashur could pick them up at his leisure.

And if that failed, he had one more trick up his sleeve that would surely work.

CHAPTER THIRTY-NINE

Gunther Weiss divided his men into two teams. One team went around to the back of the house and came at the target from the cabana surrounding the swimming pool. Weiss led the other from the street in a full-frontal attack.

They met some small resistance from a few bodyguards the target employed, a dozen or so men armed only with handguns, but that was entirely anticipated and quickly and easily controlled. Within minutes, the bodyguards were dead and both teams were inside the house.

It was a beautiful house, with high vaulted ceilings layered with solid cedar and milled mahogany panels. There were ten rooms in all, including the living room, kitchen, den, and bedrooms. Weiss found no one who answered the description of the target in any of them.

Had the target known they were coming and fled before they arrived? Was he hiding somewhere on the grounds?

They searched the entire estate, and neither the 31-year-old Johannes Burkholdt nor his young bride were anywhere to be found. Burkholdt had married an 18-year-old girl in Indonesia a month ago, but the couple had returned to Geneva after a brief honeymoon in Bali that lasted less than a week. Ashur had said they would be in the house, and Ashur was never wrong.

Weiss and his men tore the house apart looking for hiding places. They discovered an escape route behind a faux bookcase in the den, a flight of stairs that led down into a dark tunnel that went all the way under the back of the house and beneath the swimming pool to a safe place in the woods behind the house. There, they found ample evidence that a man and a woman had recently walked through the woods away from the chateau toward the city. Where they went from there was anybody's guess.

"Find them!" Weiss ordered.

*   *   *

Sara saw the first pack of wolves coming, and she tried to beat them to the creek before they had a chance to attack. But the cunning beasts moved through the thickest part of the woods as silently as shadows, and they were lined up and impatiently waiting for the tiny group of humans to approach the half-frozen stream that marked the boundary between old-growth forest and sacred land. None of the wolves could cross that boundary without permission, and Sara knew they had been sent to prevent her and her friends from crossing the creek but couldn't cross themselves.

"Oh, my God!" gasped Sara's mother when she saw the wolves.

Sara calmly stepped in front of her mother to stand between them and her family. She identified the leader of the pack—the alpha male—and pointed the forked wooden stick directly at him. She watched his eyes shift from what he thought of as easy prey to assess dual prongs aimed at his eyes. It took him barely a moment to decide if the stick posed any serious threat, and then the muscles in his haunches tightened and he bared his fangs and sprang straight for the 11-year-old with the rest of the pack poised to follow his lead.

The tip of the stick burst into bright flame as hot sparks shot straight at the alpha male's eyes, and the wolf's head and muzzle caught fire and the air became filled with the foul smells of scorched fur and burning flesh. The leader of the pack let out a horrible howl, spun completely around as if to chase its tail, and dashed headlong into the freezing water where it splashed around before sinking under the ice and not resurfacing.

The rest of the pack looked around for their leader, looked at the flaming stick in Sara's hand, and turned tail and ran into the woods. Other wolves, seeing the pack fleeing, disappeared into the dense underbrush.

"How did you do that?" asked Susie.

"Someday, when you're ready to learn, I shall teach you," said Sara. "But not today. Today I will teach you only to walk on water."

"That's impossible," said Sean. "Nobody can walk on water."

"It's impossible only if you believe it is impossible. But if you believe it's possible, then it *is* possible. Let me show you."

She walked to the creek and stepped onto the thin ice. Unbelievably, it seemed to hold the eleven-year-old's weight as she strode across to the other side.

"Now you do it," Sara called across the creek.

Sean, unwilling to be outdone by a girl, followed in her footsteps. "Keep your eyes on me," urged Sara. "Don't look down. Walk straight across. Don't stop,"

Sean walked across on the ice. It was only when he got to the other side that he noticed the thin ice had broken into chunks that floated on running water like tiny islands. There was no way that floating ice could have held him, and it was a miracle that he hadn't plunged into the water and frozen to death.

"Susie, you're next."

Susie went to the edge and stopped when she saw the open water surrounding chunks of floating ice.

"Believe you can," said Sara. "Then you *can.*"

Susie took one tentative step onto the ice. "Look at me," called Sara. "Keep looking at me."

Susie held her head up and concentrated on Sara's face. "I think I can," she said aloud like *The Little Engine that Could.* "I think I can." She took one step, then two. Another. Before she knew it, she was across the water and safely on solid ground.

"Mom, you're next."

Mrs. Nelson stepped onto the ice, focused her attention on the kids, and walked across the open water as if the creek were frozen solid. Sara talked her brothers across, and then her sister. Then she looked across the water and said: "Dad, you're next."

Herman Nelson, Sara's father, looked at the water and shook his head. "I'm too heavy," he said.

"You're only as heavy as you think you are."

"I'm too heavy," he repeated.

Sara left the safety of the other shore and walked across the water and took her father's hand. "We'll do it together," she said. "Hold onto my hand and look at the people standing on the other side. Keep looking at them. Don't look away."

She guided her father across. Herman got his feet wet, but he didn't get cold feet and stop midstream or turn back. He held onto his daughter's hand, looked at his wife's smiling face urging him onward, and kept walking as if strolling on solid ground. When he reached the other side, he broke into a sweat.

"I'm proud of you, Daddy," said Sara and hugged her father.

Sara's mother hugged both. "We made it," she said. "We all made it."

"Do you believe what we just did?" Sean asked his sister. "We walked on water. Just like Jesus. Well, maybe not just like Jesus because he walked across a big lake, but we walked across a creek. That makes us special, doesn't it?"

"Yes," said Susie, hugging her brother. "That makes us special."

* * *

"The man and woman you describe took the 6564 to Paris," said the ticket agent at the central train station. "They departed nearly four hours ago and should have already arrived at the Gare de Lyon."

"Is there transportation to the airport from the Lyon station?"

"Every thirty minutes."

"Danke," said Weiss. They had wasted four hours searching the house, grounds, and vicinity of Geneva without locating the target. Burkholdt and his bride were probably at the Charles de Gaulle airport boarding a plane. They could go any place in the world they wanted. It would be nearly impossible to catch him now.

Weiss didn't want to tell Ashur he failed twice to hit a target. He'd heard what had happened to Colonel Delacroix after several failures to carry out orders, and he feared the same fate. No, it was far better to continue the search for Burkholdt and have an answer that Ashur would buy when he called to inquire.

It was hopeless to run. There was no place on earth he could hide that Philip Ashur couldn't find him. He had no choice but to hunt Burkholdt down and kill him before Ashur discovered the man was still alive.

Weiss was less than 5 kilometers from the Geneva airport, and he knew Paris was little more than an hour away by jet. He took the whole team with him, and they boarded Air France flight 1643 from Geneva to de Gaulle. They had to leave their weapons behind in the Audis, but they could pick up new weapons when they learned where their target was headed. As soon as they landed in Paris, Weiss checked with Air France's ticket center for a man named Johannes Burkholdt and his wife. No one by that name took an Air France flight today, said the ticket agent, but someone matching Burkholdt's description had boarded an Air France flight to Chicago less than an hour ago under the name of Theodore Carnes. The man showed a valid passport in Carnes' name to the ticket agent, and he paid for two one-way fares to Chicago with an American Express card issued in the same name.

Weiss booked ten seats on the next flight to Chicago's O'Hare International Airport. If Burkholdt had gone to Chicago, Weiss would be right behind him.

*   *   *

The day was beautiful. Cool, crisp air, the smell of ozone left from lightning discharges over the lake, the sun huge now as it climbed higher in the sky, sunlight reflecting off the surface of the stilled water and from the glass panes of thousands of east-facing windows. Bob saw Diane's hawk circle the shoreline as he heard her voice whisper inside his mind. "We missed the deadline," she said. "We lost our last chance to rescue Ma. Wherever her spirit is, it can't return to the trees."

"I'm sorry," said Bob.

"Nor can her spirit find rest in the spirit realm. The doors are sealed by the abyss."

"What about Sara and the others? I thought they would restore polarity as soon as there were two male and two female Guardians to provide balance."

"Ashur has prevented Sara from joining the others."

"Would it help if we found a way to distract Philip Ashur? Make him fight a two-front war?"

"How do you propose to do that?"

"We could attack his building."

"The police still have the building cordoned off. A half-dozen police cars in front, and at least as many policemen inside. You don't stand a chance of getting close."

"Is there a building nearby that is almost as high?"

"Several."

"Any facing the window where Ashur has his office?"

"Let me see." Diane's hawk flew off and disappeared between buildings. Five minutes later she was back. "There's a new hotel a block away that might do. Follow me, and I'll show you."

Bob told the others to follow him as he followed Diane's hawk. While they were walking, Bob filled the others in on his idea.

"We left the rifles in the Subaru, and we can't get into the parking garage to retrieve them while the cops have the area blocked off. But we each have handguns, and 9 millimeters are powerful weapons at up to a half-mile. We won't get enough accuracy with a pistol to kill Ashur from a distance, but we can certainly distract him from whatever he's doing if we fire at his office windows."

"We can't do that from the street," said Tom. "We need elevation. Those windows look tiny from ground level, and we'd waste a lot of ammunition before we hit one."

"Right," said Bob. "Diane is showing us a building that might be tall enough to give us the elevation we need. She says it's a hotel. If it gives us a clear shot at Ashur's office, we could take two rooms on one of the upper floors. You and Sheila in one, Jerry and me in the other. We can even get dry and warm, and we can have room service send up breakfast and coffee. Then we'll find a way to get up to the roof and take turns firing intermittently. All we need do is knock out the windows of Ashur's top floor."

"The cops will find us," said Jerry.

"They won't know which building the shots are coming from. There are dozens of places we could be using, and it'll take time to search all of them. By the time they figure it out, we'll be checked out and gone."

"It's worth a shot," agreed Tom.

Although the hotel only had 58 floors, the roof offered a perfect line-of-sight unobstructed view of the windows along the north side of the 76th floor of Ashur's building. Bob asked Sheila to point out his office windows.

"There," said Sheila. "And the big window next to his office window is the board room."

"We'll take out both windows and let in some fresh air," said Bob. "In fact, we'll take out all of the windows on the top floor. That ought to give Ashur something to think about."

He charged the two rooms to the open-ended government appropriations listed on his orders, and the room clerk had no problem getting an authorization for billing. The same credit card numbers were used by multiple Department of Defense employees, and someone had used this hotel for government business in the past. He asked for rooms on the top floor, and they were assigned suites on the 57th floor. The fifty-eighth floor housed a restaurant and banquet facilities, but no sleeping rooms.

Their rooms were beautifully decorated with two queen-sized beds in each. They took time to shower and let their clothes dry out next to the heat vents, and they ordered room service breakfasts and hot coffee. While Sheila and Jerry ate breakfast, Tom and Bob took the elevator to the 58th floor and searched for a way to the roof. They found a locked door with a sign that read "Staff Only" and they played with the lock until it opened. Behind the door was a metal ladder that led to a hatch that opened to the roof.

The view was magnificent. Off to the east lay Lake Michigan, stretching seemingly forever. A block away, between them and the lake and partially obstructing the view, was the behemoth XIIMI building.

"We can hit it from here," said Tom. "We'll have to aim up at a sixty- degree angle, but that's not a problem."

Diane's hawk landed next to them. "Can you do it? Will it work?"

"It'll work," said Bob.

*   *   *

Those people have more lives than a fucking cat, thought Philip Ashur. He'd been inside the alpha male, and he had felt the beast's surprise and pain when fire took out its eyes. Ashur had left quickly, returning to his own body before the host died and his spirit became trapped inside.

Soon, very soon, Sara Nelson would join spirits with the other three in the sacred circle at the center of the vortex. Ley lines extended through north-central Wisconsin and connected the energy of that vortex with other vortices in the four cardinal directions. If there were two male guardian spirits and two female guardian spirits present inside that circle, then balance would soon be restored throughout all worlds. The gates of heaven would open, and spirit energy currently held captive in the physical world could migrate to the spirit realm. Philip Ashur would be left powerless.

He had one more trick up his sleeve, something so audacious that no magician in his right mind would ever consider trying it. But desperate times called for desperate measures, and Ashur was desperate.

Calling upon all the resources at his command for one final push, he invoked and summoned every male devil or demon whose names he knew. He felt his own power building and expanding as he drew the energy of the summoned demigods into himself. He visualized Angra Mainyu and Ahriman, Ba-al and Beelzebub, Mephistopoles and Mammon, Loki and

Coyote, Azazel and Asmodeus. He filled himself with the essence of every evil imaginable, and he felt his power increase ten-fold, a hundred-fold, a thousand-fold.

He had enough power to crush all those pitiful humans who wanted to restore balance, enough power to surmount the wards and petty spells women used to protect their personal space, enough power to drain the vortex itself and leave everyone and everything within its sphere weakened and vulnerable. There would be a terrible price to pay later for his foolishness, but Ashur would be a god himself by then and nothing else mattered. He would gladly pay the toll. As long as he held onto his vision, so long as nothing broke his concentration or altered his intense focus, he would be in absolute control. Nothing could stop him now!

* * *

"Aim at those two windows," Bob pointed when Jerry and Sheila joined them on the roof. "Empty your magazine, reload, and keep firing until you're out of ammo."

"What if we miss?" asked Sheila.

"We don't need to hit Ashur," Tom said. "We just need to distract him. Pepper the windows and façade with bullets. He's using real magic to keep Sara from joining with the other guardians. Magic requires action on the astral plane, and he can't work magic if he loses his focus."

"It's time," said Bob. "Everyone ready?"

They aimed their weapons at the windows on the top floor of the XIIMI building.

"Fire," said Bob.

* * *

The windows behind and above his head shattered, and thousands of shards of broken glass rained down on his naked form and sliced at his face, gouged his shoulders, peppered his genitalia, opened wounds in his scalp and arms and legs. Bullets lodged in the ceiling, and plaster cracked and crumbled.

Philip Ashur lost it all as icy-cold winds whipped through the open window and his bloodied body instinctively recoiled from the cold, snapping him out of trance and back to reality. He lost his concentration, lost his focus, lost his power, lost his last chance to become a god.

But by the time bullets stopped flying, his body had already begun to heal. The open wounds ceased gushing blood and began to knit themselves closed. He was still alive, and he would have his revenge against whomever was responsible. He would make them wish they'd never been born.

He struggled to his feet and brushed broken glass from his body. He walked to the window and peered out to see where the shots that had shattered the windows could have originated.

Ashur didn't see the hawk until it was too late.

It flew down from the sky to gouge out his eyes, and he lost his balance and fell through the floor-to-ceiling shattered window of the 76th floor of the XIIMI building, tumbling all the way down—past office windows and neon signs—to the cement pavement of the sidewalk where he barely missed one of the Chicago Police Department vehicles parked directly in front of the building. On impact with concrete, Ashur's body instantly broke into hundreds of pieces the way a ripe watermelon or Halloween pumpkin bursts if dropped 76 stories, and the same hawk that had taken his eyes from him moments before swooped down to pluck up what little was recognizable of the dead man's smashed skull in its beak and talons. Then the tiny hawk, beating both wings rapidly to provide lift necessary to carry a heavy head, flew off over the lake holding the head, soaring higher and higher, until the hawk and Ashur's head finally disappeared from sight.

*   *   *

Gunther Weiss arrived at O'Hare International Airport with no luggage, and he passed through customs in record time. Two of his men were detained by TSA and Homeland

Security for some absurd reason, but they were released after only an hour and quickly joined him and the rest of the team at the Hertz car rental counter where Weiss rented three mid-sized sedans with a company credit card.

He had no clue where Burkholdt/Carnes might have gone after landing in Chicago, so he decided it was time to call Ashur and ask for help. When he received no answer on his boss' private line, Weiss called the comm center at the factory.

Uncharacteristically, Ashur had been out of contact with the comm center for hours. The comm chief said he had no intel on Burkholdt at all and certainly didn't know his current whereabouts. He did promise to tell Ashur, however, that Weiss wanted to talk as soon as he called in, but he didn't know when that might be.

Gunther had never been to the XIIMI building before, but he had most certainly traveled to Chicago many times in the past and he knew where XIIMI's headquarters was located adjacent to the lakefront. He ordered his men to follow in the other vehicles, and he drove one of the sedans downtown himself. When he got close to the lake, he noticed an increased police presence, but it wasn't until he got close to the XIIMI building that he saw the entire area around the front of that building was cordoned off by police.

If something had happened, was it a good idea to get involved? Probably not, but he needed to know what was going on. Perhaps, if Ashur were in trouble, he might find a way to redeem himself in his employer's eyes.

He found a parking garage west of the Water Tower, and he ordered his team to stay with the cars until he called them on their cell phones. Then he walked the half dozen or so blocks to the XIIMI building where he stood as close to the police line as he could get and observed the activities of police and listened to the conversations of gawkers.

"Someone get killed?" one onlooker asked another.

"Guy took a dive out an office window on the top floor. He was naked as a jaybird when he hit the sidewalk."

"Must've been crazy, huh?"

"Yeah. Must have been."

"Who was it? Do you know?"

"Some bigwig. Nobody I ever heard of, though."

Weiss continued to listen and observe. Two of the local television stations—WBBM Channel 2 News, the Chicago affiliate of CBS, and Tribune Broadcasting's WGN Channel 9—had vans with telescoping satellite feeds across the street from the police line. He moved through the crowds to get out of sight of their cameras but stay close enough to still see and hear all that was going on. Weiss listened intently as a woman reporter for WBBM gave details in a live broadcast.

"Philip Ashur, Chief Executive Officer of the multi-national XIIMI Corporation, plunged to his death this morning after gunfire reportedly knocked out all the windows on the 76th floor of the near-northside building that houses XIIMI's corporate headquarters. Police have the area cordoned off and are searching for the alleged gunmen who are still on the loose. Chicago police ask anyone with information about the incident to please come forward. Meanwhile, John Burkholdt, grandson and heir of XIIMI's founder Theodore Carnes, has arrived to assume control of the company."

Jesus, thought Weiss, Burkholdt must have put a team in place to take out Ashur, just as Ashur had assembled his own team to take out Carnes. Whoever shot out those windows knew how to handle weapons and knew Ashur was in his office and where that office was located. They must have been pros hired by Burkholdt.

But who pushed Ashur out the window? Surely, he wouldn't have jumped on his own. Phil wasn't the suicidal type. Someone pushed him out that window, and it must have been someone he knew and trusted. And why was he naked when he took the dive?

It had to be a woman. Had he let himself be compromised by a woman? Weiss couldn't help but wonder if the new Mrs. Burkholdt was somehow involved. That would explain why they had come to Chicago, instead of all the places in the world they could have.

In one sense, Weiss was relieved that Ashur was dead. It meant that all his past failures were forgiven and forgotten.

But what if Burkholdt discovered that Ashur had ordered Weiss to kill him and his wife? Would he then order Weiss killed?

It didn't pay to leave any loose ends in this business. Weiss had no choice but to take out Burkholdt before the new CEO of XIIMI took him out. The sooner he got it done, the better.

How to do this? He regretted leaving his high-tech weapons behind in Geneva, but conventional weapons were no good to him anyway with all those cops around. He had to find another way to get to Burkholdt.

Weiss walked around the block while he wracked his brain for a solution, any solution. Surely, there must be some way to get to the man before Burkholdt got to him. What would Delacroix do in this situation?

Blow up the entire block. That's what he would have done. The Colonel believed in overkill and never concerned himself with collateral damage. He'd blow up the whole city block and make it look like an accident.

Chicago, like Paris and New York City, had an extensive underground sewer and water system to deliver natural gas and water to every business and residence in the downtown area. All Weiss had to do was find a way into those sewers, locate the gas line that ran to the XIIMI building, rupture it, rig a timer to ignite a flame, and the whole block goes Kaboom! Takes Burkholdt and all of Gunther's worries out with one blow. The plan was simple, doable, and eminently practical.

It would look like an accident, and Weiss could return to Berlin without a worry in the world.

Gunther pried open a manhole cover in an alley behind skyscrapers housing restaurants and boutiques, and he crawled down a metal ladder to the dankness and darkness below. He carried a penlight in his pocket to dilate a subject's eyes during interrogation, and he took out the penlight and switched it on and he saw the tunnel was large enough to walk upright. There were rats, of course, but they scurried away into shadows as he approached. There was water, too, runoff rainwater an inch or two deep that ruined the expensive Italian leather of his hand-made shoes. But what was a pair of shoes compared to the peace of mind closure could bring?

Weiss determined which gas line fed the XIIMI building, and he removed one of his expensive shoes and hammered copper tubing with the heavy leather heel. When the tube cracked and then broke apart, Weiss smelled the tell-tale odor of chlorine gas that American gas producers added to the otherwise odorless gas to identify a leak.

Weiss took a silver Zippo cigarette lighter from his shirt pocket. Now all he had to do was rig the lighter so the wheel would rub against the flint only after he was out of the sewer and clear of the area. He slid the gold Rolex off his wrist, slipped a small screwdriver under the crystal, and exposed the hands. Did the jeweled clockwork movement of a Rolex have enough power to turn the wheel on the Zippo? If it didn't, he was only out a watch, a lighter, and a pair of shoes. If it did, he'd be out of the tunnel and on his way back to O'Hare before the blast took out the XIIMI building and everyone in it.

He used the screwdriver to attach the watch mechanism to the Zippo, then wedged both watch and lighter between the gas line and the wall of the tunnel. He could really smell the gas now as the sewer filled with fumes.

Rushing back to the ladder, he quickly returned to clean air and mid-morning sunlight. His feet were completely soaked. He'd need to find a place to buy new shoes and socks before he left Chicago. Maybe he'd stop and shop at Water Tower Place before returning to the car.

He was a block away when the ruptured gas lines blew. The ground shook as huge fissures opened up in the pavement beneath city streets and sidewalks, and the XIIMI tower and several buildings around it collapsed in on themselves, the way commercial demolition crews demolished old skyscrapers to make room for new, a sight not uncommon in downtown Chicago.

But the explosions didn't stop there, and once gas lines began to ignite, the ensuing flames followed the flow of natural gas back toward its source. Block after square block of commercial property erupted in flames as a new Chicago fire spread death and destruction to the Magnificent Mile.

Weiss realized he had badly miscalculated an instant before flames consumed him and his expensive Italian leather shoes. He never heard the sirens of hundreds of Chicago Fire Department hook and ladders responding to what would later be called a terrorist attack on downtown Chicago. Gunther Weiss was only one of many casualties of a modern Chicago massacre.

CHAPTER FORTY

Bob checked out of the hotel immediately after he and Tom shot out the windows of Ashur's offices. Before police could seal off the entire area, the four friends hopped a CTA bus to the nearest el station, boarded a train to the loop, and transferred to one heading out to O'Hare. There, they rented a car.

They were on the Northwest Tollway, had just passed the Des Plaines Oasis heading north to Wisconsin, when multiple explosions sounded.

Distant rumbles continued behind them, and Sheila—like Lot's wife—turned to look back. Bob continued driving forward while many of the other cars pulled off to the side of the road or found exits. A dozen police cars passed by in the opposite lanes.

"Looks like someone set off a bunch of bombs," Sheila said. "I see smoke and flames all over downtown, from the Loop north to Division."

Tom turned on the car's radio and found an AM station reporting local news.

Not only had Philip Ashur been killed in what was described as a freak accident, but the building he'd been in before falling to his death had been reduced to rubble by a series of explosions. Homeland Security was already on the scene. If there were a connection between XIIMI and the terrorist attack on Chicago, they promised to find it. Chicago's Mayor claimed everything was under control and urged citizens to remain calm.

Meanwhile, natural gas service to downtown businesses had been shut off completely, and the gas company had no idea when service might be restored. Fire crews and police were busy fighting fires and evacuating people from the lakefront and north shore. Hospitals were overwhelmed with casualties. The Governor declared a state of emergency, and National Guard troops were mobilized. The President of the United States was on his way to Chicago to offer federal assistance in what he called "the worst terrorist attack since nine-eleven."

"Sounds like we got out of town just in time," said Jerry.

"Sounds like someone else didn't like Ashur and XIIMI any more than we did," said Sheila.

As they crossed the state line into Wisconsin, Bob heard Diane's voice whisper inside his mind. "I flew home," she said, "to take care of Nancy. Are you on your way back?"

"We'll be there in six or seven hours," said Bob. "What did you do with Ashur's head?"

"I dropped it into the deepest part of Lake Michigan," said Diane. "It'll eventually biodegrade. If fish consume part of the head, however, his spirit will be trapped inside the fish."

"Won't Ashur's spirit come back?"

"Perhaps someday. But before he can be reborn, his spirit will pass to the spiritual realm where it'll be cleansed and wiped free of memory. When he comes back, if he is able to come back, he'll start over from scratch. His mind and memory will be a *tabla rasa,* a clean slate. Who knows? Maybe Ashur will have learned an important lesson by then and change for the good."

"A leopard doesn't change his spots."

"Jerry did."

Bob looked at Jerry riding silently in the passenger seat. The man's beard and white hair made him look much older and wiser than a week ago. Maybe miracles did happen.

"What about your mother?" Bob asked. "Will she come back?"

"Biegolmai, Lokesvara, La Curandera, and Sara restored balance and reopened the way between worlds. Since Ma's head was burned up in a fire, her freed spirit and Nancy's spirit are in the spirit realm. There is no longer an abyss blocking the way."

"What about Susie and Sean?"

"They're safe. Sean is all excited because Sara showed him how to walk on water."

"Walk on water? That's impossible!"

"Nothing's impossible, my love. You should know that by now."

"Yeah," said Bob. "I guess I do."

"Hurry home, my love. Safe journey. I'll see you soon."

*　　*　　*

Tom went with Bob when McMichaels drove to town to turn himself in to the Sawyer County sheriff. He brought both of his children with him to prove Susie and Sean were still alive and well and none the worse for wear. Donna was so glad to hear the kids' voices over the phone, that she dropped all charges of kidnapping and abduction. She said they could stay with Bob until he was ready to bring them home, whenever that might be.

When he reported in to Defense Intelligence, Bob was informed subsequent investigation had proven him right in the previous allegations he'd made about XIIMI, including the attack on Ellen Groves. Homeland Security and the FBI had closed down XIIMI's operations in Rockford and Europe, and they were still unravelling pieces of a puzzle that had made little sense to intelligence agencies until now. Bob would receive an official commendation for his superior work, and his full leave had been reinstated effective immediately. He should plan to spend the rest of the calendar year with his family. The commendation would be in his file when he went in front of the O-6 promotion board in January, and he was virtually assured of promotion to full colonel.

Bob had his family back—his whole family now that he'd found Diane again—and all was right with the world. What more, he wondered, could any guy ask for?

Sara began to train Susie to open up to possibilities. Male and female energies were powerful forces that, when combined, could move mountains. Her job, Sara explained, was to explore her own female energy and develop it to its fullest. Someday, not too far distant, Susie would meet her male counterpart and make mountains move. Maybe not today, but sometime soon.

Biegolmai took Sean under his wing, and he taught the boy to drum.

Bob and Diane were married in a private ceremony conducted in the sacred circle by Aunt Anna and legalized by a justice of the peace in town. Several weeks later, during the Winter's solstice, Bob was best man at Tom's wedding to Sheila in the same wooded circle. Both men planned to return to active duty at the end of their authorized leaves. Their wives would remain behind and rebuild the house Delacroix had destroyed. Warriors, Diane said, needed a place and a person they could return to, and Bob and Tom would have both.

Lokesvara returned to Cambodia and the temples at Ankor Wat. He took refuge in the Buddha, the dharma, and the sangha. But he also remained vigilant and sensitive to subtle changes in energy. He was, after all, a guardian, and he took his responsibilities seriously.

La Curandera returned to Jerry Walker only long enough to teach Jerry to love life and respect the union of male and female that made all life possible. As soon as a new female guardian of the South was trained and ready, La Curandera planned to move on to the spirit realm. There, she expected to be greeted with open arms by Ellen Groves and all those who had gone before her. Someday perhaps, she would enter the physical world again to serve as a guardian.

Or, perhaps, she would remain in the spirit world as a spirit guide and be there to greet the others when they, inevitably, came to join her. For all things come to an end.

And all things begin again.

ABOUT THE AUTHOR

Photo credit: Abbye Garcia, Rock Valley College

Paul Dale Anderson

has written more than 27 novels and hundreds of short stories, mostly in the thriller, mystery, horror, fantasy, and science fiction genres. Paul is the author of *Claw Hammer, Daddy's Home, Pickaxe, Icepick, Meat Cleaver, Axes to Grind, Pinking Shears, Sledgehammer, JackHammer, Deviants, Running Out of Time, Impossible, Abandoned, Winds, Darkness, Mysterious Ways, Light* and the critically-acclaimed Instruments of Death crime-suspense novels from Crossroad Press.

Visit Paul's web pages for more information: www.pauldaleanderson.net, www.4windsnovels.com, www.amazon.com/PaulDaleAnderson/e/B00A9XFLBQ

Paul has also written contemporary romances and westerns. He is an Active Member of SFWA, MWA, and HWA, and he was elected Vice President and Trustee of Horror Writers Association in 1987. He is a current member of

International Thriller Writers, Author's Guild, and Sisters in Crime.

Paul has taught creative writing at the University of Illinois at Chicago and for Writers Digest School. He has appeared on panels at Chicon4 and Chicon7, X-Con, Windy Con, WisCon, Madcon, Odyssey Con, Arcana, Thrillerfest, Magna cum Murder, the World Horror Convention, and the World Fantasy Convention. Paul was a guest of honor at Horror Fest in Estes Park, Colorado, in 1989.

Paul is also an NGH Certified Hypnotist, an NGH Certified Hypnotism Instructor, a certified Past-Life Regression Therapist, and an IBRT certified professional member of the International Association for Regression Research and Therapies.

Be sure to read these other thrilling novels in the Winds series:

Abandoned (Eldritch Press; Crossroad Press)

Darkness (2AM Publications)

Winds (2AM Publications)

Light (2AM Publications)

Time (2AM Publications)

Stones (2AM Publications)